THE TRUTH FACTORY

THE TRUTH FACTORY

Cody McFadyen

To my friends of old. I will never forget your faces.

THE TRUTH FACTORY

PART ONE

BIRTH

I Believe
We are born;
we run through the grass, hoping;
and then we die.

—CWM

CHAPTER ONE

Once upon a time, I think, *a family lived here—and they were still alive.*

I wrinkle my nose at the odors of decay. They hang in the air, heavy and solid; and I realize (as I always do) that in a very real way, I am drawing the dead into my lungs with each and every breath I take.

It's a useless, unhelpful thought, but as always, I'm unable to shake it off. It had occurred to me the very first time I'd ever smelled the dead, and had been compelling enough to send me running pell-mell out the door and onto the front lawn.

I'd made it to the grass before barf started shooting between my splayed fingers. I had preserved the crime scene, but out front was also where the world had been. A healthy mix of cops and feds watched as I fell to my knees and retched out three-quarters of a cheeseburger and a large order of fries. The nickname "Pukenstein" had followed me for months.

I swallow, imagining that it feels, somehow, *greasy*—and shiver. The nickname was long gone. The thought remains, though, and it still compels.

"Stinks," Alan mutters, reading my thoughts with his own. His nostrils flare, while his eyes narrow. He shakes his head. "Dead people are damn gross."

"They are inconvenient," I murmur in agreement.

The murdered dead are the most inconvenient of all, of course. Murder is unexpected. It catches you while you are busy living your life, as opposed to planning for your death. Any project still not completed stays that way, undone; and every murder, everywhere, is always the end of dignity.

I stand in place, unmoving, and let it all roll through my senses. It's one thing to arrive at a murder scene, another entirely to accept its reality in more than a passive state. The desire to be elsewhere is really more of a need, and it feels instinctual.

The first time I saw the murdered dead is a memory devoid of emotion, and though I know the memory is true, it never *feels* real. The images comprising it are compositions of washed-out color, soundlessness, and tunnel vision. I can't remember what color the carpet was, but the body is always blinding in its unbearable detail. I can see the pores on her nose; the color of her painted toenails; I can even close my eyes and count the knots in that small, cotton rope that had been coiled around her neck until it cut into the skin.

This is why I learned to stand, and wait: as a preparation for the coming onslaught of denial, so that when it's time to look, I can actually see.

"Okay," I breathe, nodding as much to myself as to Alan. "Let's go."

I leave the small foyer that the home's front door had delivered me to, and walk directly forward, without turning my head. I stop when I reach the middle of the room. I can see them now—the dead—from the corner of one eye. I wait where I stand for another few moments, forcing myself to savor the weight of my own reality. I count my heartbeats and recite the mantra: *Their death is never your death. You are the living. You are alive.*

I pause for a short moment, take a single deep breath, and turn. I feel the *blink* of the missing moment—my name for that split second of rejecting what's in front of me—as a camera flash of bright, white nothing. *Last chance,* my mind is telling me. *If you don't want to know this, last chance to look away.* Then—*blink*—again, and the white light's gone. My eyes adjust, as does my mind, and I've arrived. No tunnel vision, no washed-out colors. Just the murdered dead, in all their truth, and me.

I study the dinner-table tableau. Dead faces stare back at me, expressing their endless horror in silent screams. Something I read somewhere, once, comes to me: *Some things can't be understood. They can only be described.*

I move closer, examining the gravy boat that's been placed next to the dead mother's hand, and recoil. "Is that blood?" I ask.

Alan frowns, bending forward to take a look. He grimaces in distaste and nods. "Seems so."

We are in Colorado, north of Denver. It is the first week of October, and it's a hell of a lot colder here than in Southern California. Drier, too. The bodies have begun to turn, but the smell is not what it would be in SoCal's humidity.

I read aloud the words spelled out in blood on the far wall. *"Avoiders must pay,"* I quote. *"Help us with justice, Smoky Barrett. Come and learn."* A chill runs through me again, cold little feet jogging down my spine.

It must have shown. "Never comforting to see your name spelled out in blood," Alan says quietly, watching me closely.

"No shit." I raise my eyebrows and give him a small smile. "I'm fine, Mr. Wart. That's the nature of the beast. So let's concentrate on catching him."

He gives me a hard look, searching for cracks. Finding none, he raises a single eyebrow. "Mr. Wart?"

"Yeah—you know, as in *Worry Wart.*"

"Huh. Guess it's true what they say. Pregnancy doesn't make you funnier."

"Just funnier-looking."

"Nope, no comment," he says, shaking his head. "I'm not that dumb." He pulls out the small, battered notepad that's never far from his reach, speaking as he flips through it. "I confirmed this is the only one of the three houses with a message on the wall."

Alan calls the notepad Ned, because, he said, a notepad is an investigator's best friend, and a best friend should have a name. I don't care what he calls it. All I know is that whatever goes in Ned gets followed up by Alan, period, and is never forgotten. "I need to check up on that word," he murmurs, half to himself, writing this down on the first blank page he finds. *"Avoiders.* It rings a bell for some reason."

I look at the word again, spelled out so carefully on the wall in two-foot-high, sticky-tacky red. "You're right. I've heard it somewhere, too. I think." I will the memory to reveal itself, but it eludes me. "I'm not sure. It may be just a feeling."

"Probably more than that," he observes, writing in the notepad. He glances at me, smiles. "According to Ned and the Neds that came before him, you have a pretty good memory."

"Really?"

"Fact, Jack." He holds the pad up and shakes it back and forth in his hand. "Ned doesn't lie."

Alan stretches for a moment, creaking and sighing, and it's like watching a mountain make itself more comfortable. He is a big man, my friend and colleague. Not fat, not athletic, but formidable and huge. I realized, once, that

his size informs my perception of almost everything he does, a kind of semantic creation. Alan doesn't think—he ponders. He doesn't walk—he lumbers. I
think if Alan had been a professional football player, he would have had one
of those nicknames like "The Refrigerator" or something.

He is African American, and once told me that while being big and black
didn't guarantee you'd be a good interrogator, it sure didn't hurt. This may
be technically true, but it's far from a real explanation. Alan's size is camouflage; his true abilities lie between his ears. He was a homicide detective for
more than ten years before being headhunted by the FBI, and was known for
his ability to get confessions that stood up in court. He and I have worked
together for more than a decade, and I trust him with my life.

Alan is close to mandatory retirement age for the Bureau. His face, in
profile, still looks young to me, even with all that encroaching white hair. But
a certain tiredness has settled into his eyes that I've never seen in them before,
and I know in my soul that soon, it will be time for Alan to go and live the
quiet life he has earned.

For now, I'm just glad Alan's here. It's my first time in this new spotlight,
and truth be told—I'm nervous. I'm riding a new horse, and while it is the
same as my old horse, in many ways, it is also bigger, stronger, and more
dangerous to sit on.

I spent most of my FBI career running the Los Angeles branch of the
NCAVC—the National Center for the Analysis of Violent Crime. The NCAVC
proper is based in Quantico, but every FBI office has someone in charge of local
liaison for that function. In Los Angeles, we had enough work to keep a four-
man team busy. We hunted the worst of the worst: serial killers, rapists, more.

Two months ago, we were uprooted. The director of the FBI, Samuel
Rathbun, decided to put together a kind of strike team, a critical response
unit tasked with the same functions we'd performed in LA, but on a national
level. This decision was the result of what he perceived as growing momentum
for the idea of dismantling all the satellite functions of the NCAVC, as well as
reducing the size of the central unit. There were powerful voices hinting that
the FBI should be worrying more about terrorism within U.S. borders than
the one-on-one murder of individuals, in terms of resource assignment.

"Someone's gotten people who matter to start considering the notion that
the NCAVC involves too many *duplicative functions,*" Director Rathbun said

with a snort and a shake of his head, when he'd originally offered me the position. "Never mind the fact that if you stack our post-9/11 antiterrorism budget up against the NCAVC budget, it's like comparing a skyscraper to a shack."

The director obviously didn't agree with these views, but he was a pragmatist, and he'd decided to put the strike team together on a "just-in-case" basis. If the worst came to pass, he reasoned, we'd still have a way to put boots on the ground.

"It's going to get bloody. I'll fight, but I have a pretty good political nose." He smiled without humor. "They're just softening me up. Once they figure out where I lie, the gloves will come off."

"Figure out?" I asked, surprised. "You haven't voiced your objections about this to them?"

"Right now, they're being very friendly, Smoky. Amiable deals are much better than war, in politics, any day. So if I, for example, was to want to put together a task force, strike team—whatever we end up calling it—and I hinted or allowed others to assume that the formation of such a team was my way of cooperating with their agenda..." A single eyebrow was raised; he shrugged and half smiled. "I'd guess that intra-governmental cooperation on the matter would be at an all-time high."

I whistled, then grinned. "I thought a hint was the same as a promise in DC, sir. Isn't welshing a bad move in politics?"

He waved this off. "I keep my promises, but I'm only a politician to the degree it helps my agency and agrees with reality." He gave me a look of incredulity. "Pardon my French, but I have no fucking intention of going down in history as the director who amputated our capacity to assist in the apprehension of serial psychopaths. You don't trade the ability to catch one devil in order to catch another, not when they both still exist." He shook his head once, in emphasis. "That's stupidity. I can be dumb, Special Agent Barrett, but I do try hard not to be stupid."

"You're preaching to the fully converted, sir."

He nodded. "Yes, and that's exactly my point. That level of... depravity will always be doubted to some degree, as a complete picture. But we don't doubt, do we?"

"No, sir," I answered, and kept it at that. Director Rathbun was on a roll. I wouldn't call it passionate, more... intense. But for a man with a thousand (outward) faces, it was a mesmerizing moment of truth, and I didn't want to interrupt it.

He gave the desktop an aggressive tap with his finger. "Those monsters are our responsibility. Mistaken assumptions aren't, and I don't give a raisin of a rat's turd about anyone's bent feelings on the matter." He leaned back, smiling. "In a manner of speaking, of course."

He'd asked me to head it up, and to bring my team along for the ride. We'd all agreed, for now. This was our first real case. The nation was watching, and not in a metaphorical sense.

Three families had been butchered, all on the same block, all on the same night. One of the local cops had recognized my name on the wall and had contacted the FBI. They asked for help right away, which I regarded as a good sign. It meant they were more interested in solving the case than worrying about who got the credit. It also meant they knew they were out of their depth. Which they were.

We were on a private jet within the hour, and landed at Denver International Airport a little less than three hours later.

I contemplate the diorama the killer has prepared for us. The Wiltons had been an intact family of five, with three children—two girls and a boy. The oldest daughter had been fourteen, the youngest twelve. The boy was only five. The dining table is medium-size and made of some kind of smooth, dark wood. The mother's and father's corpses have been seated at either end, naked, and their severed heads have been placed back atop their respective necks. The killer either didn't care about lining up the necks, or the heads had slipped a bit. It gives each of them a stretched, disjointed look, an image that follows you out of the room. The father and daughters were all brunettes. Mrs. Wilton was a blonde.

The table has been set for two. Mr. and Mrs. Wilton each have a white china plate in front of them, and the killer has placed forks in their hands.

"They're holding the special dinner silver," I say, pointing at the forks.

"How can you tell?"

"My mom had a set of antique formal ware she got from my grandmother. She never put it in the dishwasher, always used silver polish to clean every piece by hand. Silver reflects light differently. It has ... I don't know—it shines with more ... depth."

"Formal ware," he quoted me, teasing lightly. "You never mentioned those aristocratic roots."

I snorted. "Great-grandma was a prostitute for five years, after the untimely death of great-grandpa. That silver was payment for a 'weekend of pleasure,' so the story goes."

"Bull."

"No, it's true," I replied, smiling. "When she died, the silver was one of the things specifically willed to my grandmother, as the oldest daughter. It came with a letter that told the story of how and why my great-grandmother came to be a prostitute. It said that the silver was to go oldest daughter to oldest daughter, unless there were no daughters, in which case it could go to the oldest son. But," I raised a finger, "you could only accept it on the condition you promised never to sell it, unless selling it would prevent you from having to sell yourself."

"Wow."

"Yeah. My mother never gave it to me formally. Dad gave it to me after she died."

I remember reading the letter, and how much like a bar of solid, precious light it was to me. I was a teenager, alone in the world without a mother, but that silverware and that letter connected me to the last of the oldest who'd been forced to sell off a part of herself to survive the rigors of being a human being in a world that couldn't care less. And she'd taken a pile of that blood money, and her story, and sent them off into the future in the hopes that another of her line wouldn't have to do the same. It was as though I could feel her hand on my shoulder, rooting once again all the parts of me that had become rootless.

"Strong woman," Alan observed, quietly.

"You never stop worrying about what will happen to your children after you die," I murmur. "No matter how old they get."

"Suppose not," Alan agrees, his eyes moving back to the Wiltons.

The children hadn't been mutilated. The killer had stripped the daughters' bodies and then laid them lengthways on the long table.

I sigh. "They were so beautiful," I murmur.

"Yeah," Alan agrees, and leaves it at that.

They had skin like cream, still flawless with youth, but it lay far, far too still against their bones. That always constant, almost imperceptible tension of life that results from a constantly shifting balance of the physical self no longer fills them out, and so they seem less real somehow. They remind me of two supine and exquisite statues, chiseled from white alabaster and polished to cold perfection. The back of each one's head rested on a dinner plate, and they stared up at their parents with eyes that had already begun to cloud up and sink back into their sockets.

The girls each have the same face—their mother's—but at different ages. Nude, the contrasts and similarities are stark, painful in every incarnation of lost possibility. An image flashes into my mind: one of those ape-to-man pictures, designed to visually demonstrate evolution. If Mom had been a brunette, she'd complete the set.

"They have bruising around their necks," I notice. "And petechial hemorrhaging in the eyes." I frown. "Where's the boy's body?"

"In his bed."

"Killed the same way? Nude?"

Alan consults the notepad again. "He was smothered with a pillow, but the killer didn't undress him."

The same thought comes to me as when I first walked the scene: *This is not the work of an amateur.*

"So, four dead here." I sigh, putting my concerns into words. "One dead upstairs. And two other families murdered on the same block." I pinch the bridge of my nose for a second, closing my eyes. "That's hell of a lot of killing for anyone. Add in the lack of hesitation wounds, the neatness of the scene..."

"These aren't his first kills," Alan says, making a note in Ned, nodding agreement as he does so.

We go quiet for a moment, keeping the dead company again. Contemplating this unwelcome idea.

It's bad, of course, for this to be true. People don't understand how hard it is to kill a person. Television makes it look easy, even casual.

Words in blood, I think, gazing at the message some murderer had left me. I imagine him here, in the dark, dipping a finger into that blood-filled gravy boat. Using what he'd taken from them to spell out a dark message only he could ever fully understand.

You certainly enjoyed this, I think. *This had nothing to do with what they were. It was only about what you needed them to be. This is your vision, complete; and it's a vision that you brought with you and then imposed upon them.*

"Three families ... ," I murmur. "That means extensive surveillance. He'd need to figure out the neighborhood patterns, when people are and aren't home, and why. Maybe even a little psychological profiling if he's really thorough—which he probably is—so he can predict how they'll act." I stop, considering everything involved. "He'd need a convincer of some kind, ideally. Something powerful that would cow them right out of the gate."

Alan nods after a moment. "Makes sense. Like what?"

I think about it, studying the scene. My eyes move from one sightless face to the next. "He took three families in one night and left clean scenes. I think we can safely assume it wasn't luck. The best strategy is a decisive, crippling strike. Something that leaves no doubt about who is in control and whether he means business."

"The father makes the most sense, in that scenario. Crush the dad early, crush him fast, and most of all—crush him *hard*. The rest of the family would probably fall into line."

Stereotypes abound in our psychology at the most visceral levels, regardless of how liberal or enlightened we may be. Fathers, generally, are symbols of strength and protection to their children. *The* symbols, for the most part. Seeing a father sob is a traumatic event for most children, because of this. Watching a father get physically broken is overwhelming.

"Right." I move around the table again with Alan in tow, but slower this time, scanning all the bodies carefully. "There," I say, pointing. "The father's left arm." The arm had been left to hang loose, which is why we hadn't noticed before.

Alan gets down on his haunches for a closer look. He whistles lowly. "Killer cut off his thumb. Looks like he broke every one of his fingers, too."

I can hear the screams in my head, and wonder about that.

Wouldn't the neighbors have heard?

I frown, concentrating hard again on each body in turn, not finding any further evidence of torture. "This feels utilitarian. I think hurting them was about control, not pleasure."

"You can still see the terror on their faces," I mutter. "How did he kill them?"

"The medical examiner thinks they were decapitated." Alan gives me a steady look. "With some kind of edged weapon."

I blink, surprised. "He thinks the unsub cut their heads off with a *sword*?"

"Says the cuts are clean and that the heads appear to have come off all at once, no muss, no fuss." Alan shrugs. "It's a working theory."

"Well, it might explain how they died with their expressions intact." I take a deep breath and exhale, puffing out my cheeks. "I've never caught a case with a sword before. Never say never."

"I have. It was some messed-up Latin gang thing. The same guy liked to stick people in the center of a stack of tires filled with gasoline and light them on fire." He rolled his eyes. "Press called him the Michelin Man."

"Clever."

There's always a new way to kill somebody, I think, *when you're killing for pleasure. This is just one of them.*

I have spent more than ten years hunting evil men for the FBI. I do it because it's how I was made. It's what I'm "for." I have a gift for getting in their heads, for cozying up next to all that brackish blackness. I have felt the night sky they all labor under.

Most people can't understand evil, but that's just because they refuse to acknowledge its simplicity. Good people are complex because they take the time to fight themselves. Evil men work in fresh, straight lines, unconflicted by conscience, certain of what they want. They don't question their needs.

They creep around the edges of our light, invisible to us, watching us as we dream our dreams, raise our children, love (or hate) our lives. They watch us, and they sing their songs in whispers, songs only they, or others like them, can hear. Songs of death. Songs of suffering and blood.

I listen to the dark-singers. I'm a song collector. I'm not of them, but I can understand them. I am drawn to their music like a ship to the rocks, and I can hear where others don't because I have faced the truth: These singers are everywhere, and they look like us.

They are fathers, brothers, uncles, wives. They are the helpful teacher who touches us so deftly once our trust is gained. They are the husband who strangles a streetwalker before coming home, who then makes love to us as he gives us her face in his mind. They are the churchgoing wife who smothers the baby with a pillow because it cried too loud and had made her fat, besides.

I look into the husband's dead eyes, then his wife's. "Who were you to him?"

Who were you, period? I wonder. *Will knowing the answer tell me who killed you?*

My eyes rove, squinting for anything overlooked that might provide an answer.

Who were you, to you? I wonder. The dead don't answer, so I answer my own question with a promise: *I'll find out. The good and the bad and all the rest. I'll find out, and I'll remember.*

It's not an idle promise. I can recall all the faces of my dead.

"This feels personal," I say. "But not in the right way."

"How?"

I shake my head. "I don't know. This feels... sterile. Passionless. Like the message was more important than the act itself."

Which is all wrong, I tell myself. *Why kill the meal if it's not what you enjoy eating?*

"So what's the message?"

"No idea." A kick on the inside of my stomach makes me wince. "Ouch," I say. "You little bastard."

Alan raises an eyebrow. "You okay?"

"I'm fine. The alien is active, that's all."

He scowls. "You gotta stop calling him that. It's just not right."

Alan seems genuinely distressed, and I manage a smile in spite of our surroundings. "I could call him 'lump' or 'thingie,' I suppose," teasing him.

"Very funny."

I am more than seven and a half months pregnant, and my son is very active these days. I wonder, sometimes, if his kicks are meant to admonish me for bringing him to these places of violence. I look around the room again, and I feel him shift inside me as I do. It makes me uneasy. Does he sense that headless violence as he floats in my womb? Will the horror of their deaths imprint on him in some way?

He shifts again, as if to say yes, and I feel goose bumps run across my arms.

"Jesus," I mutter. "Way to give yourself the willies."

"What's that?" Alan asks.

"Fred. Let's call him Fred, for now. Does that work for you?"

He shrugs. "Kinda boring, but it's better than 'alien.'"

I reach a hand down and cradle my stomach for a moment, communing with the life inside. No speech is needed because we are connected.

The front door opens, followed by the sound of heels clicking against the entryway tile, and the other two members of my team stroll into the dining room. They are silent for a moment, taking in the Wiltons.

"It's bad all over, honey-love," Callie says, inclining her head toward the slaughter.

James gives her an annoyed look. "The composition is the same in the other homes," he says. "The mother and father were decapitated and given traditional seating. The daughters were strangled and stripped, and then they were all posed." I see him peer at the forks and nod once to himself. "He used the formal ware in the other homes, too."

"Did either of the other families have a son?" I ask.

"The Aymes's had a twelve-year-old boy. He was killed in bed. The killer didn't pose him as a part of the tableau. Here?"

I nod. "Upstairs, also in bed, and also still clothed."

"Strange." He frowns in thought. "Does this feel somehow … posed, to you? Less about the victims or even killing them than—" he gestures at the tableau—"this?"

I'm not surprised to hear him repeat my own thoughts. James Giron is the youngest of us, a brilliant misanthrope. His mind works twice as fast as the average bear, and he lacks social graces of any kind. He is observant, though, incredibly so, and he shares my gift. James is a song collector, too.

When he was twelve, James's older sister Rosa was murdered by a serial killer with a blowtorch. He decided at her funeral to join the FBI. James graduated high school at sixteen and then powered his way through to a PhD in criminology by the time he was twenty-one.

"I had the same thought," I tell him.

Callie cocks her head, frowning. "These scenes are unusually clean for a mass murder, honey-love, especially one with decapitations."

"We noticed."

She moves around the table, sniffing. "I don't smell any pee-pee or poo-poo, which is very odd."

"Pee-pee? Poo-poo?" I smile, teasing her a little.

She chuckles, patting my belly. "Just toning down my language in advance of my nephew's birth, honey-love."

"Don't bother." I sigh. "I can't seem to stop saying 'fuck' and 'shit' and 'bastard'—it's like my internal censor's on strike." I grin. "I think it's all the fucking hormones."

"Unacceptable." She sniffs, sticking her nose in the air. "My nephew is not going to swear like a classless construction worker."

Callie is a perpetual smile-making machine. Irreverence is kind of her hobby—or maybe it is her religion. We're not blood sisters, of course. We are close to the same age, and she has been there for me in the aftermath of all my scars. She knew my first husband, and she loved my first daughter.

I have held her through her own sufferings, too. I have been allowed to see her break, and was humbled by it. Watching Callie cry is like watching water fall up in defiance of gravity, or no longer being able to find the North Star in the sky. It's a gift of trust to be repaid with silence.

She got married this year, shattering the lustful dreams of men everywhere. Callie has a master's degree in forensics, with a minor in criminology. She's also a tall, skinny, leggy redhead with the body of a model. The marriage had shocked us all—up to that point, Callie had never been known to do more than skim the surface of a man.

Relationships are for itches that need scratching, honey-love, as she'd so elegantly put it once. *Talk is vastly overrated.* Apparently, she'd finally found the itch only one man could scratch in the way she needed.

I am happy for her, because I have always understood the truth: Callie was as alone as the rest of us, and like the rest of us, she had her reasons. Getting married was a sign she'd put those reasons to rest, and I know how rare that actually is.

"The point I was making," she says, returning to the Wiltons, "is the lack of mess. Torture is messy. Mutilation for fun is messy. I think the blood all went down the bathtub drain. Why?" She holds out her hands and smiles beatifically at us, the little people. "Because it was more about the message than the murder."

"We already said that," James replies, yawning.

"Yes, dear, but I give better reasons."

A few years ago, a bean-counting idiot (or BIC, as Callie referred to him) decided the Bureau was rife with inefficiency, and that this was costing the taxpayers. Unfortunately, as will happen in bureaucracies (Callie calls it "idiot clustering"), he was able to find a CBCD (congressional budget committee dunce, another Callie-ism) who would listen to him. An evaluator was chosen, and he jackbooted into our offices a week later.

The agent assigned to us was thirty-one but had a face so youthful it was impossible to take any of his sternness seriously. His name was Ryan. He had a background in social psychology, and for a month, he went everywhere that we went. At the end of the month, he gave us his evaluation.

"This team functions very well together," he said. "You probably already know this, but in case you don't: One of the keys to your success is in the way you information-dump and bullpen. I originally thought otherwise. I kept hearing the same idea expressed, the same information gone over, and I didn't get that." He shrugged. "I was wrong. You cover the same ground, yes, but in different ways and from different angles. It's not duplicative—it uncovers nuance. Your method actually kicks ass," he said, smiling so openly I was ashamed of having judged him before.

We were a single brain when working a case, looking at the same information again and again from different perspectives. Going over the same ground forward, then backward, and maybe sideways. I can see how it might appear inefficient and duplicative from the outside, but as Ryan had been smart enough to understand, sometimes that's exactly what's needed. Sometimes, the truth will be found in a single degree of change in one's field of view.

"So, reasons aside—" Alan asks again—"what's the message?"

We go quiet, contemplating this.

"Use of the daughters and omission of the sons was deliberate," James says. "This means it was important. The more specific the articles required, the clearer the message is to him."

"Clearer means simpler," I offer.

"Maybe." He nods after a beat. "Probably."

I consider it. "What's the simplest interpretation of this? That the parents are eating their children?"

"Ick," Callie says, making a face. "But if so, is it: 'These parents ate *their* children'? or '*All* parents eat their children'?"

A plane passes overhead. The floor creaks for no reason.

"How do parents eat their children?" I muse aloud, rubbing the place where my pinky used to be. "Sexual abuse? Physical abuse? Neglect?"

"Could be a metaphor," Alan notes. "Parents eat their children by killing off their dreams, maybe."

"I don't think it's specific to these families," James says.

"Why?" I ask.

He holds up three fingers. "Probability. Three homes on the same block. What are the odds of all three families having the same deep, dark secret? Slim. What are the odds of all three families having *any* deep, dark secret? Better, but still slim. It's more likely he chose this street because it had the victim pool he needed."

"That must be some message," Alan says, his voice grim. "Important enough to him to kill three families on the same block in the same night."

Which sure as shucks means it's important enough to do again, I think, finishing the unspoken sentence for him. *Fabulous.*

What James has said makes sense, but privately I hope that he's wrong. Solving serial murder is about making connections, as it is with any crime. The difference is in the possible connections we can make. Murder in general is harder because the primary witness is usually the victim, too. Planned murder is even more difficult because it reduces the forensic possibilities. Serial murder adds further complexity, due to the stranger-on-stranger factor, and the motivation.

Killing someone for an orgasm is not the same as killing someone for money. The difference is fundamental, and it informs everything about the crime.

A few strands of hair on the back of Mr. Wilton's head stick out as James moves past his body. It gives me goose bumps, even though I know it's the result of this dry air and the static electricity it creates.

How long have you known what you are? I ask the faceless killer. *How long have you had to prepare for this moment?*

There is a common refrain to be found in interviews with some serial killers. It is this idea of always having known that they'd kill one day. It's a form of self-awareness, and it leads them to research. They study the exploits of others and learn many things from them.

They learn that to kill for pleasure is to set yourself aside from the rest of the human race forever. When I was training at Quantico, I read something by a serial killer named David Gore that has stuck with me. I made myself memorize it.

"All of a sudden," he said, "I realized that I had just done something that separated me from the human race, and it was something that could never be undone. I realized that from that point on, I could never be like normal people. I must have stood there in that state for twenty minutes. I have never felt an emptiness of self like I did right then, and I will never forget that feeling. It was like I crossed over into a realm I could never come back from."

I memorized it because it showed me a truth I wanted to make sure I never forgot: He was clearly capable of understanding the depth of his actions—but he did them, anyway. It was the first time I made that connection: that some people could be addicted to murder. It also occurred to me that anyone capable of recognizing this gulf would probably take the stakes very seriously.

We scour the victims' lives hoping to find a link, however small. Maybe they all go to the same gym, and he's a trainer. Maybe they all graduated from the same college ten years ago, where he was once a professor.

If James is right, and the killer selected this street for its demographics alone, that makes our job much, much harder. It would make the connections completely random and thus much more tenuous.

James is looking at the words on the wall again. "The blood must still have been warm," he murmurs. "See how some of the letters have run?"

I hadn't noticed before, but I do now. Trails of red have raced down the wall's white glossy paint, all the way to the baseboard in some places.

"Interesting choice of words, too," he continues. *Come and learn*, not *come and see*. That's a very specific choice. I don't think it was an accident."

His eyes find mine, and something passes between us. "I think you're right," I tell him.

"Come where?" Alan mutters. "Learn what?"

The room gets a little bit brighter, interrupting our train of thought for a moment. The curtains to the house are closed, not that it matters. Three families have been murdered on the same block. It's lit up like a carnival at night outside, and the light show is only going to keep getting bigger.

"Quite a little madhouse you're growing out there in your garden," Callie notes.

"Only local media so far, thank God," I say, checking my watch. "But that will change soon. The whole country will be here by morning."

18

"Who cares," James says, his voice impatient and dismissive. "I don't watch the news. What I would like to know is how you want us to proceed."

I sigh, too tired and pregnant to be annoyed. *I'll have a James Classic*, I think. *With a side of butthead. To go.* I'm not too tired to file away that one little nugget of personal information, though: *James doesn't watch the news.* I add it to the others on my very, very short list.

James personifies the term *personal privacy.* We know by chance that James is gay but have never met anyone he's dating. I have met his mother, and she seems to be a sweet, warm, wonderful woman—but I would address her only as "Mrs. Giron." I don't know much about her. I heard him hum a Dylan song, once, but he stopped when he noticed me listening. The rest is a mystery.

"You and I will walk through each scene together, right now. Callie, I want you to liaise with local forensics. Make sure they know what they're doing, and fix it if they don't."

She flashes me a grin. "Already begun, honey-love. And not to worry, they have a decent team here."

"Good. I still want you looking over their shoulders. I don't care if it upsets them. Alan, I need you to do your former-cop thing. Work your magic. Get the locals to like us and then pump the well of information dry."

"Undercover buddy," he says, pretending to complain. "My favorite."

"That's because no one can do it as good as you do," Callie says, batting her eyes at him in a caricature of coquettishness. "You dazzle us with your experience."

He scowls at her. "Isn't that just another way of calling me old?"

Callie straightens to her full height and curls her lip. "I won't have such a blasphemous word spoken in my presence."

"What?" Alan grins, raising an eyebrow. "*Old?*"

"I think I'm done here." She sniffs, turning away. "If this continues, I'll have to request a transfer," she tells me.

I watch this, half smiling. I suppose an outsider might deem it disrespectful to the Wiltons, but they'd be wrong. Such banter is a survival mechanism. A pressure valve. In truth, it is an index of how upset the murders of the Wiltons, and the other families, have made them.

"We planning an all-nighter?" Alan asks.

"Bite your tongue," I groan, putting a hand to my lower back. "Seven and a half months pregnant is hell in your forties. I have to sleep eight hours, and there's no fucking 'or' to it."

"You really have become quite profane, honey-love," Callie chides.

"Bite my ass, skinny, unpregnant, very *unhelpful* person."

CHAPTER TWO

When I open the door and step outside, night has turned to day.

The street is U-shaped, with each end of the U leading to one of the main neighborhood avenues. The three homes are at entirely different points on the U, so the police aren't able to shut down the street entirely.

Instead, a squad car has been placed at each entrance to the street, and the uniforms are allowing only residents to pass. Driver's licenses are being taken and logged, and every officer has been ordered to ensure that the video camera in his vehicle is active and recording.

Each home where the murders occurred has been assigned two squad cars. One is parked in front of the house, at the curb, with the lights turning and the bright white spotlight pointed toward the front porch. The other is parked on the hiking trail behind the home, doing the same at the back-yard's gate. An unmarked belonging to homicide detectives is parked in every driveway, while a combination of white-and-orange sawhorses, crime scene tape, and uniformed police ensure the scenes are not contaminated or trampled on.

Tall, rugged, any-weather halogen lamps festoon the lawns, and extension cords run everywhere like bright orange snakes. Every home on the block is lit up, of course, and most have their porch lights on, too. The occupants crowd at their picture windows or on their front porches or lawns, gawking or scared, or both.

All the houses on this street back up to an open field, which then becomes a wood, so the entire area has been cordoned off, lit up, and gridded out. A team of trained officers and technical personnel are moving slowly through the woods, eyes trained on the ground for any possible evidence.

The local media have arrived in force, and are so far being kept off the street, but that doesn't keep them from making their presence known. They have their own lights up, and their cameras on; and all the chatter and speaking and motion, even at a distance, is faintly audible.

"What's the deal with the news choppers?" I ask, shielding my eyes and looking up.

There are two of them, both hovering in a stationary position at a safe distance, their high-candle spotlights trained on the field and woods behind the homes.

"It's possible, honey-love, that someone *might* have told them we think there's key evidence back yonder," Callie answers.

"You tricked them into giving the searchers extra light?" Alan asks, grinning.

"I know, I know. Brains *and* beauty, hard to believe, but it's true. Just ask my hubby."

James rolls his eyes and scowls. "Can we stop testing my gag reflex, and get to work?"

"James," Callie asks, sweetly, "would this be an appropriate place to observe the gay version of 'that's what he said'?"

He stares at her for a moment, and then something happens with his lips that I can't quite identify. "Not bad. I'll meet you at house number two," he tells me, and sets off in that direction.

"Was that a … *smile*?" I ask, shaking my head in some version of dumbfounded wonder.

"Kind of," Alan says. He shakes his head. "I don't know whether to go buy a lottery ticket or prepare for the end."

I notice the video camera tracking me as I cross the street toward house number two. I watch the cameraman adjust for focus, and I know when my scars become clear: He looks up from the viewfinder. He can't actually see me clearly from this distance, but it is instinctive to double-check when you doubt your eyes.

I can't blame him. It no longer harms me to look at myself in the mirror, but I still notice the scars every time I see them. Sometimes I'll trace them with my fingers, and concentrate on my reflection, trying to find the face that used to be me.

On most days, I don't care. I've grown inured to the quick glances and occasional stares. After it first happened, I hid in my home and stared into the mirror for hours, unable to find myself. When I did finally leave the house, I wore my dark hair down and let it hang around my face. I was ugly, I felt exposed, and was convinced everyone who saw me had to hide their revulsion.

My confidence grew; my pain subsided. I started wearing my hair back and tight against my head, in a ponytail that reaches almost to my waist. Originally, it was an announcement to the world: I am not afraid to let you see. Now? It's just less hot, less heavy, and more convenient. I am now that woman I never dreamed I'd be. "It's just easier" has somehow become a more compelling argument than "I need to look the best I can to the world at large."

"Screw you, world," I say, softly. "I'm married and pregnant, so I guess I look good enough to someone." The proclamation lifts my spirits a little.

Still, it's harder, I think, to be pregnant and short than pregnant and tall. I am four feet eleven, and my pregnancies *show*. With Alexa, my stomach got so big I couldn't drive. I am smaller this time (which worries me sometimes, if I make the mistake of thinking about it) but no one would call my stomach small. It precedes me through doorways; it arrives first in the room.

I glance down at my chest and smile. At least I got me some boobs, for a while. I'm normally a B cup, but am now well into a C, and probably headed for a D. Tommy, my husband, doesn't seem to care much, which pleases me, of course. Still, it's nice to have a little figure, up-top, for a change.

My ass, on the other hand, is a different matter altogether.

I've always had a big butt. I'm generally athletic enough for this to be an asset, but pregnancy is not an especially athletic time for me, and so "big" has traversed into "large."

"Not fat," Tommy had told me two nights ago, after catching me in tears, with my back to the mirror. "More of a good thing, is what that is." He nuzzled my neck from behind. "Can I be honest? I love your butt, baby."

"You never told me you were into fat chicks," I muttered, pouting.

"It's your extra-ness I'm enjoying, wife of mine." I could feel his smile against my ear. "Want some proof?" He bumped against me. "How's that? Convinced?"

I turned around, my belly between us. "Carrying a weapon isn't evidence of intent." I sniffled, wiping the tears from my cheeks with my palms.

"I'm ready to give you whatever evidence you need."

And, oh-yes-sir, you gave me plenty, I think, smiling just a little. *Because I have to admit, nothing says "you're not ugly" quite as convincingly as an erection with encores. So thank you for that, honey.*

I'm passing behind the police car stationed at the curb when the trunk flies open. A teenage girl jumps out and puts a shotgun to my stomach.

"Move a muscle and I'll shoot right through you."

I freeze in place. I freeze inside.

Time stops.

"You'll be fine, so long as you listen," she continues, in a calm, even voice. "Once I'm done talking, the gun will go away. Make a move, and make no mistake—I will destroy you and your child." Her eyes are calm, too. Deathly calm.

I'm vaguely aware, in the present, of the pandemonium breaking out around me. I hear different voices shouting at her to drop the weapon. None of it seems important. The fear is *everything* and it is *everywhere*. My senses sharpen to an unbearable point, and the adrenaline rocketing through me makes the hairs on the back of my neck stand up. I can see her eyes, those calm, focused, unworried blue eyes; and I can smell the fresh gun oil rising off the barrels. My bladder is heavy with a hot, unreliable feeling; I realize, on some level, that wetting myself is a very real possibility.

Why hasn't she said anything else? I wonder, before realizing that I haven't heard my next heartbeat yet. Time has stretched, turning a second into a warehouse-size room. I know I should say something to her, but the only word that I can think of to say is: "please."

A voice in my head speaks to me: *Fear is a physical response*, it reminds me. *In order to reassert mental control, you must first exert physical control. The easiest way to do this is to breathe. Breath in for a count of three. Hold for a count of three. Exhale for a count of three. Don't ever worry about whether or not you have time to do this— time problems are one of panic's core components. Ignore them without direct evidence.*

An unbearable sense of pressure has been building inside me. I feel like a sentient balloon understanding it is about to blow. Everything that had stopped somehow slows even further; working its way down to the atomic level. Then my next heartbeat comes, and the balloon bursts. Time races around a hairpin curve and bends to breaking—pauses; hangs—then explodes back into its normal rate. I breathe in for a count of three; hold it for a count of three; exhale.

Don't speak or act. Wait and listen. This will tell you how to stay alive.

The girl's face says she can't be more than sixteen or seventeen. Her eyes are the deepest, richest blue I've ever seen, and they say she is much older. Her hair is so blond it's almost white, and she wears it in a single, long braid that reaches down past the middle of her back. She's undeniably beautiful and in peak physical condition. She has the palpable vitality of a professional athlete—or maybe a professional killer. She's dressed in a black skintight bodysuit reminiscent of the outfit worn by a track runner, with a matching set of black tennis shoes.

I am aware—for a single, hanging moment—of crossing the border between my terror and my fear. I hear the voice in my head again. It tells me that while you can't leverage terror, ever, you can always leverage your fear. It reminds me that "fight or flight" means exactly what it says—that fighting is an option, ladies and gentleman—and your fear is there to help with that, too.

But first, the voice says, delivering its final bit of wisdom, *you must accept that you are already dead. Fear, at its core, is about caring too much.*

I register another heartbeat, and then it works. I clamber back on top of my fear and pull at its reins. My tunnel vision clears, and I realize we're surrounded by law enforcement, and that everyone has their weapons out. I see shotguns, nine-millimeter handguns, even an assault rifle. The air crackles with that intense, focused readiness that characterizes cops who've accepted the weight of certain possibilities. They're maintaining a safe distance, but every barrel is pointed at the girl, and I can feel every finger, not hoping—but waiting, committed to that duty should it come calling. The motion and din of cops and forensics and hubbub have been reduced to a near totality of hushed silence.

Alan is standing six or seven feet behind her, his weapon leveled at her back. His face is stone. He catches my eye and gives me the briefest of nods. *If you die,* that nod says, *she follows in the next second.* I've never seen him look more frightened or more terrifying.

A dreadful calm settles over me.

"What do you want?" I manage to ask her. My voice shakes a little, but it is *my* voice and under my control.

The twin Os of the shotgun pressing through my shirt feel like hot brands burning into my skin every time my stomach moves against them. I can smell cut grass on the breeze as it mingles with my own sour terror sweat. The asphalt underneath my shoes is uneven in all the usual, familiar ways, and I am reminded of my own street, in front of my own home.

The girl doesn't seem to care about all the bristling death pointed her way. She's as wholly focused on me as they are on her. "I want you to listen. That's all. To tell you that I killed these people." She says it evenly and calmly, neither proud nor ashamed.

I stare at her. "You killed these families." My disbelief makes it come out as a statement rather than a question. "Why?"

"They were not what they seem. They were the worst of the worst. Find the bunker buried under the lawn, and you'll see what I mean."

Bunker? I think it, but do not say it. "I'm sorry, I don't understand."

"There is no time. I will be dead in a moment, so you must listen."

"Dead?" I do say it aloud this time, because it makes me so very, very afraid to hear. "There's no reason this needs to end with either one of us dead or hurt."

She frowns, impatient. "There is no time for questions. You must listen."

Dead, how? I think, only half hearing her. An ant colony of anxiety gets busy inside my stomach, racing that grasshopper, preparing for winter. I will my thoughts to reach my son as he slumbers in my belly. *Honey, if we survive this—I promise to name you. No more alien. No more Fred.*

"May we record this?" Callie asks, her voice coming from the left and behind me.

"That would be ideal," the girl answers. "But let me warn you first: My finger is on this trigger, and I am resolved."

"I promise, honey-love, that is our default assumption. I'm going to put my weapon away first, and then I'll be taking a small video camera out of the bag hanging from my shoulder."

"Yes, go ahead."

The girl's calm is unnatural. It's something you see in professional soldiers or assassins, not sixteen-year-olds. Her grip on the shotgun is relaxed but ready.

She's been trained. And not by some amateur faking pro.

"I'm ready," Callie tells her.

The girl begins with no preamble, her eyes continuing their rounds as she speaks. "There are two men. They have existed in the shadows for longer than some of you have lived, and they are truly evil men. They have a plan of savagery and murder for their own enjoyment, and they bring with it the desire to promote hopelessness and nihilism. They believe you can tip the world, or a society, in an irrevocable direction by drowning it in murder and despair.

"Long ago, the extent of their plan became known to someone within the Church of the Fundamental Self, and, after a great personal struggle, this person chose not to keep the secret but instead to tell a trusted few. This small group left the church, making plans as they readied themselves, and they waited, watching, for the beginning moments that would let them know the secret had taken its first few steps of emergence into the world. They gathered others—myself among them—and we watched and readied, too.

"This thing that I'm doing now—breaking the silence of a Revealed in order to share their secret with a member of law enforcement ... you must understand—this act violates my own most cherished rules of belief. I am like a Catholic priest who burns down his church by setting fire to the confessional. Because of this action, I will die with my habit patterns unchanged, and thus carry them, and their suffering, with me into my next life."

She shrugs. "Ah, well. It is my pattern. Even this—choosing this—is a part of my pattern. I will suffer for making it less safe for the world to be honest."

Her smile is heartbreaking and beautiful, full of absolute certainty and obvious joy. It chills me. I've seen that expression before. I think of the dead families, how we kept thinking this was more about the message than the act. Of that unnatural, beatific calm.

Professional soldier was the wrong comparison. Wrong by a mile. This is martyr's joy.

I once saw a photo that had been captured from CCTV footage of a suicide bombing. The camera had been trained right on the bomber, and the photograph revealed the expression on his face just before he pushed the button in his hand. I've never seen such absolute certainty, peace, and joy. Certainly not on a nineteen-year-old boy who is about to blow himself and others to oblivion.

This is what explains you, isn't it? How a pretty young woman has the training of a professional killer, and the willingness to use it?

It changes how I see her, even now. I'm still frightened, of course, but I no longer see evil, or even insanity. This is the strength of belief. Prostitution is not the oldest profession; the exercise of power is.

"Everything points to these men coming from out of the shadows soon. We have been given the opportunity to prove this to you." She's focusing intently on me as she says this. "Agent Barrett. I am truly sorry for threatening you and your baby. Please believe me, it was only done to facilitate this moment between us. To ensure that I could speak, and you would hear."

"I'm listening," I tell her. "You have my attention."

"Two clues were revealed to us. The first was a man's name, and we soon discovered he was an Avoider—the name we give to those who knowingly and willfully turn their faces from the good. Further investigation showed him to be a construction contractor, and it was he who built the bunker you will find underneath these lawns. It was he who led me here, to the nests of those *other* Avoiders that you found. I destroyed them first, as a matter of the good, then I bled this man of his secrets and dealt with him, as well."

"Killed him, you mean."

She seems surprised by the question. I realize she hadn't meant it to be a euphemism. "Well, yes, of course."

I sigh. "And the second clue?"

"It, too, came from this man. I'll repeat exactly what he told me, though I'm afraid it's confusing and I cannot provide clarity." She pauses, clearing her throat, and then begins speaking in a pitch-perfect imitation of a man's voice. Hearing a gravelly male tenor come from her mouth makes the hair on my arms stand up. "He said: 'The Milgram experiment. Explanation was the truth, not the lie. YES, it really happened, and he wasn't crazy. No. No!'" The last *no* comes out as a hoarse shout, just short of a screech or a scream. "'Please ... that's all I know. I don't know his name. Only that! *Only that! Only that!*'" She's filled her imitation voice with fear, terror, and a deep-seated, lurching sense of physical agony. The final *that* climbs into a scream, which rockets into an ululating shriek. She stops without any apparent reason, like the flick of a light switch, then resumes speaking with her own voice. "It was all he knew, I promise you."

My throat feels thick and dry. "Did you ... " I cough into my fist. "It sounds like you tortured him. Are you aware that's a notoriously unreliable way to extract information?"

"Torture was only used at the beginning to break him. Electrodes were placed inside his anus and on his genitals and feet; and then only yes-or-no questions were asked. The rate of truth in such a setting is quite high, I assure you. The areas covered were highly personal to him, and known to us.

"We made him believe he had no hope of lying. After that, he told the truth. If he became reluctant, we simply placed the electrodes on the table."

She grins, and it's a normal grin. I've seen its twin on my adopted daughter's face as she told me about something "really cool" or "awesome," in her estimation.

I suppress a sigh. "May I ask your name?"

"I am Maya, Smoky Barrett. I have no last name, because none is needed." Her face gets serious. "Time is too short. We have waited for a very long time for this opportunity. For the proof that could not be disbelieved, and for a warrior to appear, someone we could trust without doubt." She gives me a soft, sad smile. "That person is you, Smoky Barrett. If you are ever consumed with regret about your scars, remember this—they are how we were able to believe you. Please remember it. This alone should vindicate you."

"Maya, if you trust me, then you should put that shotgun away and let me help you."

She glances at her watch and shakes her head, still smiling but impatient. "My time is nearly done. You must listen." Her voice and eyes are urgent. "You must stop the person who killed me from taking their own life, if you can. There are no trails, there is no proof, other than what I have told you and what you will find in the bunker beneath the grass. The only proofs I can offer you are these: I will die before your eyes after telling you it would happen. You'll find evil in those houses. And not long from now—perhaps weeks, but possibly months—the first of these two men will open the gates of hell."

Before I can respond, she tosses the shotgun to one side, turns, and shouts at the crowd, "I fight without the knowledge of the Father, as a member of the Rose of Swords, against the hidden tyranny of the Black Gloves!"

I'm too dazed to completely register this. Raw, naked relief is babbling away in my head. No gun at my baby anymore no gun at my baby anymore thank you thank you thank you—

"Death to all who fight under the Rose! Close the door! Close the door!"

A middle-aged man with brown hair is shouting this from the curbside of the police car, as he stands on the lawn. I recognize him as one of the home-owners, but can't recall his name.

Before I can understand what I'm seeing, the man lifts his shirt and pulls out a handgun. He points it at Maya and begins firing. Her head explodes in front of me, and I feel something wet splash against my face and chest. She pitches sideways, her brains running from her skull as she topples.

Then he turns the gun on me, and time becomes irrelevant.

I can smell the rain, Daddy, I think, a hazy singsong in my mind. *I can smell the rain.*

The year he got sick with cancer, Dad and I took a trip around the world. It was his greatest unrealized dream. I took two months off, and it was just him and me, seeing the things there are to see.

Why does a gun always look so huge when it's pointed at you? I wonder idly. I can see the brown-haired man's eyes crinkle in concentration, and I know he's getting ready to fire.

We ended our trip in Seattle, because Dad had always wanted to see the giant redwoods. It was drizzling on and off that day, but it was also warm, and the sun was out. It made us feel clean and alive.

I remember it so clearly, Daddy. That exact moment. When you asked me.

When we found the redwood, Dad was speechless. The look of amazed happiness on his face is something I still cherish. It helped me through the rougher times, when his dying started to become an ugly affair, and I have often wondered if that was part of Dad's plan all along. He was clever and beautiful that way.

"I'm going to miss the simple beauties most, Smoky-mine," he said. He closed his eyes and breathed in deeply. "Like that, right there. Can you smell it, honey? Can you smell the rain?"

The brown-haired man has the look now. I recognize the look less because I've seen it than because I know it. It's the look of commitment someone gets on their face when they've accepted the burden of killing another person.

Ah, Tommy. I'm so sorry...

Then the air explodes and shakes, and a huge mass moves in front of me; that shakes, too, and something wet rushes down my legs as the world ends and I scream and scream and scream.

CHAPTER THREE

Consciousness doesn't return gradually—it roars in, thundering like Niagara Falls.

I can hear the sounds around me—voices shouting, cop shoes banging against the pavement, a woman's scream—but they are thick and indistinct, as though the world were underwater.

I feel floaty. Some speck in the mental distance pulses darkly.

A memory.

I giggle in my mind, and it sounds horrible and wrong and yet—*I don't care. ...*

The speck rushes toward me, screaming like a freight train, growing bigger as it approaches until it fills the mental sky. It sits there, a black sun as bloated as a tumor.

How's it going? I ask the speck, determined to seem nonchalant.

Did you? it asks, grinning an obscenity. *Huh? Huh? Didya?*

I frown, feeling the question run down my spine, bone by bone. I realize I've begun to exist on two levels at once. The speck is still all. World-ending black pus still runs from each corner of its mouth—but I can feel my actual face frowning, too. I can feel the street against my butt, and something warm and soft against my head.

Huh? Huh? Did you?

Did I what?

The speck has no eyes. A slimy black tongue, thick as a boa constrictor, lolls out and hangs wrong, like a rapist's cock.

Did you misplace something, honey? Huh! Huh? Didya? Maybe... the speck licks its lips, and the air narrows in a sudden vacuum of anticipation. *Maybe... something inside you? Something wet?*

I open my eyes and find Alan gazing down at me. His face blocks out everything else, even the sky.

The question echoes in my head. Something wet?

"Water ... ," I whisper.

Everything comes rushing back, all at once: the girl, the man, the firing guns, and most of all, worst of all—the warm wet rush of liquid down my thighs. I can feel it now, turning clammy against my skin. Every muscle I have shivers at the same time.

"*Baby!*" It should be a scream, but my throat closes, strangling it to something between a whisper and a screech. Huge, hot tears run down my cheeks. Some of them pool in my ears.

"Look at me, Smoky," Alan says, his eyes fixed on mine, demanding my focus. "It's not what you think. Smell my finger. This is you." He brings his right index finger to my nose. I cringe at the acrid scent of urine. He gives me a sad smile and nods. "I checked. Your bladder emptied. Your water didn't break."

"Are you—" I draw in a single deep, shuddering breath. "Are you sure?"

"I'm sure, honey. I promise, I'm sure."

Alan never calls me honey. Then: *What's wrong with the light?*

I blink away my tears and realize that we are ringed by police officers of all shapes and sizes. They're standing in a circle around me and Alan, their backs to us, weapons drawn. We're covered and cut in two from every direction by their long shadows. As they shift and move in place, the shadows rock against us slowly, like kelp in a calm ocean.

"Took them about ten seconds to do that," Alan says softly, nodding toward the cops' backs. "Might have to adopt them all."

My mind is starting to work again, but slowly. I don't bother trying to move. My muscles are still loose and rubbery. "What's ... " I lick my lips. "What's happening?" My voice is rough and husky, like it used to be some mornings when I was still a smoker.

"Just found out we got a sniper," he says, not taking his eyes off mine.

I stare back at him, blinking. Searching for a command response that makes sense, as I lie on a street in the night with urine drying on my legs and my mind still warming up from the black cold that had delivered it. "How?"

"How'd we know?" He nods, as though I'd already answered. "One of the locals was a Marine sniper in the Gulf War. Got great eyes. He saw the top of the guy's head come off *before* all the cops nearby started plugging him full of extra holes, and before he heard the sound of a shot fired. Next thing I know, we're surrounded."

"Callie? James?"

"They're fine. Everyone took cover, but I've spoken to them both by mobile. James is on the phone with the director. Callie's off getting you some new clothes from one of the homeowners. Including some, ah," he says, shrugging, his eyes embarrassed. "You know. Underthings and stuff."

For the first time, I can see how worried he is. It screams from every clenched muscle in his jaw, from the way his eyes move up and down my body, again and again, checking and rechecking.

I look directly at him and give him a small smile. "'Underthings'?" I tease, softly. "'And stuff'?"

Alan's eyes stop roving, fixing on mine for a long moment. His face twists in pain, and though it lasts only a heartbeat, it involves every muscle in his face. I glimpse a flash of Alan as a boy, back when the world was still bigger than he was.

The moment passes. He smiles back at me. Then he grins. "She said to tell you not to worry, there should be another woman on this block with a butt as big as yours." The grin fades. "'Course, she was crying a little when she said it."

A flash of memory—the girl's head exploding—something wet on my face ... my fingers fly up to my cheek, searching, but I find nothing.

"Looking for the blood?" Alan asks.

"Yes."

"You're okay. It only got on your cheek and on the shoulder of your jacket. Nothing in your eyes or mouth."

I close my eyes in relief. "It feels like the whole world has sharp edges," I whisper. "All just waiting for me to run into them belly-first."

Alan's eyes are sad, but he smiles at me anyway. It was the smile you were given when he let his heart show fully, filled with warmth and steadiness. "Yeah, well, you know the old saying—you're not paranoid if people really are out to get you. You've had two guns pointed at you in the last half hour.

One of them was a shotgun pointed at your baby. Those are some pretty sharp edges."

I scowl at him. "You must have been talking to Tommy recently."

"It was more about listening than talking."

Tommy had been lobbying for me to take my pregnancy leave ever since I passed the six-month mark. It had been endearing in the beginning but had become much less so in recent weeks.

We'd had a number of heated arguments about it—real roof raisers. This was completely out of character for us, but we were unable to stop once it started. It's not like anyone was ever really going to get hurt—Tommy and I were ninety-nine percent perfect—it's that the arguments were so passionate on both sides. It was black-and-white, scorched earth, no compromise.

Then at bedtime we'd supplement it with some passionate, ugly, angry makeup sex. Tommy would fall asleep covered in sweat, without saying sorry or telling me that he loved me. I'd curl into my belly, a mirror image of the child inside me, and fall into a deep, happy, sated sleep. Only my own snoring could wake me.

We'd both wake up refreshed, content, and ready to face the day. It was ridiculous and beyond our control, on both sides.

In the few rational moments granted me, I understood it was simply about the unbelievable stress. Pregnancy is a pressure cooker for any couple. My past and our various personal and shared experiences conspired to make it about a billion times worse, for us.

What do two people who love each other to death do to bleed off that kind of stress? I don't know what everyone does, but we shouted with red faces and then fucked ourselves into exhausted oblivion, and held on for the ride.

"I suppose I'm not exactly proving him wrong, here." I sigh.

Alan smiles. "Sharp edges. Your words, not mine."

One of the cops ringing us puts a finger to his ear, listening. The stenciled letters—SWAT—seem to glitter on his bulletproof vest under all this false light.

"Roger that," he replies. He rotates until he faces us. "Just a few more minutes, Special Agent Barrett," he says to me. "They're closing in on the shooter's location. We'd appreciate it if you'd stay where you are until we've cleared the scene." A pained, helpless expression passes across his young face, like a spasm. "I'm really sorry about all this, Special Agent Barrett."

"You don't need to apologize to me, Officer ... ?"

"Gray, ma'am. Jason Gray."

I muster up the best smile I can for him. "As long as you're standing there being my human shield, you don't really need to apologize to me for anything."

Gray has the greenest eyes I've ever seen, and they examine my scars for a second. He gives me a half nod of acknowledgment and a respectful but grateful smile. "Ma'am." He rotates again, putting his back to us.

Alan raises one eyebrow at me. "How about that?" he asks. "Chivalry isn't dead."

"He's young enough. It's still adorable when he calls me ma'am."

Something is nagging at me from the periphery of my awareness.

A sniper, I think. *Shooting to protect me ... ?*

Suspicious thoughts on suspicious legs start winding their sneaky way up the staircase of my mind.

"How many sniper-trained killers do we know, Alan?"

He frowns. "Callie's hubby. Maybe your hubby. I don't know—I guess that's it."

"That's a fail on the sexism test," I say, smiling at him. "Think harder."

Alan's brow furrows as he thinks, clearing as he smiles. "Kirby."

I nod my head. "Yes. I smell an overprotective husband in here somewhere. Idiot," I hiss under my breath. "Fool!"

Kirby Mitchell was an assassin who looked like a California beach bunny. She was probably only a few cards short of being a full-blown sociopath—she was not conflicted about the killing she'd done or would do in the future—but in spite of this, Kirby did have a code she seemed to believe in. It revolved around loyalty, and she'd paid her dues to gain my trust along those lines. Kirby was an unlikely friend, but a friend nonetheless.

"*Overprotective* might be taking it a little far," Alan says. His eyes rove our surrounds. "Considering the circumstances."

I only half hear him as I chew away on my lower lip, worrying. "Stupid man! Alan, if he was a part of this—what he did was illegal. This is serious!"

He waves a hand in dismissal. His eyes are kind. "Like they'd ever catch Kirby red-handed." He leans forward a little, looking into my eyes with his reassurance. "Like she'd ever rat Tommy out, even if they did. Right?"

"I guess ..."

"Besides, you don't know that Tommy had anything to do with this, right?" He pauses, waiting. "Right?"

"Right." I sigh, running my hands through my hair, then leaving them there, my elbows against the street. "Christ."

"Do we need to leave here, Smoky?" He's still peering into my eyes. "Be honest with me. What's the best move for you right now?"

Sometimes it's enough to be asked. I feel myself reconstituting in his gaze. My wayward trains of thought are fading, calming, slowing.

"The very best move is to go, Alan. But it won't hurt me to stay."

"You sure? Because you just tell me—anytime, anywhere, no explanation needed. Are you hearing me?" His words and their tone are focused. Forceful. "That baby is more important than anything here, and you don't owe anyone any excuses on the subject."

"I'm okay."

"Truth? Not being an obligated idiot?"

I give him a lopsided smile. "I'm sure. Thanks."

"No big deal," he says, straightening up. Dismissing any discussion of weakness on my part, again. "I will tell you this," he says after a moment. "If it was Kirby, I'm going to give her a kiss on the lips the next time I see her."

I run a hand over my belly. I glance at the dead man lying on the street with his brains around him.

He looks so surprised. Like a light that knew it was about to be switched off in the instant before it was. I swallow. Life. It can go that fast.

"Me, too," I answer honestly.

But I hope it wasn't her, I really do.

"Something's up," Alan murmurs. "Check out the kid."

Officer Gray has bent into listening again. "Copy that," he says after a moment, turning toward us as he does. "Shooter's dead," he says. "Suicide by gunshot. Another young girl." He nods his head toward Maya's dead body.

I sit up, slowly, feeling as ungainly as a manatee. "What the hell's going on here, Alan?" I whisper.

"Well, right at this moment, what's happening is that we're getting you out of those wet undies before the press notices, honey-love," Callie says softly from behind me. I feel her hand on my shoulder. She kneels down next to me. "We're going across the street and three doors to the left. Nice couple in their early fifties."

"Thanks."

She leans in close, putting her lips to my ear. "Are you fine, honey-love? Really and truly?"

I don't know why Callie is the catalyst, but my stomach goes hollow in an instant, and my arms start trembling. I turn my lips into her ear and whisper, "Please don't let anyone see me right now, Callie." I squeeze her arm hard. My fingers hum against her, filled with the sudden electricity of latent fear. "Hurry, please."

She moves like a dancer and without hesitation. Her coat comes away from her and settles around my shoulders. I get a whiff of Callie's subtle jasmine perfume and feel her warmth. "Where's my jacket?" I murmur, noticing for the first time that I'm no longer wearing it.

"Alan took it off you, honey-love," Callie says soothingly, as her hands on one side and Alan's on the other help me to stand and remain steady. "He was checking to see if you'd been shot."

Her words come to me in dream sound, like an ocean of grass swaying perfectly on some plain that lacked horizons. "Hurry," I whisper.

It's as though a block of ice has begun to grow inside me, expanding from my center in every direction. My blood is turning into slush. The neurons in my brain are slowing their vibration, becoming silent things with dulled edges.

It takes all my concentration to walk normally, in consecutive foot-to-the-ground steps. My mind won't sync with my body. There is some kind of minute interruption or delay between thoughts, nerves, and muscles. I see it happening after I've already done it, or I will my foot to move and am still wondering why it hasn't two steps later.

They get me through the door of the home, and I burst into tears. I sob standing up, clutching Callie's arms for support, while the couple I haven't yet met looks on in distress.

One of the few benefits of being seven months pregnant (and they are few) is that people tend to give you a pass on emotional outbursts. I hate crying in public, almost as much as I hate getting angry for no reason—but I've done a little bit of both this year.

I hold onto this truth and let the flood be the flood. As the tears begin to die down, the woman disappears for a moment, returning with a box of tissues. She holds it out for me, smiling tentatively. I grab a handful of tissues and blow my nose in one long, extended, gooey honk.

"Sexy," Callie teases in a soft voice. She gently moves a lock of hair away from the middle of my forehead.

"Yeah, well, stick around and you'll see worse," I mutter. "I fart, too."

"Yes," she agrees. "I've smelt them."

The man laughs out loud, startling all of us. His wife shoots him a look of admonishment and gives him a light whack on the arm. It's all so automatic that I can tell this is a habit of his: being unable to control his mirth, needing to be scolded for it.

I like him immediately. My dad was the same way, too.

"Thank you for letting me use your home and your clothes, Mr. and Mrs. ... ?"

"Darby," the man answers, still smiling. He dips his head once in acknowledgment.

"Of course it's not a problem," Mrs. Darby assures me. "We saw the whole thing." She grimaces in distress. "When that girl pointed that gun at your baby ... " She closes her eyes tight and shakes her head before opening them again, like someone trying to shake off the devil's touch. "No more about that. You were there, too, after all."

"I'm Ben," her husband interjects. "My wife's name is Veronica."

"I'm Smoky."

They smile back, and we share a brief moment of comfortable silence. Humans who don't have any desire to hurt one another, strangers otherwise, sharing a moment by the fire. Ben is tall—six feet two or three—and he's rail thin and gangly. He has blond hair that looks the same, what my father would have called "a rioting mess of the finest order." He has the kind, open face of a man who can't hold back his laughter, but his eyes have a guardedness that seems permanent, backed by a sadness that feels forever. The contrast between the two is striking ... and beautiful. A man is alive inside that gaze, and he's seen a thing or four.

He has eyes like Tommy's, I realize. I wonder why.

Veronica is short next to her husband, perhaps five feet three or five feet four. She's a blonde, too, but her body isn't thin. She's Rubenesque. A soft stack of planes and curves made to be worshipped by some impoverished and passionate sculptor. Her eyes are a clear, soothing blue, and her lips probably belong in a poem somewhere.

I want to hate her on sight, but she radiates too much sincere warmth and concern. The very best very beautiful women have this quality, and you love its presence too much to keep the flame of envy lit for long.

"Are you ready to use the shower?" Veronica asks me, softly.

"That would be just about perfect right now, thanks."

She touches my arm absently, that assumptive touch of comfort that older women give us without insult. "Follow me." She smiles a smile of soft breezes and warm sunshine feeding a garden of vegetables and roses. *All will be well again, one day*, this smile says. I can almost believe it.

"I'm right behind you."

I nod at an old photograph of Ben on the wall at the bottom of the stairs she's led me to. He's in his late twenties or early thirties. He's wearing Marine dress blues, standing at attention and taking the moment very, very seriously with five other men dressed similarly.

"You were in the service," I say to him, tilting my head at the picture.

"Marine Force Recon." He smiles, studying the photograph with a faraway look in his eyes. "Did various things here and there." He shrugs. "Was lent out to other agencies, from time to time." He looks at me, and while his eyes remain kind, there's no humor in them. "So you shouldn't feel ashamed about crying in front of the wife and I, or ever worry that anyone else will ever hear about it." Ben smiles again. "I understand tears. Why do you think I laugh so much?"

The Darbys' walk-in shower is an obvious labor of love. It's all marble and huge, with two built-in sitting benches, steam nozzles, and multiple shower-heads—including one that hangs directly above, waiting like a metal angel to dispense its liquid luxury.

I lock the door and peel off my clothes, wrinkling my nose at the pungent smell of my own urine. This pregnancy has made my pee smell horrible, for some reason.

"Yet another sexy bonus," I mutter bleakly, folding the clothes and putting them into the plastic bag Veronica provided, tying it off tight.

The Darbys have found an almost human-size plush bathroom mat. It covers the floor so completely there's no danger of ever having to walk on the cold tile. It's incredibly soft. I almost groan with pleasure when I feel it against my feet.

"Traitors." I sigh, looking down at said feet.

In general, I have been lucky when it comes to pregnancy. I get a bit chubby, but not too much, and I have a metabolism that lets me work it off quickly afterward. I don't have the visible hormonal issues that plague some women. I don't get acne, and I had no hints of postpartum depression after I had Alexa. But my feet—they become my enemy.

"Decreased circulation, added weight, an increase of uric acid in the body, lower blood sugar ... " My doctor had smiled at me with understanding, spreading her hands at the same time in helplessness. "Pregnancy is full of idiopathic comorbidities."

"*Idiopathic* is what doctors say when they don't really know the cause of something," I'd groused.

She chuckled. "And *comorbidity?*"

"You're saying it's not my feet's fault they hurt—it's the pregnancy. And you're saying there's nothing to be done about it," I had finished, mournfully.

I move to the shower door, which is open, and turn on the hot water. I wait for the water to heat the tile and watch the steam soften my sharp edges as it fogs the mirror. I almost look beautiful, for a moment.

I adjust the temperature, keeping it as hot as I can safely stand it, and walk into the shower, closing the door behind me, making sure it seals to trap the steam. I put my back against the wet far wall and slide down until I'm sitting on the floor. Then I cantilever and waddle on my butt, feeling terminally unsexy as I do, until I'm seated under the shower head in the ceiling.

There I sit, letting the near-scalding water cleanse me. I lower my head, cradle my stomach, and give up on time and its increments of worry. I let the water cover me, as much as one can without drowning, and wait for my courage to return.

Veronica's clothes are all just a little big on me, with the exception of a black T-shirt. It's an XXL, and the words *Go Big or Go Home!* are stenciled on the chest in bold white letters. I'm guessing that it's Ben's. Even then, it barely makes its way around my stomach, and it's a tight fit. I roll up the cuffs on the sweatpants and brush my hair, regarding my cell phone with dread all the while.

Tommy called twice while I was in the shower and once since I've been dressing. I am absolutely terrified about talking to him, for reasons I'm unable to articulate to myself. It's all raw emotion.

Because you fucked up, that's why. And you know it. You refused to go and leave because you're stubborn, and your baby almost died because of it.

I sigh and pick up the phone.

He'll be pissed. Maybe crazy. He has a right to be. Don't argue with him. Just roll with the punches.

It's as though Tommy has heard my thoughts. The phone lights up with his number, vibrating in my hand so unexpectedly I almost let out a little scream. I close my eyes, take a deep breath, and answer. "Hi, honey," I whisper. "I'm fine, and so's the baby."

"Are you sure? Are you absolutely sure? Have you seen a doctor yet?"

"No, I—"

"God damn it, Smoky!" he bellows, not hearing me, not listening. "Do you have any idea what it's been like here? They showed it on the fucking news, for God's sake!"

I've never heard raw fear in Tommy's voice before. He sounds utterly hopeless, like a man literally losing his mind with worry. All the shouting is about this fear.

Back, damn darkness! Begone!

"Please stop swearing, honey," I say, in a soft voice.

Tommy never—*never*—uses profanity. It's not so much a moral point as an ingrained habit. It's just not him. This is only the second or third time I can recall ever hearing the F-word or its like fall out of his mouth.

Tommy goes silent for a moment, and I can hear his ragged breathing through the earpiece as he struggles for control of himself. "Is my wife really not hurt?" he asks, finally. "And my son?"

"Yes. I promise."

Another single, long silence ensues, followed by a sigh so bereft it breaks my heart, again. "I—I saw it on the news, baby ... and for just a few minutes, I—I ..."

"You thought I was dead."

"Yeah."

I smile, hoping he'll somehow feel it in my words even though he can't see it on my face. "Well, I'm not."

More silence. "Tell me everything that happened."

I don't think twice. Tommy used to be a Secret Service agent, and a good one. We'd crossed paths once, professionally, years before Matt died. He runs a large private security firm now, and Tommy will be a pro until he dies. He's just not built to accept his own incompetence.

Because of this, I've found the truth tends to be the best path to reassurance with him. So I talk, patiently answering the staccato bursts of questions when they fire.

"Hmm...," he muses, once I've finished. "So it's a circus of law enforcement under a media microscope—and you're in charge."

"That's a fair summation, yes."

"Crap." More silence. A sigh. "Are you doing okay with that?"

I bite my lip. "I'm intimidated, Tommy. I feel like I don't belong here, and everyone's about to catch on."

"They're not. What they're all secretly thinking is that no one could do it, certainly not them, so thank God it's you. What they're all secretly hoping is that you will. People like heroes. Just ignore them and follow your instincts." He downshifts from this profundity without warning. "I'm sending Kirby. She'll be there in a few hours."

"Not necessary. Not to mention—embarrassing."

Marriage makes one sensitive to the subtle changes. I can't see Tommy's face, but the weight of the pause that follows tells me he's struggling not to yell at me some more.

"She'll be discreet," he finally manages.

I bark out a laugh. "Discreet? Kirby?"

Tommy chuckles a little in return, which makes me feel better. "That's a fair point." He sighs. The levity sinks into the silence and is gone. "But... that's just too bad," he growls. "This isn't negotiable, Smoky. I know you can't leave. I get that. But if you stay and won't let me send Kirby to watch over you— won't let me do anything to feel like I am protecting my wife... I'll..." his voice trails off. "I'll go crazy."

It occurs to me that I've heard Tommy talk more since I've been pregnant than I ever did before. Tommy is the prototypical "strong and silent type," and he generally defines the word *laconic*.

Don't make him beg. Because he will.

The words come from nowhere, but I know they are true and should be heeded. Tommy's desperate at a distance. That's a terrible place for a man like him to be.

"I'm sorry, honey," I whisper. "Of course you can send Kirby. I miss you right now. I wish you were here with me."

"I do, too."

The silence returns, but it's more comfortable now. This has the quiet, tired sweetness of relief.

"Hey, you know what?" I ask him.

"What?"

"Almost getting killed makes me horny."

He chuckles. "Being pregnant makes you horny."

"I can't deny it, but it's also true that your naked butt, in the right light, could make a ninety-year-old nun horny."

"Really? Well, don't worry—nuns aren't my thing."

Tommy is a gourmet meal for the eyes, clothed or naked. He's ridiculously sexy, like a model you'd see on the cover of *GQ* magazine, next to a tagline that reads "This issue—Latin lovers!"

I'd met Tommy again on the first case I took after Matt and Alexa's death. It had never occurred to me that another man would ever want me again. I'd found that Tommy was only waiting for his opening. He'd touched me with honest lust, while the lights were on and his eyes were open.

"He kissed my scars and made love to me with the lights on," I once confided to Callie. "I know that sounds like a sordid reason to have started trusting him, but ... "

"It made you believe him," Callie had supplied, finishing my sentence for me. "Words would never have worked. I understand completely, honey-love. I'm a veteran of distrust when it comes to relationships."

Whatever, however—Tommy's love has healed me. It has helped return me from the precipice that hung above the darkness I'd spent so much time peering into. Maybe preparing myself for. Life is good—something that still feels like only one shoe dropping.

"Hey," Tommy says. "Bonnie's going nuts. You have to talk to her."

"Of course I will."

"Hang up once you're done with her. I'm going to get busy with getting Kirby on a plane."

"Tommy. I love you so much."

"As well you should," he jokes. That helpless silence again. "Please be careful with my wife. She's my whole life now."

He hands the phone to Bonnie before I can reply.

"Mama-Smoky! Are you really okay?"

"I'm fine, honey. I promise."

Bonnie is my adopted daughter, the first person to truly anchor my heart after Matt and Alexa died. Her mother, Annie King, had been my best friend in high school. Annie was murdered to attract my attention. The killer had tied Bonnie to her mother's corpse and left her there for days.

When she first came to me, and for a long time after, Bonnie was mute. Time has moved on. Bonnie has blossomed, for the most part. But the things she's witnessed have placed their indelible mark, as such things do. She's a gifted artist who wants to grow up and hunt bad men. She's a thirteen-year-old with eyes aged beyond mine by her experience and by her plans for her future.

She has her mother's face, blond hair, and blue eyes. She's even begun to sound like Annie, faintly. I predict gooseflesh in my future, from time to time, as the ghost of Annie continues to rise within Bonnie.

"Too much, honey," I tell her.

"Way too much," she replies.

This is our love in shorthand. *How much do I love you? Too much. Way too much.*

Bonnie, too, is laconic by nature, and I hear Tommy's brand of silence on the line. "Were you scared?" she finally asks.

"Very. I passed out and even peed myself."

I wait out that brief silence again, listening as the cogwheels turn inside her head. "But Alan and Callie protected you, right? They didn't let anyone see?"

Bonnie's differences are not so visible. They tend to come out, ironically, in the same way as they tend to for the men I hunt. It's a matter of viewpoint, attitude, and affect, as opposed to direct revelation.

Bonnie looks like the rest of us, but she is not, of course. There is a certain unflappability, a certain lack of fear. Too much willingness to look and see, when others would turn away or run.

When other thirteen-year-olds—or adults, for that matter—would have gasped, or perhaps exclaimed "Oh my God!" at being told about me pissing myself, Bonnie was instantly operational: What was done? Who did it? Were you protected?

It worries me now as it always does, as it has a thousand times before. As it probably will a million times again. But I say none of this. "Of course they did, honey," I tell her.

"And the alien?"

"Your brother's fine."

Bonnie sighs, and it startles me a little. It sounds so adult. "It's not just you anymore, Mama-Smoky. You need to be more careful." Her tone is scolding. Even a little harsh.

"Honey, I do know that, and I am careful. Of course I am—I love you guys."

"I know you do. But, Mama-Smoky? Love wouldn't have kept that shotgun from killing my brother and from killing you, too. And that would have killed Tommy." She pauses. "And it would have killed me. So if you *really* love us—be more careful."

I've always thought there was nothing worse than being correctly scolded by your child. They are rare, those moments, but they do happen. You know them when they come because they strike you dumb and shame you. "I hear you, Bonnie. I really and truly do, I promise you."

Silence. It feels like a pointing finger. "I was scared," she says, her voice careful and emphatic. "Scared like ... *then*."

"Oh, honey ... "

Her voice is calm, quiet. "I felt like not talking again, Mama-Smoky. Not for long—don't worry—but I remember how that felt, when it felt like the thing to do."

"Bonnie, I'm so sorry—"

"No." She delivers it as a statement, an absolute. "Don't be sorry for your job. Don't ever. Just be more careful, 'K?"

That's my family, I think, as I wipe away a tear. Always messing up my makeup by making me cry. "I promise."

"Good."

"And Kirby's coming."

"Better. I love you, Mama-Smoky. I still need you in my life in order to keep talking. I thought I didn't, but I still do. And everything's so great now, you know? Everyone's got smiles in their eyes again, and I have a new brother coming and ... you know?"

"Yeah, baby. I do know," I reply, smiling to myself because now, I think, she sounds a little more like a thirteen-year-old girl.

"Will you tell me about this one?" she asks.

The case, she means.

And just like that ... old Bonnie's back. My unblinking voyeur of the terrible.

"We'll see. I need to go, honey. Are you okay? I'm sorry you were so frightened."

"Yes, I'm fine."

"Too much, baby."

"Way too much, Mama-Smoky. Bye."

I stare at the phone for a moment after she hangs up, thinking about her and the things she said. I put it down and look at myself in the mirror. "You may be dressed in sweats and a man's T-shirt," I tell this self I see. "You may be pregnant, terminally short, and ugly—but you're still in charge. Take a lesson from your daughter, and get operational."

I close my eyes and tilt my head to listen. Yes, I can hear them out there. The kind of rising din only an ever-growing crowd of humans can make. Kind of like an ocean, if it whispered. I open my eyes, hoping for a heartbeat to see someone much more confident and qualified looking back at me.

Oh, well.

What's that thing they say to baseball players?

Welcome to the Show.

Then I hear another sound from downstairs, and it roots me, shocked, in place.

The sound of gunfire.

CHAPTER FOUR

I grab my weapon and fling the door open, blinking as the steam from my shower billows outward. A single rush of cold air bites into me.

"Alan!" I yell. "Callie!"

It's James who replies. His voice hums with adrenalized focus. "The homeowner's killed his wife!" he shouts.

Ben? I'm nonplussed. *Can't-seem-to-keep-myself-from-laughing, Ben?*

"Where is he now?"

"He walked into the fucking pantry, closed the door, and disappeared by the time we got there," Alan says. "Guy did a total Houdini."

"Anyone else hurt? Is Veronica dead?"

"We're all fine; she's all dead, honey-love," Callie replies.

"I want to come down. Is it clear?"

"We don't know where Mr. Darby went," she answers, "but he's definitely not here right now."

Automatic gunfire can be heard outside. It sounds like gravel being thrown at an empty pie pan.

"What the hell is happening out there?" I ask, moving slowly down the stairs, my weapon at the ready.

Ready for what? It's not loaded anymore, remember? Pregnant women. Firing guns. Remember? All those things that hurt your baby?

"No clue yet," James says. "We've been a bit distracted by Mr. Darby."

That's my James. Sarcasm in even the most stressful of moments.

I find it oddly comforting, and I hold onto that feeling of normality as I reach the bottom of the stairs. I'm breathing hard from mixed causes of effort and stress.

That'll affect your aim, I think, my eyes darting right toward the living room, left toward the kitchen. *You need to slow down your breathing and your heart rate.*

I breathe in through my nose for three counts, hold it for three counts, expel for three counts. Repeat. I feel my heart calming, my thoughts focusing. My hands stop their micro-trembling. I can hit what I aim for now. I'm ready to kill something, if I have to.

Except ... you have no bullets in that weapon, remember?

I feel the truth of it in the weight against my palm and take a microsecond to marvel at the power of learned behavior under stress.

What was your plan? Were you going to aim *him to death?*

"Where are you guys?" I ask.

"Kitchen," Alan replies. "Where it all went down."

I walk to the right, my weapon ready but pointed low, my finger resting against the side of the trigger guard. Empty or not, the sheer feel of it comforts me, and I decide to let it. I round the corner of the wall that divides the kitchen from the living room and see Callie crouched on the tile next to Veronica's corpse. I scan the room and find Alan and James peering into an open doorway. I assume it leads into the pantry.

I walk up to Veronica and stare down at her. Ben shot her point-blank in the forehead with a large-caliber revolver. The top of her head is almost completely gone.

"Notice anything odd?" Callie asks.

The moment she asks the question, I know it has an answer. I frown, looking for the thing on the tip of the tongue of my understanding. "She's smiling," I say, "but her eyes are open."

"And it's not just any smile, is the thing, honey-love. She liked where she was going."

It's true. Veronica's smile is a work of beatific perfection. She could be Mary in a painting, off to meet all the heavenly hosts.

"There's a door in here, somewhere," Alan mutters.

I go to where he and James are, peering in. "Seems like a normal pantry."

"Helpful." James sneers.

"The problem is, he closed the door first, so I didn't see what he was doing. I was there in under twenty seconds, but this is how I found it. No Ben Darby."

I examine the room again through the doorway. It's a walk-in pantry, decent-size but not ostentatious. The walls are lined with built-in shelves, and every shelf seems fully stocked. I see mostly canned food, but also some bags of pasta and rice, as well as condiments. The pantry is lit by a single bulb in the ceiling, which is on. A string hangs down from the bulb's socket.

"The exit would have to be big," I muse. "Twenty seconds is no time at all. And it would have to open easily."

"A wall or a part of the floor, perhaps," James says, nodding. "I agree."

"Then we can find it, too. We just need to do what he did: go in the pantry, close the door, and look. Shouldn't be too hard to find."

"Sure," Alan agrees, giving me a grim smile. "Unless Ben decides to pull a Phantom of the Opera on us, and reappear through some other trapdoor."

A thought comes to me. I blink rapidly, considering it. "I wonder..." I glance at James. "The girl, Maya—before she died, she said something about a 'bunker under the grass.'" I raise an eyebrow. "Maybe that's where Ben went?"

James frowns in thought, taking this idea in. "Maybe," he agrees.

The sound of gunfire—long, extended shooting—comes from outside the house.

"Jesus," I mutter. "Sounds like war out there."

"What's the plan?" Alan asks.

"You will all do nothing, of course," Callie says, from behind us. Her voice is cold. "You'll wait for SWAT to finish with whoever they're busy shooting at outside, then call them in to clear this house and locate Ben."

"Not your call, Callie," I murmur, still staring into the pantry. I can feel it pulling me forward, toward the mystery, not away from it. My default position since birth.

Callie's hand on my shoulder breaks the spell. I turn to look at her, surprised. "Honey-love," she chides. "I will hold you down, tie you up, cuff you—whatever's needed." Her voice is soft. Her eyes are gentle, too, but entirely unyielding. "You will not go diving into any further tactical situations, while I am around, until that nephew of mine you carry in your belly is born." Her hand squeezes my shoulder once. "Because eventually, the house always wins."

"I'll back that play," Alan says, giving me the same mother-teacher-daddy eyes.

James sniffs. "Frankly, I don't know why you're here at all."

"Eat shit, James," I snarl.

"No," he says, sneering slightly. "I'll just call your husband."

49

"You dirty-fighting bastard ... " I breathe, appalled.

"We wait," Callie orders. She peers into my eyes. "We wait."

I feel the storm of a fight begin to rise inside me—and then I hear Bonnie's words again. *You need to be more careful.* "Positively prophetic," I murmur. "Damn it. We wait," I agree.

"It sounds like the gun chatter is dying down outside," Alan observes.

"Take me through what happened," I say. "Ben just ... what? Strolled into the kitchen and blew his wife's brains out?"

"Pretty much," Alan says. He shakes his head. "Veronica told him she needed to see him in the kitchen—"

I interrupt him. "She asked first?"

"Yep. I only saw it because I went looking for a bathroom. I saw the gun go off, but not what led up to it."

For some reason that I can't really completely define, not even to myself, I suddenly feel exposed. Perhaps it's the way things have been going down since we got here. As though things that were supposed to seem beyond our control were actually simply dominoes being made to fall as they had been planned to fall.

I feel like we're being herded.

I clench my belly, and the alien, Fred, whatever this thing is that I've never seen but love so much, decides to bend it like Beckham and kick me in the bladder. It's as though he agrees with me. This does nothing to ease my anxiety.

"Move!" James shouts, grabbing me and spinning as he says it.

The click that caused this had fallen like a footstep, instant and consonant; and all I have time to think of is: *Please ...*

The grenade comes flying out of the pantry and bounces off the kitchen island. I see this in my peripheral vision as everything slows, once again, and I wrap my arms tightly around my stomach and crouch as deeply into myself as I can without crushing my son.

You should not be here.

When the flash-bang goes off, the sound is deafening, the light is blinding. My ears ring, but only for a moment; then they are plunged into a thudding, numbed silence. My eyes register the great white flash, and for some reason I think *Hiroshima!* and some part of me waits for the bomb winds to come and kill us all.

I blink to clear the white from my vision, but nothing happens. I'm looking at a ghost in a snowstorm. I find myself imprisoned in a room of myself, sightless, soundless, full of fear. My gun is not in my hands, and I don't know why. All I can think about is all the information that I read regarding sound, sonic impact, and pregnancy. How I am not supposed to be around weapons-fire, explosions, or other large sounds that generate waves strong enough to potentially influence the health of my unborn child.

I feel fingers on my shoulder, and I can't tell whose fingers they are. Are they Ben's? Are they Alan's? It's a big hand, but I just can't tell. "Please," I mean to shout, and I think I do, but my ears are filled with fur and packed with cotton, so I can't be sure. "Please don't hurt my baby."

But I am being dragged backward by my hair, my heels scrabbling on the tile as I scream underwater into the soundless white soup my senses have become.

It's him! I think. *It's Ben, and he's crazy—and he's one of them, the Bad Men, the kind that could carve a baby from a pregnant woman's belly and hold it up for her to see while they laugh and laugh and laugh—*

You must get control of yourself! This is what I tell myself as my mind tries to run away from me. *You are a trained FBI agent, and you know these kinds of men. You're not helpless!*

My eyes are beginning to see black lines again, to filter light meaningfully as opposed to the endless milky dive that followed the flash-bang. My ears are cluttered and muffled, like I am listening to the amorphous sound shapes of a radio being played inside a box filled with water.

I've lost a shoe! I manage to notice, for no reason that's helpful.

There is a broad blankness in the seconds following the explosion, so it's difficult for me to know how far Ben has dragged me, or even—really—what part of the house we are in now. Then I smell the scent of cardboard that's been kept in the dark, along with old dust and the faint, biting odor of safe, unleaded metal.

The pantry.

Obvious, of course, but fear makes you uncertain before anything else. It was tactically simple, which is the same as elegant, when it comes to combat: Ben had thrown the flash-bang, reached out, grabbed me … and yanked.

He's decisive, confident, and unhesitating, my mind reads back to me. It's an automatic gesture on my part, cataloging him. An exertion of control.

You call this control?

I'm prevented from telling my own mind to bite me by a series of electronic beeps and a ratcheting click. All of this happens in the space of a second or two, and then I hear and feel a medium-size whoosh of air. It hits my face, ruffles my hair with a cyclone motion.

The air smells canned. *Higher oxygen content?* I see Maya's head exploding and remember her words. *Bunker*, I think, my mind frenetic but perhaps now a little less than frantic. *Bunker under the grass. Is this where he's taking me?*

Ben is dragging me forward again, and the floor changes from wood to the rough cold of crosshatched metal. The beeps repeat, followed once again by that whoosh of odd-smelling air.

There is a silence that Ben does not immediately fill. I can see his shape in the slowly un-forming whiteness that my eyes are still grappling with. I remember a blind victim I interviewed once, and wonder if this might be a little bit of what it felt like for her. Mostly I think about those beeps and that whoosh and how final they sounded.

Oh, God. He's locked us in.

"You'll need to stand up," Ben says, firm but cheerful. "Otherwise, I'll have to drag you and your baby down three flights of metal stairs, and I really don't think you want me doing that. Because I have to be honest with you, Smoky—I really don't care for babies much. Well, not the live ones, at least!"

He chuckles at this last comment, and it's so normal, so amused and warm and yet absolutely false. *It's like he's out of an episode of* The Brady Bunch *from another dimension. The one where they finally kill off Marcia for all her bitchy bullshit, then cook her up and eat her*, I think, fighting the demanding rising tide of hysterical laughter that really, really wants to be let off its leash.

"Do you think you can stand?" Ben asks, and I can hear the easy grin in his voice; no worries, no hurries, no fuss, no muss. "We're fine here, for the moment, but I'd really like to get on with it, and I'm not known for my patience. Unless I'm trying to keep you alive for torture, that is!"

He chuckles at his own joke, and I resist the urge to tell him that he sounds like a comic book.

"I'll stand," I say in a shaky voice. At least, I think I say those words. For some reason, it's harder to hear myself speak, and the sound of it inside my head sends pain shooting through my molars, pain with hooks and sparks.

Ben must have seen me wince. "That's probably from the bang," he says, sounding just a little bit too amused. "You might have vertigo, too. Some puking for sure, if you do get vertigo. But don't worry, it'll all pass." He leans in, letting me feel the heat of his breath on my face. "If you live."

Comic books, I think again. And I am afraid, as I begin to understand why. *It's a script.*

He's a calm, confident operator. He's learned that sticking to the script gives him more time to enjoy watching his victims squirm.

In the beginning of learning anything, and in some things, forever, we are too aware of our own ineptitude. Eventually, we simply learn to drive the car instead of watching ourselves drive the car. It's the only way to survive the stupidity of other drivers—by watching them instead.

Ben's script sounds like a script. It sounds contrived, overdramatized, and hollow. But Ben doesn't care. Why? Because he's learned not to watch his hands on the wheel but instead to watch how the eyes of his victims change in the fear light.

"What just happened?" Ben asks me, his voice intent. "What made you more frightened, just now?"

There it is, I think. *That hungry need.* Sisyphus fills a hole that's never full; in men like Ben, he doesn't roll a stone.

One of the monsters once told me: *Darkness fills everything and changes everything, but only by taking things away. Even when you eat it, it's an airy, electric snack, an emptiness like no other emptiness you ever consumed before, and it always leaves you hungrier than when you started.*

He was one of my more poetic monsters. They have their insights.

"I'm just afraid," I answer, choosing honesty.

Afraid of all that quiet certitude and what it means to me.

The average person has no idea—not the faintest concept, really—of how difficult it is for a human being to finally discard every last mask. It's not just that life's a stage—we also have an inability to ever believe that we are off it. We are compelled into our roles because in the end, they are us in all the ways that matter.

So it's hard getting down to the bare metal of our own programming, to the place where we all come in moments of overwhelming agony or perhaps sustained loss; or in the days after surviving a brush with death, when the previously dim and ancient "simple things of life" resume their blinding brightness.

Life is hard. It's a world made of stone, run by tigers. So it's no surprise that we drop our masks only when we're certain we don't need them, and even less of a surprise that such certainty is very, very rare.

For serial killers, it often never happens, not even when they're jailed. They'll blather on about the crimes expected of them, but they can become almost prissy—or even shy—when pressed for the worst details of their worst offenses. It often extends even to their own recordings of their crimes, if such recordings are made. The very worst moments—when the devil appeared—are the times the camera was turned off or the sound recorder was paused or stopped.

This odd shame at the evidence of their own private vices is often the only indicator of humanity that can be found in creatures like Ben.

So who would see them, then? my fear voice questions in a purring whisper. *These unmasked, one-true faces? Go on, now—complete the train of thought: Who?*

Why ... their *victims*, of course.

Ben stuck to a contrived script because he just didn't care what his audience thought anymore.

And guess what, folks? That audience is me.

This was the cause of my trembling.

Is this why you're so calm, Ben? Because you and I, we're already committed, in your mind? Down to the bitter end and all that shit?

My thoughts remain disjointed and far too fast.

Herded, I think, again; herding my own panicked thoughts away from the truth I keep circling and seeing, again and again. It burns too brightly. The lack of hope, because of the things I know, is too merciless and too harsh. It contains no miracles.

Ben was smooth, polished, practiced, but of all the things causing fear to spike through me in this moment, it is the fact that he is so focused on his victim's reactions.

On me.

Serial killers have a specific need to fill, usually with a specific victim type, and the truth was—nothing else would do. Nothing. What Ben's focus meant was that I was more than just fine, as food; as far as Ben was concerned—I was a delicacy.

I can almost feel the fine pinpoint of his attention prickling along the outer edges of what I conceive as the "inner me." I imagine a small boy in my mind, grinning as he pokes an injured puppy with a stick. Laughing when it yelps or squeals. Jumping for joy, maybe, if it screams.

"I can smell your fear stench," Ben whispers next to my ear, making me jump involuntarily, and I clutch at my stomach. "That hormone factory in your gut makes you reek when you're afraid. Probably makes your cunt rot, too."

Rot, I file away, automatically, trying to fill my mind with thinking that was under my own control, as opposed to formless fears that weren't. *Something more about his opinion of women in general than about me specifically…*

"What is it with women, anyway?" Ben murmurs, as though he'd just read my thoughts. "You walk through your lives with a wet hole rotting out the center of you daily, and then it vomits blood monthly—unless it's getting ready to shit a child." He chuckles. "You sure can make it feel good when you're screaming, though. Cummin' in a woman while she knows she's dying—well…that's like a train ride straight to heaven." I sense his grin. "Like frolicking amidst the angels, still wearing your horns and tail."

Ben's voice, I notice—and its cadence—has changed, roughened. Regressed. I suppress a shiver.

"What do you want, Ben?"

It's the only safe question I can think of.

"I want you to start moving down those fucking steps, cunt," he replies. He doesn't sound particularly angry. He's still a blur to me, a patchwork of unformed white blotches, but I can see his eyes now. They are crinkled by a grin and gleaming with wolfish humor.

"In fact," he continues, "if you don't—I'm going to punch you in the stomach until that baby pops right out of you like a grape." Ben laughs out loud, a kind of satisfied chortle.

"That won't be necessary," I say. I'm fighting to keep my voice level, but I don't succeed completely. It's the adrenaline.

Ben notices. He notices like an animal smelling meat. "Oh, yeah…" he breathes, suddenly, excited in a low voice. "There we go: the little quaver. The sweet little tremble between your teeth. How I love it so. Honestly, Smoky, of all the things in this world—and really, I mean of *all* the things of this world—it's the thing I love the most. Hearing it. That sweet, sweet tremble...like the sound a soul would make if you strangled it to death, bent it into a bow, and then used that to play a violin. ..." He pulls up short, emitting a brief, rueful chuckle. "Apologies. I'm no writer, and I'm surely no poet, but you know how it is." He breathes in through his nose slowly, gorging himself on my scent. "Enthusiasms. They can cause a man to get carried away."

I can feel the heat of his breath on my ear, baking against my cheek. I force myself to go still. To un-exist. Because Ben is straining at his leash, I can feel it. These are creatures that spend 99.9 percent of their lives suppressing their true natures, natures that encompass hungers inimical to their own freedom. Ben called it love. What else would you call it? We love our needs the most, in the end. He's willing to die for his, to be jailed for his pursuit of it.

Ben has a plan, true. But now, in this pinprick moment, his hungers have come calling.

I sense him straining to push his monsters back down into their box, though, and so I do my level best not to give him any slightest trigger. I freeze to stone. I think of arctic circles, glacier ice, and stillness.

His nose parts my hair. His breathing is smooth—a good sign—but the breaths come fast. I'm reminded of a red-breasted robin I once saw, backed up against a wall by a cat. Its tiny little chest beat like a jackhammer drum in fear. The cat's chest hammered away, too—but with excitement. I remember how still I was in that moment, just as now. Watching.

My mind told me to step forward, scare the cat away, do something—but I'd been mesmerized by what I'd noticed: The hunter and the hunted were breathing those quick breaths in time. *Huff! Huff! Huff! Huff!* in an almost perfect 4/4 rhythm, as though the act had joined them physically. Like they'd both heard some secret song at the same time, waiting under the surface of it all to be danced to, in such moments.

I watched the cat pounce, and never intervened.

Is this what they mean by karma? So it's not about all the people I've saved—it's about the bird I didn't?

Still, still. I hold myself so very still. Ben's nose moves through my hair, back and forth, gently, gently, intimate like a lover.

I always knew there was a reason I hated birds.

The perfect absurdity has always been a kick in the funny-butt, for me, and this moment proves no different. *Oh dear God,* I think in horror as I struggle to hold back the howls of laughter that have lodged themselves, kicking, in the last part of my throat. *Don't laugh! He'll eat you alive!*

Literally!

Which sends more laughter-that-means-death crawling from up my insides, squeezing my heart with its poisonous humor.

Something about that deep need I've always had, I think faintly, with the barest edge of me, as my chest goes *Huff! Huff! Huff! Huff!* like that poor, badly murdered bird, *to give God the middle finger. Not necessarily because I'm sure you don't exist, but because... it would be cool to get struck by lightning as the proof that you do, right?*

How freaking immortal would I be? "She gave the Almighty the bird—and he smoked her ass! With lightning!"

More scuttling feet in my stomach, more jolly hands trying to climb up and out of my mouth. I hold onto the thinnest rope of self-control and dangle out over nothing, trying to escape my own death wishes.

Again, like the animal he's allowed himself to devolve into, Ben senses... something. His nose, which had been rocking back and forth slowly, stops. He goes still next to me. "What was that?" His voice is filled with ugliness and displeasure.

Dim words, training from some instructor at Quantico, come to me: *Trust your instincts in a combat situation. Hesitation is death. Trust yourself and learn to use that to stay alive.*

I opted for honesty.

"I felt hysteria coming or—hysterical laughter, to be precise. I was afraid you'd misunderstand. ... "

"So you tamped it down, did you?"

"Yes."

The longest pause I've experienced in a while lumbers by, dragging its feet.

Ben sniffs loudly, twice. "Well," he says, "I can still smell your fear, so I suppose it's all right. Besides, I can hear the pitter-patter of little feet out there. They can't get in anytime soon, but why press my luck?"

It's true, I realize. My eardrums ache, and the headache surfing its way to me is going to be a tidal wave when it hits—but I can hear them out there.

They're coming through muffled and faintly—sounds on underwater walkie-talkies. But it matters. My team is outside, and while I can't be certain they'll save me—I can at least be sure they'll do their best.

Hurry, I urge them silently.

"It's three flights down to the door, fatty, so don't move too slow—but pace yourself, Smoky my-darling-my-dear. We've got many a mile to go this night before we reach the heart of darkness." The wolfish grin again, underlying the fakery of those gentle-seeming eyes.

I can see okay now. Everything lacks edges, and it looks like I'm viewing the world through translucent white film, but I am no longer blind. It's amazing how much better it makes things. A little bit worse, sure, but mostly better.

I kick off the other shoe, shrugging inside at its loss, and then I look for the rail that had been spoken of. I find it on my left, just as Ben had said. My vision's almost completely clear. I give myself a half second to assess my surroundings, to arrive.

The steps and rail are undecorative metal, painted black. The walls are all gray concrete, and from the look of it, the pour appears fairly new—as far as I can tell. I don't see any over-darkened spots or evidence of water or minerals snaking their way in from the soil outside, the way water always finds a way. I'm no expert, but this just doesn't feel—or smell—like a fifty-year-old room.

A glance to my left and down reveals only three sets of stairs meeting a gray concrete floor below.

"Get a move on," Ben murmurs. "Times a-wastin'."

Please hurry, I pray silently again. Then I close my eyes once and take a deep breath.

You must assume that they will never come.

I take a single step down and wait ...

"What the fuck are you doing?" Ben asks. He grabs the back of my neck with one large hand and jerks it hard, in a whiplash motion.

If he gets you down the steps, is it game over? Is this that moment? That "only hope"?

My foot reaches the next step. I let its weight settle, then lift the other. It hangs in the air, and I think thoughts of leverage and fulcrums and the physics of combat. I think about my baby, about being trapped inside the fully reinforced concrete walls of an underground bunker, at the complete mercy of a man I know to be not just a monster, but a man-with-a-plan.

Ben's other hand clamps around the front of my throat and meets the one gripping me from behind. He squeezes lightly but expertly, putting the tiniest pressure on my carotid arteries and pulling up so that my chin points out. It only takes a few seconds for my vision to start sparking at the edges.

"I spent ten years killing for my country," he snarls into my ear. "Putting down guerrillas in South American jungles. Teaching Asian friends how to motivate troops and torture. I spent lots and lots and lots and lots of time watching how people behave when they believe their lives are in danger. So don't get any bright or heroic ideas. I can promise you this: Your best chance at survival is most definitely going to lie in not fucking with me."

I'm sorry, baby, I whisper in my mind. *I'm just not brave enough, right now.*

I take the next step. Then the next. I want to cry. I want to slap myself for wanting to cry.

"I could tell you if I plan to kill you or not… but that would ruin the anticipation, which is really one of my favorite condiments in these situations."

"Condiments?" I ask, automatically.

"Still barking down the 'knowledge is power' path?" Ben chuckles. "Think understanding me will help you out?"

"It can't hurt."

"If you say so," he says, grinning. "But you might be surprised. Knowledge is power—all that crap—but it's also, well—knowledge. You might not like arriving at a full understanding of all that I am." He chuckles again. Ben sure is a jolly monster, all in all. "'All that I am.' Sounds a little on the God-complex side, doesn't it?"

Don't answer that, I tell myself.

"Two to go," Ben says. "Wait till you see what I have to show you. But anyway—condiments. I'm curious. Why would you want to know? Don't you think knowing will just make you crazier?"

I grip the railing for the next set of steps and start down. I move slowly, but we keep getting closer, no matter how much I drag my feet.

"Maybe," I admit, "but I can't help it. I'm compelled to know."

"Really?" His interest sounds genuine.

"Yes."

"So it's not a job, it's a calling?"

"Pretty much, yes."

He nods, his gaze thoughtful. "I guess that makes sense. I mean, I've studied up on you, of course. We all have."

We? I think. *All?*

"—so I know you're one of the best gunslingers this side of the Pecos, or ... whatever." He grins, shrugs. "Like I said, I'm not a writer. Shoot me. Or no—I'll shoot you!"

Ben laughs again, hale and hearty. He's very good at making it feel and sound like he's laughing with me rather than at my expense. I can feel the smallest tug of gratitude at this inclusion and recognize, again, that Ben is an accomplished monster.

We reach the second landing. I can see where we're going now. The steps lead to a small patch of concrete in front of a large blast door on the wall.

"But really—tell me about it. How does it work for you? How do you come to see ... us?" That light chuckle again. "Yeah—that feels right—'us.' So?"

"It's not simple to explain. There are a lot of factors involved."

He points the index finger of his right hand and uses it to burrow into a spot on my cheek, close to the place where my upper and lower jaw hinge together. He pushes in hard, and it feels like his finger's become a ten-penny nail.

The pain is so intense and immediate that I scream without sound, with my mouth wide open. A white-hot glare explodes behind my eyes for a moment, then fades. Ben releases me, and I pitch forward, puking on the steps.

"Gross," he observes. "Now listen, I'm going to give you the same rundown I used to give the members of this South American cartel, back when I was showing them the best way to extract information. See, you have to establish your controls. Your 'baseline of belief,' I used to call it." He raises the index finger again, and I flinch. "One—never, and I mean never—fail to get an answer to the exact question you asked. That's the first bottom line. It's unalterable. Do you understand what I'm saying?"

"Yes." I nod, wiping my mouth and shuddering. The nerve he'd clamped down on crackles and jumps, moving back and forth between numbness and agony—*flick-flick-flick-flick-flick.*

"Right. I didn't ask you to tell me if it was hard to tell me. I just asked you to tell me. You chose not to, so you paid a painful price. That's the simple transaction. Understand?"

"Yes," I reply, outwardly calm.

Ben reaches over with the same finger and once again jams it into the same spot, but harder this time. And longer. Long enough for me to find my voice this time, and I let out a screech of agony so hoarse it surprises me, even as I'm consumed.

Eternity rides by, and then he stops. I am bent at the waist, as much as I can be in my condition, and I'm shuddering and vomiting and crying. I can't seem to catch my breath.

"The second thing I always taught them," he continues, amiable enough, "is that you always make sure a command is followed once you've given it. Drop that discipline and you are up the creek, when it comes to getting information out of someone. People like their secrets," he observes. "You really have to intimidate them well if you want to get at 'em."

Intimidate them well ... Ben's emphasis on *well* seems surreal in its reality. He's absolutely right in this observation, but the point that gives pause is more that he knows the difference between "competent" intimidation and the amateur version.

"I—I don't understand," I quaver, struggling to regain my equilibrium.

"I told you to move down those steps. I never told you to stop just because you were talking to me, or because you were in pain." He leans in again and licks my ear. His tongue is superheated against my skin, and slimy. "If you keep dragging your heels, you really will force me to implement the third point I always made: Never fail to enforce a promised threat if the necessary conditions demand it. I told you, Smoky: Go too slow and I'll knock that baby out of your stomach with my bare fists." His ragged breathing is so loud in my ear that I can barely hear him. "Understand?"

"Yes," I say, hearing the bleakness in my own voice and seeing him smile in response to it. I move my feet—being careful not to slip in my own puke—and continue down the stairs.

Ben squeezes the back of my neck companionably. "What a good girl," he croons, his voice full of seemingly authentic warmth. "What a good, good girl you are."

I feel that little tug again, and it horrifies me. *We respond to strength*, I think. *Whether we want to or not, we respond to strength.*

Ben is a hotbox of straining, vital, deathly strength. It beats off him in time with his breathing and his heartbeat; it burns through his eyes. Some part of my female lizard-brain is already shouting at me to give up and show him my belly.

"You wanted to know how I see you," I offer, making sure I continue moving down the stairs.

"That's right. I want to know how someone who's so good at hunting men like me gets that good. Is it definable insight? Or pure instinct?"

It's an interesting choice of phrase. It belongs to a very thoughtful monster, indeed.

"It's like a puzzle," I say, my hand sliding down the railing slowly, as I step ... step ... step ... "I don't know what picture the puzzle will show till it's done, but I always know if I got it right."

"How?"

Amazing how one word can encompass ... well—everything. "I'm not sure how to describe it, exactly."

"Just start. That's how you resolve that issue. You figure it out by talking it out. Lay all the pieces out in front of you and describe them. It'll give you the whole."

It's insightful enough to make me consider Ben with new eyes, yet again. "Well ... ," I say, nodding as I continue to make my way down the last flight of steps. "Human personalities are more like snowflakes than they are the same. People are fractals inside, defined more by their differences than by what makes them the same. But ... there is a thread to human behavior, and you can fit it into rough classes."

"How do you do that?"

"Mostly by looking for what they can't help doing. It's not always easy to know what that is, and some killers will try and hide, or obfuscate it."

"Ah, yes. You're talking about signature."

"Yes. But not just the signature of the act." I frown, trying to put words to what I mean. "Every person has their own 'life signature' for want of a better word. They're governed by all the same things as the rest of us—hunger, shelter, pain—but they have their own ... take on it. Their own style."

"And you know when you know it, is that what you're saying? You know when you've understood the picture to be the correct one?"

"More or less."

We've reached the bottom. A huge blast door is set into the solid concrete wall. It's seven feet tall or so and quite wide. A keypad and thumb scanner are placed to the right of the door.

"Three feet thick." Ben grins, running a hand over the door's surface, shaking his head in admiration. "Good luck cutting through that." He indicates my swollen stomach with a wink. "And it's not like they'll be using explosives."

Oh ... God ... , I think, as the realization hits me.

"This was always about getting me here, wasn't it?"

Ben raises his eyebrows in what appears to be genuine surprise. "Oh-ho!" he says. "Definitely not just another woman hired to fill a quota. She's smart, too."

For the first time, I notice something chiseled into the stone above the door. I read it to myself as Ben punches numbers into the keypad and scans his thumb. I fight to keep my teeth from chattering. It says:

Abandon Hope, All Ye Who Enter Here.

There is a loud click and a grinding noise. Ben turns a wheel on the door, and it opens enough to let us enter.

"Let me show you what hell looks like, Smoky," Ben says. He is grinning, and his eyes have begun to shine. He leans in so that the tip of his nose meets the tip of mine. His breath is hot but sweet, like he'd recently brushed his teeth or chewed a stick of gum. "I have things very, very few people in the world have ever seen. Special things."

His grin widens, and he lets his teeth show.

I'm so scared, baby. So very, very, very scared.

CHAPTER FIVE

"A bit of an anticlimax, I know," Ben says to me, smiling. "But it's just a short walk to where we're headed."

It's a hallway, about thirty feet long, and it leads to another blast door the same as the one we've just come through. I feel claustrophobic, and not just because it is Ben who's with me. The ceiling in the hallway is eight feet high, and the walls are set closer together than they would be in a home. The fact that it's all featureless gray concrete, and that the only lighting is from hundred-watt bulbs set into the ceiling, doesn't help. I feel as though I am marching through a shoebox that has been turned over on its side.

"So, you were saying," Ben prods. "How you know when the picture is right."

"R-right," I stammer. I am distracted by the sense of things both approaching and receding at the same time. The blast door at the end of the hallway pulls me forward, while the one behind me dwindles. It feels like saying good-bye.

"So?"

"I'm not sure ... at least, I don't understand all of it. I discussed it once with a psychiatrist who was my mentor, and he said that some people, in his opinion, quote: 'Have a greater sensitivity to and certainty of the emotional models of others.' Why that might be. ... " I shrugged. "I don't know. Maybe it's because my mom died so young."

"Or maybe because you killed her?"

My head snaps toward him as the shock drop-kicks the pit of my stomach. My baby moves inside me, restless. I freeze in place.

"What did you say?" I ask, my throat dry.

Ben nods but doesn't punish me for stopping. I suppose it's because he's enjoying my reaction.

"I said: Maybe it's because you killed your mother."

I stare at him, dumbfounded.

My mother had gotten pancreatic cancer when I was ten. She died a year and a half later. It was very bad, very painful; toward the end, the pain medication wasn't strong enough. It was a catch-22: To eliminate the pain, she'd have to be given enough morphine to kill her.

My mother had always been a devout Catholic, and she had made it clear it was her intention to survive to the end. She did not believe in suicide, and was certain—as certain as I am that water is wet—that if she killed herself, she would go to hell. Her faith was not much help toward the end. It got to the point where she would beg me to kill her a few times a day.

In moments of near lucidity, she'd grip my arm hard enough—sometimes—to leave bruises, and she would beg me with all the power she had left to kill her. To take her life. The fact that she asked, drugged or not, was the clearest sign to me of her desperation. My mother lived for me and my father. I was her dream—she had told me this many times, and I believed her. The fact that she was asking her twelve-year-old daughter to end her life, to kill her own mother, told me everything I needed to know about the depths of the agony she was in, drugged or not.

My father was not up to the task of my mother being sick. In the beginning he would stay in the room, but as things got worse he was unable to. The sight of my mother reduced to a ninety-pound bag of bones; skin like parchment paper; her red hair gone to baldness and her eyes filled with madness and pain and ringed with worse; Dad just couldn't do it. He'd been too much of a dreamer all his life, and he had always believed in his heart that there was some just order to the universe. Something vanished inside him in those last few months of Mom's suffering, and it never came back fully.

People like to tell others to grow up, and I guess my dad grew up a little bit about the world then, but I wish he hadn't. He was dead himself just eight years later or so; and while for much of it he was a happy man, and though he was always a good father, he was never as freely joyful again after that as he had been before.

I changed then. I grew up, too. I suppose that's the point where I really started being more of the parent to my father than he was to me.

One day toward the end, she appeared. It was Mom, without a doubt. Her eyes were clear, and she even smiled at me, reaching out a hand for mine. I remember how light and insubstantial her hand felt as I folded it into mine, but also how it burned. Like she was a ghost who'd died in a fire.

"I am so, so very, very sorry, sweetheart," she told me, her voice straining in her throat to become even a whisper.

We talked for a few minutes before the pain dragged her down again, and she made it clear to me that her wishes remained the same: She would not commit suicide. She smiled at me so surely and with such clarity; and I kissed her forehead, which felt like hot desert sand; and I kissed each of her eyes in turn, and each of her cheeks, both her lips, and, finally, each and every one of those fragile fingertips. She started crying suddenly, and I remember realizing that these were tears of loneliness.

"Why won't anybody touch me anymore?" she said, her voice hitched, as snot ran down the furrows that starvation had created in her face.

I will never forget that. I've seen and heard a lot of truly terrible things, but that was the most palpably lonely, miserable voice I've ever had to listen to. And it was my mother's. So I climbed into bed with her, and I took her in my arms. She wept against me for a time, until she ran down, starting and stopping a few times as she let it all out. It was good that she did it. That was the last time I can ever remember my mother knowing, fully, where and who she was.

And then, when the final time arrived, and she was again screaming and shouting and puking and shitting and begging for death... I gave my mother the only peace left to her. I gave her a little extra morphine, something I'd researched at the library, and I watched her sink into herself and pass away. *She didn't commit suicide, God,* I said to the silence inside me. *Send me to hell for murder if you have to, but if you don't let my mom into heaven, you are one real asshole.*

I had only ever told one person—a killer I had caught who was obsessed with the subjects of sin and redemption. I needed information from this person, and his trade was that I tell him some sin of magnitude I had committed and had never revealed to anyone before.

Only him, right?

I scan my memory, trying to think of the room where I'd interviewed him, trying to see if anything jumped out at me as evidence of a recording device, or if I recalled whether there had been another observer at any point. I saw nothing.

"Trying to figure it out, are you?" Ben chuckles. "How I know? It's no great mystery: He told us."

"He…told you?" I repeat his words back to him, dumbfounded. "But why…? H-how? That would have gone against his pathology."

Ben places a light hand on my lower back, urging me forward again. "Well, we sought him out, not the other way around. It was made known to him that we would seek vengeance on his behalf. All that we needed was whatever information he had. About you." He chuckles. "Good thing we moved fast—someone made him dead pretty quick in jail, didn't they?"

We are less than ten feet from the blast door, and every step I take brings my hope circling closer to the drain. My mind is filled with confusion and fear. *How could they know what they know? Why did they focus on me for so long?*

And the most vital question of all, of course: What were they going to do with me?

"That took some real fortitude," Ben says, and he seems sincere. "That hardness is a part of it all too, though." He winks at me. "I mean, have you ever considered that I'm the kind of person who could do something like that? That maybe the reason you're so good at what you do is 'cause you share more DNA with humans like me than with the rest of the 'normal people'?"

"At least once or twice a year," I answer honestly. "Of course I have."

"And?" he prods.

I sigh. "Being able to do it? I guess there must be some truth to that. But…in the end, our motivations are very, very different, Ben. And that's where all the most important difference lies—at least in this arena."

"I'll give you that," he agrees.

We've reached the door. A muffled kind of numbness enters me as I watch him key in the numbers and slide his thumb across the scanner. The same grinding sounds as before, and Ben is again turning the wheel set into the door, swinging it open slowly but smoothly.

Ben indicates the doorway with a sweep of his hand, the picture of graciousness. "*Entrez-vous*," he says, grinning. His eyes are sparkling with expectation and hunger.

I hang there for half a moment waiting, hoping. But there's nothing else to be done. Move forward or die.

I walk through the door.

The room is huge. The ceilings must be thirty feet high, and I realize those stairs are steeper than I'd imagined. The room has been organized similarly to one of those loft apartments some city dwellers seem to enjoy on TV. I see a toilet, sans walls, in the center of the room, with a shower stall next to it. The walls are the same featureless gray concrete as the hallway. It's lit well enough and comfortably warm without being hot.

"All the power comes from on-site generators," Ben offers. "They make a hell of a racket, but we soundproofed the room we put them in, and the room's thirty feet or so under the earth, so ... "

"Very smart," I observe, meaning it. "By providing your own power, you keep from generating any power spikes that might make someone suspicious. How long has it been here?"

Ben hurts my hand this time, stabbing an iron thumb into a place above the webbing between my thumb and index finger. The pain is less all-encompassing than the pain in my neck had been but much more focused. It was the difference between being burned by a fire or stabbed by a pin. Neither was desirable. I screamed.

Ben wags a finger of admonishment at me. "Next rule: Never, ever, let your target lead the conversation. The target is always the one giving answers, never the one asking questions." He scowls for emphasis. "Never."

"I'm sorry," I breathe, humiliated by the slight begging sound of my own contriteness. "I understand."

Ben smiles at this and strokes my cheek. "Yes," he said, nodding thoughtfully, mostly to himself. "It sounds like you really are starting to get it." He points to the left. "Now we're going over there. I have a nice, comfy chair for you to sit on. Then I'm going to show you some ... " His grin is bare-toothed and insatiable, full of heat and promise. He licks his lips. "Things."

We are halfway across the room now, and sure enough, I can see the chair. It's obvious, ugly purpose imbues it not with life, but with presence and coexistence, reminding me of an altar. Ben's likely a handy guy; I'm sure he built it himself. It looks like a dentist's chair that's been modified to add chest, waist, ankle, and wrist restraints. I also see, as we approach, that there is another strap at neck level.

How much do you want to bet all the measurements fit me just fine?

The straps are formed from soft black leather, made not to chafe against the skin. The kind of thing you see all the time in adult toy stores or bondage shops, for those who can afford to spend a little money on their fetish. The chair itself is black and obviously new. It gleams like it's been freshly oiled, and I imagine that it has, at that. This is where, from Ben's view, all the magic happens. His attention to detail would have been complete, his focus sublime.

Seated in front of the chair is a simple television stand. Its base is made of laminated fiberboard and it's topped off by a sheet of tempered, frosted glass. A large plasma flat screen rests on top of it, turned off. On the floor next to the TV is a desktop computer tower, and a glance shows me that it's been hooked up to the television.

So much planning. Thank God I spoke to Tommy and Bonnie before this and know they're both home and okay. Otherwise, I might be losing my mind right now.

"When we get up to the chair," Ben says, "I want you to settle yourself into it. Make sure to find a comfortable position that you're happy with, because we're going to be here for a bit."

The chair beckons, along with its black straps and all that they could mean.

At what point do you gamble? At what point do you decide to believe that death is a certain possibility? That it's worth the risk of getting Ben angry enough to beat my stomach and kill my son?

We're standing next to the chair. It's now or never. I run a hand over my stomach, trying to commune with the life inside. *Tell me what to do, son*, I beg. I look with my mind's eye toward the sky that hangs inside my mind. *How about you, God? Any good advice?*

Both remain silent. As always, I have only myself to rely on. If I make the wrong choice, I will have only myself to blame. What are the choices? Do as he says, and hope that I'm wrong? That the agenda doesn't include my death? Or hope those outside get to me before he kills me or my baby?

There is a choice to fight. To try and do one thing so devastating it brings Ben down and lets me escape. But you'll have to kill him. If you get the upper hand, you'll still be trapped here till someone finds a way inside.

You'll have to kill him.

"Take a seat," Ben orders, pointing.

It happens, in the space between thoughts and not. In the space between my fear and my stubbornness, where the land of one choice lies. I hear the voice of one of my old combat instructors, the one who had those two bright, cold marbles where the rest of us have eyes:

"If you have only one chance to strike, and you won't be able to use a knife or gun, then one of the best moves you can make is for the throat." He angled his hand up, closing it into a huge, meaty beast of a fist, which he shook before us. Then he straightened it out, as though he were going to do a karate chop. "Fist, fingers, whatever—you just need to concentrate on one thing: taking your fist and putting it through your opponent's neck. I want you to concentrate on making your hand reach the back of his neck when you strike. Like you need to grab ahold of his spine." Giving us an even grimmer look (if that was possible). "I don't care how big you are; if you do it right, they will go down. And once they do—you do not let up. You take your heel—" and he lifted up his own massive water-ski, pontoon of a foot, smashing it down so hard that we imagined we could hear the ground rumble—"and you stomp on his face and his chest and neck and knees and ankles and stomach with all your might. Like you are crushing grapes to make some wine that'll save the world. Like you are doing a goddamn Mexican hat dance to cure your kid's cancer." He'd gone silent, perusing each of us in turn. "Don't stop till his head feels like apple sauce against your shoes."

I use my elbow. I remember again: Physics. Leverage. Center of gravity. I spin with my elbow out and angled up, leaning forward at the waist to keep the weight of my stomach low. I let it lurch me with its weight and yank me along, creating a pivot that adds momentum. I feel my elbow slam into Ben's windpipe, and I watch his eyes fly open wide, first with surprise, then with pain and shock.

His hands fly up to his throat, and he falls to his knees. *Hey, look at that! Just like Mr. Lynn said!*

I drop-kick him under the chin. I had meant to connect with the ball of my foot, but when it comes to combat, everything is easier said than done. I miss and hit him with the bottom of my heel. Thank God I connect; it's the only thing that keeps me from falling backward.

I can feel the impact all the way up to my hip. Ben's head snaps back, and a crescent-shaped spurt of blood follows an arc, spraying from his nose and his mouth and chin. He slams backward onto the floor, slamming the back of his head—hard—against the stone. His eyes un-focus a little, but he's still conscious. He clutches at his throat and makes choking, gasping, gagging noises. He flops and raves. I watch as shattered bits of teeth tumble from his lips, and notice that bone from his chin is poking through the skin where I kicked it. Blood is everywhere.

I don't allow myself to believe that Ben's not still dangerous. The survival instinct is the strongest instinct there is. Barring physical damage preventing it, people will fight harder with their last breath than their first.

I scan the room for something—anything—I can use as a weapon. My eyes light on the computer tower.

No. I need to see what's on it before I break it.

I look around frantically. There has to be something.

What's that? To the right of the television?

I hurry over, and what I find freezes me in place. There, next to the television, leaning up against the wall, is an assortment of items. A genuine Louisville Slugger baseball bat. A crowbar as long as my arm. A sledgehammer. I can see a hacksaw, a cat-o'-nine-tails with razor blades attached to its ends, and a car battery next to a large insulated coil of copper wire.

I blink. They were meant for me. I'm sure of that. My mouth fills with saliva, and I blink again rapidly.

What were you planning, Ben? Were you going to tie me to that chair, then bash my stomach with the bat? Or maybe the crowbar?

A long, deep-red rage overwhelms me without warning. I can feel my eyes go dry in an instant, and some pressure is behind them. I half expect them to pop right out of their sockets.

I'm walking toward Ben. I have the bat in my hands. I can't remember grabbing it. My heart hammers with rage, and my teeth are grinding together so hard I can hear the sound of them, even above Ben's choked moans and thrashing. All I can hear in my head is a deafening hum, like concert speakers about to blow.

The bat smashes into his face, sending shocks up my arm, making the tips of my fingers go numb. Blood rockets in various directions, and I hear the sickening crunch of bone followed by a high shriek that suddenly becomes a belly grunt.

The end of the bat has caved in Ben's skull. The bat is wedged in the bone and sits in his brain. His feet thrum wildly against the floor, and his eyes are open but rolled back to the whites. One arm points straight up toward the ceiling, its fist clenching and unclenching, shucking and jiving like a Parkinsonian metronome.

"So, yeah ... FUCK you, Benny boy ... ," I croon. "You goddamn monster. ... "

I wrench the bat loose with a cackle and have a moment to consider my sanity. But only a moment.

Time ebbs away again, and in the next blink of awareness, it's over. The top of Ben's skull is a pulpy mass. Gray matter hangs loosely from the tined and jagged edge of a jutting shard of skull bone. One eye is an unrecognizable black bruise. The other is open, and the pupil's visible again, but Ben's not saying anything, not anymore.

A great gray wave rolls through me. My legs feel like two well-boiled noodles, and my bones are full of ice water. I hit my knees, seeing stars behind my eyes, and feel myself beginning to pitch forward—

Hands! Catch yourself with your hands, not your stomach!

I manage it. My palms smack against the concrete hard enough to bruise. My son is slam dancing inside my stomach, and my mind is filled with howling wind and sparks.

I open my mouth and puke until my stomach's empty. Then I collapse on my side and pass out in a pool of my own vomit, weeping till I reach the black.

CHAPTER SIX

I wake up expecting things to be different. I realize in the next heartbeat that they're not. I can smell my own vomit and feel it soaking into my shirt.

Actually, that would be Ben's shirt, wouldn't it?

My eyes fly open at the thought of Ben, at the sudden surge of need to verify his deadness.

Then I remember.

Really? You're afraid he might ... what? Be a zombie or something? Maybe you fainted a little harder than you thought ... you saw the man's brains, Smoky.

I blame the slasher films of my youth. All those Rasputin-like super-killers that kept getting back up to kill again. I lever myself up onto an elbow and look at Ben's supine form.

Yep, still dead. I feel my stomach lurch in response, ready to start rocking and rolling again. *There's more puke where that came from, boys and girls. ...*

I stand up slowly, taking care to make sure I won't just topple over again. I find my feet and then wait, breathing, checking myself for signs of shock or worse. I feel fine, or at least as fine as I can feel in the context of things. My skull has a little more light and air inside of it than I'd like, but I didn't get a head rush from standing, and it doesn't feel like I'm going to pass out again.

Jesus. Jesus. Jesus. Oh my God that was so close—

I clap a hand to my mouth to keep myself from screaming. It keeps playing over and over in my head, that feeling of being dragged toward my doom, step-by-step. I remember the moment I found the weapons against the wall, and my body is wracked from head to toe by a single long shiver. My right calf muscle tenses so hard it twists into a cramp.

"Ow ... oh shit ... owww!" I shriek, hopping to the chair as tenderly as possible and taking a seat on the edge of it as my calf shouts and shakes.

And how's that for irony? my barely there mind asks. *The killer's chair offers comfort.*

I clench my teeth and massage the muscle with my fingers, even though I know it's not likely to help much.

Time passes. The muscle finally unclenches, and I breathe a ragged sigh of relief, leaning back in the chair as I do. My heartbeat is slowing. My mind has stopped its random rocketing. I stare at my shadowy reflection in the slick black glass of the television set. This is where Ben had wanted me and how he had wanted me.

Why?

I shake my head. *No.* That's not the right question right now. First things first—find a way out of here, or at the very least, find some way to communicate with the outside. Why can wait.

A minute passes. I watch it go by. Watch myself watch it go by, and still, I don't move from the chair. I don't move at all.

I slap myself in the face, hard. That strange stutter step of sensation follows: numbness that I know is just the pain I haven't yet processed, followed by a fire that twists my mouth and puts tears in my eyes. It burns off the last of my brain fog.

Getting control of myself is really a matter of deciding whether I want to be the one in charge.

It really is that simple. Which takes precedent? Am I a pregnant almost-victim? Or am I an FBI Special Agent in Charge, head of a national strike team tasked against violent crime?

It's a real question, in the moment. Twice now, twice in the last two hours, I've found myself in mortal danger, which also means my child was in mortal danger. Now I am alone and it's quiet and ... I'm glad for the moment. Strange but true. Ben has begun, at some level, to decompose in his own juices, right next to my lumpy puddle of puke, and it means nothing to me but a chance to breathe.

Or maybe it's good you took a seat, because maybe this is shock.

I look to the right of the television again. I see the car battery, sitting like a toad, benign and ugly next to the snake coil of insulated copper wire. Ben had been planning to torture me. The copper seems to glitter through the clear plastic insulation, and I shudder.

Well, then ... I guess it's a good thing that didn't happen to me.

I manage a bleak smile and sigh. Cataloging all the 'what-ifs,' rather than exacerbating my fears, starts to calm me. I can feel the distance growing between me and my terror. My weapon is my ability to figure it—or them, or whatever—out. It's a comfortable and comforting muscle to use.

So? What's the answer? Are you still in charge, or not?

The answer comes easily, once all the factors have been considered. This was all done for me. All done to get me here, and that had been quite a commitment. This had been a big, audacious plan. The fact that the gunfire outside had been timed with Ben's attack pointed to the involvement of multiple perpetrators.

There was little reason to think anyone who would put that much work into something would now be inclined to just give up.

Since I'm a target either way, it's safer all in all to stay the boss.

Crossing this bridge of doubt recharges my batteries, and I swing my legs over the side of the chair and stand up. I rotate slowly, taking in all my surroundings. There is a lot I hadn't noticed about the room before. It's an oblong box, perhaps fifty yards long and half that wide. With my back to the television, the door Ben brought me through is on the right. I see another door on the left wall, not quite opposite the one on the right but close. It appears to be a normal door; I don't see an electronic number keypad or a fingerprint scanner on the wall. I move toward it.

It's made from gray metal. A rap on it tells both my knuckles and my ears that it's hollow. Most definitely nothing special. It has no dead bolt, just a single round, silver metal knob with a keyhole in the center. I reach down and try to turn it but find it locked.

I can't expect them all to be a cakewalk, now, can I, baby?

There's only one place the keys can be, if I'm lucky enough to have them here with me. I walk back over to Ben's corpse and, getting down on my knees, rifle through his pockets. I find a set of three keys on a silver metal key ring in the right pocket of his jeans. Bringing the keys back over to the door, I try the first one in the lock. It doesn't turn. The second key does, making me want to smile, but that feels too hopeful, so I resist. I turn the knob, and the door opens easily.

I'm looking down another hallway, similar to the one Ben brought me through when coming to this room. It has the same bulb lights in the ceiling, but there are differences that make me hopeful—this hallway doesn't end with a door; it ends in a turn. I can also see that there are two other doors on either wall of the center of the hallway, and they appear to be just like this one.

I glance back at Ben's corpse, to make sure he really is dead, and I am careful to test the knob from the other side, to be sure that it really is unlocked in both directions.

I start moving down the hallway, but then realize that I have no weapon. My eyes find the bat.

Always best to use a proven weapon...

I run-waddle back over to Ben's corpse and grab the bat. My hands are strangely dry and warm against the smoothness of its wood. Blood coats the business end, staining it in some way, forever. This is no longer a baseball bat. It is no longer radiating concepts of sunshine and hot dogs and American-pastime summer days.

I am greatly reassured with it in my hands, and my confidence is continuing to grow as my faculties regain their certainty. I feel savage, just a little. All factors considered, that's a good thing.

The hallway door on the right opens easily. Inside is another large room, not warehouse big like the outer room but more of a large office space. The kind you would expect to see filled with beige-cloth cubicles standing on gray high-traffic, all-weather carpets. It was packed with filing cabinets.

I hesitate, longing to go through them... but I resist the temptation. I move through the room quickly, checking to be sure I haven't missed some hidden opening or maybe a phone. I find nothing.

I exit and then try the other door. It, too, opens without a key. I peer inside. This room is the same size as the other, but instead of having wall-to-wall filing cabinets, I find what appears to be an electronic command center. The far side of the wall is festooned with small flat-screen monitors. They're all on.

I blink, trying to understand what I'm seeing.

Every screen has an image on it. I see bedrooms, bathrooms, living rooms, and garages. Every now and then I watch a human being enter or leave. A few of the screens show signs of violence—bullet holes in the wall, overturned furniture, corpses.

Is this real time? It must be. I nod my head, agreeing with myself, still stunned with disbelief.

I am looking at the houses on this block. There's no other explanation. Besides—my eyes have already found the confirmation: I can see the dead family at the dinner table. I can even make out the blood-filled gravy boat.

There doesn't seem to be any place that Ben wasn't interested in. Toilets and children's rooms seem like obvious choices, if perversion was what floated Ben's boat. It's less easy to understand cameras in closets and pantries and even, in one place, what appears to be under a kitchen sink. I can see the names of cleaning products, all standing out in sharp contrast, in that weird way that infrared reverses things.

I can feel the wheels in my brain hit the track automatically, figuring, figuring, figuring.

Why this behavior?

It's almost a law: If you are not a member of law enforcement or a private investigator or a spouse concerned that your partner is cheating on you, then there's almost no other motivation behind hidden-camera surveillance than the sexual. There are examples of blackmail, but they're rare and often ethnic or cultural. There are still some few cultures in the world where nothing could be worse for a woman than to be photographed in the nude—willingly or not—and then have that photograph or video distributed.

Outside those parameters, it was about perversion and control. To be able to see anywhere is to own what you see. I had once read an account of a serial rapist who claimed he could spontaneously ejaculate, hands-free, just by watching his teenage stepson's girlfriends change into their bikinis on the camera in his stepson's bathroom. Rubbing up against that feeling of power and naked need satisfied everything that was important for him.

He said he'd taken his temperature once during one of these moments and had found himself running hot. "I had a hundred and one fever, but it felt like the furnace of the Lord," he'd commented, putting poetry to what he loved, as many men do.

If that had been Ben's ballyhoo, he'd certainly given himself permission. I walk over to the console. It looks like something that belongs on the set of *Star Trek.* Closer inspection shows me that Ben must have built it himself: All the equipment being controlled is fairly usual; the flat screens covering the walls are just TVs, and I am familiar enough with micro surveillance cameras to know that they are generally economical in terms of their form factor and their parts. A wireless camera will be mated to a single receiver, whereas a wired camera will run directly into the video display source or a recorder. Ben's console looks like it's made from some kind of cheap but hardy industrial steel, no frills in the decoration department but polished and clean in its workmanship, regardless.

Ben was not the type, I realize, to do anything unless he planned to do it well. I file away the certainty. It looks like he took the remotes for each television and built them into the console. All the buttons are there to push, but they've been set into the metal. The plastic housings are gone. I also notice joysticks and assume these are for use with cameras that can be repositioned remotely.

I lean forward a little, concentrating on the console and on the wear level of the buttons, trying to get some idea of how long it has all been here. The flat screens tell me the most. They have a resolution and color clarity that put them at having been built sometime in the last five to eight years.

I also notice what appears to be a headphone jack set in numerous areas on the console. Ben had the rooms wired for sound, in many cases. I look around for any headphones and find them in a cardboard banker's box placed next to the console. I lift them out, position them on my head, and plug them into the farthest left jack.

I don't see a volume knob anywhere, so I'm concerned for a moment that my eardrums might get blown out unexpectedly. I needn't have worried. Ben's attention to detail was in evidence here as well. I can hear a man and a woman talking, but the sound level is almost perfect. Not too high, not too low, and the sound quality is superb; I can make out every distinct word.

"This is the end," I hear a man say in a tired, haggard voice. "The living fucking end. They'll never believe us."

I look for the monitor that matches the sad man's voice. Ben had numbered each station on the console, and I guess that his logical mind would have laid out the screens in a similar order. I find that I'm right. I've plugged the phones into station number one. On the first and topmost screen to the farthest left, I can see a middle-aged couple, their backs to the camera, as they peer nervously through a crack in the curtains of their living room picture window.

"We don't say anything!" the woman snaps at him, but there's more fear than anger in her voice. She's clearly terrified.

"I don't know. ... " The man sighs, shaking his head slowly.

He's a tall man. It's hard to tell exactly on camera, but based on what I know of average ceiling heights and picture windows, I'm guessing he's a little over six feet tall. Everything about him is slumped. His shoulders, his head, even his hands hanging loosely at his sides; all mirror a self-assessment of a failure worth dying over. Although he looks like a man in his late fifties, he's taken care of himself and is well muscled; I can tell that from here, even though he is fully clothed. He's wearing a collared pullover shirt, and the sleeves hug his biceps and triceps. Even in defeat, he poses unknowingly with that perfect equilibrium of the fit and ever ready.

The woman spins on him, so that I can now see her in profile. Her face is like something cut in two; the one eye that I can see is wide and wild with fear, while the side of her face I can witness has twisted in anger. She stabs one of those well-muscled biceps with a long-nailed finger. I raise my eyebrows because I realize she has poked it hard enough to snap the nail. It breaks clean off.

"What don't you know?" she says to him in a kind of strangled shriek, like she wants to scream but can't afford to make a sound. "You don't know whether or not you want our granddaughter to die? Or maybe to experience something even worse than dying?" She stabs him again, and I watch as a drop of blood pops forth and rolls down his arm, falling from his elbow to the carpet. He doesn't seem to notice. "What don't you know? That we'll go to prison? No matter what we say or do? That no one will ever believe us, no matter what we say or do?" She leans into him; he has married a woman almost as tall as he is. All her anger and her terror are building in every part of her. You can see it everywhere in her stance, in the way her body seems to vibrate so hard it almost feels like it should float off the floor. "We have no proof! If we stop now, it's all been for nothing!"

The man is silent. Silent like a rock face or a hot country road. Silent and empty. He shakes his head again, still peering out the window, still not looking at her. "Look out there, Carolyn," he says. "It's all coming apart. It's all coming crashing down." He turns to face her for the first time and grips her arms gently with his large hands. His gaze on her is tender, and I can tell by the way she looks back at him that this couple loves each other as a given fact, true each night when they went to sleep and waiting there when they woke up every morning. She turned to him now the same way she always had, and he to her, because it had always been the right choice, and because they always found their love where they had left it. "The things we've done ... maybe we need to stop surviving. Maybe some things are so bad, it's better that our Sheila dies than for her to ever know we did them."

Tears are running down Carolyn's face, and I am transfixed. *This must be what it felt like for Ben*, I think. This incredible voyeurism. This forbidden enlightenment. The woman stares up at her husband and begins to sob. She reaches up and puts a hand on either side of his face, a gesture of her own that's as tender as his gaze. "Oh, my poor man," she sobs haltingly. "My poor, sweet, man! I'm so sorry. I'm so sorry. If I just hadn't filled in that raffle ticket. ... " She collapses against him, crying.

He smiles for her comfort and strokes her hair. "Shush ... be quiet now. Don't say silly things like that. This kind of evil is no one's fault but the ones that make it so. Shouldn't be anything wrong with filling out a fucking raffle ticket. So don't talk stupid."

The woman just keeps crying, and he hugs her close, stroking her hair and wounding with his words of comfort. Some time passes, and even though I know perhaps I should continue searching for a way out of here or a way to communicate, I just can't help myself. I have to see where this is going.

"Well ..." The woman sniffles after a bit, wiping her tears with her fingers in that way that women sometimes do when they are trying to keep weepy eyes from ruining their makeup. "What do you want to do?" she asks him. She seems as tired and full of failure as him now. I can hear the dull defeat in her voice. "Whatever you want us to do, I'll do. Even die." Her face twists for a moment, and it reminds me of the cramp in my calf muscle. "But what about her? What will happen to her?"

The man turns, smiling, and brushes a lock of hair from her forehead. It seems like such a comfortable motion for him to perform, and I understand that these two have been together for a very long time indeed. "Haven't you figured it out, my darling?" he says to her in a general tone that chides as a peer, the one that always said she was only as stupid as he was, too. "All this time, what's the one thing they've never failed to pound in the hardest? The need for secrecy. So what about all this? Doesn't seem very secret to me." He looks into her eyes. "That can't be good, my love."

She stares up at him for a moment, her mouth fallen open in surprise. Then she snaps it shut, hard enough for me to wince at the loud click her teeth make when they come together. She swallows like she's gagging. "Do you ... Do you think they've already killed her?"

The man kisses her forehead. "Do we really want to know?"

She doesn't answer. She doesn't have to. I can see it all in her eyes and in the way that she sags further. *Acceptance of Defeat*: If she was a sculpture, that would be her name.

"I love you, honey," the big man says.

The gun appears in his hand. The sound of the gunshot is so sudden and unexpected, I scream out loud. The woman's loving eyes become a mist. It's a big gun for a big man: a .357 Magnum. Carolyn's head is a ragged stump. And then, again—another explosion just a half second later—and once more I jump and scream. I rip the headphones off my head and fling them away from me. Shuddering.

Sweat runs from my hairline down my forehead and finds the bridge of my nose, racing down it like a ski jumper. I try to think: *What would be so terrible that the risk of it being true and knowing it was true was more fearful and more important than being certain their own granddaughter was dead or alive?*

CHAPTER SEVEN

The turn in the corner had revealed two doors: one at the end of the hallway, and another on the right, catty-corner to the first. The door on the right, blissfully, had turned out to be a bathroom.

I sit on the toilet now, trying not to groan with the sheer pleasure of releasing my over-swollen bladder. The acrid smell of my pregnant-pee—what Tommy has charmingly referred to as "permanent asparagus at midnight," wafts up to me and makes me crinkle my nose.

When you gotta go, you gotta go... and those aren't just words when you're seven months pregnant and you gotta go...

A sudden memory comes to me: the first time I ever heard a man groan with a sound of sexual pleasure while he pissed. It had been Matt, of course. Matt was the source of all those early firsts. I was still lying in bed, luxuriating in the new smell of our morning sex sweat, and I heard him through the door. For some reason, it had given me a shit-fit of the giggles. I'd buried my face in the pillow and belly-laughed.

Now I understand.

It occurs to me, as I take in the bathroom, that with the door closed, I could easily pretend I was back at the office. It's the same perfect square, with the same single, non-glass mirror, one toilet, one urinal—Ben had even installed the handicap rail, which for some reason makes me stare and gives me shivers. It's that attention to detail, in everything.

I finish up and wipe myself, then pull up my panties with a series of unsexy jerks and grunts, thinking, as I do, how much these simple actions make me look like an uncoordinated hippopotamus. I wash my hands in the sink and wonder how much time has passed. It's just me and Ben.

And Ben can't tell the time anymore.

I stare at my reflection and bite back a giggle. My worry about this is dazed and faint. It comes from a distance. I know that really, at some level, I've just been wandering since I killed Ben. I recognize my inappropriate affect for what it is. The silence is beginning to feel like a tomb. It has started eating away at me, just little bites, but when you have only your own thoughts for company, it's hard to tell the little bites from the big ones.

I think it's the inability to tell time. It wears on you like water. If you lose the ability to track time after a life-threatening incident ... well. The literature is clear. It can give you the sense that you've been lost at sea alone.

I shake my head to clear it and splash my face with cold water from the sink's faucet. The water is very cold, indeed. My fingertips screech and go numb when the water hits them, and I gasp at the sting of it against my cheeks.

It helps.

I notice a soap dispenser, filled with pink liquid hand soap, mounted on the wall to the right of the mirror.

Pink—just like the soap in the office bathroom.

I stare at it and frown. I stand up straight and let my eyes take in all the details of the bathroom again.

It didn't *resemble* the bathroom in the hallway by our offices; it was an exact duplicate. I consider for a moment whether I'm imagining things. Not so much because it's an impossibility, but because I can see no point to it. Why mimic the bathroom only? So far, nothing else in this place has reminded me of home or of my home away from home at the FBI.

Because it's not for me. The thought shudders into place in that way that tells me it's found the right place.

It's just Ben being Ben again.

This finely granulated replica was built for his own needs. It makes sense. This must be how detail-oriented monsters like Ben dream. I lean forward to get a closer look at some scratches in the upper-right-hand corner of the mirror. Someone etched words into the metal, and I know them already by heart. They will read: "Profilers may not do it better, but they'll always know why they do it." The same letters and the same words had been scratched into the metal in the office bathroom, an attempt at humor so lame and pathetic that it had been allowed to remain, maybe out of pity.

I think about the wall monitors and the feeling of power that seeing into others' lives must have given him. This was the same, in a way. More for him than for me, a way of showing himself he was already inside us, like a tumor or a deadly virus. Parked up close, cheek to cheek. I glance down at the shiny toilet porcelain and see my face reflected in the water.

When you pissed in that bowl, did you feel like you were pissing on me? I bet you did. Even more when you took a shit, probably.

My skin goes clammy, the way it does during a sudden, hard shudder. When it comes to what the monsters do—and why—there's nothing new under the sun, once you reach the base of it. Serial killers are all stalkers at heart. They want what they want, and it is all that they want.

It's not uncommon to see many of the same manifestations of the classic stalker in the stalking of a victim by a serial killer. Trophies that are not related to the victim's death, but are instead about the victim's life. Photographs, email conversations they copied using spyware placed on the victim's computer. Knickknacks known to be precious memory touchstones. To seize such things is to seize the victim's innermost soul, to hold the things they thought beautiful hostage. It's a very special form of rape.

Like any stalker, they lie for hours dreaming. Thinking of their chosen; turning them over in their careful, watchmaker-sensitive mind-hands; pondering every aspect of their victim's life and future fate as though each separate part were a separate piece of the most precious gold. And in many ways, I suppose—for them—they are gold pieces, after all. What else would you call the most valuable thing to you in all the universe?

He'd leaned forward, a life-size pointing finger of emphasis. "Just don't lose sight of the bottom line. In the end, it's about prolonging the release, because the longest prolonged is the strongest result. The very smartest and strongest can build whole worlds inside themselves, with a level of detail in imagination that would stagger you."

I close my eyes, breathe in the scent of perfumed toilet water, and my stomach twists. It even smells the same. How would he know that? I regard myself in the mirror again.

Did you stand here, Ben? Watching yourself as you owned me, soaking my essence in through your pores? Did you grin with both teeth and come in the sink?

I'm incredibly pale. My skin is a clean, milk white, but my cheeks have been savaged by strawberry blotches. The effects of stress and threat and killing a man. I have the sense, again, of floating unconcerned when maybe I should be running.

"Oh, to hell with it," I mutter, dropping my eyes from the mirror.

Timeless time marches on. Wearing at me with its un-measurement.

I dry my hands and exit the bathroom. I study the door at the end of the hallway, wondering less about where it leads than about the size of Ben's operation. This was obviously a mammoth, long-planned, expensive undertaking. It would have needed many people, loyal people. His wife had apparently been just fine with getting her head blown off, and then there was the sad couple I'd watched on the television screen.

Let's not forget poor Maya, with her incomprehensible message. Or the girl, just like her. The one who saved me and then killed herself.

I consider the awful scenario on the television. Those poor people were obviously being blackmailed by Ben. He'd put them under an incredible strain—one so terrible that death became preferable. Based on the number of screens I'd seen, it seemed obvious that he'd done the same thing with everyone on this block. Riding herd on that would be a full-time job.

Human beings resist oppression instinctively and emotionally, and some resist forever. A large part of successfully controlling a group with terror, blackmail, or any other form of external threat is being able to separate the wolves from the sheep.

The sheep are victims who break quickly, break early, and then accept their fate. The wolves are those individuals who will never—truly—give up. They'll never quit looking for a way out, and they never stop making trouble. One wolf is all that's needed to organize the sheep, because although they've given up, the sheep, in the end, will obey the wolf if he only pushes hard enough.

Most ruthless criminal organizations will always put the wolves down. The wolves might be culled from trafficked women or from overambitious members of their own organizations, but the point is to recognize that form of strength, to identify early that type of person who would never truly accept being broken.

It's the same equation faced by anyone planning to rule people like cattle or who came to power through violence. How do ten thousand control a group of one hundred thousand or one million?

Controlling a suburban block was an awe-inspiring act of social psychology. It required a knowledge of how groups function as groups and all the quite fundamental ways in which groups of people think differently from how they think alone.

It would also require incredible ruthlessness, I think. *The kind of ruthlessness most people would find unbearable to manifest. Or experience.*

Hell—even to conceive of.

I stare at the knob. I have a schizophrenic mouth; it wants to go all cotton dry, but it's just not sure it *needs* to.

What are you going to find if you open that door? A chamber of horrors? A broom closet?

Or the possibility I'm really worried about: more of Ben's friends, or at least the kind of man he would consider calling a friend?

Because—oh, yes, I'm certain—with something of this size, there's more like Ben involved. Monstrosity has settled in here and gotten comfortable. When the monsters get comfortable, they tend to become magnets. They find one another, in ways not always definable, but undeniable.

I grip the handle of the bat with my right hand, not satisfied with it as a weapon but at least comforted a little by the warm feel of its wood-grain in my palm and by that red-black stain soaked into the business end of it.

In for a penny, in for a pound. And if anyone's waiting, I'll pound your fucking skull till I see your brains, too! I shout silently, to nothing.

I think for a moment about what must be going on aboveground. How frantic they must be. Everyone on my team knows what to expect from a monster like Ben, and I would imagine that this is a burden of knowledge hard to bear.

Oh ... oh sweet Jesus ... I breathe, bringing a hand to my mouth. *I hope to God no one's let it leak that Ben took me. Tommy would lose it utterly. And Bonnie ...* I remember her words. How she'd admitted she still needed me to have a reason to keep on speaking.

This thought makes me angry. Angry in a way that rockets slightly out of my control, all white-hot unreasonable and unwilling to entertain compassion.

"Motherfuckers ... ," I snarl lowly, thinking about Tommy and Bonnie and their awful, helpless terror. In this moment, I almost hope to find a brother of Ben waiting on the other side of that door.

Maybe it wouldn't be so bad to have another one of you down here. *Batter up.*

I turn the knob and open the door. And groan. I put a hand on my stomach. "That's another sucky set of stairs, baby," I complain. "Another three flights, from the look of it."

Baby kicks me. Baby don't care. *Baby sure can be a hassle*, I think, in one of those uncharitable moments that late-term pregnancy hands you daily.

Baby's probably got the right idea, though. Complaining converts air. It's really not very effective for much else.

It took a lot less time and effort to reach the bottom of the stairs, compared with the ones I'd staggered down with Ben.

The door is the same style as the others. I'm beginning to understand Ben's logic on security, at least in terms of how this place has been laid out. The outer entrance we came through was concealed inside the pantry. Even knowing it was there, it would be difficult to find.

If you did find it—then what? The door was constructed to function as a blast door. It created an airtight seal and was thick enough to withstand serious explosives. Opening it required two-factor authentication: a series of numbers punched into the keypad, and a thumbprint.

Then, a set of stairs leading you almost two stories down into the earth, ending at another blast door. The walls were all thick, reinforced, hardened concrete.

Once you were through the first two points of entrance, the security level dropped. The doors had single-key locks, but those seemed to be mostly for show. I'm fairly sure that a nonpregnant, non–terminally short person could kick most of the inner doors open, locked or not.

The bunker had a functional elegance that was also telling: Ben was effective, but he was not paranoid. It was an important tactical point. He took great pains to ensure that even locating this place would be difficult and then practiced impregnability at its entrances. Once past those portals—it was feet in the grass, free to roam. Ben may have been focused, but he hadn't been crazy.

Having thought this through, these three flights of extra stairs trouble me. Ben hadn't felt the need to place another blast door, but whatever was below was valuable enough to him that he'd decided to bury it two stories deeper than the rest.

It can't be anything good.

I open the door and walk through it. What I see takes my breath away.

I'm standing in a large new room. It's not as large as the admitting room (as I've now labeled it in my mind), but I have found my answer to Ben's need for depth: The ceiling in this room must be forty feet high.

The reason for this is obvious: A giant photograph has been wrapped around a circular pillar standing in the center of the room. The pillar runs floor to ceiling and is not freestanding. I can't clearly make out yet what the photograph is showing me.

I walk up to the pillar, checking to my right and left, rooting out the corners with my eyes. I am alone. The room is not so large now that I'm inside it. Twenty feet by twenty feet, at the largest. Nor is the pillar its only feature. It's just the one you can't stop looking at.

The photo shows, in grainy black-and-white, a living tower of terrified Asian people being formed as a result of their own desperate strivings. The bottom is a base of corpses. I cannot see what they are running from, these people, but they appear to have come from every direction. They collide in the center. The only place they have to continue running, then, is up. They scramble up and claw over one another, a horrible, rising pyramid of death. Mostly, their features are grainy and unclear, but even on old film, the horror is obvious. Most have O's for mouths. I assume that they are screaming.

I gaze and I gape, and I cannot stop doing either. I know what I'm looking at now. It is hidden history. What I'm seeing should not exist.

In 1937 the Japanese invaded the Chinese capital city of Nanking. What followed was an unprecedented slaughter. The atrocities committed were the kinds of things the word *atrocity* was invented to describe, an absolute representation of the worst of the worst.

One of the most extreme accounts involved the slaughter of unarmed prisoners by Japanese soldiers firing machine guns. The Japanese surrounded a mass of prisoners—largely civilians—and opened fire. The Chinese tried to flee, but since the bullets were coming from all points of the compass, so were those running to escape them. Many died as they ran, of course. But the rush of bodies inward from all the outer edges kept the corpses standing upright. The living began to clamber up and over them and up and over one another, creating a tower of humanity that strained toward the sky like a living finger of useless hope. Eventually, the tower would collapse, but the Japanese would start again, and the whole building process would begin anew.

"I remember you," I whisper to the photo-encrusted spire. This event was part of my psyche.

One of my greatest secrets as an agent has to do with the first time I ever saw hard-core child pornography. The secret is in the way it ruined me. Those images were like depth charges. They dotted the surface of my mind, and then they sank until they reached my center, where they exploded again and again and again.

It hadn't been even all that significant, from the standpoint of my career history. It was an unsavory and unwanted detail, and I was the new kid on the block. The crap work fell to me. I accepted this easily, with the equanimity that any profession requiring real competence demands from its newbies.

But then... I whisper silently to myself.

I saw her picture. She was eight, or maybe she was nine or ten. It's hard to tell with little girls sometimes. It hardly mattered. She was far too young to experience what happened to her.

In the first photo, she was begging. Her hands were twisted together in prayer. Her face was contorted into itself, and her eyes had been consumed by fear. The camera had really caught that expression cleanly; you could see it roaring there, like a fire inside her head. There was no way eyes could look like that for long without staying that way forever. She was crying rivers.

The photographs that followed showed that her prayers had not been answered. For the first time ever—and the last, I hope—I saw on film and in video the reality of an adult man raping a child. The moment cratered me.

It had been subtle but pervasive, and it never let up. I dreamed of that girl, and I would wake up biting back a scream or would be shaken awake by Matt because I was sobbing in my sleep.

I had gone through every photograph and movie of that monstrous collection, and the doing so had clobbered my mind with hammers of horror. I walked in feeling fine and left feeling old and spent.

The real difficulty, I understood over time, was that I couldn't find a form to contain its truth. It was a vivid but wordless event in my mind, and it was both timeless and absent of any existential context, like the memories of a young child.

This terrified and marooned me. The ability to know the shape of truth when I saw it is one of the primary tools I have always used to face the world. It's not an act of prediction, but of recognition. I know it when I see it; I know it without a doubt.

This is how I was with people, with killers, with my life. I did not leap before looking. I was spontaneous only on the outside. In reality, everything I did was considered and based on observation.

Each time I would think of that hot afternoon (and this was one of the strange things: I always think of it as a hot afternoon, but I know it took place in an air-conditioned office) and remember all the staring and watching and listening that I did there ... I once described it to Dr. Childs as a long-term memory that contained no short-term memory within it. It was like looking at an animation done in watercolor that has been run just a bit too fast. The tree was a tree, and you remembered seeing a tree, but you only ever really saw the object as a whole. The details were thick and opaque and fuzzy.

It drove me crazy, even more so because I knew the shape of this particular truth within myself. I understood that this phenomenon had occurred to protect me. But I also was aware that all the damage had already been done, forever. It didn't matter that the lines were blurred: I knew what I'd seen, and that was the whole problem.

It was the first time I finally understood that there are some things just so awful, so terrible, that we will never believe they are true in our roots without proof.

That afternoon is one of the greatest regrets of my life.

It had been Dr. Childs who seemed to understand this concept of the shape of things and its importance to me. He had been the one who'd suggested that I go looking for something to compare my experiences to, as a way of helping me contextualize them.

"Find some awful thing that, once you put it up next to your memories of that afternoon, makes you say: 'Yes—it was exactly *that*.'"

The story of Nanking was the closest I ever came. Specifically, that account of the living, human spire.

I gape at the giant photo sculpture, and I think the same thoughts again: *This! This is it. That's what it was like.*

I can't really know with certainty, of course, that these are genuine photographs from Nanking, and in fact there's no history to support it. Nanking was a walled city. The Japanese had closed the gates, letting no one leave or enter. The citizenry was trapped inside a giant, savage box, with an army intent not just on destroying them, but also on enjoying the process.

Most of what we know comes from letters written by foreign nationals who were living in China at the time or from photographs and film smuggled out under the noses of the Japanese. There were mercifully grainy images of dead babies lying in a ditch, and of beheadings, but I had never heard a whisper of any photograph in existence depicting this particular, unique horror.

I know this is authentic. I don't know why I know, but … this is the shape of truth.

I walk around the pillar. Something tugs at my understanding. These are not separate photographs cleverly cut together. This is an unbroken set of images from top to bottom. I can't figure out what it is that I am seeing, and then it comes to me. These are photos extracted from a movie. Sharpened and enlarged to life-size.

I notice for the first time that part of the far right wall is not a wall at all but a giant viewing screen. A large red button is set next to it. Below the button, painted in blue onto the concrete, are block letters: PUSH ME. I walk up to it and stare at the dull red plastic. It looks squat and ugly. Dangerous. I lick my lips and push.

The screen flickers into black, then the movie starts. It's grainy and fuzzy, and parts of it are cut in such a way that you can tell that sections of the film must have been damaged beyond repair at some point. It's only two minutes long. Ben has looped those two minutes so that they play again and again, and they are probably the worst two minutes in the world.

There's no sound, and it was shot from a height, so that the camera was angled slightly downward. I watch the split second of the beginning, again and again. The Chinese people standing and staring, afraid but not yet terrorized.

Then the gunfire, beginning at the outer edges. Bodies fall like cut wheat, and the ripple is visible as an actual wave, something that makes my stomach jump in nauseated rejection. The running and scrambling is the shape of desperation, the bottommost limits of terror.

I watch a face come clearly into focus, right toward the end of the film. An older man, of all things—white-haired and wrinkled—is the King of the Hill. The man is panting like a dog, and his eyes are white saucers. He is screaming. He is the last peak that this particular human spire has. The cameraman catches him just before a bullet finds his forehead, just before the human mountain fails and topples. The man falls, and all those he had clambered over cover him with their death. I watch for a time, numb, and then push the button, and the screen goes blank. I am trembling.

Ben has images of the Nanking Massacre... in a secret bunker under the earth... of a Colorado suburban neighborhood?

I suddenly feel very alive.

Unmeasured time moves on, creaking.

The far back wall has some kind of message mounted on it, and I walk over to get a closer look. Each letter is carved from some dark hardwood and then sanded and polished to a smooth, glassy gleam. I see evidence of Ben's perfectionism in the exact, straight lines the words are laid out in, in the way every letter is of a precisely identical height. I guess they are almost a foot tall. It's marvelous workmanship, regardless of its provenance. I read the sentence to myself out loud:

"Some things are so evil they *must* be denied, until proven by evidence of the most undeniable kind."

I can't confirm it in the mirror, but I'm sure that my face has gone bone white again.

Anyone could think those words, true... but do they have to be *those* words, so soon after just thinking them myself? I take a deep breath and close my eyes, and when I am steady, I read the words to myself again.

It's like a museum foyer.

I notice something on the far left wall. It wasn't obvious because the walls are recessed and because the room behind them is dark, but there is a set of enormous glass doors there. I walk up to them and peer through.

I can't see a thing. The giant doors have enormous handles to go with them, and I pull on each, feeling like Alice. The doors open easily, with a slight pneumatic hiss. Once fully open, they appear to lock in place, and in the exact moment that they do, the lights in the room come on.

I can only blink and gape. It's all that my mind is capable of doing, under the circumstances. It's not just the sudden rush of light into all that darkness, it's what the light reveals.

I clap both of my hands to my mouth, dropping the bat to the floor with a clatter. My eyes are wide and blinded by the impact of what I'm seeing. The stillness of my thinking carries a clarity that hurts, like the razor edge of a knife made from glass.

Museum, I think, dully. A museum to stop all the clocks and dull the shine from the stars.

The single room revealed is the largest one to date, by far. It truly is like an aircraft hangar, one of those buildings so massive it can have its own weather system. I understand now why Ben had dug down another two floors to hide it. It is a treasure room of the unimaginable.

Ben's attention to detail peaks here. He gave this room all his focus and the best of his abilities. Row upon row of clear boxes made from Lucite stretch in all directions, all of them perfectly symmetrically aligned, no stack too high, too left, too anything. They are all that's visible in this enormous room, almost as far as the eye can see. If they were all empty and filled only with light, it would be breathtakingly beautiful. Kind of like walking safely on the surface of the sun.

These lights are on, but only to ensure that viewers can clearly see the darkness inside every box, and each one holds a separate nightmare vision.

The first thing I see when the lights go on is the large glassed-in diorama. It's a rectangle turned on its longest side, and it stands about six feet tall. Letters have been painted onto the glass:

The Perfect American Family!

Inside, the stuffed corpses of a family cavort in unnatural ways. The father lies with his daughter, wearing a rictus grin of devil's pleasure. The daughter is not even a teenager, and Ben left the expression she died with on her face: formless terror.

The mother is placed on all fours, wearing a dog collar, clearly chained to the bed by dear old Dad. A stuffed teenage boy masturbates forever in a corner, looking on gleefully. The bodies are real. I know what corpses look like. Nothing has quite the same authenticity as death.

A television set placed on an entertainment center in the "bedroom"— both quite retro in their way—displays a running loop of some twisted highlight reel of child pornography. A brief glance shows me that Ben had been thorough and museum-like there as well.

A set of headphones hangs, plugged into a jack mounted in the glass. A small sign prompts me: *Add to the Experience with Audio!*

I decline.

It's only the first. The first of so many. I start walking through the room, dread running through every part of me. There's no obvious enemy or danger, but I've rarely felt more afraid.

My son does nothing to calm these metaphysical fears, deciding to get more active now than ever. I rub the bottom of my stomach with my right hand and do the same with my left at the top, willing my touch to be a comfort of velvet.

Am I hurting you by having you here while I see these things, baby? I don't usually believe in things like that, but this... it's almost enough to change my mind.

My son goes still and silent again, as if to call me on my lie. I sigh. It's true, of course. I was never going to change my mind. I could feel the weight of the unknown in this room, tugging at me and urging me forward.

I take a deep breath and enter the room fully. I notice a difference in temperature and odor. The air is colder and more canned. It's also extremely dry. Some form of climate control runs while all these bad faces slumber in the dark.

I decide to head all the way to the back first and then make my way forward. I'll see what I can see before I'm rescued.

If you're rescued. And who really cares?

Static rushes through my mind, bringing a surge of fear and fury, then is gone, like it had never been. I wonder what it was I'd just been thinking...

Oh—right. Head to the back.

I'm familiar now with Ben's need to enforce order on his arrangements and keep them loyal to a chronology of some kind. I figure the oldest things will be in the back, with the exception of the selected items—like the family—handpicked for display up front.

I want to start with the old. It's always my favorite kind of mystery: the ancient knowledge that just gets lost, and once lost becomes secret. All those things and buried bones that normal people and civilians will never see, laid bare and lit brightly.

I've walked and walked and walked, and I'm not even a quarter of the way across the room's distance yet. I walk through a gauntlet of horrors, visible only in the periphery of my vision. They come to me in little flashes, and my mind fills in the holes.

Inside one large glass box: what appears to be an authentic, ancient, wall-size ink drawing on an old piece of parchment. It displays a woman tied down to a wooden rack, naked. She's obviously terrified, but the people drawn seated around her appear to be oblivious. They are smiling, holding wineglasses, chatting away to one another like it's all just about a Sunday brunch or a spot of tea.

Under the parchment the legend explains:

This is an early depiction of an old form of entertainment: watching someone get skinned alive. It was popular in all the best circles, once. Red wine with those screams, anyone?

Then:

Push the Big Red Button to Watch the Movie!

I pass it by, but even glimpsing it changes me.

Not all of it documents Ben's personal work. I pass a desk with a set of gloves on it, placed next to a lamp with a leather shade. The gloves are small, made for a woman's hands. The smallest black swastika has been stamped into the leather. Lying next to the gloves is a large book bound in the same leather. The title stamped into its cover reads *Mein Kampf.*

Genuine Jew skin was used to make those gloves and the lampshade! You can't buy those in Kmart. The leather for the book was stripped from the back of a particularly troublesome rabbi. They flayed it off him in a single sheet.

This edition of Mein Kampf *has been autographed by Hitler.*

I almost open the book to see, but I resist the impulse and walk on. It's a discipline. A kind of talisman, really. When you spend most of your time marching through the muck of existence, it's important to make sure you can still do that one thing the monsters can't: deny yourself.

Ben's placement of lighting is creative, and the cumulative effect is awe-inspiring. Fiber-optic cables snake everywhere, along with LEDs and ultrahigh-wattage conventional lighting. It is exclusively white. No yellows, no reds, no frosted bulbs. This is meant to be a clean, pure light, the kind nothing can hide from or should want to.

I think contrast was important and meaningful to Ben. I see it in his displays: on one side, the drawing that promised a skinning—horrible enough; on the other side, the incomparable reality. Bright white light, in the context of his museum, provides a contrast that permeates everything. It signifies that all the evil, hidden things in this huge room would always be uncovered and exposed.

Light is truth. What truths were Ben's lights divining? Nothing good. The truth that sometimes black, dark, shady things can live just fine in bright, warm light; and that good things can be made to crawl and learn to like it. Maybe the truth that it doesn't matter that it's daytime and that all the lights are on; the light alone will never be enough to make you safe.

I am halfway through the room when I hear a scuffling noise to my right. I've been walking at a left-leaning diagonal, passing by rather than through the true center of the room. The sounds are coming from there.

I hesitate, but only for a second or so. I turn and move slowly toward the noise. Still, I'm glad that I remembered to pick the bat back up off the floor. Its death-flavored wood comforts me. The same noise comes again, and my knuckles go white as my grip on the bat tightens.

I understand that it's a zoo only when I'm directly on top of it.

There are four large glass cages. Human beings—or what used to be human beings—live in each one. The bottoms of the cages have been lined with sawdust and wood shavings. They had been hamsters to Ben, not people.

A woman, maybe fifty years of age, is in the first cage on the left. She's nude and insane. She batters herself against the glass when she sees me, snarling and raving the way some primates will when you visit them in confinement. She claws and snaps her teeth, leaping and shrieking and beating her chest. I lean forward a little and peer into her eyes, but I see no flicker of recognition that she's a human, too.

"I'm sorry," I whisper to her, my voice low and dull.

Next comes a man roughly the same age as the woman. His behavior is worse than the woman's, more self-destructively insane. He claws at the glass so hard that he actually tears a fingernail loose. I watch it stick to the glass for a moment, then topple off into the sawdust and shavings.

It seems Ben had filed all the man's teeth to sharp points. I notice some scraps of raw meat, slabs of it an inch thick, lying loose in a dog bowl. The man notices me looking and follows my gaze. Once he realizes it's his food I'm considering, he throws back his head and howls. He sounds so much like a wolf that I jerk in my shoes, and I imagine I can feel the goose bumps rise on the bone of my spine rather than on the skin above it.

"I'm sorry," I whisper again.

All this shouting has gotten the children going, too. The boy is fourteen or fifteen; the girl is perhaps a year older. Both have gone feral, probably irretrievably so. They all begin racketing at once, mixing screams with hoarseness. It's a bleating, primeval cacophony.

"Oh God ... I'm so, so sorry." I am weeping. They keep shouting.

It's impossible to tell how long they've been here. This kind of breaking down and conditioning is not done overnight. It takes dedicated work over a period of many years. It involves, at its heart, merciless repetition and the extinguishing of hope. Actions are given to be performed, and they are performed again and again at the exact time they're supposed to be performed, regardless of their value. The lesson is simple: The point of the action is not the point at all. The only point to anything is that you do what you are told.

Along with this rhythm of demand and reward comes the punishment. An unending barrage that becomes, in their small worlds, the only thing they know. It's a heartlessly simple equation: People need people like they need air. If you are the only person available, and you keep it that way, and you base their survival on that fact—it won't matter how badly you treat them—they'll have to love you, in the end. They'll have no choice.

The repeated actions are varied over time for different reasons. Some promote the totality of obedience. Others promote regression, such as forcing a man to method act as a monkey for a year without ever breaking character. Or making a grown woman suck on a pacifier and speak only in baby talk. It's Pavlov and his dogs built for the apocalypse. The worst kind of thing man can do to man.

Suddenly, I don't want to walk all the way across this shitty room. In fact, I'm so tired in this instant that I sit down on the floor right where I'm standing, and I allow myself to bruise while my sorrowful eyes watch people who once knew they were human act like apes. I know the truth, that it's not likely any of them will ever recover.

They seem reassured that I'm not going to hurt them or steal their food. They settle down, though they remain watchful. The girl turns her head to and fro, staring at me with open curiosity. It makes her seem so much like a caged monkey that I cry a little.

"I'm sorry," I whisper for the last time. "But at least I can promise you that Ben won't hurt you anymore."

I sigh, my head hung low. Then I stand back up and prepare to walk back to the entrance so that I can leave this room. I'm ashamed of admiring my curiosity earlier.

As I turn to go, I notice something. There are another two dioramas of size off to the right of the caged family. They catch my attention because their placement belongs to the center of the room. They are on display here because Ben found them especially important for some reason.

I walk over and see the contents of the first. I freeze in place at the same time as every atomic part of me begins to hum and squeal on overdrive.

Here's what the word thrum *was invented for.*

I'm thrumming!

Processing information is hardly a straight line. It passes through many filters before reaching its final meaning. Denial is a key one, and it kicks in fast, even before we can be aware of it sometimes. So yes, the walls are made of glass, and my vision is fine, but it still takes me a moment to believe what I'm seeing.

A little more than seven years ago, a man I was hunting by the name of Joseph Sands broke into my home. He tortured and murdered my husband in front of me, and he caused the death of my ten-year-old daughter. He raped me, and then he spent ten minutes disfiguring the left side of my face.

The scar is continuous. It begins in the middle of my forehead, right at the hairline. It goes straight down, hovering above the space between my eyebrows, and then it shoots off to the left at an almost perfect ninety-degree angle. I have no left eyebrow. Sands carved it off as he meandered across my face, imposing his own vision. The scar travels across my temple and then turns in a lazy loop-de-loop down my cheek. It rips over toward my nose, crossing the bridge of it just barely, then changes its mind, cutting diagonally across my left nostril and zooming in one final triumphant line past my jaw, down my neck, ending at my collar bone.

He used a cigar on my breasts and belly. I saw my pregnant stomach in the mirror yesterday and realized for the first time how symmetrical he'd been; the scars bisect my belly laterally in an almost perfect straight line. In the right light, I look like an alien with multiple belly buttons.

In the course of a single night, the trajectory of my life had been altered forever. I had lost my family, a face that I recognized in the mirror, and most of my hope. I've been in danger since then, but I've never again felt quite as palpably close to death as I did in the months following the event. There is something about wishing for death that opens a door that can never be closed again. Once you cross the line between an unquestioning desire to live and the acceptance of death as a possibly preferable option, you never completely return. You know the truth: It *can* seem so much better to die.

The life I have now isn't something I could have conceived of back then. Had anyone told me in those darkest first months that it was possible for me to rebuild, not just myself, but a life—full of love, and a family—I would have thought they were crazy, and said so. Somehow, all of this had happened. I'd lost my whole world, and regained it. It was not the same world, true, and I could still find time to mourn the one that was, but it was a world worth living for. Sands and his actions no longer defined the present but had receded to a memory.

But now... I blink, my mouth hanging open, shocked to my core.

Ben has re-created my bedroom and Alexa's bedroom on the night that Sands raped me and killed Matt and Alexa. He has done it lovingly. He found stand-ins for all of us, and I can tell it might have taken a while. They are as close to perfect matches without actually being doppelgängers as anyone like Ben could have hoped for.

This includes Sands, too. I hear someone whine, then realize it's me. I put my hand over my mouth and look around instinctively, embarrassed. No one else is here, of course. Just me and the family. They're looking at me, and around, concerned. Probably wondering if they need to worry about whatever it is that frightened me.

"No, no, it's okay. I was just surprised."

They cock their heads to and fro, pretending without pretending to be the perfect human-monkeys.

I take a deep breath and look again. It hadn't been surprise. That had been an autonomic whine of pure, animal fear.

Sands.

The likeness is incredible. So much so I have to wonder about Ben's obsession with detail, maybe mixed with a little bit of homemade plastic surgery. I can't seem to stop feeling afraid. It can't make me run, but neither can I clear the weak feeling from my knees.

Sands is the man who changed my life by killing my family. By torturing and raping me. He is the only person on this earth who has ever seen me beg. The only one to make me beg, even while he laughed at me, even when he made me beg again.

I'd begged him not to kill Matt. I'd begged with everything I was, and I promised him anything, whatever he wanted, no matter how base or low. This happened while Matt looked on, agonized, all his gift of childish wonder dying in him right before my eyes.

Sands had been the only man who'd ever truly broken me. No one knows the details of this. I've never even told the story to Dr. Childs. When Sands tortured Matt, and once Matt died, I gave up. I surrendered. I sobbed like a child, and I kept on begging, even though it was just for me.

I did things for him, like a passive child. Like a wolf that's been bent into the shape of a sheep. He even petted my head once and patted my cheek and told me he was proud. Calling the experience humiliation is like calling death a wound.

But then I got to kill him, to see him dead with my own eyes and by my own hands. To be sure he'd be the only one who knew me in that way forever. Now he's back—and so is the me of that moment.

Ben had found my own most excellent likeness, too. She's stuffed and lacquered, but Ben had worked his artistry at some point, with all his heart and soul. This is evident in the expression that she died with.

He couldn't have known, right? This is just what he does.

Right?

She looks like me when I was broken. She looks exactly like me. How I know I must have looked in that bottommost moment.

I jerk in my shoes again, and the spell breaks. I blink. Shake my head to clear it. *It's not that he knows. That's just what everyone looks like when they break wide open.*

There's a marble bench in front of this display. A marble bowl sits on the floor before it. I peer into the bowl. It's filled with a crusted mass I recognize as dried semen.

I guess Ben really enjoyed spending time here.

Something about it is so pathetic, so human, that I snap back into myself again. I'm no longer terrified, only badly shaken.

My eyes turn toward the replica of Alexa's room.

No.

There's no part of that memory that I can survive twice. I put my back to it, to all the replicas of that night, and move on to the final diorama.

The last one is strange. The cage is more of a big box, really. A pedestal sits inside, centered. Atop it is a skull. It's been stripped clean, down to the bone. The teeth are all there, though some of the front ones are oddly discolored. This speaks to me, but I can't connect the intuition to any concrete memory. Hanging next to the pedestal is a flat-screen monitor. Ben had suspended it from the box's "ceiling." Wires run from the monitor down to a small electronic box that's been mounted on the floor. Wires run from this box to another one of Ben's red plastic buttons.

As before, words underneath the button give their command, in that always up and never down kind of way: PUSH ME!

I hesitate. The lack of any hint about what would be seen if you did push the button is telling. This would be an ambush of the senses.

Screw it. I push the button. *Can't be worse than a life-size twin of Sands.*

But I'm wrong. I recognize the girl's face the moment it appears. I have never met her, but this hardly matters. I have seen her photograph too many times not to know who she is. I watch, transfixed, while he does what he does to her, as he makes her scream and die, and it removes any remaining doubt. This is the right death. It's authentic.

Oh, man, I think. *This is bad. So very, very, bad.*

I find myself racewalking toward the double glass doors. I support my stomach and I pray that all this malignant radiation hasn't already ruined the parts of my son's DNA that are reserved for luck and for siding with the good.

I am as superstitious right now as the first caveman-mother ever was. Nothing about simply standing next to all these glassed-in horrors is actually going to change the physical composition of my son. I know this, but it doesn't matter because I've seen the shape of this place's truth, and it's wrong-shaped to be here with my child, unborn or otherwise. End of story, period.

This is the second time since his life began to grow inside me that I've been a captive. I feel like a crazy person who's suddenly gone sane. I finally see it all the way Tommy must see it.

I quicken my pace.

I must have been out of my mind to come here pregnant!

No. Worse.

I'm a bad mother for being here pregnant.

The words burn, but only because they're true. Hell, I don't even have the excuse of doubt. I know children under my care can die. I've watched it happen, right before my eyes. I am fully briefed on the awful truth that a mother's love will never be a shield.

Sands knew of my family because of my work, and they died because I was hunting him. Then there was Annie, killed by a monster because that monster wanted me to chase him. On and on, my endless, selfish stupidity.

I reach the doors and pass through, pulling them closed behind me, letting the darkness reclaim all that awful light. I can still hear the family, hooting and howling for a second, but they quiet down after just a moment. I wonder briefly if some part of their ruined minds sees the lights come on and thinks of it as morning.

"It's nighttime now," I murmur. "Go to sleep. Someone will come to get you soon."

I feel crazy. My skin feels flushed and prickly hot. I go to the bathroom again and splash my face and hands with that numbing icy water. It's the perfect thing, like a sunrise burning the morning fog off a lake of cold, black water. I stare at myself in the mirror. I'm so haggard. I look older than I can ever remember looking.

"Now *that's* the face of a woman who's been taken hostage, terrorized, and then killed a man," I tell my reflection, giving two thumbs-up and winking. "Hold that look!"

I whine again. I'm so afraid right now. The blackness is back. Where did it come from? I've been rebuilding myself for years, getting more solid and stronger. I'd started at the foundation and hadn't skimped on the introspection, as far as I knew.

So why?

Something Dr. Childs once said comes to me.

People can only take as much as they can take. Once they reach their limit, they're generally surprised. They're also helpless to change it. He was looking right into my eyes when he said it. I'd thought it was an anecdote, but now I understand that he'd meant it as a warning.

I begin to shake. I will it to stop, but it won't. This scares me more than anything else.

I can't go back to that place. I can't!

"Smoky?" the deep voice calls, faint but unmistakable. "Smoky? Where are you, baby?" Louder now. A shout.

"Alan ... ," I whisper. "Please help me."

I decide to step out into the hallway. My feet stay rooted where they are. I frown. Had I really called his name? Or had I just imagined that?

"Smoky?"

He's right outside the door. I try and call out to him, but my throat is closed, and my mouth's gone dry. I will him to find me instead.

The bathroom doorknob turns.

"Smoky?" His voice is careful. So are his eyes. I wonder what I look like. "Are you hurt?"

No, I think, but cannot say. Not in any visible way, at least.

His eyes travel down my body and stop at my leg. It's shaking. Shaking like I'm a scared old dog. He looks back up at me, and now his eyes are sad.

Alan's face is a rolling ocean of raw, random emotion, each and every one of them riding the raggedest edge. He wants to kiss me and slap me and sob for his own fears. It's all written large in the way he looks, in the twist his face becomes. I know his signature of emotion because he's one of my oldest friends; and of course, it has always been my friends that I've turned my gift of understanding on the hardest.

Alan takes me in his arms and holds me there until my leg stops quaking. "You may be the luckiest pregnant woman alive," he whispers in my ear.

I find my voice. "Get me out of here, Alan. Right now, please. I don't want to talk to anyone or see anyone or explain anything. Take me and my baby away from this evil before it kills us." I'm proud of how little I sound like I am begging.

Alan doesn't hesitate or even blink. He nods once, says nothing, and drapes his jacket around my shoulders. "I'll get you into the car and take you to the airport, right now. I'll drive right through the media if I have to." He grins, obviously relishing the thought of mowing down reporters in a Crown Vic. "Hmm. That might even fix this day."

I can't reply. I can only smile, but it's an important smile, in the moment. It's the smile of my strength returning to me.

I burrow into his shoulder. *Take me home, Alan,* I think at him. *Take me home to my Tommy and my Bonnie.*

I remember that last diorama I saw as we are on our way to the car. I'm so tired. I want to close my eyes and remain mute. Even though not telling Alan could destroy the life of someone we both care for—I can feel only reluctance.

I wonder if this is what it was like for Bonnie. Wanting to talk but just not caring about anything enough to do so.

"Alan ... ," I croak. "I need to tell you something. It's important. Whatever you do, you can't let him see it."

"See what?" he asks me, frowning.

I tell him, and make sure he understands. He does.

"I'll take care of it," he says, his expression grim. "Christ." He seems lost for a moment, old and scared and cold. He shakes it off. "Let's get you in the car, and I'll deal with it before we head to the airport."

He tucks me in, gentle as a giant handling a baby. I hear the click of my seat belt sliding into place. "You good?" he asks me, peering into my eyes. "I can be gone for five minutes?"

"Yes."

"You sure?"

"I'm sure."

He nods once, then closes my door and jogs off, presumably to find Callie.

I watch through the window as the media all clamor and point their cameras toward the car. I'm not surprised. Alan's told me a little on the march back up from the underworld. Every family on the block, except for one woman, was dead. Some were suicides; some were murders committed by neighbors who then committed suicide. It was an inexplicable horror orgy of death and mayhem, as though Jonestown had come to Colorado. This wasn't just U.S. news. It would go international, if it hadn't already.

Wait until they find out about the bunker and the museum. And the family. It'll be a feeding frenzy.

I don't care. I can't even summon anger. I'm exhausted. I can't think about death and pain and people being transformed into monkeys or about all the separate parts of a mystery that looked massive enough to be its own world.

It turns out that my sense of time had been severely kiltered. I'd been convinced there was no way I was down there longer than three hours.

I was wrong. A full day had passed.

A day!

I shiver and hope Alan comes back soon. I wonder what happened during all the time I can't remember. Or if there's time I can't remember. Maybe it's all there and I just have the fast-forward button locked in the on position inside my brain.

I don't think so. I really don't. What I think is that I lost my mind. That the building of me cracked and tumbled.

I think that happened for a reason.

The shapes of things apply to the shapes of my truths, too. In this moment of rushing water and absolute confusion, I trust the instinct that tells me: If you want to raise that building again, you'd better run.

Fast.

I take a final look, then close my eyes. I resolve not to open them again until we're gone from this place.

This is the shape of me quitting.

But then, a loud tap from loud fingers against the glass of my window, and Alan is staring in at me with eyes louder than the rest. With a look of such ... awfulness. My lips tremble against each other.

Something terrible has happened.

PART TWO

SILENCE

CHAPTER EIGHT

(The following two articles appeared in the editorial section of the *Denver Post* and in a weekly column of the *Los Angeles Times*, respectively.):

Death Museum in Colorado Sealed— Revisionist History in the Making?
—By Andrew Kent, Contributing Staff Writer

The so-called Death Museum got its name from the only witness to it who has ever talked about what he saw.

According to Denver SWAT team member Nathan Hogue, the underground room is "as big as a football field, or maybe a little smaller. It's packed with Lucite display cases, and inside those cases… oh, man… the whole thing is a death museum."

The very next day, Officer Hogue stopped talking. When approached by the media with follow-up questions, he refused comment but not before saying: "It's been explained to me that there are national security matters involved. I had to sign a secrecy agreement with the FBI."

The FBI spokesperson, Christina Nueves, had this to say: "Officer Hogue misspoke. The secrecy agreement is not due to national security concerns. We have a lot of material to go through—one of the largest forensic jobs in history. This is material that spans, in some cases, decades. It's possible that some or much of this material will inform older cases or open new ones. We want to ensure there are no legal missteps and also that there are no leaks to victims' families should that become relevant."

Ms. Nueves would not comment on whether or not it had yet become "relevant."

We do have one specific description from Officer Hogue. "It's the first thing you see: a life-size photograph of Chinese people crawling all over each other.

Thing reaches to the ceiling. There's also a video to go with it—the photos were taken from the video, I guess—which I watched. I'll never forget seeing that. It's hard to describe. Supposed to be related to the Nanking Massacre back in 1937."

Curiouser and curiouser. Well, I'm sure some will scoff, but if there was ever a time a strange event itched to be turned into a good conspiracy theory, this is it. The machine that churns them out has already gone to work, certain that someone finally found where they hid those pesky Area 51 alien corpses. The writers of the blog oswaldTIMES3.com—who believe that a three-man team killed Kennedy, not a lone gunman—have stated that they "know" "the truth" will be revealed soon.

Really? The truth? Wouldn't that be something?

I'm not much of a believer in conspiracies. They require a lot of intelligence and loyalty, and these aren't factors I see much evidence of within our government. No, my greater concern is what we will not be told about things that "don't matter" but which will be withheld, regardless, "for our own good."

The dying human tower of Nanking is an excellent example. Yes, Officer Hogue has already talked about it, so no doubt it will be released. But consider this: What if he hadn't spoken of it? Nanking is a very old Japan and a long-ago China, but the wound has never fully healed on either side. Can you see a politician (or a politician in uniform) deciding to file it away somewhere? It wouldn't take much. All he'd have to claim is the truth: He didn't know it had any historical significance.

And how about theft of artifacts? Imagine the value of such a video, if it does exist (and Officer Hogue has no apparent reason to lie). I'm not trying to imply that law enforcement is corrupt or crooked or incompetent. I'm implying that they are composed of human beings and that human beings have a history in this area. Talk to any Egyptologist, and he'll tell you the same.

You can always count on horror to leak like water, eventually; even with the crackdown, rumors have begun to circulate from reliable places. The discovery of a myth is just one example: a lampshade, made of human skin, that appears to date to the Nazi era. Or another: a grainy black-and-white film supposedly documenting the suicide of Hitler himself.

I'm not saying that those in government would overtly destroy such artifacts, or even—once the dust settled—suppress the facts of their existence.

I'm saying this: I already have a big brother, thanks. And CSIs, no matter how skilled, aren't historians—they're a part of the law enforcement machine. In my opinion, we need outside-trained civilian observers to make sure this train stays on the tracks all the way to the finish, and to see to it that history—potentially one-of-kind history—is correctly cared for and preserved.

This should not be a decision that belongs solely to the federal government and its representatives. The "museum" exists in Colorado, and we Coloradans should both have a say about, and feel some responsibility for, its handling and disposition.

If ever there was a time for transparency, I'd think it would be in regards to this "Death Museum."

Let's hope we end up hearing the whole truth once the dust has settled. In the meantime, we'll have to trust that the FBI and local police know what they're doing, and trust them to do the right thing without civilian oversight; and that nothing worth millions, or hundreds of millions of dollars, disappears into the black market, never to be seen or heard from again.

I imagine you can guess where my optimism lies.

Los Angeles FBI Director Sells Out His Own

—From Richard Whitman's column "The Weekly Truth"

I have written about corruption in both the local and federal government enough, over the years, for my own view of the subject itself to evolve. In my wide-eyed, beginning days, my shock ran deep, along with my outrage.

As time has gone on, and while my shock is often still present in regard to the details, my outrage has (largely) disappeared. It's not that I've become cynical. It's that I've come to understand: Where power and money are available for misuse, you can count on a certain percentage of human beings to take advantage of that fact.

Getting outraged every time a politician is caught with his or her hand in the till (metaphorical or otherwise) is like getting outraged at the yearly presence of hurricanes in Florida. The hurricanes will continue, regardless. The lesson to learn, then, is not to stop caring about them, but to never stop watching for their approach.

People are human. That's like saying that water is wet, I suppose. But in the arenas of power and money and sex, it's more rule than cliché.

I've seen the hand-wringing and shows of wide-eyed disbelief from news-people and politicians at the recent discovery that a veteran agent of the FBI, who was also the assistant director of the Los Angeles field office, had betrayed his own people for money. I can understand their reactions. The facts alone are shocking. The results—including the death of an agent's family member and the loss of Special Agent Smoky Barrett's home to a fire, just to name a few—are shocking.

But again, all of this only underscores the same lesson: Hurricanes happen, and we must never stop watching for their approach. Perhaps if the FBI itself had been better at this, the results would have been different.

Still, when you examine the record of Assistant Director David Jones, even this writer can forgive the extending of at least a modicum of trust to the man.

Jones joined the Federal Bureau of Investigation in 1977 and worked his way up by merit. He was commended no less than three times for personal bravery in the performance of his duties and was wounded by gunfire during the rescue of two kidnapped children in 1983, where his specific actions were attributed to saving the lives of the children involved.

Sources say he had "the right kind of record": a large tally of wins on one side and, on the other, a smaller tally of black marks for ignoring the kinds of orders—and superiors—that should be ignored. An agent's agent, in other words, incorruptible but human.

According to sources, David "Davy" Jones was also that rarest of bosses in a large government bureaucracy: a man respected by his subordinates. He was fair but ruthless and was still trusted to "go through a door," should the need arise.

He also stood up in defense of agents under his command on at least two occasions, when to do so meant swimming against the bureaucratic tide. One source tells me that these actions led to delays in promotion for Jones.

So why, then, did a man like David Jones go so against what he clearly worked so hard for all his life? He was not a rich man, but he had no out-standing debt to speak of. His credit rating was fine, and he owned a home. He lived within his means, and according to neighbors was generally helpful and polite, if distant.

There's much we still don't know. What facts we are aware of are these:

There are items in the so-called Colorado Death Museum that were stolen from FBI evidence storage, and these thefts are directly attributed to David Jones by sources within the FBI itself.

In Cyprus, a bank account containing close to five million dollars was found in the name of David Jones. Attempts to trace the funds have been fruitless, but according to our source at Interpol, this is not the first offshore account Mr. Jones has used. There's evidence of accounts going back more than twenty years.

People are human. Hurricanes happen. Surely, then, anyone can understand the allure of five million dollars to a man on a government salary? And who knows if this was the five million he had left from a larger amount, as opposed to something he grew slowly over time?

Perhaps what they don't understand is the cruelty to one of his own agents, one he was supposed to have had personal regard for. Perhaps they don't understand why anyone would do something so despicable. It's certainly hard to come up with any scenario that could ever possibly justify it. It's the one part of the whole story that's made this writer feel the old outrage again that he used to feel in his early days of investigative reporting.

The fact known is this: Hours after the release of the grotesque video that's now being called The Missive, another video was circulated on the Internet, posted from an Internet account that belonged to Jones. It has been verified as genuine. This video lasted approximately forty minutes and is unedited and uncut. It shows the torture and rape of Smoky Barrett, special agent of the FBI, as well as the torture and murder of her husband, Matthew Barrett.

The video raises more questions than it answers. The man responsible, Joseph Sands, was killed at the scene by Agent Barrett and thus had no opportunity to remove any recording equipment. There has never been a mention of a video made by Sands or by anyone connected with the case, officially or otherwise. The FBI has verified for this writer that the case files contain no record of a video made by Sands. Yet, clearly, it exists.

The video is graphic and horrible. Anyone who keeps a "copy" should be ashamed. I'm not sure I've ever witnessed anything more private. I find it hard to blame Agent Barrett for her recent hermitage, given all that's occurred, and I doubt I could find many who'd disagree with me. The losses she's incurred—doing the job she does—are breathtaking. They are horrendous, and no one could fault her for refusing to bear it further.

Jones did not report to work the day the video was released. When agents were sent to his home, they found his naked corpse, a leather belt around its neck, hanging from the showerhead in the master bathroom.

Both the FBI and the LAPD have issued joint statements confirming that no suicide note was found with the corpse and have classified the investigation as "ongoing."

Perhaps Mr. Jones felt that a note was unnecessary or that no note would suffice in explaining his actions.

Maybe the lack of a note is his message: I was a hurricane, and you should have been watching.

(The following is excerpted from an article written for an online blog; a mention of it occurred during a network news show, after which it was picked up by Reuters and distributed nationally by various papers and publications.)

The Wolf and the Maiden— Where Is Smoky Barrett?

—By Aaron Wilson

The man in the video never calls himself the Wolf—though that's what the world has come to call him. He talks, instead, about a world of wolves and sheep, and says that all of us exist as either one or the other.

He contends, then, to prove his point by committing a series of violent and horrible acts on camera, for all "the sheep" to see.

The Wolf chose to film in high-definition black-and-white, stripping the events of their color and leaving them to stand alone. We have to add what's missing ourselves. We know that blood is red, even if we see it on the film as black. As for screams, well, they have their own colors, too.

This writer will not render the Wolf's actions into words here; to do so would be redundant. It's a media world now. The infamy of the video has carried it to the farthest reaches of the Internet. It can be easily found if a person's so inclined.

In many ways, its message is incoherent—or at least unclear; and this writer is not the only one to have made the observation. Various ex–intelligence agency analyst types—hired guns for news organizations with deeper pockets than yours truly—have discussed the conflicting nature of the Wolf's actions, stated intentions, and words.

"The best analysts locate anomalies, not trends," said Michael McKay, who spent twenty years working for the CIA. "Anomalies in that... material abound. On the one hand, it's the act of a sadistic individual pursuing just those aims, without remorse. On the other, it's the product of an unbalanced mind attempting to justify the acts he's committing with pseudo-psychological rationalizations.

"There are the semi-revolutionary statements, which are themselves entirely broad and no more specific than the call for 'the sheep' to 'rise up' against 'the wolves'—but he leaves it to the sheep to define who the wolves might be.

"Finally, there is the specific nature of the comments regarding Special Agent Smoky Barrett, as well as proof of knowledge of the attacks against her and members of her team. This is the great anomaly of the video, really, in that it's the most specific aspect of it. In all ways, in this video, the man everyone's calling 'the Wolf' is broad and general. Look past the violence, and he is almost stereotypical.

"When he speaks about Barrett, and about the happenings in Colorado—here is where he reveals something about his true intent, in my opinion. The question becomes: What is that intent, and what does it mean? 'Why her?,' in other words."

This writer imagines that Special Agent Barrett would agree, were she engaging on the subject with anyone. She has built a career hunting men who kill for sport, and it's well-known that in hunting such men, the victim is always your best lead—even when the victim is you.

It is also worth noting that the nature of the museum itself, in terms of its sheer size, reveals that "the Wolf" is no loner but must be part of some larger group.

As for Mrs. Barrett, she has refused all contact with the media. We know she delivered her baby. We know that her home was burned to the ground. We know that she has not returned to her job. Beyond that, she has been successful in hiding herself and her family, and her current whereabouts are unknown, despite all efforts of those with aforementioned 'deeper pockets' to locate her. ...

CHAPTER NINE

I am dreaming of the ending to the video again. I have watched it while awake only twice in the six weeks that have passed since my time in the bunker, but I have dreamed its entirety, from beginning to end, over and over again. None of it is good, but I have seen variations of most of the evils it contains. It is the ending that makes the rest of it matter. Knowing it's waiting, understanding what's to come, lends its horror to the moments that precede it, like falling for an hour toward the open mouth of a monster that waits below.

In my dream, I am fixed in place, and I can hear the sounds of horror rushing toward me.

It's not thunder. It's not even the roaring of the ocean, really. It's more like a screaming in the distance, in this distance of my mind. The scream becomes a roar that fills the world, given from a mouth wide enough to eat the sun whole. It fills the ears of my inner self until I am so deafened by it that I cease to exist. It is all that there is; and after a time, it becomes all that ever was.

Then, a sense of inner straining reaches me, signaling a change. I become aware of it only by realizing that I am once again aware of myself as separate from the sound. The separation is the width of a hair, or the sung-spun blur of a hummingbird's wing reduced to a specific nano-moment, but it is there. Or rather, I am again. The roar becomes a scream becomes a murmured wail, like the water of the ocean struggling back out to the embrace of its larger self. The end of the world is swallowed—and the world itself returns.

I dream that I shift in my sleep because when I am aware of my dreams, they require logical continuity. These are dreams that disturb my sleep, and even while I am in them I know that I will wake up tired. I sense that I could blink once, on purpose, and disturb the surface equilibrium of the dream liquid that holds me under, but I do not. Even this is part of the dream: the power to wake and the choice not to.

I must wait for the ghost train that's coming and watch the horror cars go by on wheels of blood and bone. The shape of the train changes from time to time, but the content it carries mostly remains the same. Its horrors seem to anchor me.

Very little does, these days, so I wish it toward me and hear the speeded-up sound of its *clack-clack-clack* respond, because in my dreams—unlike my waking life—my will is all.

Horror or not, I wish I could sit in the sand (it's made of diamonds of every rainbow color) next to these tracks (lines of ivory the color of a dead man's teeth, strong and rustless as titanium) under the eternal moon that I can see from the corner of my eyes smiling at me (it smiles only when I look away, and then with mindless hunger). I'd sit here forever and scream as the train rocked by, chortling its black bass notes of anthracite evil.

But at least I would sit with certainty, with my mind under my own control. I lust for this like sex; I long for it like water. The blood in my veins is desperation, distilled to its purest possible form.

The roaring in the distance is the train now, and it approaches less with a roll than at a speeding shamble. It's been fitted with Gabriel's horn, and the roaring song is all again, drowning out my own screams when they arrive in my throat with their feet of nails and thorns. The train arrives in the same moment, and the first car is every car, and each car is an image, like a movie projector—*clack-clack-clack*—going faster and faster until no car is separate and the image is all. It fills my mind till my mind is gone. *It's a clue!* is the last thing I tell myself before I disappear and forever comes again.

It's a movie. It has been shot in black-and-white, but that's a reflection of design, not a marker of age. The blacks are too black, the edges too crystal sharp, to have been shot on older equipment. The definition is so high I feel like I could step into the picture as it plays and smell the coming violence.

"Once upon a time," the voice speaks, a calm alto, "Americans understood the truth of violence. We were no smarter, as a whole. But because we knew that death was real, that blood was red and smelled like sweat and pennies, there were some lies we could not be told. We didn't check on our children at night because the good Lord told us to; we checked on them because we knew they could die in the dark, we knew it in our hopes and bones.

"Ugliness was a brother, a mother, a sister, a father. It crippled kids with polio, and hung black men from trees till their faces twisted into bloated, purple fruit. Men shot each other in the streets and then undertakers put their bodies on display in coffins to rot in the sun for the crowd to gawk at. Women were beaten by their husbands till they slurred their words for life and were told that speaking less was the best protection, anyway.

"Alas, times have changed," he says, without a hint of either amusement or regret, "and as always, we have changed with them."

The camera lens has been fixed on a tabletop, shot at a downward angle. The table is wooden, stained but unpainted, the fine grain made more vivid for being shot in black-and-white. Three items lie side by side, aligned with the grain: a scalpel, an M1911 .45 handgun, and a blowtorch that shines so brightly it looks like it had been chrome plated or cut from a block of pure silver.

A single hand appears, palm up and gloved in black leather. The leather is smooth and supple, and it gleams under the harsh lights he uses. There is an odd texture to the glove that I recognize but cannot recall. It tugs at my mind horribly, like the tug of stitches at a numbed wound; you watch yourself bleed without feeling. The hand sweeps once over the table, indicating the four items as though the indication alone would serve for meaning.

Which it does, doesn't it? my mind croaks once before resuming its scream.

The hand leaves the camera frame again, and the voice resumes its placid, documentary drone. "Those who do not understand suffering and death are unable to completely understand life. The unintended consequence of a constant, homeland peace is that war becomes a movie. Something exciting, even desirable. Rape becomes an issue to discuss instead of an abomination. And torture? Well ... torture can be redefined by those who do it, which action will be believed and thus supported by the sheep who believe that wolves and sheep can coexist peacefully."

The gloved hand appears again and wags a scolding finger at the camera. "Wolves eat sheep. No law passed by man can change this. But all that is required these days is that they eat their sheep in private and leave no carcasses to be found. Eventually, no sheep can be found alive who has personally witnessed a wolf taking a violent meal. Only tales survive. Over time, tales become fables or cynicism, or perhaps even discrimination against the poor, misunderstood wolves." The hand disappears again. "No one remembers what a dead man in a coffin smells like in the hottest part of the afternoon, or the sound a sheep makes when it is murdered, or the way the wolf smiles when a dying sheep screams."

The speaker moves behind the table now, placing tented fingers at either side of the displayed implements. "There are more wolves roaming the world now than ever before. They have never left, never become more 'peaceable.' They have only gotten smarter. The wolves of today have learned the primary lesson: Eat in private and you can eat your fill, and the sheep left alive will only believe in the peace. We're always the most eager to believe in our greatest hope."

A gloved finger touches the scalpel and strokes it along its length. For the first time, more than the speaker's hands are revealed. I see a tanned Caucasian forearm, shaved smooth and of indeterminate age. He's rolled the white sleeve of a pressed dress shirt in a perfect cuff up to his elbow. The gloves, I realize, are in the style of motorcycle gloves, tight around the fingers, ending at the wrist. They reek of quality and speak of violence. They are the functional gloves of a serious man.

"I could pull this blade from my pocket while walking through a subway station or perhaps 'the mall' and so long as I kept on smiling and appearing agreeable, most of you would let me get close enough to cut you dead. Why? Because you do not *believe*. Death is an unfortunate event that happens to others—perhaps because they've earned it? Perhaps because you are luckier or better or more deserving than they are? All these fantasies run through your heads, like sugarplum fairies of stupidity. In a choice between my intent as good or deadly, you must assume the best of me because there is no way, in your houses of denial, that the worst could ever come knocking on *your* door." He pauses, and his finger stops, too. "Every one of you I've ever killed was always so surprised. You could not fathom, in a thousand years or a million days, how chance had chosen you out of all the others available for plucking.

"And do you know something? None of you quite believed it until the first time I sliced into the fat beneath your flesh." He points at the blowtorch. "Or burned it black and crackly like a campfire marshmallow.

"And do you know something else? You were always so surprised at the *ugly* of it all. The horrid stench when you shit yourself in fear. The snot from your nose mingling with the stew of vomit hanging from your chin in a god-less, goopy waterfall." He chuckles. "Oh! The humanity! The sheep look up!"

The gloves close into a fist for a moment, then relax and disappear from the camera frame. "But possibly, I should ridicule you less, yes? Because in the end, to paraphrase, I come not to eat the sheep—but to save them.

"The point of the lesson is not horror for the sake of horror but horror for the sake of education in the truth. The truth, dear friends, is simple: They're making sheep burgers out there like never before, and you think it's all some-how hypothetical or distant.

"Watch what follows and learn. Put down your childish hopes and dreams and see the world for what it is: a place where wolves eat sheep, not because the sheep cannot defend themselves, but because they want to believe the wolves have changed."

The train is gone by now. Metaphors die quick deaths in dreams. I can see only what I've already seen—what the man with the gloved hands will show through the lens. I'm still sitting in the sand, but the railcars are gone, replaced by a flickering silver movie screen that stretches from horizon to horizon, as far as the eye can see.

It is the end that counts. The events that come before it speed by too quickly. Their only reason for being is in the waiting they provide, the feeling of inexorable forward motion toward an inevitable destination. I am unable to move from my viewing place, but at the same time, I am falling, tumbling, being dragged. It's as though I can hear my own future screaming in the distance.

All my senses strain, even as I wish they wouldn't, each one fine-tuned to its utmost point of clarity.

I can smell the wood of the table: unvarnished pine, freshly cut and finely sanded. The faint, hard bite of soft, cured leather wafts off the killer's gloves, making my nostrils twitch and the hairs on the nape of my neck rise and quiver. There is the clean smell of oatmeal soap on sun-washed skin. It reminds me, for some reason, of a confident man who shaves himself with a brush and straight razor. Finally, layering itself over everything, the patina of the coming storm. The slowly oozing, oily aroma of terror—like nickels and dimes boiled in soy sauce and urine left on the stove for too long in the hottest part of a humid afternoon.

My ears hear the sounds of the world straining. Cords that can't be snapped, pulled tight till they should. The mosquito shouts of wood chairs on wood floors, creaking in choirs of protest, while bare sweat-slicked skin squeals and burns as it slips across some oaky smoothness. The body runs in terror even when it is bound, moving whatever patch or part of itself it can, to get away.

The Wolf, as the world now calls him, had captured six people for the beginning of his show: a Catholic priest, three men, one woman, and a teenage girl.

"First we take a symbol that demands you regard it always and only as a sheep."

There is a moment when the camera is still, and I can hear the smooth-soled shoes of our killer moving with purpose across the floor. Then the lens moves, and a man appears. He sits fully clothed in a chair, wearing the collar of a Catholic priest. He is gagged, bound, and almost mindless with fear. His eyes rove wildly, jitterbugging in his skull like a crack addict's. *He's older than the others*, I think. Perhaps in his late fifties, with gray-white hair and a thin, gaunt body. He is fraying everywhere. Dandruff flakes dot the dark shoulders of his shirt, which has been washed into a worn-looking "half black." His shoes are clean and shined, but the leather is like an old woman's face.

He's an impoverished holy man, the only kind I trust. Stretching his dollars when he has them, eating less when he doesn't. Working for something, using nothing and less by choice. I may not agree with his faith anymore, but I can see how unprepared his simple life has made him to face this horror. I can hear it in the creaks of the chair's wood as his body shakes against it. I can hear it in the cracks of his shoe leather as his feet writhe inside them.

It's the sound of protest a rope makes in the instant before it breaks, and in truth, it comes from every part of him. I can hear his knuckles crack and his neck tendons whine, and his skin is drawn so tight against the bone it reminds me of a rubber band stretched to the snapping point. In his terror, it's as if he were trying to rip his soul from his own body.

I've been in his position, so I think: *Maybe he is.*

The gloved hand appears, and it now holds the scalpel, which it points at the priest's head. The priest's eyes clatter and jitter, trying to see it all while denying it at the same time.

"The collar and the cross. Take either or take them together, and you are allowed no choice but to *believe*. This man cannot be a wolf. He is a priest! As a human, he has sacrificed the sweet feel of a woman's cunt slipping and sliding against his need and the sometimes even sweeter feel of dollars running through his hand like a river of gold that can make any dream come true. He must be a sheep. Why, after all, would a wolf choose such weakness?"

The scalpel shines in black-and-white, held like a lover by the unnatural leather. It caresses the priest's ear and parts the thin hair on his trembling head. No blood is drawn, but he shakes even harder.

"Did you know there was a time that a failure to attend church on Sunday was punished by cutting off the ears of all involved? Fathers and mothers and brothers and daughters, held tight while the sides of their heads were made smooth and bloody. It's true. So many lost their ears, in fact, that it was one of the driving reasons behind wigs becoming so popular in Europe and elsewhere." He chuckles. The priest trembles harder, making his chair chatter against the wood floor like the teeth of a man freezing to death.

"So the wolves put on their sheep coats and their sheep collars and donned their sheep crosses, and then assured and reassured those most unfortunate failures of attendance that this was not the action of a wolf, no. It was the sheep helping each other keep their fetlocks fully placed on the trail that would lead them where all sheep long to go: an infinite world of eternal peace.

"So children watched as their mothers and fathers shrieked at this sawing of the gristle and waited their turns; and looked into the eyes of the men who held the knives; and knew without doubt that what happened was deserved, not enjoyed; and was meant to do naught but ensure that one day, all the sheep would graze on the greenest grass possible.

"This blood and fear was being spilled, they knew, to bring them to that final place where they would be free from the wolf that life itself is, in the end." The scalpel paused against the priest's flesh, which drew taut in my dream like the skin of a human on some cannibal's drum.

The violence is sudden and shocking in its suddenness, like all true violence. The hand without the scalpel grabs hold of the hair on top of the priest's head and yanks it back, holding it still. Then the scalpel carves, smooth and curved and certain, following the lines of the priest's ear with the care of someone using a stencil or tracing paper. The gag does almost nothing to stifle the sounds of the priest's screams. They are a mix of a soprano singing and a bull snorting and a pig being choked to death.

The cutter grabs hold of the whole ear without letting go of the scalpel, and he pulls with tremendous force. The ear tears loose without much resistance. The cutter brings it close to the camera, till all that fills the lens is the ear, the scalpel, and the glove.

It's human skin, I realize in my dream, sitting on the sand of diamonds by the train tracks made of bone. *The glove. That's why it bothered me. It's like the ones that I saw in that museum under the ground.* I scream in my dream at this realization, without knowing why. It's certainly not worse than the ear or the priest in the background, but it makes me scream in a way that they can't.

It's a clue, the same voice whispers to me again in my mind. *Pay attention now, and don't you dare stop. Now's not the time for looking away.*

"Denial," the voice of the filmmaker says. "It is the way the mind protects itself from what it cannot survive. You, dear sheep, are experiencing that right now, in this very moment. You do not believe this is an ear, not really. It must be a simulacrum of latex rubber or a special effect of some kind. Life is not the place where hope suddenly dies. That is how sheep think, because it is what they *must* believe."

He drops the ear, and while I do not see what happens to it when it leaves the eye of the camera, I can hear it slap the wood. It's like a *crack* that's been transmuted to a *thud*. It's a sloppy sound. The sound of something important being tossed away and lost forever.

The camera moves again, coming around now in a few moments of jerky motion until finally settling to face the priest directly. He is crying with abandon, snot running from his nose. His eyes are full of a mixture of begging and unbelief.

"I come to save you sheep, remember? We must rid you of your denial. The ear was real. To believe this—to be sure of it—you must be sure that the man himself is real." A gloved hand pulls at the gag until it hangs around the priest's neck like a scarf. "So tell us, Father—are you real?"

The priest leans forward and vomits into his own lap. "Please, dear God in heaven, please—stop this! No more! No more. Oh, God—please!" Snot and tears and fear hang from his chin. He is shivering so hard I imagine I can see each pore in the skin of his face moving as separate dots of darkness, like all the stars turned inside out. "Please! Please! Please!" he begs and sobs.

It is here where my own denial finally dies. Because, of course, the filmmaker is right. Even knowing that outside my dream, in the real world that I will wake up in soon, this very same video exists and has been played around the world in all the ways that such video finds ways to make itself known—I did not believe, for just a moment, in that ear. I did not believe in the scalpel, or the priest, or the gloves made of human skin.

But language is where we humans find ourselves as human beings most, in the end. We make sounds that mean things to one another and to ourselves. Over time, those sounds grow roots that reach into every last piece of ourselves, adding more and more meaning with fewer and fewer words. Hope has a sound, love has a sound, hate has a sound; and each of them has a million roots of sensation and connection and singular truth that we cannot escape the feeling of without literally carving out parts of our brains.

"Please—Oh, *God*—please!" the priest screams. I hear hope and horror, terror and pain; and I hear, in the quality of the way he says that word— *God*—the sound of a man pleading for help. It's the sound of a son begging for help from a father, or a mother, or a brother.

The sounds and the language send a shock through me, appearing as whole forests of meaning; not as something from nothing, but as *everything* from nothing. Denial doesn't just disappear in this moment—it's murdered. Yes, I realize, that is another human being, and he is real, and his suffering is real.

And so the ear was real.

This is the problem with my life, I think, on the diamond sand. This is the clue the whisper meant. I understand too much with too little. I *know*, whereas others are allowed to at least be unsure.

Yes, the whisper agrees.

That part of me that has made me what I am—a hunter of men who cut the ears off priests—calculates toward its own understandings, too. The moviemaker knows *all* of this, and it's why he's chosen the method he has. It tells me a lot about him. I know what's involved in arriving at such certainties, so it tells me that he has been practicing his subject for a long time.

It tells me, too, that he is not a liar. He *has* come to teach the sheep. Not in the way that I think of them or because of any morality we share, but because his stated goal is not a lie. It is his plan to bring the unbelievers to a state of certainty—that the wolves do exist, and all those possibilities hinted at in horror films and crime dramas really are true, at least somewhere.

"Fucker," I mutter in my dream, wondering as I do if I also mutter it in my sleep.

I hate him for it, because it's a shitty lesson to want to teach the world.

"Now, Father, tell me the truth: Who would come up with such a lesson about the discipline of faith? The sheep? Or the wolves?"

"Please. ... " The priest weeps. "Please, just—just stop. Just that. You don't have to do anything else. Just—stop." His grief is quieter now, but this is only because it has deepened. He, too, knows that the ear is real. That loss of denial has carved banks on either side of his soul, letting what was just a possibility when hope still existed become a river or the rain.

"Stopping would not be the truth, Father," the filmmaker chides. "Stopping would allow for the presence of doubt. Some of the sheep want to believe so badly in your inability to be a wolf, and I have no intention of allowing that."

The priest weeps harder now. "Why are you doing this?" he begs. "All I've ever done is give my life to God. Since I was nineteen years old, I've done nothing else. Nothing!"

The filmmaker laughs out loud, and it's a genuine laugh, I can tell. Jolly and straight from the belly. "Nothing?" he chortles. "Are you *sure*?"

I see it in my dream as I saw it in real life, the very first time I watched the video: the shift to defiance. It is slight—almost imperceptible—but under the circumstances, it puts up my antennae now, as it did then.

"I have given my life, and all that I am, to the Lord my God," the priest states, staring into the lens of the camera. His voice is firm and steady, and there is no slightest evidence that his statement lacks certainty.

There are many reasons that a man of faith, particularly if that faith is strong, could find inner reserves of resistance and strength. But there is a pattern to human reactions and the movements from one emotion to another, and despite what many people think, their sequences make sense more often than not.

The priest's visceral terror and agony had reeked of authenticity. So much so that they reached deep into me and shook me hard, in spite of all that I've seen. Just a moment before, he was the true picture of a man who would do just about anything—perhaps even sell his soul—to get the torture to stop. Then the filmmaker had challenged a single assertion, just once, and it had transformed him. It had taken away his fear.

He has something to hide, I think. Something worth more than the loss of another ear or any of the other possible events staring him in the face.

Sequences are where psychopaths fail the most when they are faking behavior. They choose the wrong reaction as the next one in the sequence, not simply because they don't understand what the next reaction would be, but because they don't understand why it *should* be the next reaction. Their greatest Achilles' heel is when they attempt to build models of "normal" behavior, while lacking the emotional motivation that drives it. One of the aspects of being able to authentically present oneself as being good, in other words, is the actual desire to be good. Wanting to fake it is not quite the same thing; and in this context, "quite" can be an inch, or it can be a light-year.

"Ah, Father," the filmmaker chides. "When will the wolves of your ilk understand: This action of falling back on your slogans reveals you more than it conceals you? Never, I suppose. Why change what works most of the time just because of the few times it doesn't, right? Those who see through you are always in the minority, anyway."

"Yea, though I walk through the valley of the shadow of death...," the priest intones, his eyes gazing toward something only he can see, *"I shall fear no evil."* His voice doesn't tremble, and his spine is like a rod of steel, straight and true. He has become an archetype in the space of a heartbeat.

Liar, I think.

"Liar," the filmmaker intones, all hint of irony or amusement now absent from his voice. "What you mean to say, Father, is that you don't fear doing evil, particularly that evil that you love so much, isn't that so?"

"Thy rod and thy staff they comfort me...," the priest drones on. His force of will to ignore the filmmaker utterly is palpable, and it stinks of a performance.

His ear bleeds freely down his body. The pain must be immense. I am reminded again of how instinctively we hold onto our most important lies, not only because of what others would think of us, but because in truth, they are a part of what makes us who we are—even to ourselves.

"Ah, yes, 'thy rod,' Father. That's always been the problem, has it not? Thy rod and where you put it? Such as into the mouths and anuses of those altar boys you called 'Father Michael's Favorites'?" The priest goes silent and still. "Did it comfort them, Father? Your rod? Did they 'fear no evil' when you fucked them in the rectory or substituted your ejaculate for the blood of Christ?"

"I did no such thing, you filthy creature!" the priest spits out, finding his voice again. But his denial comes with a tremble this time. His fear has changed and deepened. I can see the sweat rolling down his skin in sheets.

I have seen this movie before, in my waking life, and I know what is coming. How the filmmaker will come up with photographs and videotapes that Father Michael was stupid enough not only to make, but also to keep. How the filmmaker will say: "An eye for an eye, Father, is it not? What, then, should be exchanged in your case?"

How he will take the scalpel and answer his own question with a slow, studied precision. The cars whip by, revealing the same to me again, showing me in a heartbeat what took ten excruciating minutes to reveal in real time.

I understand the things Father Michael did. The terrible crimes, and what they meant, and what they did to his victims. *But still...* I can never stop finding his suffering as anything but wretched. It doesn't matter how much he deserved it. Watching his torture turns out the lights in some parts of my soul forever.

His begging is like a flock of crows cawing themselves to death. There's no victory to be found in it, only the truth the filmmaker is striving to reveal: Wolves exist, and when they exist, wolves do what wolves do—*they eat.*

I am no one's food, but neither am I a wolf in the way of the filmmaker. I understand his point intellectually, and there are parts of it I can understand emotionally in ways that most people in society cannot. In the end, though, still...I do not understand the final act, the thing that closes the curtain. I cannot understand getting so close to another human being, skin to skin, and sucking down their emotions as they suffer.

The flickering images on the screen begin moving forward even faster. *The end is coming soon,* my mind croons to me. *Are you ready? Can you feel it? Have you prepared your mind and heart?*

It's the other victims I see next.

There is a white man in his sixties, with a grim, acne-scarred face and a crew cut. He has a bit of a beer belly, and his eyes are flicking back and forth like a hummingbird's wings. There is a young African American man who appears to be in his thirties. He seems to be in pretty good shape, and his eyes are dry, but the front of his blue jeans are stained with urine. The last is a Latino gentleman, who I would guess is in his midforties. He has long, thick, black hair, and his shirtless torso exposes a mural of tattoos covering a muscled frame. He is moving his weight back and forth from one leg to the other. His eyes are a mix of resignation and defiance, hope warring with knowledge of the inevitable.

The woman looks like a housewife from the suburbs, a bottle blonde in her midthirties wearing a yellow dress and no shoes. Her head keeps darting around, looking first at the camera, then at the teenager to her left, then at the men to her right, and back to the camera again.

The teenager is about fourteen, and in my dream, she is the one who makes me cry tears of moonshine and diamonds that sparkle as they fall and add themselves to the sand. She has exquisite blue eyes, red hair, and skin the color of milk in the way that works—not pale and unhealthy, but beautiful and rare, like fine china destined for adventure in some faraway place. She's only just started becoming a woman, and everything about her speaks of possibility. She is at once nostalgia and the now, an image of the way we all mostly see one another inside forever, because she is at that age where you really become the "you" you remember as yourself; and that moment is always the present one, moving forward.

They've all been handcuffed by four-way manacles: cuffs on each wrist leading in separate chains to a center point, from which two chains lead down to the cuffs around their ankles. Each has a manacle around his or her throat that is made of steel and has been chained to a bolt in the wall. Their mouths have been taped shut.

The filmmaker has set them up to be targets and nothing else. They can move only to shift their weight, and if they fall down, they'll be strangled by the manacles around their necks.

It is a masterful mix of personalities for the filmmaker to have chosen, and this truth is only heightened by the ways in which we are not allowed to know them. They have no names, no voices, no history. The Latino man could be a singer or a father or a gangbanger. The woman in the yellow dress could be a mother or a housewife or a CEO. The young black man is both brave and terrified, and the fact that he has wet himself while keeping his eyes dry and defiant only increases his value to the viewer as a person.

The older white man—is he ex-military? He has that look, but his eyes are the worst ones to watch, too. It doesn't matter that he's not young; you can tell that he is gripping his life as hard as you grip your own.

And then the teenager. She is a hope. The hope we all start with, the hope we remember losing, the hope we have for our children. She is the future and the possible. Her beauty, which has only just begun its transformation toward full womanhood, makes me think of a waterfall or a sunrise. Something wonderful in motion, too alive to ever remain completely still.

"Here you could be" is what the filmmaker says to us with this selection. The final touch is the black-and-white. It reminds me of home movies on reel-to-reel projectors or of old movies watched with family in the living room. Color can be anything, but black-and-white will always be paired with the concept of memory in the mind.

The fact that I don't know their stories, that they are all empty glasses, only makes it worse. It allows my imagination to run wild and roam free. They get to be anything that I think they might be. Which means, in the end, that they are people. Humans who I pass by in the street, or who I stand with in the checkout counter, or who I watch movies with in the theater. They are the other drivers in the cars on the highway or the other passengers on the plane. They are the names that I read on headstones in the cemetery, names that matter despite that they are the names of strangers; because one day I know someone will read my name on a stone in just the same way.

"I took all these people in a single afternoon, using a single vehicle. I was able to take them not because all of them are inherently weak, but because of that core disbelief I'm attempting to demonstrate. I was able to take them because each of them believed they would somehow survive, that a wolf would somehow not end up acting like a wolf. I showed them a hard face and a gun, and I gave them a combination of demands and promises. 'Do what I tell you, and you'll live,' I'd say. 'Refuse, and you'll die.' Each believed the promise, and as a result—each one will now die."

As he speaks this last sentence and they hear it, the five panic and become a strange visual phenomenon of motion. They pull and stumble and choke. They strain and dance and jerk frantically, all to the sound of jangling chains and throated screams blocked by taped-up mouths.

Still, my own voice croons again, *even this is not the end.*

The weapon comes into frame. The filmmaker sighs, and it is the patient sigh of the teacher again. "Let me show you the truth. Watch and see—do these people survive? Does some force majeure arrive to save them? Does respect for age save the old man? Does the injustice of dying young save the girl? Will they survive their wounds, miraculously?"

Then the gun is blasting away, and every bullet fired gives its answer. The ground doesn't open, the sky never falls, and once the weapon is empty, all five of them are dead. The facts of life without the intervention of magic or any larger, guiding justice.

Remember, though—even this is not the end. ...

The sand I'm sitting on has gone cold.

I want to wake up, I hear myself wishing. *I've seen this last part already. Really, I have. I made myself watch it all, and I've learned anything I could already. I promise.*

The film is speeding up. The sand that was cold just a moment ago has suddenly become uncomfortably hot. I feel like I'm sitting on the asphalt of a parking lot in July.

Please, oh please oh please ... I want to wake up. Just let me wake up now, now, now. ...

"Let's discuss this magical construct of a 'just universe' that inevitably doles out good for the good and bad for the bad, little sheep," the Wolf says. "Our last little lesson for now."

Please, oh please, oh God, please. ...

"Here we have a genuinely decent and admirable woman," the Wolf intones, calm as a documentarian. "She is a churchgoer—a Catholic, in fact. She was a faithful wife when married, and a good mother.

"She lost a daughter to a serial killer, many years back. Some gentleman who liked to burn just-pubescent young girls and defile their charred corpses."

The Wolf's voice dies off. I get the sense that he is pondering her. "He burned her daughter alive, and it almost broke her. But this good woman had a son who needed her, so she found her strength and proved her mettle. Somehow she found her smiles again. Extraordinary. Really—you can trust me on that. I've seen enough weakness in the world to be an expert on the subject. This fine lady defied the odds.

"She raised a son who's become a credit to society. He's brilliant, and he works in law enforcement catching some very bad characters indeed."

The woman's gone wild with fear. She struggles in panic against her bonds, and any of the shrieking I couldn't hear through her gag, I can see in her eyes.

I've stopped begging to wake up. It won't work, now. We've reached the turn in the road, the place, once we pass, where everything is revealed.

"But tell me—if there is some guarantee of the good—why in the world wouldn't it protect her from this?"

The quick, low *whoof* of a gas flame being lit is heard. An unceasing dragon hiss follows, with the volume turned low and the treble set to maximum. It reminds me, in my dream, of water blasting from a faucet or of an ocean wave crashing forever in the distance.

The woman looks like she's trying to crawl out of her own skin, until he starts to paint that skin with flame. He's a surgeon with a fire scalpel. He takes off the gag to let the camera hear her screams, and I wake when the first eye boils out of her skull. I wake to the echoes of her hoarse, manlike shouts mixing with my own.

I rush into porcelain arms and vomit till I'm puking up air. I can't get the thought out of my head: She shouted like a death-metal singer when he burned her eyes.

James's mother—Catholic to her finish—had sounded like someone possessed by the devil.

I wipe my mouth and put my head in my arms as I sit on the bathroom floor. I feel like if I don't hold myself together, I'll collapse and fall apart. The holding has become a full-time job lately.

"James, James, poor James," I whisper in the darkness. The pain is too huge and awful for tears. I have not yet comprehended it, not really. I know this.

He did everything right, and his mother died like his sister. The killer laughed in his face and shit on his whole reason for living, and ...

And ... ?

And he saw the video.

I rub my forehead against my arms, scratching at the itch of my misery. It's buried too deep, like a bone on the mend or a phantom limb. One couldn't possibly comprehend this much injustice in the universe and take one's next breath.

Of course he saw the video, I think. *By this time, who hasn't?*

The filmmaker, as I always think of him, is world-famous. Both the video and its accompanying missive have made their way around the world and back again.

After murdering James's mother, he'd ended with two final messages: a call to arms—of sorts—and then a placing of the blame.

"The difference between being a sheep and being a wolf is this one, simple thing: Sheep believe there are no wolves or that the wolves that exist have reformed. Wolves know that there will always be wolves and that the wolves will always eat sheep. This is the world that we live in.

"The time has come for you to choose. I've shown you reality. Death is real, and it is final. When a person harms you, they are not helping you, regardless of what they say. Guns do more than make loud noises; and God, if he exists, is a watcher, not a referee.

"What world will *you* choose to make for yourself? What will you choose to teach your children—the reality or the dream?

"Many will ask why I have done this. Most will question my motives. My reasons and my motives are simple. I gave one of them already: I have come to free the sheep, not to eat them. This is a nation of disbelievers in reality, where the sheep grow greater in numbers and the wolves grow stronger day by day.

"Do you want justice? Then I am afraid you will have to grab it for yourself. Tired of your children being molested by priests? Tired of the rich stealing from the poor without punishment? Tired of a government that spies on its populace in the name of liberty? If this is truly so, then the solutions are simple: Become wolves, and go to war for what is yours.

"So long as you wait for things to change, then that is how long they will remain the same.

"I am a wolf, and always have been. I prefer a world full of wolves and challenges over a world of easy pickings. Wolves who are cowards might as well be sheep. My message to those wolves who disagree: Go fuck yourselves.

My message to those wolves who demand my blood: Come and get it, if you dare.

"The only difference is a choice. Make a choice—any choice—and then prove it in your actions. Put some blood in these streets again, and teach our children the truth: This world only gives you what you have the power first to take and then to keep.

"This is the only truth. There is no other.

"As to why I have chosen now as the moment, for this you can thank only Special Agent Smoky Barrett and her team of wolf hunters. She chose her profession over all else; then by doing so, she located and uncovered the most precious of my lairs. It took some time and some resources and some years to build up what has been revealed in Colorado.

"Wolves value their privacy, and no true wolf would ever allow such a violation to go unanswered. I commend Barrett for surviving the encounter, of course. It is not a result I would counsel her to expect a repeat of, should our paths cross again."

Then he paused, and in that moment the first time I saw the video—it seemed like the longest pause ever in the history of the world. "You are a wolf, Special Agent Barrett. The fact you're a woman, that you are pregnant—none of these things fool me. You are a wolf. If I find you again, I will kill you, and your family, and all you hold dear. I have your scent now, and your measure.

"Let us hope that you have mine."

A similar written manifesto accompanied the video and has also gone viral. Combined with the fact that what we found in Colorado was related to the filmmaker, and all the other things that have happened both to me and my team. ...

(*But we won't think about those right now, no sir.*)

The world's buzzing in the news cycle of it all, and it's a story that won't seem to turn itself off or go away.

James, I think, wiping tears off my cheeks. *I'm sorry, so sorry. I'm sorry I'm not strong enough. Everything's gone upside down, and I don't know what to do to make it right anymore.*

It's too big, whatever it is. I don't know what to do. I can't see the whole picture or make it make sense. I just ...

The burble of my son's voice comes through the baby monitor I'd snatched off the nightstand on my way in here, cutting into and ending this mental litany. Christopher has woken up and is hungry.

I sigh and smile. Nothing's as unjust as a hungry baby, and this particular injustice was entirely within my power to resolve.

It would be nice to have one night go by where I don't dream the video, though. I wish I could resolve *that* problem.

I have to. *Otherwise* ... I shrug and stand up, heading toward my hungry son.

Otherwise, it's going to destroy me, plain and simple. The world will become that wolf that eats me.

What will you see, my blue-eyed son ... ?

I sing-think this in these wee hours as I watch my son draw his life from my nipples. The tug-tug-pull is as rhythmic and regular as the tide coming in or my heartbeat. It comforts me in the same way that mountains not falling or the sun continuing to rise comforts me. Rain is supposed to fall. The ground is supposed to lift your feet, not open beneath them. And hungry babies are supposed to eat.

"Not a problem for you, it seems," I murmur, watching him.

I count his fingers and toes in the glow from the lamp. Ten and ten, I am pleased to see. This has become my comfort food, verifying his normalcy. He came out the long, slow, hard way, and a month early, to boot. After everything that had happened during my pregnancy, I couldn't help being paranoid.

Let me see him! I remember shouting, out of my mind on a combination of pain, drugs, and fear. *I need to count his little fingers! I need to count his little toes!*

I cringe now, thinking about it. "Mama sounded like a psycho Dr. Seuss character, honey," I whisper to Christopher as he suckles.

"He doesn't seem to mind," Tommy murmurs from behind me.

"That's because he's got his priorities straight." I look up at Tommy and smile. "Why are you awake?"

He smiles back, but not before I catch the shadow that has just vanished from his face. "I heard you get up. I'm a light sleeper."

I nod as a reply, thinking: *If you say so, husband mine. ...*

"Is it weird that I'm a little bit jealous of this?" he asks, inclining his head toward our son.

"What?" I raise an eyebrow. "You want back on the boob, too?"

He half smiles, lifting the gauze patch over his eye with a cheek as he does. "Jealous of you, honey, not him."

"Oh. No." I shake my head once, emphatically. "That's not weird at all. You should be jealous."

There's nothing quite like nursing. I had forgotten. Much like pregnancy, it is both far more and far less than you expect it to be. I think most women have very romantic notions about both.

Really, though, there's nothing romantic at all about either. Pregnancy is a marathon of endurance, with multiple side effects, and a finish line of terror and pain. Post-pregnancy is mostly about fear. Will I do it right? Will I do it well? I look at my son. *Will you grow old after I die? Will you love and be loved, or will this hard world swallow you, slowly but whole?*

Nursing is the same, in its way. It's painful—your breasts ache from being over-swollen with milk, but your nipples are gummed and sucked till they're raw and burning. It's also incredibly exhausting. Newborns eat every one and a half to three hours, so there's never any respite.

Babies bite down much harder than anyone would think when they're startled, and it can be anything from a door slam to a dog bark to me shifting in my chair to get more comfortable that causes it. Nipples aren't made of iron, and even the newborn jaw has PSI to deliver, so there's plenty of pain to be had. It's hurt enough, from time to time, to bring tears to my eyes.

It doesn't help to feel so "unpretty" all the time. My boobs are huge, especially for my size, and they are an embarrassingly leaky ship. I didn't get fat per se during my pregnancy, but I sure didn't get skinny, either.

"You're pleasingly plump," Tommy had argued when I mentioned it to him.

"I look like a middle-aged woman who's still carrying around her baby fat from college!" I wailed, followed by some sexy postpartum sobbing and an even sexier runny nose.

Then, of course, son... I think, sighing. *There's all the other stuff that's happened, too.*

Your uncle James's mom getting murdered, and your uncle James's subsequent flip-out and disappearance, for one.

Men attacking our home while Mommy was away in Colorado. Almost blinding Daddy in one eye. Burning down our house.

Christopher's mouth works away like a machine built to make the future. *Mommy losing her marbles...*

I push this thought down as quickly as it rises. It is forbidden here now.

I will not pass my sorrow on to my son! I will the words to myself with a firmness and certainty that I honestly find surprising each and every time, all things considered. I have no ground beneath my feet anymore, but this one thing contains no doubt. My son is the ship towing me forward, even as I protect him from being sunk by the weights of a world he cannot yet face alone.

He's chosen the worst time to be born, the most inconvenient moment possible, but I know I'll never see it as other than the best moment he could have arrived. That inconvenience has been the rope that lashed me to the mast in the early parts of the storm. I have become responsible for him during a time I could barely be responsible for myself, and thank God for that.

I have sat in darkness and sunrise and twilight and watched his mouth working its hope. Surviving the experience at first, becoming bonded to it as the marathon continued, thinking: *This is how family becomes family.* Not simply because the memorable moments are shared, but because of the commitment to *all* the moments, the wondrous, the anguished, and the banal. Waking, eating, sleeping, loving, cleaning, kissing—these are not separate experiential islands. Attractive or not, they are connected life.

Many things may happen to my son, and most of it I won't share with him. But no one will ever have had this but me. This moment-by-moment, day-in day-out, long run of suffering and love to keep him alive when he was at his most vulnerable. The root of all parenting is in having seen life when it needed you most. It is a bell of commitment that can't be un-rung and a bell of beauty in depth of being that cannot be unfelt.

"Still going in the morning?" Tommy asks me.

Only the baby keeps me from snapping at him. "As I've already said—yes. I'm going." I try to stop there, but then that's the problem these days. "I'm sorry you have a crazy wife."

It's random and cruel—my current specialities. The fact that it bounces off him without leaving a mark only infuriates me further.

"Crazy or sane, you're all mine," he half smiles again, and as I watch the patch covering his injured eye move again, I'm flooded with remorse.

I grab his hand. "Sorry... really."

He frowns. "Sorry? For what? It's not as if I had to squeeze a nine-pound baby through my penis, or something." He squeezes my hand back, kisses my cheek, and ambles out of the room, looking like more than I deserve and like something I'll never give up. Rumpled hair, white T-shirt and boxers, and all.

Your father's a keeper, I tell my son with my mind.

His mouth moves and works, an endless piston sparked by life, no fossil fuels required. I watch it, riding the pain, creating the world that will outlive me.

I don't want to think these days. I don't want to think about how it's been a month since I've returned anyone's calls or about the fact that my house is now a concrete foundation buried under the debris of a burned-up life.

I don't want to think about how I've never helped look for James or about the time I lost in the bunker.

Definitely don't think about that...

I don't want to think about the thousand or so letters, cards, emails, flowers—what have you—that people have sent or tried to send me since the whole story went global. Or how I never (never) go outside now unless it's to throw all those unopened cards and flowers in the trash.

And I really, really don't want to think about my old boss. About how he betrayed me—betrayed all of us. And then killed himself.

I want only to watch my son, and feel his hope, and watch another sunrise without it bringing a day of pain or sorrow. Then I'll keep my word, because my son and my family are a clock that forces me to keep marking time. Their light is too bright to ignore with my weakness. I'll swallow my terror and go out in the world and see if it's possible to ever be whole again.

"He's so small, but he eats so much."

Bonnie is standing in the doorway watching me. She's mostly shadowed, barely lit by whatever moonlight has managed to sneak past the curtains. She is thirteen now, existing in that coltish space where she's so obviously not a woman but is also so obviously no longer a child.

The memory of her mother's voice comes to me without warning, and with such clarity, I almost start in my chair.

Burgeoning, Annie said, and grinned, looking at me in the bathroom mirror at school. She turned to view her profile, indicating her new breasts with a flourish. *That's the word mama used. She said I am a "burgeoning young woman."*

Burgeoning, indeed. The word had been invented for Annie as a teenager. She'd been the hot one, the girl who made eyes pop and heads swivel. She drew bad men because she was never beautiful enough to dispel her own doubts. She was the supermodel you could buy at the dollar store. Her lack of self-confidence was her weakness, and I never learned its source.

That's one thing Annie didn't give her daughter, at least. Bonnie's one of the strongest people I know, including the adults. She seems impervious to the concept of approval of others, at least in terms of needing it.

"He's an eating machine," I agree. "But so were we all, right? Eating and pooping in our pants? Over the mouth, past teeth and gums, look out diaper—here it comes."

She scrunches up her nose a little and smiles. "I guess, but ... gross."

"Can't argue with you, there. I thought about packing some of your brother's poop in a box and sending it to the military—you know, for use as a weapon. But I realized they'd probably have to classify it as a weapon of mass destruction."

She giggles, a sound that lifts my heart in the mostly dark. For a moment, Bonnie sounds her age. It's rare enough to cherish.

Bonnie is my daughter now. We've crossed that doubt long ago, and it's only a blessing in the end, once all the cards are laid faceup. Bonnie came to me a silent, injured child who'd suffered because her mother was my friend. In the beginning, I sometimes think, only the fact that she needed someone to take care of her kept me alive. I am built to need others to care for. It's the best and worst mix of my mother's strength and Catholic guilt, combined with my father's idealism. Most of the time it's a burden, but now and again, it will save my life.

Bonnie needed me when I didn't need to live, and ultimately, whether you walk fifty miles because you *want* to or because you *had* to, you find yourself in a different place than before. I ended up in the land of being glad I was alive. And while it's true that seeing Annie's ghost in Bonnie's face can be a knife in my heart for a minute or two, those minutes always pass and give way to a better truth: She is her mother's heartbeat, living on in defiance of the world that ran her down. Every time I look at Bonnie, I have a concrete reason to doubt despair.

She walks into the room and stands next to my chair, looking down at her baby brother. "Are you worried about him?" she asks. "I mean, do you think you'll be afraid for him when you leave the house tomorrow?"

I don't lie to Bonnie about these matters, if I can help it. She's survived too much to be condescended to. I try to protect her as best I can, but I always have to remember that she's been aged at the roots before her time. "Yes. A little bit. I guess in the morning I'll feel worse."

She nods, thinking, still watching Christopher. "I understand. After Mom died, and I couldn't speak—do you know why?"

"I could only guess, honey."

"It was two things, really." She brushes her (*her mother's*) blond hair behind an ear with one hand. "One was that I wasn't alone. Something was in there, in that silence with me. I can't really give it a name or shape. It was something shaped *wrong*, though... because it was built from the memory of what he did to her in front of me and what happened after. Parts of it were made from how she screamed while I watched, and then there was the biggest part." Her eyes close, hold, then open, the only hint that what she's saying is also something that she's feeling. "The biggest part, which was about that long, quiet time I was tied to Mom's body. How she looked. How she stiffened up against me." She puts a hand on my shoulder, and I feel the barest tremor. "How she started to smell. And her eyes. Every time I opened mine, her eyes were there, looking back at me. Then they started to change. They got dead, too. That's when I really knew she was gone."

I reach out and take her hand in mine, squeezing it gently. "Oh, honey... I'm so sorry. That's not saying much, but... " I sigh and shrug a little.

"I know, Mama-Smoky." She squeezes my hand back. "But when I was quiet, you see, I wasn't seeing it all because I *couldn't*. I could see pieces of it but not the whole. Even though, really, I had seen everything, smelled everything, felt everything—I couldn't *remember* it that way—at least, not in the beginning—because I knew if I did, I'd go bonkers. It took everything I had just to keep from going crazy forever, you know?"

"I know."

She pulls her hand away. "The other one—the other reason—was because I knew once I started to speak, it would all be true. And I just didn't want to care again about a world where I could see *all* the monster and have him not be something magic, or some devil, or anything like that. I would have to see he was just some crazy guy who had a crazy dad, who liked hurting women a lot. I'd have to see that my mom died for no reason at all. She died because he liked hurting people and sometimes you have bad luck in life. Why would anyone want to be absolutely certain of any of those things?"

Her hand is back on my shoulder and my son is still feeding, but I am speechless and mesmerized.

"I know it was too much for you, Mama-Smoky," she says, her voice soft. "You know I do understand that kind of thing. Maybe more than most people. I know it's not like they say on television. People can't just watch bad things happen all the time, and have bad things happen to them all the time, and be afraid all the time—without something breaking down eventually. Nobody is a superhero, Mama-Smoky.

"I know that fighting inside yourself is all you can do right now. But at some point you'll have to decide if you want to start talking again. Sort of." She frowns. "It's a—something we learned in English class. ... "

"A metaphor," I manage to say, faintly.

"*Yes,*" she says, nodding. "A metaphor. You'll have to decide if you want to start talking again. If you don't, that's okay. Whatever you want to do, I'll take care of you and Christopher, even if it's for the rest of my life. If you're too broken to be strong anymore, I'll still love you, Mama-Smoky."

A beat of silence passes that I don't fill. My throat's a little too full of my heart, and my heart is suddenly too bloated with love and pain to swallow.

"I hope you decide to keep going. Maybe it will have to be different than before, but we're still here and we love you." She leans forward and kisses my cheek. I am flash-frozen, terrified by the strength of my love and by her simple, perfect tenderness. I'm afraid that if I move or even breathe, it will be like trying to hold a soap bubble in my hand. "But whatever happens, I'll never be angry or mad and I'll always be with you and help you." She whispers in my ear, "You made it so I could talk again, Mama-Smoky. If you need me to talk for you, I'll always be ready. I love you so much."

She turns and leaves the room without saying another word. I remain there, rooted and still as an ice-covered statue in winter. Feeling the pull toward the cliff that she's offered me because really, this is what has struck terror into me. It is not guilt at her words but fear at my overwhelming desire to give up and let her care for me. I want to cease being strong and start being safe. I want to be selfish and weak for the rest of my days, and I don't want to see monstrous people or hear about monstrous things anymore. I don't want to be responsible.

This, more than anything, is a guarantee that I will leave the house in the morning. I feel my own mother's stubbornness rising in me, half or more of her ghost spreading through me, cell by cell, via her DNA. It is the simple idea of being told I can't finish the race that rankles me enough to run it.

Bonnie knows this, of course. I don't doubt her sincerity, but I can see her hoping that it might also be a challenge. She's a layered thinker and has the requisite arrogance to allow herself such manipulations.

Christopher's mouth stops moving and pulls away. *Still, you and I both know she meant it. And that means we love her ten times more than before and twice as forever.*

I sigh.

"Which means we're screwed, little dude—or at least I am," I whisper to him. "I have to find a way to start talking again."

It feels right. True, there is still that lacking that I've become familiar with. It's the feeling that things are set pieces. Two-dimensional expressions inside myself of the reality around me. Ideas, emotions, people—I know intellectually what I should feel, but I can't seem to muster up the third dimension that gives them life, that makes them bleed and makes me bleed in their mattering.

But for a moment, I had felt the shape breathe. When Bonnie offered her life to me, without thinking, without hesitation—I sensed a breath before the return to stillness, like seeing movement out of the corner of your eye in a morgue.

I rock my son and look for solutions to my fears. Soon I will have to leave the house we've rented under another name. I'll have to walk out the door and into the great ... wide ... *open*. It's late November. The moon is a frozen stone in a stark and starless sky.

Worry's waking up. Worry eats breakfast and becomes anxiety. Anxiety drinks her lunch and after that she's serving up panic for dinnertime, followed by terror all night long.

I stare at that rock of a moon, and I pray to it with a blind, religious madness that I never even knew I had a talent for. I show it all the places that I'm broken, where before I always used to hide my scars. I imagine myself talking to the first woman. Not Eve, nothing biblical, but literally the first woman, period.

I see her as something bestial but sensate. She is as real as an axe through screaming meat but able to conceive of heart love by a hot fire. The first woman to be aware that she was not an animal per se but with no mother or father who could say the same. She formed the first female thoughts, interacted with the world, and made the first female decisions. She is not godlike in the least to me. She's a hundred percent human being, which is why I can trust her image.

I don't see her as real, of course. At least, mostly not. She doesn't literally talk to me; I don't hear her voice in my head. She is a construct, a kind of mental bootstrap. A way to hold onto myself as the rock in the flood.

I have never been as lost as I am right now. Tell me how to do it. How do I get up in the morning and walk toward that door? How do I open my hand and grip the knob and turn it?

My son makes a noise. I'm overwhelmed with longing when I look at his face, already diving deep into slumber.

What's happened to my strength?

I imagine her answer outside myself (though most of me knows it's all a mental trick, a way to find the answers my own mind's doubling away from), and it belongs to a ruthless voice. To the pitiless speaker of the truth:

You can choose to be a mother who is strong enough or a mother who is not. That is all. Survive or die. If you choose to die, the world will swallow you up without looking back, and you will be as worthless as a stone in the dirt because you will have failed to be enough for your son.

Then she turns from me and walks away. Her contempt is clear.

I rock my son and moon-pray and hope for sanity, all the while trying to remember a time I was able to find a doorway through the barrier of my fears.

CHAPTER TEN

I stand in front of the office building, staring up at it with trepidation. I feel displaced and uncomfortable, and that all by itself is unsettling. It's been only six weeks. It feels like six hundred years.

Get out of the open. The inner words come to me as a command.

"Hey," Kirby says, speaking to me in a soft voice as she stands next to me, "don't worry. No one is going to get you without going through me first." Her eyes study me, then scan the streets and sidewalks around us, surveying every face in a cold blink that does, in fact, reassure me.

"I hate leaving Christopher," I murmur. "This is the first time I have since he was born."

"I know. But no one is going to find that house, and the three guys I have on patrol there are the best." She grins. "Besides yours truly, of course."

I grin back. Kirby's grins have always been infectious, and I'm glad of it at this moment. "Of course."

"Are you packing?" she asks me, a hint of curiosity in her voice.

I flush, feeling a shame I cannot define spike through me. "No."

The grin again, a million moments of reassurance in a second. "No worries. I am. Times three." Faux puzzlement fills her eyes. "Or is it four? I guess if you count the knives, it's five."

I smile back again but more shyly this time. "Wouldn't expect any less."

Her eyes scan the environs again, then come back to me. She seems hesitant, something I expect is a foreign emotion for Kirby. "You really gave in to his one demand, huh?"

I sigh and shake my head. "It's the only way he'd agree to the rest." I shrug. "I needed him for the rest, and he wouldn't budge unless I agreed to the first part, you know—first."

"Prick," she replies, flashing the easy grin again. "Though, as pricks like him go..." that flash of hesitation again, followed by a mirror of my own shrug, "he could be worse, you know. Talking to him might not be the worst idea you've ever been forced to swallow down at gunpoint. Maybe it'll be like gulping down cum for the first time; you know, like 'ooo, ick, why does it feel like snot?'—but then in the next moment, you realize it's really not that bad, right?"

I have seen Kirby in a rare state and been trusted with it by her: total helplessness. My team and I rescued her from a very bad individual who'd been torturing her. I found her and took her to a bathtub, where I cleaned her up myself.

Just before I did, she'd whispered one of her life's biggest secrets in my ear. The revelation of something so personal, I had understood at the time, was her way of thanking me by giving me what she treasured most: a part of her most private, inner self.

It's a trait we share, in our way. It's the reason she's followed me here, and why she's the only person who knows everything that's about to happen. I told only Tommy about the first part—the agreement I was forced into by my own request. I knew it would comfort him. Kirby knows about the rest because she was the one to carry my written request to the person I'm about to see. She'd been subjected to his questioning and to the eyes that went with them.

"Gross metaphor, but...yeah. He's one of the rare good ones," I answer, my voice quiet.

"He knows the score," she murmurs. "The real score, not the silly song everybody else dances to."

I nod. "I know," I say. I glance at her and realize that she is waiting for my reassurance or maybe my promise. I force my gaze to steady on hers and force a certainty into my tone that I don't really feel. "I knew what his demand would be. I think it's part of why I thought of him. So don't worry, I'll talk to him. I won't waste his time, I promise."

Kirby studies me, and we are connected, for a flash of a second, in the same way we had been in that bathtub. Then she blinks and grins, and the moment is gone. "I'm not saying you shouldn't make him fight for it a little, or anything. Never give for free what you can get paid for, that's my motto. Except when it comes to sex, of course."

I grin back, infected again. "Of course."

"You ready?"

I tremble inside a little but manage one last diffident shrug. "As I can be."

"'K. So I scoped it out already. I know you've been here before, but it's been a while, so I figured you'd want a refresher. The glass doors lead into a reception area, which has a desk in the center. The elevators we want to get to are around and behind the desk. We go straight in, walk to the right, and then head to the elevators. We'll be taking the one closest to the wall, even if we have to wait for it, and you'll be next to the wall. I'll stand next to you and between you and everybody else." She pauses. "If you get panicky, just follow those steps, do those actions. Don't worry about how you look or anything else. Screw the strangers and all their damn opinions.

"If you need to get out, all you have to do is tell me. I won't ask a single question or make you feel guilty or anything. You say the word, and we are gone in a heartbeat. Got it?"

"Yep."

"Then let's get this truck moving, for gosh sake! Time's a-wastin'!" she exclaims, with a wink and a last glance around.

No time like the present, I tell myself, mixed up by my own fear of the moment and by my gratitude at the way Kirby's handling me.

I take a single deep breath, then hurry through the automatic glass doors, letting the bleak November sun pine for summer on its own. The air inside is comfortably warm, but little knobs of gooseflesh have popped up on my arms, and they won't go away. This is my first time back out in "the world," doing something that involves decisive action. My various responses to this have overwhelmed me. I can't get ahead of my rising panic or get rid of the itch between my shoulder blades that tells me a target's been painted there.

I hurry into the reception area, aware of Kirby just a little behind and to the left of me, aware that my skin's gone clammy. I can feel thin lines of sweat making their way down from my armpits, bisecting each side of me as they lope toward my waist. My hairline's gone damp.

Anxiety disorders can bring about agoraphobia, I quote to myself from some Internet entry on the subject I read, one bleary-eyed and sleepless night. It's avoidance. Anything to avoid the possibility that something will re-trigger the panic. Panic, it seems, is a kind of wholly involving agony. It crackles every neuron, sets the nervous system on fire, and sends the endocrine system into overdrive. Panic—true panic—overwhelms any sense of time, freezing you in place in a moment of abject helplessness and terror.

I've found myself behind a locked bathroom door in the wee hours, crouched in the shower, shaking to the bones while my teeth chattered and rattled in my head. I've sweated so much, shivering and biting my knuckles to hide my terrified moans, that the T-shirt I was wearing grew stiff with salt. These moments are huge enough, involving enough, to become their own source of terror. I will do almost anything to avoid the experience, and I can never be certain of what will bring it on.

Will it happen here? I wonder. Fear gnaws on my equilibrium, while shame carves out chunks of my pride. *God, I don't think I could survive that. Not even with Kirby.*

The urge to turn on my heel and run rises in me so urgently I almost accept my inability to resist it. Almost. But then I stub my mental toe against a crack in the concrete of this imperviousness, and I know in that moment that I could keep myself from leaving if I wanted to. It will feel like I'm on fire and burning alive, but it's within my power. This crack was made by the action of coming here. Self-confidence is built, or rebuilt, in layers that are held together by the mortar of demonstrated ability. If you can walk, you can accept that you might run.

If you leave now, you'll never come back. My mind whispers this to me in the voice of truth. And I believe. I am certain of this truth because I know what certainty is these days.

That's the biggest problem with losing your mind: the lack of certainty. What should I be thinking? What is the right way to feel that will prevent all the wrong ways in the future? The very fact of worrying about questions that are as automatic as breathing for most people is stressful and depressing.

Certainty is rare. So when it arrives, you tend to know it. The shape of insanity is a shape full of significance but lacking in time and sound. Things become brighter and louder to the mind, but they send off muffled echoes that leave you frowning and full of questions. It is the shape of a hammer banging against a wall of cotton, sending forth sparks of white, cold, smokeless fire. The vision blinds, but the ears are left hungry, and so there is no balance.

If I leave now, I will never come back from this brink. I will lose track of the crack in the concrete, no matter how much I search for it. I'll live at home forever and force my family to deal with that and bend their lives around it.

I see all of this clearly, an unalterable future truth stretched before me as plainly as an open road. I push my feet into the ground. I imagine them as anchors, as tree roots, as too heavy to be lifted on my own.

"You're doing fine," Kirby murmurs, a guiding hand touching my elbow briefly. "Keep to the right now, and then back to the elevators."

There are a handful of people in the lobby, moving in one direction or the other toward their own destinies. The floor is made of older, slightly beaten marble that I remember from a past that seems a lifetime ago.

"Got it," I reply, swallowing with a dry mouth. I take the next step, and yes, I am still moving. Away from the possible future I'd just glimpsed, toward one that I cannot. I can see the elevator lobby beckoning, and note with almost unhinging relief that no one else is waiting there.

We pass by the receptionist, who glances at us as we pass. Her eyes are clear blue and she has hair so blond it's almost white. They belong to a sun-scrubbed pixie face, which sits atop a compact beach-lover's body.

California, I think absently, *thy names are Young and Blond and Woman.*

She gives me an automatic smile before returning to her own concerns, showing off teeth too perfect and white for envy. They're a sign of youth; she's young; she earned them.

"There you go," Kirby says, using that same murmur, giving me another guiding touch of reassurance. "Past little miss beautiful and straight to the elevators."

I have stopped sweating, and this seems like a victory. I can feel it drying on my skin and wonder, for no reason, if the salt will leave marks on my blouse. "*Little miss beautiful?*" I murmur back. "Sounds jealous."

Kirby snorts out a sneer. "Please," she says, her voice haughty and cold as a queen's. "Not even when her best day is matched up with my worst."

We reach the elevators, and then I am against the wall, with Kirby standing guard between me and the world.

Safe.

We take the elevator to the eleventh floor, riding in silence with strangers. The Muzak is progressive, as far as Muzak goes. It doesn't conjure up images of lounge singers or white man's overbite. We get off without company and head left, then turn right. The door is at the end of a short hallway, the only one in it.

Ready for this?

It's a stupid question. *Ready for terror? Ready for fear?*

Yeah, right.

There's no nameplate affixed to the faux wood paneling of the door, and when I turn the knob, I find it's locked. I feel my skin going clammy again, and suddenly, I want nothing more than to be inside. Behind the lock.

Safe. Secure.

Then I actually think:

They're coming!

Whoever "they" are.

I feel Kirby's touch on my elbow. It calls me back to reality, like a switch being flipped. "We're good, boss-lady," she murmurs, her tone cheerful. "No bad actors anywhere. You might want to try knocking. Either that, or I can karate-kick that door down for you."

"I'm not sure he'd appreciate that," I say, smiling. "Let's try a knock, first."

"Sounds good to me, but really, I'm fine either way."

I knock twice and soon hear the shuffling sounds of shoe leather on thick carpet.

"Coming, coming," the voice says, patient and amiable.

Hurry, hurry, I think pleadingly. Feeling the sweat begin to bead and roll again as my body cries its tears of panic, which has returned; the switch flipped without warning.

I hear the lock click, and the door opens. Dr. Childs smiles when he sees me, a wide, warm, genuine smile. "Smoky!" he exclaims. "It's been too long. Please come in. Hello, Kirby," he says, acknowledging her with a similar smile.

"What's up, doc?" she jokes, grinning.

I push past him and enter, not caring that it probably makes me look hurried to them both, that it makes me look, well—crazy. Kirby follows me in. I watch as she closes the door behind us and engages the dead bolt.

God, I'm nervous.

"Rest assured," Dr. Childs murmurs in a kind, quiet voice, "this is a very safe, very private place. It's swept for bugs, cameras, and other surveillance devices weekly. It is not rented under my name, but the name of a trust."

"I know," Kirby replies. She raises an eyebrow. "What? You thought you were dealing with an amateur?"

Dr. Childs bows his head once. "Never, my dear. If nothing else, I am reassured."

"That's one of us," I mutter. My eyes rove everywhere, looking for dangerous, hidden things.

Dr. Childs studies me for a moment. Smiles again. "You're nervous."

I don't answer.

"That's normal," he reassures me.

"I know ... "

"But?"

I sigh, looking at him—really seeing him and not my fear—for the first time. "It's not a normal kind of nervous." I bark out a laugh with razor edges on both sides. "What's up, doc? I'm fucked up, that's what. In fact, I think I've lost my marbles."

Any future words are sucked out of me with the sudden, soundless finality of someone absentmindedly opening a window on the moon. The instantaneous totality of this silence makes it profound. It's the first time I've said it out loud to another person: *I think I've gone crazy.* It feels wrong to speak it, like all the dread of approaching doom the world can muster hangs in a sword above my head.

Kirby seems to have faded into the background, standing silent as golem by the door.

Dr. Childs doesn't ask me to clarify this statement. His eyes don't fill with pity or worry. "I see," he says, his voice gentle but confident. Strong. "Well, why don't we see if we can do something about that?"

It's hard to remain terrified in the face of such certainty and aplomb. *I've seen it a million times*, the tone of his voice says. *Yours is yours, and it is unique, but even so—I've seen enough of the same not to be intimidated.*

I realize that this is what the surviving family of the victims I deal with feel when I do my job right. Their mother/daughter/wife has been raped, skinned alive, murdered. The world should split apart from speaking such words out loud. From making them true.

The world doesn't, and this is the state I find them in: the aftermath of the world continuing to turn in the face of something that should have ended it. No one is born knowing how to handle victims of these particular shapes of monstrosity. It's not knowledge that's intuitive—you have to seek it out. I suppose that dealing with insanity is very similar.

"Thanks," I mumble in a soft voice, staring at the floor.

"Think nothing of it." He smiles, underlining the statement. "Now let me give you the quick tour again. Not much has changed, I know, but it's been quite a while since you were last here. As agreed, you have given me two hours of time involving just the two of us, after which our guest will arrive, and we will discuss the other business you asked for my assistance with."

I follow him, only half hearing. I'm too busy enjoying the sound of my heart beating at a regular pace, as opposed to jackhammering away like a metronome on meth. Stress is stressful. Its absence after a long constancy is like a cool breeze in hell.

"I'll wait out here," Kirby chirps. "Don't worry about me. I could do two hours standing on my head."

I don't really need a tour, and Dr. Childs knows this. He's giving me time to arrive, to inspect and verify my safeness without bringing the subject up. This oblique handling of obvious pain has always been one of Dr. Childs's gifts. He'll chase you till you give up when it comes to a direct confrontation of key issues, but in most other ways he'll do his best to give you your dignity.

I watch him as he walks, and wonder, in my current state of mental disrepair: *How does he do it? He's seen at least as much as me. How does he stay sane?*

Dr. Kenneth Childs is a forensic psychiatrist. He's in his early sixties and has spent the majority of his life doing his own version of what I do: peering into the darkest darknesses. Searching them out and looking closely.

True, it's taken a visible toll. He looks older than his years. He's been white-haired, including his moustache and beard, for as long as I've known him. But he's still got all his marbles. He's not running through the open spaces like a frightened deer or sweating at the drop of a hat even when the air is cool.

Equilibrium. *That's the word I'm looking for. He still has his equilibrium. I don't.*

Why?

There are crimes that can be understood by any human being. Theft, murder—even if we are not built to commit these crimes ourselves, empathy isn't impossible. We don't need to commit the crime to understand what it meant for the criminal. Then there are those crimes that defy empathy. You can approach understanding but never fully reach it unless you are that criminal. Child rape. Murder for sexual pleasure. Necrophilia.

Instead, we approximate, always aware that approximation is as close as we'll ever get. But even approximating a howling darkness hurts your ears. I've watched other profilers grow thinner, harder, and become incurably closed off over time. Divorce rate is very high. Suicide occurs, something we never speak of but are aware of as a possibility. You can't think it would never be you once someone you've respected and admired kills himself.

Dr. Childs, though, has never shown any cracks, not really. I've seen him get angry and sad, but I've never watched him crumble. His calm, quiet affability has always seemed invulnerable.

I've known him for most of my time in the Bureau, and I think he was the first to recognize my potential. He'd let me visit when I had questions as a rookie, and the relationship has endured. Not only because I trust his professional insights even more than James's or my own, but because he's always been there to listen as another human being. Life's taught me that real friends are an anomaly, not the norm.

It is a combination of these reasons that led me to approach him with my request for assistance and then got me to agree to his one condition: two hours of talk-therapy time with him, alone. I trust therapy about as much as I trust God, which is not saying much at all. I acknowledge the possibility of the usefulness of his existence, but have not seen enough proof to be counted among the truly faithful.

"Is it as you remember?" Dr. Childs asks.

"Hmm?" I blink, feeling more like I woke from a sleep dream than a daydream. Par for the course, in these dazed days. "Oh—yes—actually ... " I look around, then smile. "Almost nothing's changed."

He chuckles. "Patients, few and far between the living ones might be, tend to appreciate that. Continuity comforts in a chaotic world."

It's a large space. Dr. Childs once told me it was a little over fifteen hundred square feet. It had originally been a back-office space, possibly a small clinic of some kind. It had since been broken down into four offices and a large, open, empty space that I assume was once a waiting room.

The carpeting is thick and comfortable enough to walk on barefoot. The lighting is bright without being glaring, and all the lights can be dimmed or brightened at will. The furniture is minimalist, with light, bright wood and cushions just comfortable enough to be inviting without putting you to sleep.

We've ended up in the hindmost office, which is the largest. The back is all window, looking out on the grungy greater glory of the San Fernando Valley.

The room is a marvel of design. There are no real walls—there's not even that much furniture—and yet one never gets the feeling of being exposed. Dr. Childs has been very clever in his placement of accessories, furniture, and other decorations, including bookcases. The result is a feeling of sitting inside a courtyard, protected, viewing everything without everything viewing you, kind of like sitting in a one-way fishbowl.

"We can sit over here to the left," Dr. Childs indicates. "It's by the windows. I find, sometimes, it helps to talk if you have something permanent and larger than you to focus on."

"I'd like that," I murmur, pushing hair away from my eyes. Still nervous. Nervous, nervous, nervous.

He's right, of course. Sometimes, what you are looking at inside your head seems so much bigger than you or anyone else, for that matter. Like a mountain-size darkness you're expected to balance on the edge of your soul.

I'm glad to sit down, besides, and I ease my feet out of my sandals, stifling a groan of pleasure at the feel of the carpet against my soles. Pregnancy had been hell on my calves and feet.

"No couch?" I joke. "Isn't that like a requirement for you guys?"

"Yes, yes, I've never heard that one before," Dr. Childs says. But there's good humor in his voice.

There is solidarity even in our stereotypes, I think. When things are the way they are supposed to be, it comforts us.

"I did once smoke a pipe," he admits with a rueful smile. "But it wasn't just an affectation. I picked it up honestly from my father. It's my strongest memory of him—the faint, sweet smell of pipe tobacco that followed him everywhere. It's what lingers for me."

"Why did you quit?"

"I quit the day I learned that my father had been a child molester."

I gape openly. I can't help it. I can't last recall—and it might have been never—a time when Dr. Childs shared something truly personal about himself. "Holy crap ... wow ... Uh—when did that happen?"

Smooth as always.

Dr. Childs looks off, taking comfort from the city, but only for a moment. He turns his gaze on me again, studying me. There is a deep and permanent sadness wrapped around his gaze, along with great patches of star-filled darkness-peering, but there is little in the way of regret. I wonder again: *How does he do that?*

"My father was a gifted research therapist. He specialized in the study of childhood development, which obviously gave him access to children. Much of his work was with orphans or the children of criminals. Supposedly along the lines of his studies, but really it was about their vulnerability." He shrugs. "It wasn't a dramatic story, Smoky, or even a unique one. It was a normal story. The type you and I hear about all the time. He got greedy and touched a few too many. He grew comfortable and calm, and believed, like so many of his kind, in the press releases of greatness his grandiosity demanded from his ego."

"Someone talked."

"Someone talked," he agrees. "And that was that. He was finished." He shakes his head. It's a sad, curious gesture. "Strange, when I really think about it, it's not so much the molestation that woke me up. He never touched me; he was smart enough to see that my mother was not a weak-minded woman. That's probably what saved me," he confides, glancing at me. "No, it was the fact that he broke so quickly. He was so weak, they didn't really have to pressure him at all. And when he broke ... " Another shake of his head. "He shattered. He turned into a simpering puddle of calculating fear."

"You saw this?"

"In a manner of speaking, yes. They came to his home to arrest him, and I happened to be visiting. When they told him why they were there, he turned to me and my mother and began to sob. He told us that he was sorry. I believe he was, in that way that craven men can be sorry. Do you believe that?"

Even though I recognize what he's doing, I can't help but be ensnared by my own interest. Dr. Childs knows this, I'm sure. The beginning of all therapy is manipulation, he'd once told me. He's sharing with me because he knows this is the only way to ease me into sharing with him. Dr. Childs knows my deepest fears, and his insight is intimidating. I'm sure he's seen things in me that I have no idea he's seen.

Now he's asking me a safe question, one that is not personal to me but steers the conversation in the direction of human behavior. The fact that he's asked this question in relation to personal revelations about his father creates reciprocity. I really have no choice but to answer.

I understand what he's doing because I do it myself all the time. Good interrogation is an illusion of negotiation and compromise. In reality, it is an application of force toward getting the truth. Though the force applied is psychological, not physical, it is no less persuasive, and probably more so. Even the arrangement of the room is a direct parallel to interrogation techniques. It comes down to the fact that once you control the environment, you control perspective. When you control perspective, you control reality.

"You are asking me if I think that child molesters can bond in a fundamental way with other people?"

"I suppose I'm asking if you think it's possible for it to be genuine. Or is it always a strategy driven by selfishness?"

It's one of those questions that seemed wrong when you were staring at the results of a psychopath's work. Perhaps even blasphemous if you were looking at the body of a child. It's a useless question, asked to fill an unbearable silence, and we ask it all the time, silently or otherwise.

"There is a school of thought that believes psychopathy exists on a continuum," I offer.

"And you agree with it?"

I consider it. "The things I've seen... I'm dubious. I don't believe they are capable of feeling truly selfless remorse. I think it's more self-serving. But I can't deny that I've encountered one or two who really did seem to love his mother or his mate." I frown and shake my head. "But even then... I think it's more about loving the quality in them that particular psychopath prizes. I just haven't seen truly selfless remorse from a man who gets off on murder. I tend to side with the instinct that says it's probably not much different for pedophiles. I don't believe it is driven by any form of love. I think they get off on it as rape, and because it's rape."

"Your tone tells me you have strong opinions regarding pedophiles. Any specific reason why?"

"I was never molested or anything." I shrug. "I've seen the material. Extensively. It was one of the worst moments of my life. I still think about it sometimes."

He nods slowly. I search for condescension in the gesture but can find only concern. "And are there other things from your work or life experience that you tend to think about often? Anything you feel you consider too much?"

And there it is, I think. *The opening salvo*. I have time to be aware that I'm viewing therapy as an adversarial activity, but there's probably not enough time in the world to solve that particular problem. It's innate. It goes hand in hand with my lack of trust in general. "Are you asking me if I have post-traumatic stress disorder, doctor?" I smile.

"Please don't do that." He's frowning and shaking a finger at me. "Please don't try and think ahead of me. If for no other reason than it's unhelpful to you. I give you my absolute and ironclad word, on my honor—which is a meaningful phrase for me—that anything you say is safe in this place. And I will hold to that trust no matter what. I'll hold it under torture, theoretically." He smiles a lopsided smile. "Of course I can't guarantee how long that would last. All that I ask in return is that you not look for the subtext in my questions. I can promise you, most of the time no subtext exists. The earliest lesson I learned about dealing with the minds of others was this: You don't know. The moment you become the kind of therapist who thinks he does, it's time to find a new profession."

"Is that why you tend to work for the dead rather than on the living?" I venture.

He raises his eyebrows, amused. Dr. Childs is apparently used to the parrying that goes with interviewing law enforcement. It makes me wonder if in fact he's had more living patients than I imagine. "How about an exchange?" he offers. "We'll spend the next hour or so talking about you. So long as you do this, I will answer your question once we're done. How's that seem?"

"Like something I'd tell a criminal if I was interrogating him," I say. I raise a hand in surrender. "But it would be a fair technique, and I wouldn't be lying, so—sure. Why not?"

The best police—Alan likes to call them the *real* police, the ones that have it running through their veins—fear the interrogation room as much as the next person. They know that no one is immune, not if they are human.

I am no exception. It doesn't matter that I recognize his methods; I am still subject to the rules that built them. I know he's given me an illusion of choice, but it feels and tastes and smells just like real choice, and ultimately, that's all that matters to the mind.

Bargaining, when it comes to information, is almost always a false conundrum, something put in place as a way to save face. False dignity, too, tastes as real in the right light. Soon, I know, I won't even be breaking it down anymore. There will be no more play-by-play examinations of his methods. Because Dr. Childs has the deadly trio: He knows his subject inside and out, he has an innate understanding of rapport, and he controls the milieu completely.

Stockholm syndrome, here we come. Except I think they call it transference, in therapy.

"So, my question: Do other things, memories, come back to you often? And if so, what happens when they do?"

I am quiet for a time, considering this. "To be honest, if you'd asked me that two months ago, I would have answered no. I would've been certain I was telling the truth."

"And now?"

I stare out the window, drawing strength from the city. "Now I think I've been fooling myself for a very long time."

"In what way?" he prods.

I am irritated that he has to ask. Mortified that he has to ask. I know everything I want to say. Why is he having to drag it out of me?

"A ... a great, black ... *horror* sits inside my gut, blocking all my forward progress. It keeps me stuck in the moment, in the right here and now, but not in a healthy way. In a way that makes me feel ... crazy." I blurt all this out before I really know what I'm doing.

Dr. Childs is silent for a moment, but only for a moment. "Explain," he says, with that same, broad, constant equanimity. He is silent and ignorant of all the clocks, an open door waiting for me to pass through. Every single line of him says that he's as comfortable as a mountain, and that he can take all my rain.

I will myself to speak again, to answer, but my tongue has turned to stone inside my mouth.

"What is it, Smoky? Don't worry about answering the question for now. Tell me instead what's happening to you at this moment."

My voice restarts itself, all on its own, and the words come spilling out of me. "I feel ashamed. I feel stupid. I feel ... I feel like I have been pitying others for having the same problems I do."

"Go on."

November in California is when the cold—such as it is—has settled in for our version of winter. It's now mid-December, and the world has gone still and cold. The palm trees live on. I watch the gray sky and think I'd almost prefer snow to being teased by a sun that never gives warmth. There's a certain cruelty to taking away the warmth without giving anything in return. "I've said I'm fine a thousand times and believed it. I never thought I was lying."

"But now, you do?"

I rub my arms against the sudden chill that runs through me. "Now ... I feel like I've been lying to myself all along. Like, at some level, I've always known this was just building up and waiting to explode."

He smiles gently. "Have you considered the possibility that, indeed, you have always known?"

"I don't understand."

"Think about what it is you do. Why you're good at it." He peers at me, ensuring I am hearing him. "Don't you think it would make sense?"

"Maybe," I answer, still doubtful.

"Let me put it another way." He steeples his fingers, collecting his thoughts. For someone else it would be an affectation. "Let's say you met a stranger. A woman. And that woman tells you about her life.

"You find that, before she'd even reached her teens, she watched her mother die of cancer, slowly and painfully. Her father died before she was twenty-one. She overcame these losses admirably. She married a good man and had a child. She found a profession she believed in."

He pauses, looking off at a memory. I'm still, my throat dry as dust. Transfixed.

"As a result of her profession, she became known to a very, very bad man. This man broke into her home. He tortured and raped the woman, tortured and murdered her husband while she watched, and murdered her firstborn, her only child.

"In the years that followed, many good things happened. She healed, more or less. She met another good man. But other terrible things happened, too. She's become known to more bad men—she's famous, even, it would be fair to say. And they have disfigured her further. She spent time in captivity. Her best friend was murdered due to one of these bad men, and this friend's daughter—newly orphaned—has been put into her safekeeping." He waves a hand, finished. "I think I've listed enough misery to make my point." He leans forward, and I marvel at the depth of warmth I can see in his eyes. "Let me ask you a question, Smoky Barrett. Imagine you met such a woman. Now imagine that she is fully recovered from all these events." He snaps his fingers, startling me a little. "Completely functional. If you met such a woman, doing what you do, knowing what you know—with your experience with victims: How do you think you would see her?"

My mouth clicks when I open it, my lips peeling away from each other. My tongue feels slimy, moving between my teeth. "I ... " I clear my throat. "I guess I'd think she was Superwoman or something."

He laughs. It's an A-plus laugh; he approves of my answer. "Yes! Therein lies the problem. Because you see, my dear," he says, more somber now, "there are no superwomen. There are only women. You'll never meet the woman I posited, because she can't exist—and be human." He smiles. "There's only you, and you are human, after all. The mistake is thinking it's otherwise. That you are the exception to the rule. The reasons that drive it are admirable, without doubt, but—admirable or not—they aren't factual. You have limits." He points a finger at me, and all I can sense, in all the forcefulness surrounding this gesture, is his gentle hope that I hear him. "You have limits. You don't believe you are allowed to. You think it is shameful to need them. All the same faulty, lovely logic that's driven soldiers and law enforcement personnel and parents who care, since humans started trying to live up to an ideal outside themselves. It's lovely, but only until it begins to kill you."

The logic is obvious, unassailable. My heart resists. "It flies in the face of a self-image I've always believed in. A self-image I need."

"Oh, balderdash," he scorns gently. "You mean it's the best one you could build under the circumstances. But it's an impossible ideal. I invite you to consider: How could trying to be something no human is capable of ever being be healthy, in the end?"

"It's kept me alive," I mumble.

He shakes his head once. Emphatic. "No. It's kept you upright."

The statement stops me cold. It's such a small difference in quality. But I feel the shape of this truth; it feels correct, even if I don't know all the reasons why.

"You're an incredibly strong, highly internalized woman who's learned to rely on her own strength and judgment. The number of mental tricks a person has to go through simply to survive life's pyrhhic journey is immense." He spreads his hands apart and smiles. "It's hardly a mystery why you developed the solutions you have. And the truth is, they have their place."

"But?"

Dr. Childs nods. "But not as a mechanism you are unaware of. Not as a motor you can't turn off if you need to."

"Why now?" I can hear my own fear and frustration. "Doctor—life's *better*. Not just in my mind—it's *better*. I have five times as many fundamental things to be happy about now, as opposed to five years ago. I get what you're saying, but why *now*? It's not logical."

He shrugs, but it's more Socratic than dismissive. "Oh, it could be many things. My guess would be: Some straw broke the camel's back. Simple as that. If you want your sanity to submit to your logic—well..." He leaves the obvious contradiction in terms unstated.

I get up from the chair and begin pacing, my eyes fixed on the city outside the window. "But then, why... I'm dreaming about victims, crime scenes— that I put to bed emotionally a long time ago. Things I saw and remember seeing. Most of all, things I remember feeling deeply about. I thought about them, cried about them, died a little inside about them. I didn't bury them or engage in a bunch of denial. I took it *in*." I look at him. "So? Why are they suddenly all back and screaming in my face? Why *now*?" I run down, deflate, and take my seat again. "Why am I suddenly terrified for no reason ten times a day?"

"There's a difference between feeling, Smoky, and feeling *enough*."

I frown. "I don't follow."

"I've known you for some time. How do you do what you do?"

"What—you mean profiling?"

"Yes."

I think about this for the millionth time. The answers had so many shapes and colors. What quality endures?

"Let me help you," Dr. Childs says. "Is it more intellectual or emotional?"

"Emotional," I answer without hesitation.

"Yes," he encourages. "Describe that for me."

"It's like a puzzle. When I start, it's two-dimensional—like a blank outline of a person. As I go along, I begin to find pieces of the puzzle and slot them in place."

"How?"

"By not looking away. By only looking closer."

"Looking at what?" he presses, pushing at me gently but inexorably.

"Well—everything," I answer, blinking. "How the victim must have felt, but also how the perp would've felt in response to that. What it would have sounded like, smelled like ... " I shrug. "Tasted like. Once, my killer was into chocolate—"

"Excuse me," Dr. Childs interrupts. "Did you say chocolate?"

"Yep. He'd melt enough to pour over his victims once they were on their last leg. They'd drown in it. The autopsy showed third-degree burns in some of their lung tissue."

"Remarkable. And?"

I frown, remembering my frustration. "I just couldn't get it. Chocolate. I've never disliked it but never really cared for it, either. So I went and saw a chocolate expert." I smile. "A chocolate *gourmand*. I had him teach me all about chocolate. I saw how it was made. Smelled all the different smells. Ate a ton of samples and gained ten pounds in the process."

"Did it help?" He doesn't bother trying to hide his fascination.

"Yes," I respond, slowly. "Not right away or all at once. But it helped me understand him."

"Do you find, in these instances, that you are able to put all of what you understood into words?"

"No."

He looks off, pulling at his beard absently. "This is mostly what I expected." He returned his gaze to me. "One more thing. Tell me about the very first time you learned that the world outside your family could go wrong. That other people could come to bad ends."

The memory comes without effort. "I was six years old, at the playground near our house. Mom was off talking to one of the other moms, and I was minding my own business, digging in a sandbox. I think it was a Saturday."

The boy.

The boy had been blond, with deep, dark, sad blue eyes. He had the most serious face I'd ever seen. I noticed his shadow first, as he stood between me and the sun.

"Hi," he ventured.

"Hi," I replied.

Amenities satisfied, he sat down and watched me dig. We were alone for the moment, as sometimes happens when young children are in motion, as they ebb and flow.

"Whatcha doin'?" he asked me.

"Digging."

"That's cool," he said, nodding.

I accepted as to how this could be true but stayed focused on my project.

"Can I tell you a secret?" he asked, after a time.

"Sure."

"You have to promise not to tell."

"I promise." I made this promise automatically, without really losing focus on my project. I suppose this makes sense. How bad could I have expected his secret to *be*, at six?

He looked to the right, then to the left. I didn't perceive it this way at the time, of course, but in my memory it's a sad, pitiful thing to see. Too fearful, secret, and furtive for a child. "My daddy hurts my mommy and me. And he sexes me sometimes."

"What's *sexes* mean?"

He looked off, and in my memory, the depth of his discomfort is plain on his face. It's an expression of sharp edges. Someone who can't wake up from a falling dream. "He ... you know. Puts his penis inside me."

"Oh," I replied, though in reality I was still mystified. "I'm sorry."

"Yeah." He scuffed the dirt with the heel of his sneaker. "Promise you won't tell, 'K? My daddy said if me or Mommy tell anyone, he'll hurt us really bad. Maybe even kill us."

Dr. Childs cocks his head, curious. "What did you tell him?"

"I told him that I promised. That I wouldn't tell."

"And did you keep your promise?"

"Until now, yeah."

"Why?"

I think about it. "I suppose ... because I believed him. I didn't know his father, and it's not that hard to scare such a young boy, so—who knows for sure? I was absolutely certain the boy believed it."

"You never discussed it with your mother or your father?"

"No." I search my memory for anything, even a small slip of the tongue. "Nope. Not a word, ever."

Dr. Childs strokes his beard, thoughtful. "Were you frightened by the experience?"

"Sure. I had nightmares."

"I can imagine. Was that the only time?"

"No. I'd see him every now and then at the playground. He'd always come up and sit down and talk to me. Sometimes he just talked about kid stuff, but most of the time it was about his father's abuse. It went on for about a year. After that, I never saw him again."

"You never learned his name?"

I sigh. "Never. He didn't offer, and I didn't ask. We were both six, and ID is a lot less important to children at that age. I remember making another friend that summer. We said hi, played nonstop for five hours, and shouted our names out to each other as we were heading home for dinner. So that was part of it." I shake my head tightly. "But not all of it. Some of it was instinct, I think, on both our parts."

"Very possible," he agrees. "Contrary to popular belief, children can be very, very good at keeping secrets, even big ones. Perhaps especially big ones."

"I know. I wish I had learned his name, though. I thought about him a lot after I joined the FBI." I pause. "I still think about him."

"Let me ask two questions, Smoky, and please give it some thought. It's not a gimme. Did I say that correctly?"

Dr. Childs is the prototype for who and what he is. He speaks the King's English and never swears. Slang sounds like a foreign language coming from his mouth.

"Yep."

"These are my questions: How do you feel when you think of him? And: Has the strength of that emotion abated?"

Something large and scary and ugly moves around inside me, opening a single lidded eye to regard the world. I feel a vast shutting down, demanding my surrender, burning on the edges of myself with a blue flame.

"Smoky?" Dr. Childs prompts gently.

"I feel … sad. It's as strong now as then. Maybe worse."

"Why?"

I consider this. "I suppose because I have more context now. I didn't really understand what was being done to him then. Now I do."

"Hmm … ," he agrees, his voice thoughtful. "That makes perfect sense." He gives me a soft smile. "Indulge me further."

"I don't know," I mutter, astonished (and dismayed) at the edge of anger and hostility I hear in my voice. "I don't like this. I feel like something bad's about to happen."

Dr. Childs leans forward a little. He'll never touch me or take my hand, of course, but it is the meaning of the gesture; I can feel it. He is closing the connection between our two points in space because ultimately, comfort comes from others, and loneliness is only ever solved with intimacy. "Please. I promise I won't let you leave here in a bad state."

I can't meet his eyes. "Whatever," I mutter. "Go ahead."

"Thank you. My last question: What do you feel, more generally, as *yourself*, about that memory? Of course you are sad for him. I'm asking … " He purses his lips and looks off, struggling to find the words. "I want you to tell me what it makes you feel about the world and life and people, in general."

"Is that all?" But I manage a small smile, and the anger's gone now. I can hear my own faint amusement.

"My apologies. Please indulge me."

I stare at him, thinking. He returns my gaze, looking as unflappable and patient as the Buddha. I only feel his waiting, and it seems bottomless, ready to accept anything. It calls to my inner weakness like a siren song. I want to curl up in his nonjudgmental bubble and be safe.

How do I feel about the world? About life? And why doesn't that seem like a silly question that I should deflect and ignore?

"I'm very concept oriented." I hear myself speaking without really having registered making a decision to do so. "Feel?" I shake my head. "Not the best way to approach it, for me. You ask me how I feel about life because of that moment, and I hear 'Tell me how you *see* life as a result of that moment.' Do you understand? And is that weird?"

"I do understand, and I'd be more likely to call it insightful than weird. Allow me to rephrase, then: Tell me how it makes you see the world and life and people, in general."

The ugly, moving through me again, like a serpent. It has the bulk of a leviathan. I see it from the corners of my eyes as its massiveness slides across the world of me before disappearing into shadow. I am afraid of myself again.

"I see ... " I squint, trying to see a thought with my eyes. "I see a world where a young child screams against the wood."

"The wood?"

I blink like a sleepwalker coming awake. "What? Oh." I clear my throat. "Our apartment—the one we lived in when I met the boy—had wood floors everywhere. Back then, I assumed everyone had wood floors."

"I see. Please, continue."

What is the answer to this question? I ask myself. Because I know there is an answer to be found. I am not a big believer in closure through conversation. I hear too many lies to believe in full disclosure as something that happens broadly. I don't believe in some great, as yet unseen answer that will cause the walls to come tumbling down and solve all the mysteries of me.

But I do believe in truth. And if there is a shape of it to be seen, I have to see it, once I know it exists. There are words here. Words that matter.

"What do I see? I see the truth that incident extrapolates. I saw it the moment he told me: This is a world where little boys can scream against the wood. Not that all of them will. But they *can*. And ... " I feel the words before I say them, like a sucker punch to the heart: " ... and it always will be. No matter how many abusers are locked up, there will always be more. That's what really accumulates—that particular certainty."

I am possessed now. I have found the shape of this truth, and it's as though everything I need to say about this is all there in my mind at once, as a whole piece. I am not speaking—I'm keeping my mouth open while the words run out.

"It's not about being cynical, or bitter, or anything like that. It's not 'a viewpoint that's been skewed by my job.' It's a reality that's skewed by others' ignorance of the truth. I don't worry that everyone I pass on the street is a killer or an abuser. I know they aren't. I just know the truth: Somewhere between two and four percent of the population are pedophiles. A smaller number will be serial killers. That's just the way of the jungle, the way things are.

"It's not that I take a dim view of people in general, even. It's that I can't 'un-know' the truth: These people are real, and they exist. Knowing this changes everything."

"Yes," Dr. Childs agrees, nodding. "It does. But Smoky … why do you think you hold on to the emotion about your victims? Why do you keep it fresh?"

It's one of those answers I know only because he asked the question, but I know it immediately. "Because they were beautiful and human, and most of the rest of the world will forget them. Even their families. Someone should remember." Tears are running down my face. I jut out my chin, daring him to shout me down. "Some wounds should always be ragged. It's not right to let the world … exist like that. Like it doesn't care, in the end." I look up at him bleakly. "Even though it doesn't."

"But you do," he says in a soft voice.

"Damn right."

"Even though you know caring in such a way will change nothing?"

"Even more because of it."

Dr. Childs looks through the window, thinking. I grab some tissues, and I wipe my cheeks and blow my nose while I wait. I feel drained and filled to bursting, simultaneously. Feeling anything strongly, I've found—even grief— can be as exhilarating as it is exhausting.

"Thank you, Smoky," he says. "I know that I pushed you a bit. Thank you for being willing to struggle through it."

I shrug and eke out a small grin that I hope doesn't come across as a grimace. "You're the doc, doc."

"On that note. I just want to check in on the things you discussed with me by letter."

"Sure."

"Still having panic attacks?"

"Yes."

"Difficulty sleeping?"

"I'm not sure *difficulty* is the right word. I barely sleep. How's that?"

"Better? Worse? The same?"

I shrug.

"The same, then," he says, nodding. "Night terrors?"

"Those are better. I was getting them three or four times a week. It's down to one or two."

"Better, but I'm familiar with night terrors. I know even once is too much."

Night terrors. What a fantastically perfect name. Some part of me loves the person who coined it. They could have decided, no, *terrors* is too hysterical ... let's call them night *problems*. Yes.

Being woken up by your own screaming; waking up dizzy because you've been hyperventilating in your sleep; waking up in the middle of the night with your teeth chattering in your head; these are not problems. These are terrors. When they first started, I was afraid to sleep. I feared the time between 1:00 and 4:00 A.M., when the monsters came out to play.

"How are you doing with the emotional control?"

"No better. I get mad too easily. Bonnie doesn't seem to care—"

He interrupts me. "Truly?"

"The first time I apologized, she told me it wasn't necessary. She said that she knew the difference between me being mean because I was hurt, and me just being mean, and that the first one was quote 'irrelevant' to her."

"Remarkable," he says, shaking his head. "I'm sorry, I interrupted you. You were telling me about the anger. That Bonnie was dealing with it."

"Right. But Tommy ... every time I snap at him ..." *Oh shit*, I think. *It's going to happen here. Oh no.* "I—I want to die. I look at that ... that ... eye. ..."

I cry like a baby these days. It's a zero-to-sixty-in-a-second-or-two phenomenon, and it's generally an explosive and shameless display. I don't weep— I sob. I hate it. It makes me feel weak and insane.

But Tommy, oh, Tommy, his eye!

The floodgates open wide, whether I want them to or not. I bawl without stopping, remembering. They called us on the plane. I was in the air when I was told that killers had come to my home, burned it to the ground, and attacked my family. That Tommy had blown them all out of their boots but one. That they'd fought, hand to hand, and it had been an equal and brutal battle. That Bonnie was unhurt but Tommy was in surgery because a ring on his opponent's fist had almost ruined his eye. They were able to save it, but it was a close, close thing.

He had two cracked ribs, and his nose was broken. His body was bruised, practically from head to toe—big, fist-size marks that could turn black as an eggplant, yellow as a jaundiced eye, blue as the blue that lives just before the black. His left eye had been swollen shut, and he'd needed stitches in his lips, knuckles, and in three places on his torso. Only his teeth were spared, God knows how.

His pain had been immense. The cracked ribs made breathing painful. A trip to the toilet would end with him curled into himself in our bed, shivering in silence.

And the worst, oh the worst, and he can't ever, EVER know I saw.

I continue to bawl, mouth open, head back, eyes closed. I don't need a tissue, I need a towel.

It had been the middle of the night. I woke up because Tommy was not in bed. He didn't move unless he had to, and I'd grown sensitive to the times he'd get up. It could have happened only because his ears had been swollen from being boxed in the fight. Normally, Tommy has the hearing of a bat.

The light to the master bathroom was on, and water was running in the sink. I walked barefoot to the door, which was open just a crack, and that is when I saw him. Tommy was swaying in front of the mirror but not looking into it, and he was weeping. Not sobbing, just weeping, like a man who was physically overwhelmed.

In our bed, he would shiver and shake or curse; one time he cried out in pain. He never shed a tear in my presence.

I was so terrified he'd see me. I was a trespasser, there, in that moment. I crawled back to bed with a knife in my heart, but I didn't cry. When he returned, I pretended to be sleeping, and so I heard him when he kissed my cheek. He didn't say it in my ear, and it was said in the barest whisper, but I heard him.

"I'm so sorry, honey," he whispered thickly, with those stitched and swollen lips. "I didn't save your house. I fucked up."

I screamed inside my own skull in silence until the sun came up, and I felt like I wanted to murder the whole world. I've never been so bloodthirsty or felt so impotent. The two in tandem were pure torture.

The man he killed had been Russian. Ex-Spetsnaz, I'm told, the Russian equivalent of our Navy SEALs. When I saw the photographs of his corpse, I had to go vomit in fear. He'd been a giant, almost six feet seven, with a body like a tank or a shark.

"He fought that man, with one of his eyes already not working right, Mama-Smoky," Bonnie had said to me one evening when we were alone downstairs, while Tommy writhed in the bedroom above our heads. "They fought like animals. It was ... " She frowned. "I don't know how to describe it. It wasn't human—but, yeah, it was ... which made it ... *more*. More of everything. Do you understand what I mean?"

I had, but then again, I had not. It's one of those things, like child pornography or a murdered family, that can't actually be grasped until it's been seen. I can describe to someone what a dead child locked in a house for four days in summer smells like, but it will never be known to them, because it's not a thing to be known. It's a thing to be witnessed.

I could imagine, a little, from the photographs of the dead killer. His face was a nearly unrecognizable pulp. The right ear had been virtually torn off his head, as had his lower lip. He hadn't been as lucky with his teeth; the rictus grin behind his lips looked like a broken piano.

Tommy's knife work is what had ended the fight, and this, too, was evident in the photographs. The man's throat had been slit from ear to ear, but he'd also been gored in a straight line that ran from his sternum to his groin. The arteries on both his arms and legs had been severed, and Tommy had completed this circle around the man's body by burying the knife in the roof of his mouth, angling it up into his brain.

"He was so fast once he had the knife, Mama-Smoky. Once he could get the knife because I stabbed the guy—wow—it was like I was watching a martial arts movie." Her eyes are wide as she says this, not in fear or flippancy, but in wonder and respect, something I'm more than conflicted about. "*Whish! Whish!* He sliced the guy's arms, and then *whish! whish!* he'd sliced down the guy's chest and stomach! Then the leg arteries, and the other man was down on the floor, already dying. Tommy cut his throat and slammed the knife in his mouth." She shakes her head, all hero worship and no fear. "I don't think it took more than six or seven seconds. Then we had to get out of the house because the house was filling up with gas from the stove, which got ripped away from the wall during the fight."

Tommy had dragged the giant man out onto the lawn, for reasons that remain unclear. I think the reasons *were* unclear, that Tommy was barely holding on and thus running on automatic. He can't remember anything after the injury to his eye, not even killing the Russian. I think he saw a man down and did what he had once been trained to do, back when he worked for the Secret Service.

My sobbing is abating; it appears that the big squall has blown itself out. I wait for it to finish and concentrate on not hyperventilating.

Once he could get the knife because I stabbed the guy ... every time I thought this phrase, my heart stopped beating for a moment. I was infinitely, unbelievably proud of her, on the one hand. The knife had saved them, however it had ended up getting close enough to Tommy for him to grab it. They might both be dead if she hadn't. On the other hand, of course, was the truth: She'd been lucky. Defy-the-odds, beat-cancer lucky. Which meant they'd both been lucky. Which meant that while I was boarding the aircraft to fly home, for just a second of a moment, everything I loved had hovered on the knife edge of being lost, with luck as its only armor.

Every time I thought it out, it always felt like madness. Like playing Russian roulette with five out of six cylinders loaded and after giving it a spin.

I'm in a state now where tissues are enough, and I use a handful to wipe my face. I hadn't worn any makeup, because I don't wear it these days. Too much crying without warning.

Everything had fallen apart so quickly, I think bleakly, as I soak the tissues with my salt.

All my structures had shattered, inside and out, and I'd set myself adrift with no destination beyond survival and endurance. My terrors remained terror-ful, and in the middle of it all, my son was born, like a big bright burst of light.

And while none of the hurting has abated since he entered this world, neither has any of that pain dimmed his glow or meaning. He is a pure happiness, an unquestionable good. My love for him is something too deep and boundless and fierce to be understood by anyone but me. I've never doubted I'd survive all this, because I have to, for my son. We're all he has, and this is not a job you can fail at if you want to call yourself a human being.

This is why I'm here now. It's why I reached out to Dr. Childs to begin with, why I agreed with his one demand. It is the tether of light that keeps me from doubting the final outcome even when it seems that I am drowning in an ocean of doubt or flailing in a hurricane of it.

God help me if I were alone and responsible for no one.

"Sorry." I sniffle, clearing my throat. I smile a little. "But you did ask."

Dr. Childs chuckles at this, and in that moment, I see some of the shape of him. Because the chuckle is genuine, which means he understands: That even if you're only laughing away the tears, laughter at all levels is a grounding, cleansing thing. It serves no practical purpose. It doesn't make it rain money or put food on the table. Laughter is what happens when there's too much joy, or in defiance of too much pain; or sometimes, just because the day is kind. Like love and sex and children and singing, it's free solid gold.

"That was an excellent cry," he offers, still smiling.

"Thanks. I was pretty proud of it myself."

"Let me ask you one last thing. This is less diagnostic for me than something I want you to consider for yourself. While I understand that the anger is out of proportion to the circumstances, based on what you described—do you really feel that your grief is? Or is it the lack of control that bothers you more?"

I find myself blank and wordless. Confused. It's as if someone asked me to consider whether the sky could have been green once, before it was blue. Not only would the question never have occurred to me, I don't really understand why it would ever be asked by anyone. This feels the same.

"What ... I'm sorry—are you asking me if I think soaking my shirt with tears and snot, because I'm wailing like you just chopped off my arm—all of a sudden—is normal?"

"No, I'm asking you to consider clarifying why you feel it's not. Is it because it's in my presence and not under your control? Or do you honestly feel that your grief is out of magnitude to the occurrence it mourns?" His gaze on me sharpens, becomes more intent. "Is your grief trivial, Smoky? Is it worthless and silly?"

The rage that washes over me leaves me breathless. "Well ... ," I say, after a moment, "I suppose since I felt like killing you for asking me that ... I suppose my answer must be no."

He smiles. "I agree. I agree completely. I find your grief—on all counts—entirely reasonable. The reason it keeps its strength, for you, lies in your own gift: your ability to empathize. Not just with the parts you approve of, but with the person as a whole." The smile becomes a gentle grin. "Reasonable, not crazy."

I sigh, then nod, allowing the possibility. "Fine. But not being able to control my emotional state isn't reasonable. That's crazy."

"What a terrible word, *crazy*," he says, frowning in disapproval. "So loaded. So judgmental and divisive."

"*Nuts?*" I offer.

"*Suffering from a mental illness* would be my preference."

In spite of the lightness of our banter, I feel something inside myself go silent at this proclamation. "*Mental illness*," I repeat, rolling the phrase around on my tongue. Savoring it. I grin at Dr. Childs. "Let's use it in a sentence! 'I have a *mental illness*.'" My voice sounds hot and tight. The words glitter in my ears, sharp-edged as a dream you're trapped in.

"Yes," he replies. I wait for him to say more, but he does not.

"And?" I demand, frustration and fury (*and let's not forget desperation!*) threatening, from nowhere, to spark into a full-roaring flame.

His eyes have changed somewhat. They are the same in gentleness but have increased in strength, and their focus on mine is absolute. "But nothing," he answers, his voice calm and kind but oh-so inexorable. "You chose a profession, holding knowledge that, once known, can injure or unhinge the mind. As a result—" and now he leans forward again, slightly—"you have been injured. You have been harmed. And so, yes, you are—right now, as of this moment in your life—suffering from a mental illness."

The rage that appears shocks me to the roots, not only with its size, but by the suddenness of its totality. "*Screw you!*" I scream at him at the top of my lungs, no ramp-up at all. "I am *not ... a fucking ... VICTIM!*" I come out of my chair as I say this and am dimly aware of myself as a spectator, watching myself as I lose all control. I wonder where the crack in the sidewalk has gone, that place for the toe of my mind to find and know: Here is where one thing ends and the other begins.

"You are a victim of the violence done to your body and your mind," Dr. Childs says. His voice is quiet but clear. "That doesn't equate to victimhood as a habit or behavior."

I sneer, hard and deep. Self-contempt carves bloodless furrows through the skin of my face as I tremble and reel. "Poor, poor, *poor* Smoky ... ," I whisper in a low, reedy, breathless voice, each word cut from a block of ice. "Did she get a boo-boo on her—her *mind? Huh?*" I'm shouting now, and see myself mad-eyed. "On her fucking *soul?*"

Dr. Childs keeps his seat, and his eyes never leave mine. They are focused, not impassive, and they send a single, maddening message of lovely, terrible, precious certainty: *I am here.* No matter what you say or feel or reveal or do— or *are.* I am here.

It is a look that simultaneously enfolds me in comfort and pins me in a spotlight. My emotions rocket in an endlessness of opposites. I am kissing in cannon fire. Pinning the now to the now forever.

"Not at all," he says gently, inexorably, a train of unstoppable certainty. "Or at least, not in that way. I am saying that sanity is always a current and potentially temporary state. It does not exist in a monolithic fashion, but as a state of equilibrium. Sometimes—something overwhelms what allows the balance of that equilibrium. It can be a large moment or it can be small, but it is rarely one moment only—which is why the small ones that turn the boat over surprise us the most." He pauses, studying me, and I am aware of his words and their meaning penetrating my consciousness. Getting through to me with their simple logic. "It is also your answer as to why those past faces have returned. Not because you denied their existence at the time, but because you never allow the strength of their memory to dissipate; thus they are always there, waiting to return if they are invited.

"Why did they not return in the past, as compared to now? The answer is to be found, again, in that answer of equilibrium. It is their meaning that has changed for you, not the memories themselves. The memories are as they have always been: three-dimensional, fully realized, completely, empathically understood, in both their pain and their glory.

"Think of that state of equilibrium as the current sum of all the meanings you have assigned to both the good and the bad occurrences in your life. When that sense of meaning becomes overwhelmed or distorted beyond our ability to control it—that is when we are suffering from a mental illness. It can manifest in too many ways to possibly list and can last for a moment or a lifetime.

"It is the source of your panic and of your inability to control the shift between what you consider a normal reaction and an abnormal one. It is not an indictment of weakness or even something that need have some deep, holistic, life-altering meaning. The return of complete sanity—of the full control of you *to you*—is simply a matter of returning you to a state where the sum total of those meanings adds up to a sum you can live with in comfort, or at least live with in the absence of fear."

I am not speaking, not yet. But I am sitting again, and I have stopped shaking in anger, and I am listening intently. This has the form of certainty; I can smell it. It has the shape of truth.

"As I am aware you are a result-oriented individual, I will speak with you frankly: Your chances, in my opinion, are very, very good. Many people cannot return from moments of great despair or posttraumatic stress. You have done so in the past. What's more, I believe—and it is factually the only reason I agreed to assist you in the other matter—that the solution, for you, lies in your ability to seek out the evil that's external to you.

"The fact you can bring bad men to the justice they deserve—here is where what tips that sum balance of meaning and your equilibrium lies. The fact you are willing to attempt it, in whatever state you are in, is a very, very good sign for your recovery. I am not saying it is the only solution nor the only one we should aspire to implementing, but where I would advise many patients to move away from what initially deranged that equilibrium, in your case, I am firmly comfortable in advising you otherwise.

"If you want to seek out the man or men behind this—in other words—then I believe you should, and that doing so will be therapeutic. I think it is in the doing of the actions of this, and perhaps a little behavior modification therapy, that you will find your balance again."

He spreads his hands and smiles warmly. "You have made your profession and what it means inextricably a part of your life, Smoky. And more than that, you have made it a part of *who* you are. We could spend much time debating the wisdom of this, but I believe that it would be time wasted. We are what we make ourselves, and at some point, consequently, what we have made ourselves is simply who we are.

"Fine, your balance was knocked out of kilter, terribly so. Most understandably so. AD Jones is only one amongst many symbols that, in my opinion, upset your certainty in that one thing, that singularly most important sum of sums. I believe that an inability to be sure of that one thing—if of nothing else—is what is making life itself unbearable to you. It's what we must restore, if we are to restore you.

"And that certainty is this: That while the world can be terrible, and while this is forever so—while there will always be a child somewhere, screaming against the wood—justice can always be brought, in the end, if you desire it." He points a finger at me. "If *you* desire it."

Dr. Childs stops, and I know he's done now. He's had his say. He watches me gently and with a compassion that I can tell he was born with, that is as inextricably a part of everything he is as the things he's stated about me. In that moment, I feel the squall coming but also sense its finality with a relief so great, so complete, I feel like I'm going to shatter into dust in the moments before I become whole again.

Life is the story we tell ourselves. The words come to me unbidden, from somewhere. Some old sense memory, charting its way up from the depths. I'd heard them from a friend or read them in a book or something, and now here they were again.

I start crying at the same time I begin speaking, but it's okay this time because I understand why each thing is happening. My tears are my mourning, and my mourning exists as a response to the truth of all that has happened, recent and past, to me and to others. My speaking is a purging and the need for a witness to it. To know and to see that at least one other person walking this earth understands this thing I am looking at and weeping for, in the same way that I do. They don't have to feel the same way or be the same person as me, but sometimes we need a witness to finalize our most resolute and fundamental truths of self.

"I think I can take anything or see anything, as long as I know I can make things mostly right, in the end," I say, as I weep. "Really. It doesn't matter how bad it is. I know that sounds arrogant, but in my case, I think it's true. It's not how bad it is that gets me. It's my concept of how much right can be made in spite of it."

"I think that's a most beautiful and quite excellent expression of the way in which we all feel about that particular form of balance," Dr. Childs replies quietly.

"With Matt and Alexa, the hardest part about that wasn't that it happened but that it happened because of me and the job I do. But I killed Sands; I shot him myself. Then Annie was killed; and again, she was chosen as a victim because of me. But I caught him, too, and then there was Bonnie, and I was responsible for her...and then there was the job. Making sure I did it the best way possible, better than anyone else could, when that was possible." I weep mournfully, letting it waterfall out of me like toxic rivers or acid rain. "The thing is, I was good at my job. Sometimes, really good. I had a great team, and we grew close. Then there was Tommy." I drag my palms across my cheeks, wiping away sheets of tears. "I got pregnant again. Me and my team were good enough to get chosen as the resource for the strike-team initiative. Life was getting better, not worse, you know?

"So, sure, bad things—terrible, awful, horrible things—had happened. But I was able to keep my confidence that I'd stay ahead of it all. That in spite of all the bad things I knew or saw or even experienced personally, I was winning more than I was losing." I stop speaking, and my chin drops nearly to my chest. I stare into my lap.

"But...this. AD Jones. James—what that man did to poor James's mom. Tommy and Bonnie almost getting killed. My house getting burned down." I wipe away more tears and hear the childish misery of my own voice. "I'd managed to stay in that house, where Alexa was made and where she and Matt died, in spite of all that had happened there. I survived their ghosts and built a new life in the same place; that let me celebrate rather than mourn them. I mean, it was just a house, but to have it...burned away like that...along with everything else."

I can't stop crying. These aren't the strong, heavy sobs of earlier, but the tears are continuous. Less a thunderstorm than a steady rain. The kind that cause rivers to rise and flood, catching towns by surprise as they wash them away. "AD Jones was my friend. He was my mentor. He knew Matt and Alexa, and he also knew Bonnie and Tommy. He knew everything I'd gone through. How could he betray me like that? How could he betray James and my team?"

I shake my head. "I know people think the video of my rape is such a big deal to me, and I guess when I first heard about it, it was. I mean, it's horrible to have that out there. But I don't know—I've already been through all the public aspect of that and overcome it." I gesture at the scars on my face. "After it happened, every time I walked around with these and saw people reacting to them ... it felt like they were seeing the rape." I shrug in anger and misery and wave my hand dismissively. "I guess it should be a bigger deal, but that's not what really bothers me about the video.

"It's that AD Jones must have been the one who provided it. He's the only one that makes sense. Add in the reproduction of the bathroom—our office bathroom—in the bunker ... " I sigh. "Who else could it be? When I think of the video, I think about him. And that—that's what really hurts me. It hurts me so much! How could I trust someone like that for so long and have them know me and so much about me ... and then have them turn out to be such a fraud, to such a degree?"

The tears are lessening now. I can feel things winding down inside me. A great purging is coming to an end, and while it will have been a good thing—I can feel this—it has also exhausted me. Not just the action of the grief itself, but because I can sense the beginnings of everything that will follow, too. The searches for answers. The rebuilding of self. Nothing about any of it will be easy or small or given, and the thought of it all is enough to make me bone-weary.

It is a part of my fear, too; I can see this now, and I tell Dr. Childs. "I'm also just ... afraid. I've almost never really been afraid of the guys I'm after. I mean, I have been, in the moment, or if I actually allowed myself to visualize the possibilities. But part of the job, especially chasing these kinds of criminals, is the ability not to worry. Either you have it, or you develop it; because otherwise, it would devour you."

I look up at him for the first time since I started speaking. "Whoever, whatever this is—it's not just big. It's huge. The resources involved ... " I shiver and hate myself for it. "You didn't see that place in Colorado. It's massive. It represents action over a very long period of time, involving a ton of money, and on a global scale. When I start to consider all the variables—including those that involve the qualities of the kinds of men capable of something like this—I feel outmatched. I don't feel confident about winning. I've never felt that way. Never. I've felt all kinds of things about the men I've gone after, but one thing I *never* questioned was that I had the ability to win. All I had to do was find them."

I look down again and sigh. I feel less wretched than when I walked in here, by far, but much more drained. "That's an alien sensation. I really have no comparison to it. So if I'm not sure that we can even win, how can I possibly ask my team to put themselves in that kind of danger? What if we lose?"

I look back up at him and feel my eyes go wide and horrified. "What if they *die* because of it?" I shake my head rapidly back and forth. "Oh, no. Hell, no. That would be the end of everything. It would end me for good, without a doubt. It wouldn't matter how amazing and incredible and right you were about putting what I was feeling into words. The loss of *that* balance? There'd be no remedy." I feel my face twist and the shame burning in my eyes. "I'm afraid of that, Dr. Childs. Afraid like I've never been afraid of anything. And I can't seem to put that fear away. I need to, but I can't."

I'm done crying. I feel different inside, tectonically so. A distant part of myself is amazed at how the ability of a man to state the exact nature of my problem could make such a change inside me. Dr. Childs was right, and brilliantly so—I am solution oriented. My inability to profile myself had left me without even the hope for a solution. His explanation of balance, about the sums of meaning, and most of all—his ability to put my specific need in regards to those things into such precise and perfect terms—was half the battle, perhaps a bit less.

At the same time, the problem with revelation is that it reveals. I am aware of all that I have no solution to, as well. All potentials that do not include resolution include the potential for a repeat of or continuance of my problems.

I am finding that one of the fears you gain as a result of losing your marbles is the fear of losing them again, and it's a terror.

"What do you fear most, as a result of not solving your fears?" Dr. Childs asks me, as if he'd been reading my mind.

I consider it but don't have to think about it long. The answer is shameful, but I give it anyway. "Death. Killing myself." I try a smile. "I'm not suicidal or anything. I haven't been recently, either, even with everything that's been happening. But if there was no hope of a solution, ever?" The shiver runs through me again. "It's like … everything I know and understand would be turned against me. It's one thing to accept that the worst things possible will always be happening in the world, somewhere. It's another thing to get, like you said, knocked off balance about your view of that. It's something else entirely to know that and lose everything that keeps it from eating you up forever."

I stare off. Thinking of my father and my mother, of the ways in which they passed on to me both their weaknesses and their strengths. "People think I'm strong. I suppose I agree with them most of the time. But when I look down that road—at that possibility—I don't know … I just feel weak."

Dr. Childs smiles at me. "Ah, Smoky. Don't be too hard on yourself in that regard. Most people simply live in denial of a particular truth, and healthily so: that anyone can be brought to that point and that place. Anyone can be broken enough by life that they truly wish to end it. Part of wanting life and of desiring to remain alive is the defense such denial gives us. You lack that protection, but only because of what you went through. It's a very important point to remember, and one you should already know: Simply because you can conceive of something does not mean that you will do it, or even that you are capable of it, in a meaningful way.

"You've surely run into the great fantasizers, who are full of guilt at the certainty they could murder for pleasure or rape for the thrill, when the truth is: They are as far from the nature of the true, sadistic psychopath as you or I."

"Yes," I acknowledge. "That's true."

"So? This is really no different from that. You've been forced, not by choice, to look too far down *all* the possible avenues your life could *ever* take. This has forced you to consider all the possible solutions you *might* arrive at to these various scenarios." He shrugs, dismissing the world and my fears. "That has a great deal of validity in terms of addressing your fear levels and difficulties in the present. It has no relevance to the truth of your strength in the moment. Can you see this, at least a little?"

"I suppose so," I allow. And when he puts it that way, I can.

Thinking isn't doing. It's not that it can't be a relevant predictor, but in some areas, the gulf is too wide. Dr. Childs is saying the same is true in terms of suicide, and when he puts it in those terms, it feels true to me, even obviously so. My lack of desire to die right now is the best contrast of truth to this concern about what I could do in some possible future.

"Good," he replies. "Now, as to the fear and the reasons behind it, these seem entirely understandable and valid to me. Only someone very foolish or perhaps very stupid would disagree. Whoever or whatever arranged for these attacks is, as you say, a formidable opponent." He grimaces. "I can't help you with that truth, beyond giving you the opinion I've already given, which is that facing them, therapeutically speaking, is the only real resolution to your current mental difficulties."

"Great, thanks," I say, managing to smile a little and managing even to feel it a little.

He returns the same smile, raising an eyebrow of "Ah, well." "However," he says, raising a finger, "I can help you therapeutically and am advising you specifically to take advantage of it."

I hesitate, but only for a moment. I sigh. "I'm ... not opposed to the idea."

He nods. "Good. I understand you're reluctant. I can only ask you to trust me. At the moment, you are feeling the relief of abreaction—the 'good' wrung-out feeling of a purging of bad emotion. Once you take the first steps on the road to action against your enemy and are firmly committed to it, you will continue to feel permanently, *generally* better. And this will be so; you will be better in fundamental ways. This does not mean, unfortunately, that your panic issues will resolve themselves at the same time. Fear that has overwhelmed us is a strange thing to the mind, particularly when that fear has been validated. It does not disperse so easily. You need tools that will help you in combating it, should your fear levels rise. These exist and are fairly simple things. They mostly involve redirecting your fear or helping you to delay acting on it until you've regained your equilibrium."

"Okay."

"You are still nursing, yes?" he asks.

"Yes."

"Normally, I would recommend a mild antianxiety drug, too, but that's out for the time being." He shrugs and smiles. "That's life. I think you'll find the exercises we devise for cognitive behavioral therapy quite helpful, regardless."

"I wouldn't have been wild about the idea of being on drugs, anyway," I reply. "How could I carry a weapon? I'd probably be decertified for field duty."

"True. Then again, as fearful as you have been of late, tell me the truth, Smoky: Did you bring your weapon with you today?"

I look away. "No," I answer, irritated by the insight. I sigh. "Do you actually think I'll beat this, Dr. Childs?"

"I think your chances are excellent, Smoky, I truly do." He shrugs, the smallest spark of sadness in his eyes. "There are no guarantees, however. I won't lie to you: PTSD and related agoraphobia can be resistant to change. So, while I don't see it as the most probable outcome for you, it is the outcome for some. It's always possible you'll fall into that smaller percentage."

I try to swallow with a throat that's gone dry. "Great."

He raises a hand of warning. "That's not all. You have to give me your promise, and it must be absolute: If you don't experience the permanent fundamental change I spoke of, if you leave this office and find yourself simply frozen again—you must tell me."

The fear trembles inside me again from a distance, like a hint or an echo. "And if that's the case? What will it mean?"

Dr. Childs waits for a moment, then sighs. "It will mean that your difficulties may not resolve through the action of direct confrontation. It could mean they never will."

"And what would you recommend if that happened?"

He gives it to me straight. "I would recommend you retire immediately and that you allow your husband to use all that money he's made to take you both, and your family, somewhere you love to get on with your life in the best way you can. There are other treatment modalities we could attempt from that point, in terms of the most difficult symptoms, but the primary treatment would be to remove yourself from the environment that has caused your condition. Nothing else would make sense or be medically sound."

"Jesus," I manage as a reply. Then: "Wow."

"I would need your promise, Smoky, regardless of that possibility."

Even the thought of a return to how I felt earlier makes me feel like taking one of those pills right now and weaning Christopher tomorrow. The loss of my career forever? It was unfathomable to me. Still, it has that same shape of truth that I can't deny, and I know that both the promise and the possible result are the right things to do. "Okay," I agree. "I promise. If things go bad again and stay bad, I'll tell you." I swallow. "I'll even agree right now that if that happens, I'll have no choice but retirement."

"Thank you," he replies, bowing his head in acknowledgment. "On both counts. Now, before I release you, I want to reassure you and perhaps warn you on a few topics."

"There's more?"

"First, regarding yourself and how you generally feel: Don't be discouraged or assume the worst if you leave this office and then later tonight feel a return of the old fears at the same levels. Instead, if that occurs, I'd like you to do the following: I'd like you to examine your own perspective on the matter at that moment."

I frown. "I'm not sure I follow."

"Expectations, both good and bad, can influence our assessments in the moment. You recall the old saying: 'The only thing we have to fear is fear itself'?"

"Sure."

"Well, this can be much the same. Your fear levels, in terms of having night terrors and panic attacks, have been extreme. Fear of a return to those same levels, as a result, becomes its own fear, requiring its own questioning of perspective when you have the feeling that the same symptoms are returning."

"You're saying I could psyche myself out, in other words. Think the same thing is happening, when it's really just a lesser version of it?"

He nods. "Exactly. On the other hand, even a full-blown panic attack at this point shouldn't be allowed to convince you that things are hopeless. Again, this is not a single-visit, one-conversation problem. And as I've said, the fear can be the last thing to go and can be quite resistive. Fear operates at the level of instinct and has a very good reason for doing so. Convincing the whole that the part is no longer necessary can take time."

"That makes sense," I allow.

"Good. Next, consider the truth, as well, that you'll be throwing yourself directly into the path of not only your general fears, but also the ones that make intellectual sense. Your agoraphobia is quite intense when it kicks in, yes?"

"Yes." I don't even bother trying to deny it.

"Expect more of the same, perhaps even worse. Realize that this is rooted not only in emotion, but also in emotion with intellectual *proof*. To wit: If people are out to harm a person, it makes sense to stay indoors. Try and remember this when the agoraphobia threatens. Remind yourself that when dealing in real terms, one is not striving for a guarantee of safety, because such a thing can't actually exist. Instead, you are dealing with a continuum of safety."

"Risk management," I supply.

"Yes," he says, inclining his head in agreement. "Forever and *only*," he stresses. "Remember: There is no guaranteed risk prevention other than already being dead." He leans forward. "Constant fear, really, is a behavior. What we want to do is remember that fact, while reconditioning you to behave differently. This is not something that can be done overnight or even necessarily in a month's time. The behavior itself will continue, to whatever degree it does. Part of reconditioning yourself is being aware of that fact and having strategies in place to deal with it, should it occur."

"What kind of strategies?"

"Well, primarily, you want to acknowledge what's happening and then distract yourself from it. Direct resistance—'biting the bullet,' as they used to say—is not the best approach. Fear is too instinctive for that. Instead, develop ways to refocus your attention until the fear passes. Over time, your intellect and your instinct should sync up, meaning that you should no longer experience fear in the absence of a true, current threat."

I blink a few times, surprised. "That seems ... very intuitive."

Dr. Childs smiles. "Much in the arena of behavior modification is. It makes sense when you hear it. That's because it generally does. Make sense, I mean."

"Anything else?"

"The strategies. The best approach is a planned one, not ones you devise in the moment. A common one recommended by some therapists, for example, is a rubber or elastic band around the wrist. When the person feels the approach of fear, of a panic attack, they snap the band against their wrist as a distraction. Some people take a walk or simply change whatever they are doing at that moment and refocus their attention. Whatever you decide, you should generally have decided beforehand, and the key is that it truly refocuses your attention."

"I'll have to give that some thought," I say, "but I understand the concept."

"Excellent." He tilts his head, observing me for a moment. "You should take the most encouragement from your reaction to my little speech regarding the balance inherent to sanity and the feeling of relief it gave you in terms of a possible solution."

"Why is that?"

"Because it points toward your current state as being the result of recent events rather than the result of a long-term building-up of pressure due to exposure to trauma. If the first is so—and that is my belief—then the solution of action should recover you fully. If the second is so—which is not my belief—then retirement is the most likely outcome."

I stare at him. "Wait a second—your little speech? I thought you were giving me gospel then. It sure sounded like it. It definitely felt like it."

Dr. Childs raises an eyebrow and smiles. "When it comes to the mind, and particularly to the healing of the mind, very little is gospel, Smoky. There are only creative attempts based on knowledge, with a little hope added in for good measure."

CHAPTER ELEVEN

One of the rooms in Dr. Childs's office is a small conference room. It's been an hour and a half since he finished his therapy session with me. Our guest called to say he was running late, which was fine with me. I'd needed the time to reorient myself.

Walking through the mind is akin to crossing chasms with single steps. Time is irrelevant. You can spend a few hours in an office, as I just had, and come out to find yourself in undiscovered country.

I feel washed-out and jumpy at the same time. The moment I walked out the door, I felt the doubt Dr. Childs had alluded to. Even leaving the smaller office to reenter the larger space made me feel briefly exposed.

Kirby examined my face, and I imagined that I saw approval in her eyes, or at least some form of it. I hoped it was true. It meant that whatever change had occurred was visible to another, which would make it easier for me to accept as true.

"Everything hunky-dory, boss-woman?" she'd asked.

I had smiled. "Not everything. But maybe something."

"Something's better than nothing, yeah?"

"A one is better than a zero, I suppose."

She grinned. "Now there's the optimism I know and love. My cup-half-full girl."

"I'll ensure some coffee's made for our guest," Dr. Childs had said.

"No rush, doc," Kirby replied. "He called to let us know he was running late."

So coffee was made, and I had time to collect myself as well as I could. I feel stabler, stronger, but still lacking the vision of a plan. All of this was only the result of me reaching out on instinct, a state that's still the truth. I am feeling my way forward, half blind.

I haven't spent the last six weeks or so in a state of permanent panic or pain. I've also had plenty of time to think. In many ways, it's the only thing I have done. Nurse my son and think. Survive an attack of night terrors and think. Cradle Christopher in my arms and think.

I've never been able to turn off my mind at will. I even took some meditation classes once, something Callie had managed to talk me into, but it didn't take. Calculating the future is an unstoppable force inside me, particularly where crime of any kind is involved. Unanswered questions require answers be found, and there never seemed to be an end to unanswered questions.

I thought about the Wolf and the death museum and Ben. I thought about the couple who'd embraced in sorrow before killing themselves and the things that they'd said about their granddaughter.

I considered the time I had lost and the most disturbing fact of all, when I allowed myself the time to really think about it: the missing computer towers. The ones that contained the footage from the surveillance cameras. They'd been there when I first saw that room, when I'd put on the headphones and listened to that couple mourn their situation and then watched them die. Someone had taken the computers. Either it had occurred during the time I lost, or it had occurred not long after my rescue.

There was a visible record of their existence: Whoever had pulled the towers hadn't bothered to get rid of the cables connecting them to the wall—but the towers themselves were gone.

Sometimes when I was sleeping, I would dream of the time I had lost. In that dream, a man without a face glided down the underground hallways, computer towers under his arms. He carried them effortlessly, with arms stretched out unnaturally like rubber to surround them all. He'd come up to my supine form passed out on the bathroom floor as he waltzed toward the doorway leading into the museum foyer. He'd stop and then stare down at me, with my big, pregnant belly, in my helplessness. That moment would always last forever in the dream. I could feel him deciding: live? or die? I could sense how little it mattered to him because his power to choose was so total, so utter.

"Don't eat this sheep," I'd whisper, even though I was unconscious.

His formless face would say nothing, but I could hear his silent laughter in my mind and smell his amusement sweating out of his pores. It was the smell of electricity and power, with just a hint of clean rain.

CODY MCFADYEN

Then he'd continue his glide, letting me live, for no reason but a whim. I'd know, in the dream, how very lucky I'd been. My survival in that long, lingering moment of his regard had been a matter of a coin toss or even less. He hadn't killed me because he just didn't care enough about it one way or the other. I didn't matter to him, dead or alive, and he had other places to glide to, other things to do with his knowledge and his power. Perhaps if he'd had just a little more time, he'd have un-rubbered an arm long enough to choke me or break my neck.

Time had been short, and so he'd moved away, uncaring, without even the need for a shrug or a second thought about his decision.

It was a dream I had back when I was still having night terrors, and it would often precede them. I'd wake up with the smell of clean rain in my nose, and the afterglow of his formless face etched on my eyeballs, and the screams of my own fear on my lips. I'd race to the bathroom, trying (usually without success) not to wake Tommy and trying at the same time not to wet myself in a catharsis of terror.

I'd had time to think about all of it, even in my dreams. My thought patterns have a discipline and a duty; they follow a structure. As they began their walk down inevitable paths, I began to understand not so much what I did know, but the important aspects of what I didn't. I needed advice and expertise of a particular kind, but I wasn't sure exactly what it was. In all the articles I'd read about either myself or Colorado or the Wolf, only one person had expressed ideas that resonated.

I'd asked Kirby about our guest, based on her past CIA and NSA experience, wondering if she'd ever heard him mentioned.

"Him?" She grinned. "I know more about Mr. Man than that. Let's just say that his penis and my vagina have actually crossed paths in the past." Then a frown. "Which might prove to be a problem, actually. Mr. Man is a little on the stiff and proper side, and he was married at the time, so ... " She snapped her fingers. "You know who else knows him? Dr. Childs."

"Childs? Really?"

"You betcha." She pursed her lips, examining me. "The good doc has a serious past. He's what they call 'a respected man in many circles.' Mr. Man likes and respects him, too—which is saying something."

"Why is that?"

She rolled her eyes. "Mr. Man is one of those smart guys who knows just how smart he his. I'm not saying he's arrogant—he's actually pretty nice, if you like the type. But he puts everyone he meets into a box pretty quick, and once you're there ... let's just say, it's a life sentence."

Her comments about both men had intrigued me; and, following that blind instinct, I had made the decision to have Kirby contact Dr. Childs on my behalf. Now here we were, sitting in a conference room waiting for our visitor to arrive.

A light knock on the door, and it opens a moment later. Dr. Childs appears first, followed by the person I'm here to speak to—ex–CIA analyst Michael McKay. I rise to meet him, sticking out my hand for him to shake.

"Thanks very much for agreeing to come see me, Mr. McKay," I tell him.

He takes my hand and gives it a gentle shake. He has a strong grip but soft hands. They hold onto my own for a moment longer than is really necessary as he looks into my eyes. "It's my pleasure and my honor," he says, in a voice like his hands, soft but strong.

McKay is as average-looking as they come. He's about five feet ten, with thinning brown hair, brown eyes, and a face that manages to hover between normal and handsome. He's lean, with long arms and longer legs all fitted into a very expensive, obviously tailored gray suit, which he wears with a vest and tie.

His eyes are his most captivating feature. They are the one thing on the outside that reveals what and who he is on the inside. They belong on an eagle or a hawk. They are depthless, intelligent, and piercing. I feel pinned and very much seen by that gaze.

I smile a little. He surprises me by smiling back. "I know, I know," he says. "I look exactly how you'd expect a CIA analyst to look."

I glance at Kirby, who grins and shrugs. "Mr. Man can be a little unnerving like that," she chirps. "He definitely takes those eyes to bed with him, though, I can vouch for it."

McKay colors a little, then smiles and sighs, turning toward her. "The inestimable Miss Mitchell. How are you? How have you been?"

"Like you'd expect, Mr. Man. I'm still just me, me, and me all the time."

The smile drops to a faded grin. "Just what I'd expect and hope to find," he murmurs, in a voice thick with memory. He glances at me. "Since she has no concept of privacy about some things, I'm going to guess that Miss Mitchell told you she was my one indiscretion?"

I shrug, embarrassed. "Ah ... well. You know. Kirby."

McKay grins, and it transforms him. It's all brightness and strength, and it matches his eyes. It's like watching a curtain being pulled away from some hidden inner fire. "Don't be embarrassed for me, Mrs. Barrett. I knew what I was getting into with Kirby Mitchell. She's not responsible for the loss of my marriage; she was just one of the many barometers that predicted that outcome as the most likely."

McKay's naked grin is infectious, like Kirby's, and I return it. "Thanks. But call me Smoky."

"As long as you'll call me Michael."

"But never Mike, isn't that right, Mr. Man?" Kirby teases.

"'Never' is an understatement, Miss Mitchell," McKay replies coolly, without missing a beat. He rolls his eyes at me. "She's always called me that. Never varied it, either."

Kirby shakes her head and rolls her eyes in return. "Well, duh—that's your name, Mr. Man." She purses her lips. "It's not like anyone's ever spent much time calling me Miss Mitchell, either."

McKay inclines his head. "Point taken."

"Do we want to get seated and begin, then?" Dr. Childs asks. "Can I get anyone a cup of coffee? It's a fresh pot and a delicious blend." Kirby and I decline. McKay accepts. Dr. Childs nods once. "I'll be right back," he says, heading out the door.

"He didn't ask you how you like yours," I say to McKay.

He smiles. "He never forgets how anyone takes their coffee. At least, I've never seen it."

"So you've know each other a long time, then?"

McKay shrugs. "Longer than some, shorter than others."

Kirby chuckles. "Mr. Man is not a big sharer. *Big* believer in the 'no answer, answer.'"

"Guilty as charged," he allows, without a hint of defensiveness. "Old habits die hard. I'm a big believer in protecting the privacy of others once they entrust me with it."

"Me, too," I say.

"Yes," he says, nodding, appraising me with those hawk eyes again. "I'd expect that. It's one of the many reasons I agreed to your request to come and talk. Using that as a lead-in, I want to be clear about two things: I won't ever reveal any information that is covered by past security agreements I've signed or that would be outside your clearance. Secondly, you can count on my discretion and silence regarding anything we discuss today." He frowns. "I know some call me a hired gun due to my paid media consultation, but you shouldn't let that worry you. Money is money, and money is nice, but money is not the truth. The truth is important to me. You don't need to worry that I'll ever get the two of them mixed up in my head."

"I appreciate the reassurance, Michael," I say. "And I believe you."

"You should," Kirby pipes in. "Mr. Man's even stood up under torture, haven't you?"

A considered silence passes that gives me the sense that Kirby has almost, but not quite, pushed too far. "A story for another time," McKay finally says, in a tone hovering between cheerful and subdued. "But thank you for the reference of confidence, Miss Mitchell."

"My pleasure, Mr. Man," Kirby says. "Sorry if I said too much."

He shakes his head and flashes that grin again, letting it clear the air. "I trust you with my secrets more than most, Miss Mitchell," he says. "You know that. Just as I know you never say anything without thinking about it first or by accident, whatever else you might want people to think."

"People can think what they want, Mr. Man," Kirby snaps, but then she winks. "Point taken and point received. I'll watch those lips and sink no ships."

It's a fascinating conversation for me to watch between these two secretive people. I have known Kirby for a few years now. I count her as a friend, and I trust her with my life and the life of my family. Aside from that one secret she gifted me, however, I know very little about her past.

She and McKay are porcupines of a feather: smooth on the outside but thorny and brambly on the inside, with hidden grottoes and valleys that few—if any—will ever see. It dispels any mystery about their coupling. That shared inner mystery is what drove them together, however they were together.

Dr. Childs breaks into this when he arrives holding two cups of coffee. He places one in front of McKay, keeping the other for himself. "One sugar, no cream, that's correct, Michael?"

"You know it is, Doctor," McKay says and smiles, followed by a sip from the cup and a nod of genuine appreciation. "That's good coffee."

Dr. Childs takes a seat on my side of the table but three chairs away. McKay has taken the seat across the table, in front of me.

"Do you want me to leave, boss-woman?" Kirby asks.

"Actually, no," I tell her. "I'd like you to stay. You might have something to offer on all this that would help me."

"You're the boss. Besides, if I'm not mistaken, that door has a steel inner core and a pretty fancy alarm system to go along with it. Am I right, doc?"

Dr. Childs sips from his cup, nods. "Of course. Security can never be a hobby and still be called security, after all. The walls of this office are similarly protected. It would take quite a while for even a dedicated and well-armed individual to gain entrance, by which time we'd have exited via the private elevator in my back-most office."

"Still the strategist, I see," McKay says, raising his coffee cup in a toast of approval.

Make that three porcupines of a feather, I muse, gazing on Dr. Childs with new eyes.

McKay gestures in my direction. "I'm here for you, Smoky. Why don't I let you have the floor?"

I struggle to gather my thoughts, wishing I'd made some notes to refer to. This is the whole problem, of course, and the reason I'm here. Focusing on this helps me.

"If you don't mind, I'd appreciate you humoring me first. Give me a layman's explanation of what it is you do, and assume that I know nothing."

He smiles and nods. "It's the most common request I get." He relaxes back into his chair a bit, thinking for half a moment before beginning to speak. "An analyst reviews information for the purposes of providing future predictions about it. This could be in response to a current threat, but most analysis is a constant ongoing action. The ideal for any analyst is not catching bad guys after they become a problem, but recognizing their potentials before they have the opportunities to fully realize them. In the best-case scenario, analysis should be more about prevention than response."

I consider this. "But both situations must have their own protocols, right? One's an active chase, while the other's a preventative maintenance action. The whole approach must be different for each."

He nods. "In the case of a current threat, focus narrows. The same basic tools are applied, but more assumptions are allowed because more real-world data is known. We're no longer dealing with an unknown number of possible outcomes or avenues of attack." McKay gives me a pointed look. "At their base, though, both methods are guided by the principles of structured analytic theory."

I smile, raising my eyebrows in query. "Which—speaking for the remaining ninety-nine-point-nine percent of human beings—is what, exactly?"

He considers for a moment before answering. "Structured analytic theory examines, reverse-engineers, and models the actions of heuristics in thought. Heuristics are the internal patterns that our actions of thought *follow* in order to arrive at conclusions regarding the information life presents us."

I blink, trying to assimilate this intellectual mouthful. "I'm not sure I completely follow."

McKay smiles, undaunted. He's been at this particular nexus of confusion before and is confident in his ability to navigate us through it. "You have to think of it this way: In heuristics, we are not concerning ourselves with the content of the information itself, but with the literal, structural ways in which that information is processed. Doing so reveals the presence of enduring patterns, ones we all share."

He shrugs. "Speaking literally, heuristics *is* the human behavior of information processing. The goal is simple: greater and greater economies of thought. How to reach the most correct answer necessary at the fastest possible speed." McKay glances at Kirby. "You tell me, Miss Mitchell—in a race for survival, what's the best way of ensuring you get to that right answer first?"

Kirby grins. "The best way, of course, is to already have the right answer, Mr. Man. Thinking is dying, once the time for action's arrived."

McKay returns her grin, nodding his approval at the same time. "That's exactly right. Which is why the primary action of heuristics is the reduction of the necessity of choice in regards to information. This is primarily accomplished through the actions of pattern recognition and by the combining of smaller parts into larger meaningful wholes which require them."

I hold up a hand to stop him. "I'm pretty sure I'm following along, but you're seriously stretching my brain here. I need some concrete examples."

"Sure. But first, let's look at one last little bit of theory. Take a look at the word *information*. What does it mean, really? Well, the simplest way of viewing it is as a functional reality: It's not information unless some kind of relationship is involved. That is, until the meaning of one thing becomes relevant to modifying the meaning of something else, the concept we recognize as *information* doesn't exist in any functional sense. Do you follow?"

I give him a thumbs-up. "I'm good."

"Okay, so then for your example, let's look at driving a car. When you first begin to learn how to drive, every time you enter the vehicle and during all the time you are driving, to some degree you are required to note the interrelationships of all the parts involved constantly and to recognize them newly in every moment that passes. Nothing is on automatic yet. As you go along in the process of learning and your confidence and ability grow, the number of relationships you're required to be aware of reduces, as well as the number of new moments in which you are required to note their presence. The actions of driving the car itself probably become almost entirely automatic." He spreads his hands. "This is a good thing: It frees up your attention to be placed on events exterior to the vehicle; for example, the actions of other drivers. You are now able to do more while thinking less about it as you do.

"The point being, the action of heuristics is just that: You are reducing the number of *relationships* that must be newly examined in each new moment of application and reducing them to as close to zero as possible.

"Imagine yourself as a child, as a newborn infant just learning about the world that surrounds you. In your world every relationship, being new, is potentially as important as every other relationship. Through the process of learning, heuristics creates rules of thumb, patterns to recognize, and so on, that allow for greater economies of thought. Where less is required to be considered before more is put into action.

"Mostly, it's a good thing. As a process, it's endured because it works more than it fails." McKay's gaze on me is filled with self-amusement. "The problem, of course, is that it does fail. Reduction of the number of choices you're required to consider speeds up the process of thought, true. But, as it does this by allowing for assumptions to become more or less permanent, it also forms the basis for bias and for all assumption-based error."

I purse my lips, frowning—and then I smile. "I actually follow all of that."

McKay nods. "It only seems difficult from a distance. Examined, it's intuitive."

I consider everything he's told us so far. "Back to structured analytic theory, then. What's its role in all this?"

"To quote myself: 'Structured analytic theory examines, reverse-engineers, and models the actions of heuristics in thought.' What benefits does this confer? It allows us to recognize common errors in information processing and to thus account for their potential."

He holds up a finger. "For example: There are protocols for brainstorming sessions that specifically call for allowing anyone to present any idea, no matter how ridiculous, radical, or off-the-wall. No heckling of any kind is allowed. The idea is to free up thinking in general." He smiles. "But one of the patterns identified in structured analytic theory was that the presence of a boss could hamper the brainstorming process. Underlings were more likely to censor themselves in some way when in the presence of someone higher up on their command channels. The solution? You can limit brainstorming sessions to groups of peers, or you can have the senior person remain but have them openly acknowledge this stumbling block. They can then declare a moratorium on any consequences for what one says during the brainstorming session and make it absolute and without exceptions."

"Makes sense," I say.

"It does," he agrees, nodding. "Most of structured analytic theory is that way—and should be. It's an entirely pragmatic field. Remember 'theory' isn't 'philosophy.' In structured analytic theory, we're trying to create the purest observer possible, that's all. Not the most morally correct observer or the one with the most popular conclusions." He taps the tabletop to underscore his point. "We want the one who will derive the most *applicably* correct conclusions from the information he's presented." He cocks his head as he looks at me. "That's the short-form explanation of my field. Do you need me to lecture some more, or ... ?"

"No," I say, nodding and smiling my thanks, "that was perfect." I look off, collecting my thoughts. "Michael, it wouldn't be melodramatic for me to say that a bomb went off in the middle of my life and the lives of my team. We weren't just attacked—war was waged against us."

"I can't imagine anyone arguing with you about that," he answers, his voice quiet.

"So now, I'm going to gather these people back up. Then, I'm going to send them—and myself—back into the same fight that just blew them apart." I look at him. "Now, that alone I could deal with. We've been to that place before. The problem involves what we're adding—and that's a problem of scale."

He frowns. "I'm not sure I understand."

"I read an article that quoted you on some of the things you said regarding what happened in Colorado. What resonated with me, mainly, was your observation of the conflict between what we saw and what it all seemed to mean. Was it personal or political? On the one hand, we have that video the Wolf put out, which for all its production value, is ... strange. It's almost prototypical, in a way that could be authentic—but might not be.

"Then there is the museum itself, the sheer size of the place. Clearly, that's a lot of resource, and it sure doesn't involve just a single person."

"True."

"Add to that fact that, when you examine the timing, and I mean the timing of everything: my team being called to Colorado; the girl who jumped out of that car trunk and first threatened me, then warned me, then was killed; the discovery of the museum itself and the whole operation—it appears deliberate, like we were drawn there on purpose. But then the Wolf says the discovery of it all by us was a violation, one that's made him angry. Which is true?"

"You said it was a problem of scale."

I nod. "Yes. I'm used to hunting the lone killer. The single individual or, sometimes, a killing team. It's very rare for me to be considering the motives of a group larger than two or three people." I pause, thinking. Looking for the words to explain the one part of the puzzle that bothers me so much.

"I ... I know the shape of these guys. I know their authentic scent—their true reality, in form—when I see it. That doesn't mean I can always see it. The point is more that I know it when I do. Serial offenders are serial offenders and nothing else, once you see their true faces. The hunger, the need, the acts, and what drives them—no other criminal is quite the same. It's not something that can be approximated, you understand? It's the real deal, or it's not, and there's just no wiggle room."

"I do understand," he says, quietly. "Terrorists are quite similar, in their most realized form. The true fanatic is unrecognizable as anything else, once you've seen them."

I lean back, running a hand through my hair. Feeling my frustration and my fear rise inside me. "That's my problem. Really, it comes down to two men. Ben, the man who kidnapped me into the bunker, and the Wolf."

He frowns. "How do you mean?"

I spread my hands. "Ben was the real deal. He was right up next to me, whispering in my ear. I felt the heat of his ... his *wanting*. His *need*. He wasn't there to do his duty or to throw anyone off the scent. He was there for me, and it was the best and most important moment in the world to him."

"And the Wolf?"

"Again: authentic. I don't care how prototypical or stereotypical that video was. And it's true, there may be aspects of it that were designed to be misleading. The authenticity was in the acts. In the choices of victim. There was a—" I struggle for the words—"a cruelty in his choices that was just too visceral. He may have shown off some lies, but he also revealed himself, at least to me. He was there, doing those things, because it's exactly what he is. It's the only place he wanted to be."

"I see," he muses, looking off into the distance, thinking.

"Ben and the Wolf are serial murderers. That's not a temporary hobby or something you put down once you've picked it up. It's who and what you are *first*. Everything else is built around it, comes second, or serves it. So that part—those two men—belongs to me. Two individuals, and I hunt individuals.

"My problem of scale comes when you add that to everything else. Serial killers don't hunt in groups. They just *don't*! It requires too much trust. Historically, it's not the smartest strategy. Duos or teams almost invariably turn on each other in some way or become the reason one or the other gets caught."

"The Hillside Stranglers," Dr. Childs offers. "Bianchi testified against Buono for leniency in his sentencing."

I nod. "Sure. There are a number of examples, especially when it comes to male-female teams. Karla Homolka comes to mind as a particularly egregious one."

He raises an eyebrow. "Indeed."

"The point is, what they do is private, because in reality they know what they do can't be accepted by anyone. Not even by another like themselves." I nod my head once, an underlining action of self-agreement. "What they do is ugly, and they know it. Torture of another human being for pleasure is ugly. You look ugly when you're doing it. I've seen the evidence of that myself. It's not something to share or to have an audience for." I meet his eyes and shrug. "It's shameful. They can claim otherwise until the cows come home, but deep down inside, where it really counts, they regard what they need as shameful."

"But the Wolf had an audience when he put out that video," McKay counters.

"True—except that you never see his *face*. So you don't really see *him*, as far as he's concerned. You only see his actions, and he can enjoy that. He can get off on the thought of the horror or repulsion he creates in you. What he can't accept is being seen in totality, by you or the world in general, while committing those actions." I consider this truth for a moment, rolling it around in my mind. "You can't dress up the final act. There's no way to make it pretty. It can only reveal all the worst possibilities of the person involved." I look into his eyes. "I can't overemphasize the truth of this. This is why packs of serial killers are just never found."

"I think I'm starting to see your point. About your problem of scale, I mean."

"It's a problem of too many factors. The street—an entire block of people—being watched and controlled by Ben, with the help of his wife. The museum. The girl and the religious tie-in." I pause. "The betrayal of my own assistant director." I bring my hands into each other, forcing the fingers to bounce off one another. "These things don't belong together. I don't know how to view them, or the right way of thinking about them, to lead me to what does belong to me."

"The Wolf."

"Yes. The Wolf and whoever else is working with him." I sigh and smile. "This is why I asked to see you. I need you to help me understand *how* to think about this problem. I'm not asking you to come up with the answers for me—I'm asking you for some guidance in how to view the motives of a murderous group with the same confidence I view the motives of a murderous individual." I stare down at my hands and feel the great darkness at my back. "Lacking that, I'll still be too ... off balance to gather my team back up, much less to do any of the rest of it."

A long silence follows. McKay clears his throat. "I can give you some advice. But I want to make sure I have all the facts first. I don't know anything about the involvement of an entire block of residents, for example, or the fact they were all being watched. Do you mind taking a minute to fill me in on everything—start to finish—after which I'll tell you what I think?"

So I do. I tell him about Maya, the girl who'd put a shotgun to my pregnant belly, and her shouted warnings regarding the "Black Gloves." I tell him everything that happened in the bunker; about what Ben said and did; about the museum and its atrocities, including the captive family of humans-become-animals. I explain the surveillance setup I found and relate the story of the older couple who'd killed themselves, and about how they'd seemed more like hostages than willing participants. I explain how the computer towers, along with the footage each contained, had gone missing. I tell him everything, leaving nothing out other than my own reactions in the aftermath.

"I'm not asking you to tell me what all this is or means," I say, when I'm done. "I'm hoping that you can point me in the direction of a ... a way of thinking about, or looking at, all of it that doesn't just add up to more and more confusion. Each time I look at the whole, at all the variables involved, I get lost. One thing contradicts the other, and on, and on." I smile. "I need a logic machete of some kind. Something that'll help me pick a path through what looks like an impenetrable forest."

He is quiet, for a time, once I finish talking. He clears his throat. "That is quite a story, Smoky, and I've heard some that would stand your hair on end. I like your analogy, though: a logic machete. I'm happy to offer my views, and I do think some of them can be helpful." He sips from his coffee cup, then sits back, hands clasped on his stomach, and stares at the ceiling for a few moments. He blinks rapidly a few times, a sign of collecting his thoughts.

"The greatest part of what I do, in the end, is to identify patterns of thinking that lead to bias. Once those patterns are identified, I list them out—literally—so that they can be used in a deconstructive way." He gestures, but his eyes aren't really here or seeing us. He's dropped into his own brilliance, the thing he was made to do. "I mean, what is bias, basically? It is just another form of certainty. What is certainty? A factor you don't believe needs to be reconsidered in terms of its established truth." His hands move toward each other, flat, fingertip to fingertip, then apart. "One makes the other, because they're the same thing ultimately, and it's a constant process.

"Cognitive thought, at its heart, is really the action of comparison. As new information comes into the system, it is compared against all the existing conclusions in the system. The result is either the modification of existing conclusions, the formation of new ones, or as a corollary, the rejection or modification of the new information itself." His eyes refocus for a moment, drilling into mine without effort, seeing me before disappearing again into his internal wilderness. "This is why specific identification of bias as a broad action works. The action of searching for it forces you to reexamine information that you've assumed doesn't require it. It's a deconstructive, resistive, unnatural action. A discipline, as opposed to an instinct."

I glance at Kirby and am surprised to find her attentive, devout without a hint of an eye roll or a sarcastic comment waiting in the wings.

"I have a saying I came up with that then leads to another saying," McKay continues, smiling faintly in self-irony, letting us know he doesn't take himself as an author of truth, just a talker about it. "The first is that an analyst should be detail oriented but cannot be obsessive-compulsive. Why? Because the obsessive-compulsive *must* have the answer, and that's just not always on the table. The analyst must always understand that there are going to be questions left unanswered, and that it's not the finding of *all* the answers that's required to solve the problem—only the finding of the answers that matter.

"Which leads into my other clever saying: Sometimes you must ignore the forest and look for *the* tree. It's not that you want to let go of the ability to see the big picture. It's that you must discipline yourself to deliberately ignore it from time to time in order to force yourself to reexamine your assumed constants—your ever-potential biases." At this, his eyes refocus on mine, and he is fully back with us. "Which is what I believe my best advice to you would be, in your current situation."

I frown, seeing the larger concepts he's communicated but not their specific application to me. "How so?"

He spreads his hands wide and shrugs. "If the problem is scale, then you have deliberate actions you can take in analyzing it. The first and most obvious one would be to ignore it. Stop looking at the big picture. Accept that perhaps the scale *is* too large to be known—and move on. Focus on the details until you find that one fact that you can establish as undeniable truth. Squeeze all the bias out of it, like you'd squeeze blood from a stone, and establish it as a fact. That fact will then lead you forward to other discoveries."

"Like one of those one-thousand-piece puzzles," Kirby offers. "Right, Mr. Man? My dad and I used to do them. You find the corner and edge pieces first, then you build inward from there."

McKay inclines his head in acknowledgment. "That's a nearly perfect metaphor."

"Well, that's because I'm a nearly perfect person, Mr. Man," Kirby says, grinning at him and giving me a wink.

"You said there were two options when scale is a problem," Dr. Childs says, a gentle nudge to remind us of the bookmark in our conversation.

"Yes," McKay answers. He purses his lips. "The second is not so much a strategy, in the same way as the first. It is more of an additive—a practice in perspective. Look at the fact of the scale itself as its own whole and fully individual detail. Why did they use a forest? Why *not* just use a tree?" He tilts his head and raises his eyebrows. "Think about it. As I mentioned before, in my line of work, scale can be an identifying factor of the player. Similar to your concept of signature. If the resources involved are excessive, a big player is involved. It's a natural reflex: If you have the money or the spies or the armies or the—well, you get the idea—why not use them?"

"Yes. Still makes sense."

"What if the act itself is huge, while the resources involved are relatively small? The events of nine-eleven come to mind. Just four planes to change the world. This is a signature all its own: the signature of statement. To attract attention, to sow terror and fear. Statement, as a signature, generally couples with the psychology of scale: the need for big acts which the world will witness. This speaks of belief. Of commitment." His eyes are on mine again, and I catch a brief glimpse of a large, tired sadness. It surfaces, then dives again.

"Of the fanatic. Surely you must be familiar with this in your line of work? In relation to the kinds of men you deal with?"

I blink at him as I realize—he's one hundred percent right. "It's one of the very first things I understood about them," I say, hearing the faraway softness in my own voice now, with that unfocused quality of the present due to the presence of some internal monolith—one your life revolves around. "How empty they are and how aware they are of their own sense of emptiness. It's constant and crushing. It's what drives them to do what they do: You need huge things to fill huge, empty spaces."

McKay nods. "That makes perfect sense."

"But it's also the fact of what that emptiness is. I mean, what it really is. It's that they can't sense themselves fully until they've understood how others perceive them first. They don't exist, really, until they know they've been seen."

"Couldn't you really say that about any of us?" McKay asks.

I give him a lopsided smile. "You could—except that most of us, for the most part, live as who and what we really are. The process goes in reverse for serial killers: The normal face is the mask. It is *not* them. So they aren't actually seen by us until we see the results of the actions that belong to their hidden faces. They are what they love."

"So are we all," McKay observes.

He's right, of course. We are attracted to our own obsessions magnetically, inexorably. What we love is really just another word for what we cannot do without. Sometimes it's something you stumble across, like the love of movies or of reading a good book. Other times it's an inevitable result, the sum you are drawn to by something within you.

I am able to look at all the horrors and all the awful results of the terrible men I hunt because in the end, I love the result of what I am able to do with that looking. When I am building their pictures in my mind from nothing, and a piece clicks into place that I know belongs—it's a rush. Sometimes it's brief and small, sometimes it will be large and expansive, but a burst of pure pleasure, without a doubt. Without that payoff, I would be unable to integrate the things I've seen.

I glance at Dr. Childs and find he is looking back at me in return. He smiles, as if he knows what I'm thinking. I suppose he does. This was his point to me earlier, given a different form or shade of nuance. Because I have the ability to find those answers, I am able to balance the results, to me, of the horrors I witness.

I feel something, a leviathan something, tumble slowly through me. A sense of companionship outside my family, of being with like-minded people who understand me, if only professionally.

I miss my team. I understand this truth as it vocalizes inside me. *I miss what I do.*

It's an uplifting, empowering truth, for all the bittersweet it brings. My heart clenches once in a single, deep ache of longing. But then, this is not the same as the pain that drove me underground. This is the pain of the need that will drive me forward, and so I grab onto it with both hands and hold it tight, letting it hurt me the way only the things we love can.

"Don't stop now, Mr. Man," Kirby says, but her watchful gaze is on me as she says it. "You're on a roll." I can feel her own attentiveness, for a brief moment, just as hawklike in its own way as McKay's is when he makes direct eye contact. Then it passes, seeming satisfied with whatever it had found.

"Some other observations on the subject of scale," McKay says, picking up from where he'd left off as though he'd never stopped speaking. "One would be: Just because it's big doesn't mean it takes a lot of people to run it. Perhaps it's simply efficient or run by a small and ruthless group—or both. One of the fundamental components of terrorism is that it leverages fanaticism, allowing a small number of individuals to create carnage on a large scale.

"The same fundamental applies to the beginnings of most revolutions. They always start with a small, dedicated core group, which is why the usual result is not freedom, but a transfer of power."

He pauses, studying me. "Look, Smoky—at some point, every analyst has to commit to a hypothesis. It's a difficult thing. But once committed, the point becomes not to start big, but to start small. You have your beginning hypothesis? Good. To use Kirby's apt analogy, that's one of the corner or edge pieces of the puzzle. Now go and prove it. Find the next piece that fits.

"Your basic assumption is that the men involved in this are genuine in terms of their desire to kill for pleasure. Next is your assumption that men of that type don't operate in large groups. Fine. I can give you many examples of single men who control large groups, through ruthless actions, to fulfill goals that are entirely personal to them. There's nothing wrong with your hypothesis on the surface.

"Instead of focusing on how the scale involved disproves your hypothesis—*commit* to it. Ignore the forest; focus on the tree. Consider how such a large-scale operation *would* be run by a small group of men, or even just a few men, rather than allowing the scale itself to deter you. If it's impossible for something to be, and yet it is, then either it's no longer impossible, never was, or what you think you see is an illusion."

"Ruthless blackmail of some kind seems to be a factor, maybe," I allow, feeling the statement drag its feet as it comes out of me. Fear and uncertainty have been the most stable features of my life lately. Certainty and a commitment to knowing are difficult. Expressing certainty feels almost fraudulent and comes with the pain of an atrophied muscle being put back to work.

McKay doesn't seem to notice. He agrees with my statement, encouraging it. "An old, well-proven tool, with plenty of past and current use by intelligence agencies and dictatorial governments."

"Not my personal favorite, though," Kirby muses. "Either your operative resents you for it and is always looking for an angle to get himself out—meaning he hates your guts. Or he doesn't care because the relationship satisfies some other personal interest—meaning he's some kind of weirdo or psychopath with something extra-special icky worth blackmailing him over." She grins. "I'll take a good lie over the haters and the nutters every day of the week."

"You make valid points," McKay agrees. "Of course, no one hates as purely as the true believer once he or she has discovered they've been lied to." He glances at me. "Which is something for you to keep in mind as you pursue your investigation, Smoky. Based on your hypothesis versus the scale involved, it could become relevant."

"I don't think I understand."

He purses his lips. "Well, it's a conspiracy of some kind. Conspiracies, like the men you hunt, don't spread the truths of their nature over a large group. The whole truth is known only to those who formed it."

I consider this, nodding. "Makes sense."

"Conspiracies, unlike their usual portrayal in books and movies, tend to arise organically. The opportunity presents itself, and then the potential for the conspiracy is recognized, as opposed to the other way around. This holds true for most criminal conspiracies."

"Also makes sense."

"If we follow your line of thinking and your hypothesis and compare it to the size of the operation, what's one of the components required to make it work? In a purely functional sense, I mean."

I draw a blank for a single, long moment, and then the obvious answer comes to me. "Proxies. Cutouts." I pause. "Innocents." I consider this, and as I watch the parallels and corollaries it sends my thoughts chasing after, I realize that I'd been right to consult with McKay. "It's not uncommon for highly organized serial killers to have families and for those family members to be unaware of their 'other' activities."

"The BTK killer comes to mind," Dr. Childs chimes in. "He was married for thirty years or more, as I recall, and I believe he had children. None of them suspected."

"Right," McKay agrees, nodding. "When Miss Mitchell referred to her preference for a 'good lie,' she was speaking of something quite similar to the lies your organized offenders tell their families. The masks they wear. How do such people react, once those masks are removed?"

"It depends on the type and length of the relationship," I answer, "but it pretty much ruins their lives. Particularly in terms of their ability to trust in the future."

"I can imagine. So expand that dynamic to the group conspiracy, which operates on a larger scale and through multiple layers. The proxies are not familial, but organizational. That organization could be religious, political, or even simply business based. Any legitimate organization of strangers who come together to forward a common purpose, even if that purpose is simply 'to do business' do so with an understanding that there will be rules everyone's expected to follow, a framework everyone will agree to operate under or within." He shrugs. "Betrayal, in a group sense, is when a smaller subgroup is benefiting in some way by violating the agreements the rest of the group expects them to be following. The greater the benefit, added to the degree the rules were broken to achieve that benefit—the greater the betrayal."

"I can see that," I say.

"There are other potent factors, too, of course. The more personal the group purpose being forwarded and the more dearly held it is by the various members of the group, the greater that betrayal becomes. The more other members of the group give up or risk to forward the group purpose—again, the greater the betrayal perceived.

"This is why betrayal on Wall Street, while reviled, is less surprising than betrayal of one's revolutionary compatriots or the fellow members of one's religious organization."

"The liar: revealed once, never trusted twice," Kirby quotes.

"Who said that?" I ask her.

She grins and inclines her head to indicate McKay. "Mr. Man, of course."

McKay seems surprised, then smiles sheepishly. "I suppose I do tend to enjoy my memes when I teach, don't I?"

Kirby reaches over and pats his hand. "Only in the most effective way possible, Mr. Man. I have to admit, they're pretty mnemonic."

"Always good to hear. But then, you were hardly ever the airhead you pretended to be, were you, Miss Mitchell?" He grins. "Well, you were—but only in the most effective way possible."

She sticks her tongue out at him. "I'm not responsible for the misconception of others."

McKay returns his attention to me. "If it turns out that your problem of scale does, in fact, involve large numbers, then the true believers are always one of your points of entry." He waves a hand, as if to indicate a number of different options. "The honest worker who finds out that the company retirement fund is being looted. The churchgoer who never misses a tithe and then sees her pastor wearing Armani suits, driving a new Mercedes, and buying million-dollar homes. The true believers—especially when they have kept the faith expected—are the weakness of any criminal conspiracy, because they become its greatest enemy once the conspiracy is revealed.

"The core of any conspiracy is that it is hidden, so it deals in lies. It obfuscates with deliberate and planned intent, often through many layers. The cleverest have many layers indeed, some of which—in the same way as your lone offenders—are designed for the sole purpose of leading one away from the truth.

"True believers are different. They are not, or were not, knowing members of the conspiracy. Once the conspiracy is revealed to them, their information is not designed to hide, support, or obfuscate the conspiracy. They may not know everything you need them to, but the information they give will tend to be the most reliable. When what you are searching for is cloaked in lies, reliable information is your most priceless commodity." He smiles. "But then, you know this already. Every good law enforcement person does, I'd imagine."

"Nothing scares a crime lord more than a wife who's just found out he has a young, blond mistress," Kirby says, winking at me. "Speaking from experience, of course."

"A man's wife once led me through an acre of woods, in the middle of the night, to a small shed her husband had put up on their property," I say, my voice in a murmur as I lose track of them all just a little, the memory becoming too vivid, in the way the worst memories do. "She was still wearing her nightgown and a fluffy pair of slippers. The shed looked normal inside— just a rocking chair and a small table, with some cigarettes, books, and girly magazines. But we found a hidden entrance under the table, and it led us underground to this earthen room. He'd tortured, murdered, and buried six teenage girls there."

"She had no idea about her husband, but she took you straight to the shed?" McKay asks, frowning.

I nod. "She noticed him leaving after she'd gone to bed, maybe two or three nights a week. One night she decided to follow him because she was sure he was cheating on her. She was pretty puzzled when he didn't even get in their car but just started walking into the woods. She followed him all the way to the shed, but there were no windows, so she went back home and to sleep.

"The next day, while he was working, she crept back out there. She found the cigarettes—which he said he'd quit smoking—and of course all the other misdirectors he'd left there for her to find and feed her denial. Which they did. She was so relieved to find out that her suspicions about him cheating were wrong, she stopped suspecting anything else."

Her face comes to me, and her name: Denise. "Little Denny" is what her husband called her, and it was apt. She'd been a small woman, just a hair over five feet tall, and she was slight in all ways, as some women are. Quiet, shy, self-effacing. Her husband had been a quiet type, too, but tall—he towered over her when they stood side by side. She was young, just twenty-seven, but they'd gotten married when they were both nineteen, straight out of high school.

"We dated the last year in high school," she'd said, speaking so softly I had to lean closer to hear her clearly. She'd pointed at the wedding photographs posted, along with so many others, on their living room walls. "John was on the basketball team. I did some volleyball—though I wasn't really that good. He was the first man I ever slept with, on our wedding night," she'd added, coloring as she realized what she had just revealed.

When I called on her in the dark of the night, I learned that they had three children. The oldest was just seven, a chubby, cute little thing who woke up to ask what was going on, rubbing her eyes and yawning as she did. I watched Denise grow strong in an instant, in that warm, calm, firm, earth-mother way. "Everything's fine, honey," she'd said, in a voice that left no doubt. "Go back to bed."

The child had obeyed without a hint of concern, wholly mollified. It was the one place where Denise wasn't slight, and it had given me some hope for her. I had latched onto this one, visible strength, letting it lead the terrible words I had to speak to her.

"Denise, I'm afraid I have some very difficult news to give you. It's about your husband, and no, he's not dead—but still, it's going to be very difficult for you to hear. I need you to prepare yourself and to try and be strong for your children. Okay?"

Denise had been extraordinarily pretty, with big, dark, luminous eyes, cream-perfect skin that I instantly envied, and black hair that fell loose to her shoulders. I remember, now, how shiny her hair had been, even in the half-light glow of her living room lamps.

I remember how still she'd gone and how quickly, like a river that had been frozen in an instant by a photograph or a spell. Only her eyes had changed, going wide and round, becoming twin, bottomless lakes lit by moonlight. She looked like a deer caught in the headlights of her own life.

"Okay," had been all she'd said in reply. I waited for more, but nothing came.

So I went on to tell her my terrible things. How we'd been called by the local police because her husband had been arrested trying to kidnap a fourteen-year-old girl. About the battered, black leather briefcase that had been found in his trunk and the items it had contained: a hammer with blood and hair dried on it lying atop a huge pile of Polaroids, which depicted other young girls in various states of terror, dismay, or death.

She remained in that same state of silence and preternatural stillness through it all, but I watched those eyes turn from lakes into wounds. They darkened with shock and deepened in dismay, and then they just bled tears. She cried silently, without her lips quivering once.

When I finished, a full minute went by without her saying a word. "Denise?" I asked. "Do you understand what I'm saying to you?"

Denise had not replied. I wanted to look away from those eyes, from the awful oceans they'd become, but I could not. I was as transfixed by her as she had been by the words I'd spoken.

Without warning, she'd stood up, heading for the front door. "Follow me," she'd said, speaking with that lifeless tone that always seemed to belong to the freshly murdered heart. "There's something you'll want to see. Something important." Then she was out the front door and into the night, and I was hurrying after her.

"Denise," I had said, "you should put on some clothes first, or at least some shoes." But she didn't seem to hear me. She was a woman on a mission, running away from her life and herself as she ran and led us toward the truth.

The moon had been three quarters full, a bright, white coin. It was late September, and I recall the slight chill in the air. As I chased her into the woods, I had time to reflect on the nature of denial and the components that guided it within us, into our minds and our hearts. Three acres of land, with trees, in Southern California, meant money, of a kind, for example.

Her husband, I thought, *was a good provider. They have a big house and three cars. All his smiles, in all the photographs I have seen, appeared effortless and genuine and warm. Happy.*

But then, I suppose he probably was happy. Why wouldn't John be happy? He was self-employed, making great money; he had a family that loved him and suspected nothing; all of which allowed him to do what he really loved without much effort. Nearly all the most heartless psychopaths I have encountered have had great smiles, just like John. The result, I suppose, of the satisfaction of all their self-illusions, in all directions, even while plying their evil on the world.

Denise had been the one to firmly answer that common question so many of us ask: Was it really possible for the wife of such a man to suspect nothing? The answer was yes. Of course it was possible. Most human action is involved with finding ways to ignore the truth. Denial is one of the strongest and most primeval forces within us, especially when the basis of that denial is love.

I kept pace with her, my flashlight unnecessary under the strong moon glow, until she stopped. "Here," she said, pointing at the shed. It had looked lonely and small, outlined in shadow and outdone by the trees. "I must have missed something about it. I thought I hadn't; I even came here in the day-time and looked around inside, but there must be something I didn't see." A pause, and it's an awful moment of silence, as a memory. "I guess I've never really been that smart."

Denise took me inside and took care to show me the magazines, the pack of cigarettes with an old Zippo lighter lying next to it, and the ashtray full of butts. She explained her conclusions about each, how they'd been a source of relief when compared to the possibility that he was cheating on her. I'd been patient, not rushing her, making sure I listened and that she knew it. Because by then, I'd understood that her need was as much about explaining it to herself as it was about explaining it to me.

"We spoke a few years later," I tell them, coming back to the here and now. "I don't generally revisit the families of the victims or the killers, but I had never really been able to shake her. How she'd been that night."

"And how was she?" Dr. Childs inquires.

I smile, remembering. "She was... okay. Not amazing, not awesome, not remarried, but okay. I was right about her children being the strongest part of her, and she even told me so."

"Rare," Dr. Childs observes. "I don't know that 'lucky' would ever apply to such a woman, but she most definitely beat the odds."

"Yes, she did," I agree. "It didn't ruin her. It changed her. She went through some pretty difficult times, but she survived. I got to see the kids, too. They were protective of her, naturally, but not more than you'd expect. Which is a minor miracle in itself."

"I'd call it extraordinary," Dr. Childs says.

"We talked for over two hours. Denise did most of the talking, and I listened. She told me the most dazing thing about that night was not just the news itself, but how quickly she'd flipped into a state of full belief and understanding. It had been the shed, and the way he'd always wait for her to fall asleep before he went there. Once she heard what I told her, she knew. I think if she'd never discovered it, the outcome would have been much different. She might have stood by him without irrevocable proof. But that shed and his timing ... " I shake my head. "It all came together and she understood her own denial in an instant."

I go silent, hearing and seeing her in my mind again. *"I mean, really—why go to so much trouble just to smoke and masturbate?"* she'd told me she'd asked herself. *"If you'd never shown up in the middle of the night to tell me about his arrest, I suppose I would never have asked that question. But once you had, nothing else made much sense. I knew that if you weren't lying about the arrest, then it was all just ... true."*

"Anyway," I say, smiling at McKay. "Denise is a good example of your concept in action, from my own experience."

He nods. "I'd say so. All you need to do, then, is remember that the same principle applies, regardless of scale. The innocent, true believers are your first sources of truth that are reliable, when it comes to conspiracies, and every conspiracy requires them." He grins. "There are laws, after all. Generally speaking, a person can't walk around committing acts of evil with impunity. The same is true for groups of people, whether they happen to be governments, churches, or hedge funds."

"I understand now what you meant."

"Good." He studies me for a moment. "Is there anything else?"

I shake my head. "No. Or at least, not right now. You've helped me get a grip on how to view it and how to balance what I normally do with ... whatever this turns out to be, in the end. Now I need to do that. Consider it. Think about it." I smile, glancing at Kirby. "Find those corner and edge pieces." I put out my hand. "Consulting you was the right move, Michael. You've helped me a lot."

He takes my hand, shaking it, holding it for a second in that soft-but-firm grasp as he gives me the full benefit of that hawklike gaze. "My best advice? If these men are what you believe them to be—trust your instincts, Smoky. They've proven themselves, time and again." He lets my hand go. "And of course, if you ever need my assistance, don't hesitate to ask." His lips thin, in the barest hint of anger. "I've seen those videos, too. The man or men who made them must either be killed or caged, and I'll be more than happy to lend a hand if needed."

"Thank you. I appreciate that," I tell him. "Both the advice and the offer of assistance. I'll keep each of them in mind."

"On that note," Dr. Childs says, "I think this would be a good place for us to end." He's watching me as he says this, and he is smiling.

Yes, I think, *you are right: I am ready to start doing something outside of this room, and my home, for that matter.*

"I agree," McKay says, rising out of his chair, causing each of us to do the same. He nods to Kirby. "Miss Mitchell. All in all, very nice to see you again."

She grins at him. "Likewise, Mr. Man."

"I'll show you out," Dr. Childs says.

McKay inclines his head to me one last time. "Smoky. A great pleasure, minus the circumstances, of course."

They leave the room together, and my eyes follow them, but my mind is elsewhere now.

"Kirby," I murmur. "I need you to give me two days. Then I need you to do two things."

"Which would be?"

"Find Callie and Alan, and bring them to me, and then … ," I say, sighing. "Then I need you to find out where James is hiding, and take me there."

"My pleasure on both counts," she answers cheerfully. Then she snorts. "All that talk about wolves and sheep." She shows me her killer's grin. Her eyes go flat and empty before filling back up with an arctic night. "I guess he got too caught up in complaining about the sheep to hear the flip side of his own lesson plan: Not all wolves are the same, either. Some hunt and kill better than the other wolves do."

I return her gaze, allowing myself a moment to consider, once again, the dichotomy of having a guiltless assassin as a personal friend—and then let it go. "I suppose I'll drink to that," I reply.

I look through the doorway to the conference room and am surprised at my confidence. I know the fear will return, and even the panic and terror, too. I'm not so self-deceptive as to believe you can heal a broken mind in the course of an afternoon.

But I also feel another pull, and its existence creates its own certainty, just as inexorable. It is the feeling of answers existing and being within my ability to grasp. I can sense the tumblers, turning and clicking inside me, along with the feeling that if I concentrate hard enough, they will reveal the shapes of their truths to me. This is a process that, once begun, can't be stopped. You'd have to kill me.

Not if I catch you first, I think, sending this off into the ether toward the man who made those videos.

I wonder, for the first time since this all began, if he thinks about this possibility from time to time and fears me just a little, too.

It's a good feeling, one of the corner or edge pieces to my own internal puzzle.

If you don't think about it, Mr. Wolf, then you should. Because first I'm going to put my team back together, and then?

Then we're coming for you.

PART THREE
SPEECH

CHAPTER TWELVE

"This is the place?" I ask Kirby, staring up at the broad façade of the hotel as the ever-present crowds of the Vegas Strip swirl around us.

"Room 11343," she answers.

"How did you find him?"

She grins. "After searching for weeks and coming up with nothing—and I mean no trace at all—I asked myself: If you were a really smart guy who wanted to hide but couldn't break the law to do it, how would you go about it?" She snaps her fingers, engaged in a conversation with herself. "The answer: a personal favor. The problem is, James doesn't have many friends." She pauses. "Or any, to be honest. At least not that I could find, and I looked pretty darn hard."

I sigh. "That's ... consistent."

"No, that's sad, but anyway—I still thought the idea was right. So I shifted from personal favors to professional ones, and then added in a little bit of smart. You've read his personnel files, right?"

"Sure. I reviewed them before I interviewed him. I got my position during a time the FBI was restructuring my unit. I got to handpick my team. That's a rare wish to have granted, so I took my time looking around."

"*Restructuring.*" Kirby snorts. "I know that code—it means 'someone screwed up, and the powers that be needed heads on their spikes and blood in the hallways.'"

I smile faintly. "That's fairly accurate. It wasn't a full-on bloodbath, but there were some major holes created that no one had previously expected to exist for a long, long time."

"Were they right?"

"Who?"

She rolls her eyes. "You know. The guys who usually get it wrong. The powers that be. Were they right about the need for, um, *restructuring?*"

"Strangely, yes. Rare, I know, but true." I point a finger at the hotel. "Back on topic, please? I'm getting..." I hesitate and pluck briefly at the band on my wrist, feeling the panic begin to ride in from the distance. "I want to get inside," I finish, lamely.

It's not bad, not yet. I'm not really sweating or shaking yet. It's more like a tremor in the ground that I can feel in the soles of my feet. Like wild horses or a herd of bison still blocked by the hills but coming my way.

"Can't blame you," Kirby chirps, smoothly ignoring the real issue and giving me my dignity again, something that's become a habit. "It's freaking chilly out here! Isn't this city supposed to have been built in the middle of the desert?"

"It's January, Kirby. And the desert's known for getting cold at night." I point to the hotel again. "James?"

"What division was he in for a few years, prior to the one he was in just *before* you grabbed him? Think, and it'll come to you. It was exactly the kind of place you'd put a Mr. Smarty-pants like him."

I frown, drawing a blank. Then it comes to me. "White-collar crimes. That's how he got onto my radar, actually. His clearance rate was phenomenally high when he was in that division. So high that everyone in Los Angeles had at least heard of him, even though he was posted in..." I look up at the hotel, understanding. "Vegas."

"Bingo," Kirby says, smiling and pointing a finger of approval in my direction.

"He was given the choice of his next division," I murmur. "He chose Organized Crime in Los Angeles. It's where he was from and where his mother still lived."

"The important part of all that is that he used to work here. Sin City is a heck of a place to hide if you're an insider."

"Makes sense."

"I usually do. It's one of my gifts, like how I'm sexy, or how I can kill someone with a cardboard tube from inside a roll of toilet paper. Anyway, I had Callie call his old boss, who jumped on it pretty lickety-split and got back even faster. Seems like James did a pretty big favor for the chief of operations at the rainbow behemoth, there, and used the favor to check in under an alias and pay cash." She grinned. "The old boss had to lean on the C of O pretty hard not to rat us out and warn James we were coming."

"Really? I know James's old boss. He's a crusty, scary guy. What was the favor?"

"James closed a case that would have cost the C of O his job during a time the C of O's wife was preggers."

I sigh. "That would do it. Are we sure he didn't warn him?"

She grins. "Like you said: That old boss, he's a crusty, scary guy. James is still up there. He's there pretty much twenty-four/seven, per the C of O. Room services everything and then pays the C of O in cash, who then reimburses the hotel."

"That might make someone in his position nervous after a while," I murmur. "No one needs an FBI agent losing it in the hotel they're responsible for." I run a hand through my hair. The feeling of incipient panic is still there, but the rumbling doesn't seem to be getting any closer. You can get used to the ground under your feet shaking in a constant tremble. It's the feeling of something coming *closer* that's the problem. I snap the band on my wrist twice, then straighten my spine. I'm ready but not ready, which is the same as being ready, when you're scared. "Okay. I'll go up alone and then call you when I'm done."

Kirby frowns, shaking a stern finger at me. "No ... I'll go up with you and watch you go up to the door alone. Once I see you've gotten inside, I'll hunker down by the elevators. You'll call me when you're ready to leave, and I'll come into the hallway and meet you there. 'K?"

I can't imagine Kirby hunkering down next to anything. For all the carelessness she pretends, she moves with a constant, killer's grace. But I am grateful. "Sorry, you're right." I glance at her. "And thanks, Kirby. Not just for how you've been taking care of me, but for finding him, too. I really appreciate it."

She feigns a yawn, then blinks and grins. "Oh, sorry—touchy-feely, mushy-gushy—puts me to sleep so *fast*. Ready to get out of this crowd and the cold?"

I smile. I speak Kirby, and I know this is her way of saying "you're welcome." I nod. "Lead the way, my fearless bodyguard."

"Fearless, deadly, super-*beautiful* bodyguard, you meant to say," she quips, then sets off with me following close behind. She parts the crowds without effort, moving with the grace of a deadly ballerina.

On the way up, in the elevator, I consider the nature of favors. They aren't considered an honorable currency by the decent or the strong, except in the most exigent of circumstances. In a very real way, they don't exist until you become desperate and see no other road to take.

Like me, with Kirby, these past months, I think. I study her back and am suddenly overwhelmed by a wave of gratitude that punches me in the heart and leaves me reeling.

Once the favor road's been chosen, you never forget the ones who said yes. I'll never forget what you've done for me, Kirby. Never.

I can't imagine James calling in a favor from anyone. It's as disorienting and unexpected as the first time you experience an earthquake. You don't really believe that the world could move under your feet without warning, until the moment it does. It ruins the rest of your day, or maybe your week, depending on the earthly violence involved.

The whole idea of James just ... running away ... that was even more alien. That was more like the first time I heard the thunderclap of a gunshot from a gun in my own hands. It was so unexpectedly *loud*, nothing like what I'd heard on TV or in the movies. It was terrifying, not empowering, and it sent adrenaline shooting through my body, along with the visceral demand to run, run fast, now, far. The shock was gone by the time the first clip had been emptied, but I had also been changed forever. The world had become a more dangerous place, in an instant.

Some events that change us become a certainty of the existence of the good. They become the tinder we use in the dark times to relight the fires of our hope. The first time another person kisses us, loves us, accepts us in our nakedness, metaphorical or otherwise. Other changes make us understand our mortality; and while not necessarily bad, they can't support us through darkness, because the certainty of our own death never belongs to the light. It can only be accepted; our reaction to its immobility, transformed. Gunfire and earthquakes fit the last, not the first.

I wonder if other people have been made to feel that way, because of me? I grimace and sigh. *Probably. And on more than just this occasion. This is the worst, not the first.*

Matt and Alexa and Sands, that had been the first. I'd run, far and away, and much like now, into silence. My friends had waited, but the waiting, I imagined, had changed them. The world had changed with them, around them, representing an increase in that knowledge of mortality rather than a distraction from it.

The elevator stops, and a *ding* cuts through the air, stilling my maunderings. Kirby reaches over and pulls the emergency stop button. The elevator freezes in place. The doors stay closed.

"We're here," Kirby says. "You ready?"

"More than I'm not."

She shrugs and winks. "Shucks... sometimes that's the half-second difference between who pulls the trigger first and lives."

"Your metaphors need some work."

Kirby grins at me. "I can only speak the truth, boss-woman."

"Aside from that statement itself being a lie, you mean."

"I don't lie. I never lie. I just say things other people end up believing are true."

The loud *ding* had jolted me. My already startled heart had jumped from a jog to a sprint in the space of a breath, and as calm reasserts itself, I realize this is why Kirby had pulled the emergency stop button in the first place.

"I'm ready now," I tell her. "Thanks for giving me a minute to catch my breath."

Her gaze back is uncharacteristically serious. "Just remember, Smoky-dokey: You can move at your own speed. There's nothing wrong with making the world wait. There's a heck of a lot more wrong with running on sore feet and falling flat on your face—or your ass."

"My ass."

She raises an eyebrow. "Sorry?"

"I'd rather fall on my ass. It's got built-in airbags."

Kirby gives me a dazzling smile and nods her approval. "Well—so long as you know...."

She pushes the emergency stop button back in before I can reply. The doors open, and I hesitate for only half a second before walking out onto the eleventh floor.

I'm standing in front of the door to James's room when the desire to run seizes me. It grips me violently, without warning, like a stranger attacking from behind in the dark. I raise my hand to knock, and watch my fist tremble. It's visible, more of a shake than a rattle. I could be an alcoholic in need of a drink.

What will I find once that door opens? The unknown is a vacuum that we fill with our fears. My fears are black, giant bats, too warm and too wriggling in the darkness. They are heading my way in a constant slow lope that seems crafty.

Will he be crazy? Drunk? On drugs? Perhaps he's suicidal, and he's sitting in there right now, staring at his gun. Guns can sing to you in the darkest times, black metal Sirens with round mouths made from shadows. *Pick me up*, they harmonize. *Put me to your head and* pull, *and I will give you peace*. The existence of an option can become comforting when it seems like the pain will be forever.

I turn my head and see Kirby, staring back at me. She has watchful eyes, like all predators. She does not grin or wink, because she knows I am afraid, in that way all predators know such things. She waits, meeting my gaze with her own, showing me just how steady she is. Kirby is as ever-ready as a rock, comfortable being still but waiting to be thrown.

It comforts me, as it's meant to, and I knock without thinking. *Rap-rap-rap*, three times, short and loud and hard. *Cop-knocking*, Alan once called it, and I had agreed. No one knocks on your door quite like the police. It's a sound carrying two simple messages: You will open this door, and I am not going away until you do.

I wait, craning my ears for the sound of motion, feeling both my focus and my anxiety increase. They are twin brothers, for cops. Closed doors are a threat, an enemy. They engender any possibility you could imagine, when you are the one with a badge and a gun. You learn to harness that anxiety toward creating greater focus, in the name of surviving whatever might answer.

Nothing. I knock again—four raps this time—and add my voice to the mix. "James? It's Smoky." Silence returns, but there is a minute change in the air, as though an ear or two eyes had just turned my way. "It's just me," I say. "Nobody else."

That instinct, that he is hearing me now, grows louder inside me. It's like listening for your own heartbeat in the dark. It is a sound that's always there, every day of your life, but most of the time it's tuned out. You turn your gaze inward, and it comes to you, a blood metronome, the car engine of your life. Only you can hear it in this way, but there is no doubt in that sound.

An exterior noise—that of feet shuffling across carpet—drives the inside away. The sound stops at the door, and there is silence again. "James?" I query, staring into the peephole. "Will you let me come in? Just me. Kirby is the only other person here in Vegas with me, but she's down by the elevators." I pause. "I need to talk to you, James. And I know you need to talk to me."

"Why?" comes drifting through the door, barely loud enough for me to hear it. It's more than a whisper, but it has the same reedy qualities. "Why do I need to talk to you?"

It feels like a riddle, and I hear the hoofbeats of my heartbeats again. If I give the right answer, he'll open the door. If I give the wrong one, he won't.

I'm not worried. I know the answer to this particular riddle. We are on familiar ground for me, and that is the point and the answer. "Because I have the one qualification someone in your position requires: authenticity. You know that I know what you're going through."

Weighted silence, like water, fills a pause. I glance down at the band around my wrist and realize that for the first time since I put it on, it's become meaningless. Crossing the line that would bring James and I face-to-face so that I could help him was like being in the groove of my own record again. Its familiarity aligned all my atoms, righting that sense of my own density. I was standing in my place in the world, the one that belonged to me because I had earned it.

"James, you need to open the door. Maybe I can't help you, but at least I'll be able to talk to you as a peer. And in your situation, that's a pretty rare thing."

I hear the sounds of locks clicking, and then the door opens, and he is there. His eyes meet mine. James is never vulnerable, and this always makes him seem older than he is. His gaze now is full of the weariness that constant agony creates. Weakness of any kind is such a foreign thing to see in James, it strips the years away instead of aging him. He is a walking open wound wearing the face of a boy, bleeding out on the carpet in front of me without even the ability to be ashamed.

"Oh, James...," I whisper. "I'm so sorry it took me so long to come and find you. I was weak. You deserved better—and sooner. Please forgive me."

They are mournful words, spoken in a tone that aches with regret. I hear both and feel them, but they increase my strength, not my sorrow. It is our actions that tell us who and where we are, I think. I'm only ever at my most certain when I'm facing out toward others, not in at myself.

James's lips tremble, and his eyelids flutter once. A single tear appears in the corner of each eye, wobbles once, then they both fall like stones, cutting each cheek with a sharp line of water. He sighs, and it is a sigh from his bones. It is the sound of the beaten, the self-imprisoned, the deserves-to-be-dead.

"Well, you're here now," he says. "So I guess you can come inside."

Normally, these would be sarcastic phrases, built to bite. At the moment, they're just words, barely delivered. James's eyes leave mine again and return to whatever horror he's been watching. He sways, and I get the sense I could topple him over with just a push of my finger.

He turns around and shuffles back into the room, leaving the door open behind him. I glance at Kirby, nod once, then follow. The sound of the door latching closed completes the circle of my own focus and drives the rest of the world from my awareness.

No one else exists, or has ever existed, but him and me, are the wordless words that run through me. They thud with great certainty, these wordless words, and they exist in forever, disregarding time.

The hotel suite is large. It has a living room and a separate bedroom with its own door. Where I am standing, just inside the entryway, it is dark. James is inside the bedroom with all the bulbs switched on. He's left the door flung open, a rectangular invitation of soft, bright light.

We are on a ledge, not in a room. In the land of the hopeless, where the soul starves to death.

More wordless words, and my strength only grows in the stillness of the silence of this one timeless moment. I move toward the light, made eager by having finally been relieved of the unbearable burden of worrying about *me,* ready for anything, anything at all.

Bring him food.

The back wall of the bedroom is a single, long window of glass. We are on the "good side" of the hotel—looking down on the lights of the Vegas Strip from on high. The sidewalks are fast-running rivers of people, but the streets are packed solid with cars and taxicabs. They move slowly, as a unit, ponderous as mud.

Two chairs and a small table sit off to one side, placed so the occupants can enjoy this view. James is seated in one of the chairs, gazing out of the window. As I enter, he does not look up or move at all, for that matter. He's approached the motionlessness of the dead, weighted down by all those heavy, heavy bricks of sorrow.

I know the place where he is living right now. It hurts to move in that place, a pain that is almost physical and nearly actual. Every second drags by as its own eternity, unbearable but never-ending. Suffering that cannot be borne becomes cancerous, growing like a tumor, dragging at you from every direction, until any motion at all feels like swimming with all your clothes on. You *could* swim, but if you're not going to drown, why make the effort? This becomes a habit, and that deathful stillness sets in.

Suffering is timeless. It measures its movement against the clock of its own existence. I remember, in the first month after Matt and Alexa were murdered, sitting in one place for hours at a time, unaware of the day slipping by. I cannot remember thinking anything. I can only remember feeling everything. I waited. I breathed. That was all.

I glance around the room and see the fraying edges here, too. James is not obsessive, but he is always fastidious. This room is much cleaner than my own bedroom became when I was in the same state. But the dishes from yesterday's dinner are still here, along with an untouched bowl of breakfast cereal. The bed is unmade, and I can tell from the slightly stale smell in the air that James has not requested new sheets or towels for days.

I return my attention to him, studying. He has not allowed the neglect to spread to himself yet, and this gives me hope. His hair is still damp from a recent shower, and he has shaved. His clothes are clean. He is wearing blue jeans with a black belt around the waist and an unwrinkled, unstained white shirt.

I blink, realizing in this moment that I've never really seen James, in the physical sense. The weight of his personality has always been his most defining feature.

He's beautiful, I think, wondering how I'd never noticed this before.

He wasn't masculine beautiful, like Tommy. James was literally beautiful: like a Spanish prince. His face was perfect and aquiline, his skin olive and unflawed. He had a trim, fit figure. His dark hair was only loosely styled, because it rested in a subtle, natural wave that any woman would envy.

And young—how did I never notice how young James is?

In reality, though, this is no great mystery. The answer is simple: James has never been young. His tremendous intellect, the murder of his older sister when he was really just a boy, combined with a single mother who would have needed his support in the aftermath—that was a powerful trio. More than enough to make any young boy become a man inside, and quick.

I have always mostly tolerated James. I have admired his abilities, and I have never questioned his loyalty. Friendship, though, has always seemed out of reach to me, and his fault for being so. For the first time since we've known each other, I am seeing James as a person and realizing the similarity of our histories. Not in content, but in meaning. We both grew up inside too early and learned about the sharp, pointed end of the stick of life too young.

Both of us had allowed these events to define us, but James's devotion was far more consuming. My mother had been murdered by cancer and had only been put out of her misery by my own young hand. It had been awful but random, not evil. My mother had died from her own bad luck. James's sister, on the other hand, had been murdered by a man. It had been a deliberate, horrible act. I had experienced the casual unjustness of life when I was young, while James had experienced true *injustice*.

It's made a difference between us, I realize. *Something subtle but pervasive.*

I had married—twice, now. I had experienced carrying a child, the birth of that child, and of watching her begin to grow into a person. I now had an adopted daughter and a new son. My life was more full, in terms of personal relationships, than James's. His injury was deeper and earlier. In the end, as a result, his work was his life, and his devotion was pure. It was priestlike, engulfing.

Hard not to admire.

But it makes the murder of his mother all the more crippling and significant.

I sigh and move to the table, taking a seat in the open chair. I leave the silence where it lies. Opening that door was a huge sign of trust. I'm content at the moment just to be sitting across from him.

I give myself time to collect my thoughts. The opportunities to reach him will be narrow and fleeting. Communication is motion of a kind, a distraction from the surviving of suffering. Unnecessary communication would be more than unwanted—it would be ignored. I remember tuning out entire conversations simply because they became too bromidic and pointless.

I needed to say the *right* words to James, the ones powerful enough, interesting enough, to tear his gaze away from the internal, spinning diamond of self-fascinated horror that his suffering had become.

What I really hoped was that he would speak first and give me a clue or two. The deadliest thing I could do, in this situation, would be to assume I understood what he was going through. "Wrong" had a broad geography in the land of suffering.

You probably think you'll never get past this, someone had said to me in the first two weeks after Matt and Alexa's deaths.

I had not replied, but on the inside I had hated the person who spoke, just a little. He'd had the arrogance to assume that he understood the nature of my pain, and the greater arrogance of getting it wrong, of making it two-dimensional.

I had not been worried that I would never get past it. I had been worried that I *would*. Mostly, I had barely considered the existence of the future at all. I was too busy trying to figure out the best way to kill myself.

Later, as sanity returned, I forgave him. His intentions had been good. But during that time of no perspective, trust was obliterated as a result of this action. I don't want to make the same mistake with James.

So, I wait and watch the rivers of people and the mudflow of cars. I study the lights of the hotels, and most of what I see is new to me. I've never had the inclination to gamble. This is probably only the second or third time that I've been to Las Vegas. It seems unreal and cartoonish. Everything is too bright and too huge and feels placed with the purpose of distracting its customers from some darker truth. Like a lie built from lights.

"Do you believe in God?" James asks, breaking his silence. "Or have you ever?"

"I don't know," I answer, honestly. "When I was younger, I felt like I believed. But sometimes I think I wanted more to *believe* that I believed. My mother was Catholic. Her faith was pretty strong." I smile. "So was her personality." I shrug. "I wanted her to like me."

"I've never believed in God," he says. "I lied to my mother and told her that I did. She needed that belief to survive my sister's death. It helped sustain her. She would have worried about me if she knew I didn't believe."

"Then that's a pretty nice lie," I murmur. "In my opinion."

"I never told her I was gay, either," he says, as though I hadn't spoken. And maybe, for him, I hadn't. "She was Catholic, too. No fags allowed in heaven, you know. No cocksuckers allowed through those big, pearly gates." He glances at me. "She had a very literal picture of heaven. Just like that. You know—fluffy clouds and little baby angels with harps, all that silly, ridiculous bullshit."

"She probably needed a solid picture to look at," I say. "Something tangible that she could see in her head. She'd need that, to be able to see where your sister was."

James's face twists, like a rag being wrung. Tears slice his cheekbones again. He clears his throat. "Yes," he agrees, his voice shaking a little. "That's what I thought, too." He stares at me, really seeing me now. "But you know something? I was starting to hate her for it, just a little. Not a lot. Not a *lot*. But yeah—just a little. I wondered what would happen if I told her. 'Hey, Mom, look: I don't believe in your big guy in the sky, but I'm pretty committed to sodomy.' I wondered if her love was unconditional."

His face twists again, there and then gone. "That haunts me, Smoky." His eyes are wounded and full of desperation. "That doubt. It *haunts* me. How could I have doubted my mother like that?"

"James," I chide in a soft voice, keeping it gentle. "You get to be human. And that's all that it was."

He goes silent again, but his eyes don't leave mine this time. I feel that we are still in motion, as though the concern he'd just expressed was a kind of metaphor or the tip of some iceberg. You have to work your way up to the biggest horrors in small bites and slow, careful steps.

I say nothing for a moment. I make sure my eyes stay locked with his and choose my words carefully. "I can take anything you need to say," I tell him. "Anything you need to feel. Anything you need to show. I'll never tell a soul, and I'll take it all to my grave."

"I know," he whispers. "I believe you." He is struggling to keep looking at me. His face twists again, and then his eyes go wide with horror. "It's my ... " His hand flies up to his mouth, covering it. His eyes go wider. "It's my ... " More tears appear, and this time, they do not stop. The dam inside him is about to break, and I brace myself for it. "It's my ... *fault*, Smoky! It's my *fault*!" The hand drops. "It's my *fault*!"

The words are like a mantra and are approaching the level of a shout. We have arrived at the edge. He is looking at it—his horror—in all its fullness and trying not to disintegrate as he does so.

"It's..." He draws in a breath, far too deep and long. His mouth twists like he's being strangled. His pupils are small dots in an ocean of white. He freezes in place and in time.

We've arrived, I think. *He sees it.*

"It's my *fault*, oh my *God*—it's *my* fault that my mother is dead, Smoky!" He turns to one side in his chair, doubling over, and vomits onto the carpet. He looks down at the vomit, then at me, aghast. "I'm sorry!"

I stand up and walk over to him. I look down at him and take his face in my hands. "Shh," I tell him. "Don't worry about that. I need you to listen to me, James. Look at *me*, and listen to *me*." I shake my head, a gesture of firm denial. "No," I tell him, my voice soft but firm. "It's not. It's not your fault. It's his fault. The man who did this to her. It's his fault, not yours. Not ever yours. Do you hear me?" I ask him, without expecting an answer. "He killed her, and it happened because he wanted to do whatever it was that would hurt you the most. So he took her from you, and *all* the fault for that lies with him. Not with you." I run a hand through his hair and cup his face tightly in my hands. "It is not ever going to be your fault that your mother was killed, James, any more than it was your fault that your sister was murdered. Do you hear me? I'm not lying to you, I promise. It's the truth. But if you don't find a way to believe it, you'll die inside. It's a lie that will kill your spirit."

His arms fly around my waist, and he pushes his face against me, burrowing into my belly as he howls. Howls and howls and howls, like an animal being burned alive. I hug his head to me, and I let myself cry with him, a witness to his pain.

"Not your fault," I whisper to him, as I weep and he howls. I say it over and over, again and again, willing the words into his soul. "Not *ever* your fault."

It went on for nearly five minutes, gradually lessening in strength. He winds down into silence, and his arms loosen a little around my waist, but he keeps his face pressed against me. I stroke his hair and match his silence. A few more minutes pass, and then he sighs. He turns his head so his cheek rests against my stomach.

"It's okay," I murmur. "You can stay there a little longer, if you want. I'm fine."

James doesn't reply, but he doesn't move, either. He stays that way for another few moments, letting me be the lee against the storm of life. I stroke his hair, thinking nothing. Not waiting, because waiting is a form of leaving, not a form of comforting.

He finally pushes himself away from me, and I let him, but I don't return to my chair. I gaze down at him, overwhelmed with tenderness. "It won't be the last time," I say. "It'll sneak up on you over the next few weeks, out of nowhere. But that gets better over time. If you believe what I told you, it gets better." I lean forward a little, staring into his eyes. "Do you? Believe?"

A long moment passes, and then James nods. It's a small nod, nearly imperceptible, but it's a nod. "Yes," he says, in a voice almost too faint to hear. "I do. Mostly, I do."

"Good," I say, encouraging him. "That will get better, too. It takes longer, but in six months or maybe a year, you'll be sure. One hundred percent sure."

His eyes search mine, looking for a sign that I'm lying. "Really?" he asks, his voice laced with doubt. "One *hundred* percent?"

He is afraid of not believing. Afraid of going back to that same state of horror, ever again. It's a pit of nightmares, filled with all the yammering monsters that ever made you scream. "Yes. And you know why? Because: It's the truth. More than that: It's an undeniable truth." I resist the urge to reach out and touch him again. "Suffering can become ... addictive, in a way. It tires you out so fast, it's easy to find yourself on the edge of a cliff and out of fuel. You have to find a way to resist that urge, without suppressing what you need to feel." I cock my head. "Do you understand what I'm saying, James?"

He tries to clear his throat and fails. "Yes," he says, a little bit hoarse. "You're saying that wrongheaded regret is poison and death."

I grin, chuckling a little. "Yeah. You got it."

James reaches his hand out, hesitates, then completes the motion, taking one of my hands in both of his. He cannot meet my gaze. "Do you know why I'm such an asshole, most of the time?" he murmurs in a low voice.

"No, I guess. Not really."

He strokes my hand as he speaks. Turns it over, palm up, pulling gently at the natural curl of my fingers. "It's something I learned early. Something about being too smart for most people. It's easier to keep people away from you than it is to spend all that time helping them catch up." He pauses. "It gets tiring. I know that sounds fucked up and arrogant, but it's true."

"I can see it," I say.

"If it gets tiring for too long, it gets too easy to start hating people. It got to be a habit. One I can't break." He sighs, and then he turns my hand back over, leans forward, and kisses it. It feels like a butterfly landing. He looks up at me. "Thank you for coming here. Thank you for helping me and for being someone I could trust enough to help me. I'll never forget it." He smiles. It's the faintest smile possible, and it is brief, but he smiles. "I'll probably still be a dick, though."

I laugh, caught off guard, and another one of those faint, fleeting smiles flashes across James's face. It's like watching the sun break through a cloud. "I'll consider that a promise," I tell him, with a grin. I let the grin fade. "And you're welcome, James. But thanks aren't necessary. Plenty of people have been there for me in the same kind of moment, more than once. We're all indebted to one another, constantly, hopefully forever. That's a part of what family is: paying it forward, in circles. Over and over, again and again."

"Blah, blah, blah," he jokes, dropping my hand. "But yeah. And still." He leans back in the chair, looking spent. "So what comes after this?"

I return to my chair and sit down. "The best antidote ever," I tell him. "Justice as vengeance."

He stares at me. I watch a series of complex emotions run across his face and through his eyes. Three predominate: pain, anger, and hope. "That..." He nods. "That sounds pretty good, actually." His voice is stronger now. He studies me, and I am gratified to see the focus in him building. "Do you have a plan of attack?"

"To a degree," I say. "But it's not something I can do alone. I need you, and we need the team."

James studies me for another long moment before turning his gaze back to the window. I watch him thinking as he watches the Strip below. He turns his eyes back to me and gives me the weariest smile ever smiled in the history of the world.

"I need five minutes to clean myself up and ten minutes to pack. Can you wait?"

I feel my heart clench. Tears well up, but I force them back down. My grief doesn't belong, here. When I speak, my voice is clear and calm.

"Of course I can wait," I tell him. "Take as long as you need."

CHAPTER THIRTEEN

I dream of the second atrocity, and can call it nothing else. I do not say the words aloud in the dream. I'm not aware of any specific point where I think this phrase in my mind. It simply exists, in an undeniable state. Where the first video had seemed to encompass the sickness of the twisted fanatic and true believer, the second atrocity was a testament to a belief in nothing.

I'm dreaming, I remind myself in the dream. It is less than lucid, but at least I am allowed to know that this is not reality.

I am sitting in the middle of a desert at night, a desert of silver-white sand that glitters and glows under a full and fluorescent moon. I can't feel the chair in which I'm seated but somehow still know that it is made of the same polished gunmetal as the table in front of me. I turn my head left, then right, and find only horizons made of sand. The starlights are fully connected circles, like one of those time-lapse photos of the nighttime sky.

There is no time here, not so long as I sit in the chair.

This is nowhere-place, forgotten by the universe it came from. It is all the turnings left when you would normally have turned right that have ever, or will ever, exist. A warm breeze blows without ever stirring my hair, slow but constant, and comfortable as the womb.

A metal box is in front of me, its top level with the top of my head. It is not separate from the table but seems to have grown from it. It extrudes from the tabletop seamlessly, made of the same black metal. It gleams under the moon and starlight.

There are two perfect, glass-covered holes cut at my eye level. They are horizontally parallel, and the space between them is the same as the width of my nose. All I can see behind the glass is darkness, but somehow I know that if I put my own eyes to those two perfect circles, I will see everything. The box reminds me of one of those old stereoscopic viewers for dirty movies, where you'd crank a handle to make the film move by. Topless women would shudder past your eyes in grainy black-and-white as you fell into a world of imperfect illusion.

One of the men I chased and captured lived in these older versions of the world. He dressed in brown pinstriped suits and a vest and wore a brown bowler on his head. He listened to his records on an authentic and ancient Victrola, and we'd found one of those viewing apparatus in his trophy room. He'd filmed his killings—all done with an axe—in black-and-white and had transferred a series of selected frames onto actual movie film, which he then used his own wooden playing box to view.

He'd appeared in my dreams more than once. I saw him hunched over his playing box, eyes pressed into the viewing holes, panting and sweating as black-and-white horrors danced past his eyes and screamed through his brain.

I lean forward and put my eyes to the holes. For a moment, I'm staring into blackness, and then a light flickers. Slow at first, it picks up speed, until the evidence of motion disappears. The light becomes an unbroken whole, and I fall into it as the white-silver sands and the slow-blowing breeze and the circles of starlight disappear. I am in a movie theater now, but the top, bottom, and sides of the screen can't be found.

"Hello, there," the voice says. It is cheery and disguised. The man who made this movie used something electronic to turn his vocals into a chorus that harmonizes with itself.

The movie begins, and it is the second atrocity. The movie is in color, so vivid it's almost painful or beautiful, perhaps both. It seems far more real than reality. It bleeds with life and clarity, like the mind or the dreams of a child.

"I am the Torturer," the chorus voice sings, "and I have come to teach you how to make a soul cry."

The camera has been pointed down, toward his shoes. They are formal shoes, made of black patent leather, with laces to match. They are surrounded by grass so lush and green I can almost hear the color as a sound.

"Admiring my grass, aren't you?" the chorus voice sings in a shout, amused. It is a moment of false telepathy, but it still makes my skin shiver against my bones. "It was not easy to grow indoors, I can tell you that. Even harder to do in secret and keep secret."

The camera jostles, then moves in a panning motion, showing us the walls of his tabernacle, this place where the deepest parts of him pray. They are made from natural stone, and no matter how hard I strain my eyes, I can't find the places where the separate pieces must meet. They disappear into the grass at their base and round roughly to become the ceiling at the top, like a cave. "True UV lamps for the grass to grow require a series of deep-cell batteries, if you want to run them without creating a power spike. Water has to run regularly but also without access to utilities, and so, sometimes, it rains in this room. When it rains, the lighting dims, and you can listen to the sound of thunder."

The camera pans further, coming to rest on an altar of stone the length and width of a human being. I know this because of the human being stretched against it. It is a woman, and her head lolls as the camera zooms. She seems dazed, shocked, her eyes full of a distance that never receded. I squint to peer closer, and let my own distance enter me, putting space between my emotions and her suffering. She is nude, young, and beautiful. She has the body of a dancer or an athlete, not just in form, but in the way her skin glows and breathes. She is the picture of health, the woman every woman wishes she could be, in a physical sense. I would guess her age at twenty-three or twenty-four, and the beauty of her youth makes me hurt.

"Every torture is like a painting," the voice harmonizes, breathy, full of its own pondering of wonder. "You are painting with human, in the color of pain. I have never titled my works, because each stage is a life all its own, with a name of its own. I call this moment—this instant before the jump—'The Impending Scream.'" He pauses, and the young woman stiffens, searching for the strength of resentment or outrage, but failing. Her fear has pervaded her. It's hooked into her mind and her soul and become greater than her will.

The camera zooms closer, framing her without losing any part of her. I am now able to see clearly how she's bound. This killer has built his altar with the same attention to detail as all the rest of this room and has built the steel he hooks her restraints to into the stone itself. Iron manacles encircle her upper arms, her arms at the elbow, and her wrists. A single, thick link of chain hooks each manacle to the half-circles implanted in the altar stone. Each link is long enough to allow them to lie next to her against the altar top but still short enough when combined with the placement of the manacles to hold her tight. Her legs are similarly attached, with manacles at the ankles, knees, and upper thighs. A single, large manacle encircles her waist like a cold iron belt.

"The preconditioning period is important," he continues. "It is vital to the success of the installation. Think of it as you would think about the marinating of a fine meat in a good seasoning sauce. Leave it too long, and the meat will be too soaked through, too heavy, with the taste. Don't leave it long enough and the taste won't be strong enough to satisfy." He pauses in his speak-song. "But find that sweetest spot, that place in between the mind straining and the mind breaking, and you will have achieved an optimum of fear." A black-gloved hand comes into the lens, just the hand and no more. It touches her head, strokes her hair. Gentle. Loving. She moans and begins to weep. It's a weak, faraway sound, as though not just her body, but also her mind, was listing and intoxicated.

She's drunk on fear.

The hand drops out of view. "It is overwhelming, this beginning place," the voice continues, fluctuating from bass to soprano a hundred times a word, doubling back on itself ten times a second to form endless harmonics, sounds with no starting or finishing place. "One has been shown enough reality to know, intellectually, that what's coming is true. But at this level of reality—the walking path between normality, agony, and death—the mind is protected by itself from arriving at actual belief. What the painter achieves, then, is not hysteria but instead an endless drowning of the self. An unending, overwhelming fear saturates every moment that passes by, but until the pain begins, until that first cut or burn or shock occurs, no belief arises." He pauses again. She stiffens, then freezes. Her eyes go wide and stare fixedly at a single point. Her chest begins to move up and down rapidly, a whole breath in and out every half second. I have the sense he is gazing down on her, letting her see his eyes and all the dark and endless promise within them.

"This is a pure moment," he sings, and I can hear in his voice, even in its altered state, that he believes this. "This is a moment of undeniable life. It is the last time she will ever be the person she was, and she knows this without believing it. Try and hang in this place for as long as you can. Drink it in till it leaks from the pores of your mind forever. Only humanity, by the simple action of existence, forms this perfect note. Savor such sounds with your eyes and yourself. Listen close, and you will hear it, in this silence: Gabriel's horn blowing for a single life. The end of the world, in a song of tears." She writhes against the stone. He must have leaned closer to his camera, because he speaks in a whisper that blows his breath against the microphone. "Listen."

A beautiful, horrible sound fills the cavernous room this killer has built. It is the song of a hundred screams and a thousand horns, amplified and mixed and altered to create a harmony of ten thousand pipe organs played beautifully. It draws me toward it, but it also freezes me in place, and my jaw drops as much in horror as it does in wonder.

"It's taken me a lifetime to build this sound," he whispers, seeming awestruck. "The screams of the tortured, the most confident horns, the playing of a pipe organ when played by a person in a state of the profound, mixed and mastered, trebled and tweaked, until perfection appeared. Do you want to hear the apocalypse? Here it is, dear friends. Here it is."

The first time I'd heard it, I'd puked. I had to grab a garbage can. It had gripped me too quickly, leaving me no time to reach a bathroom. It was a screaming, screeching noise transformed into a song that would kill its singer. Its beauty made it unbearable.

He lowers the volume without turning it completely off. If I cock my head and close my eyes, I can still make it out. "Torture has been my life's work," he speak-sings, and his voice is strong again. It fills the room with its tone and confidence. He is not laboring to prove his ownership, ability, or command. He is as comfortable and certain as a god.

He probably feels like one right now, I think.

"I have chased this song without knowing first what it would sound like. It was something I knew I would know, once I'd found it. I knew I would recognize it like a father recognizes his own child at birth. It was so," he says, quietly. "Those voices you hear came from the throats of women and children and men. It is the music of the damned, when I was their devil.

"Soon—in just moments—I will be her devil, too. She will warble from the pit of her belly and beg and scream until her tongue bleeds from the roots. You believe, perhaps, that you will be repulsed. That what you will witness will be a sickening terror. I urge you to wait on judgment and to watch instead. Your reaction might surprise you. If you find yourself, for example, getting hard while wishing you felt sick, then it may be that you need to accept the truth of yourself, not the lie.

"It is true, not everyone is built for bloodshed. I don't claim superiority—only difference. I am different than most others, I and my kind. We lack the worry about the morality of our actions that belong in most. This does not mean that I have no code, only that I do not have *your* code. If you believe that an inability to hold to your code is the same as having no code at all—then who is the fanatic here, really? You or I?

"The answer is, we both are. We believe in such things not by choice, but because it is who we are inside. I am what I am. I have no choice but to be what I am. If I were to fight my most basic nature, it would erode me slowly until either I failed or went insane. Insanity would bring death in short order. I cannot live outside my own skin any more than you can."

There's a perverse logic to it, I had thought when I first watched this video. Still, he's overlooking a pretty big factor, in the end.

His next words had addressed this very thing, in another instance of false but still eerie telepathy.

"It's fair to hate me for what I do. I reach into your masses and pluck from you those you love. I harm them into death, using the most painful and depraved methods possible, and I do so knowing what I am doing, what it means to you, and what will happen to the person involved. So, yes—hate is warranted for my actions. But blaming me for an inability to change my DNA alone, belief that I can remove the spots I was leopard-born with, is only irrational. If you catch me, you should neither forgive me or hate me. You should kill me.

"I am what I am. And I love what I do. I love it more than life itself. It is my child, and it is an only child."

The young woman has been listening, rapt, to every word. I have watched her as he speaks. He has made her the centerpiece of his tableau, and she is compelling in that role. Her eyes go wide in terror, sometimes, and horror in others. Her mouth opens and closes, like a guppy on the kitchen counter, searching for the air that belongs to freedom from the moment she's found herself in. Once, she closed her eyes, and her lips moved in a slow, soundless whisper of prayer. I find it strange that she never speaks, not even to beg.

"There is nothing uglier than hypocrisy in evil. True, I don't believe in the concept of evil in the way that most human beings do, but I do understand what their belief encompasses. If you believe as most do, then I am evil. The difference between me and many of my kind is that I embrace what I am and allow self-love to flower. I have refused to hate myself for being born with a different nature than the majority. Over time, this has led me to an important understanding: that I am not driven to do what I do by a hatred for those I torture, but by the love I have for their states of pain."

There are ways this is true. Twisted ways, but this kind of understanding is part of what I do and why I'm good at it. I have sat across the table from too many murderers, men who live for the kill and the moments before it, with a heart deliberately emptied of anger. Empathy, not confrontation, is what brings their secrets out. Serial killers spend a majority of their time doing alone what they love the most. They live in disguise, hiding their truest face from the world and the people around them. Friends and family are presented with a mask, not the truth.

I enter a room, a short woman with a scarred face, usually the woman who caught them, and give them an offer many can't refuse. I tell them I will listen without judgment or repulsion, that there is little they can say that I could not imagine or haven't already seen. I make it true, even when it isn't, because it must be true. Until they're dead, or all their victims are known, it's best not to burn any bridges of trust that I've managed to build.

Some of these relationships can last for years. This kind of empathy blurs the lines, over time, forced or not. At some point, pretense becomes difficult to distinguish from its corresponding reality. The line is found by feel more than sight, and maintaining the equilibrium is ultimately an act of will.

Still, this pretended moral blindness ultimately provides the greatest clarity. Serial killers are willing to put their lives at risk, to gamble their entire future, in order to do what they do. They never feel more fulfilled or alive than they do in the moment of truth, whatever that moment may encompass. They feel godly, all-powerful, and alive. A failed or botched fantasy can drive them into terrible rages or great depressions, or both.

Serial killers are all secretly married to a wife named Murder, and there is no husband more faithful, no love that runs deeper. They are willing to kill for her, die for her, go to prison for her. Metaphor or not, what else could you call it if you can't call it love? Insanity, maybe, but love and insanity have always been fraternal twins.

This understanding is safer than contempt. There is less danger in being prepared, and recognition of this fanatical love keeps me on my toes around them all. I treat them like the addicts they are, always understanding that I am one of the people standing in between them and their next fix. I could always become a substitute if I let my guard down. Some of them tell me this openly or write me long letters disguised as guilty confessions, spelling out in graphic detail all the things they've dreamed about doing with me. Some of these letters will arrive from men I haven't caught yet.

Every now and then I will feel like I've woken from a dream. My inability to be afraid of all these dark men dreaming of me will seem insane. In those moments, I'll wonder if I am just them in reverse. I'm gambling my life and my future and all the people I love in order to hunt them down. When the hunt has a scent and the chase becomes close, my focus becomes absolute. I feel completely alive, every line in my life drawn in black ink on white paper. Then, I will think or remember that there is a great difference in the results of our actions and the motivations behind them. I will return to my dream and become fearless again.

Life and death, however, are not semantic states. This is the line that never blurs. I could no more be the men I hunt than they could be me.

But yes, I think in the dream as I listen to him preach, *they love what they do, and it's a true love.*

"I said I don't consider my state of being as superior to that of the moral. The same doesn't apply to my own kind. Every group has its subsets of the incompetent, the stupid, and the insane. We are no different. Most of what you know of us comes from knowing this subset. You learn from idiots like Bundy or fools that keep young women locked in basements and end up believing these young women love them. You learn from the caught, and feel safe.

"You shouldn't. Because of the news stories you see, and even the fiction you watch or read, you believe that law enforcement is competent and actually solves most of our crimes.

"They do not. The truth is perhaps terrifying to you but infinitely simpler: They are unaware, for the most part, that any of our victims exist. It's easy to get away with murder. All you need to do is prevent anyone from finding out that murder ever occurred. The earth turns. The days roll by. Memories fade. The lonely, friendless girl or boy who didn't show up to work one day leaves barely a trace of themselves on the world and the people around them.

"Sloppy fools and idiots kill and leave the carcasses to lie where they fell, slathered with their DNA or with obvious personal connections to their victims. You hear these stories, you read your novels, watch your television shows or movies, and feel secure. Good is winning over evil; the world is guided by some inborn justice.

"None of this is true. It has been said that the United States has anywhere from thirty to fifty serial murderers roaming within its borders at any given time. Regardless of what you see or read—do you find it credible that law enforcement is keeping up with this tide? Of course not. For the most part, they are plucking their wins from the low-hanging fruit. Dahmer was insane. While on the hunt, Bundy called himself Ted to anyone who would listen. Kemper turned himself in the moment after he'd murdered his mother, realizing that this was in fact the itch he'd never been able to scratch. Son of Sam took orders from his dog. Does this sound like a cast of the best and the brightest?

"What of the Zodiac killer? Never captured. Jack the Ripper? To this day, no one can be certain who Jack really was. Why has the FBI only recently realized the virtue of setting up a task force devoted to locating killers on the highway? Over ten lazy fools caught and put in prison so far, but long-haul truckers and hungry men in automobiles have been riding the nighttime highways for decades. They have been driving through the shadows between your city islands of light. Only the willfully ignorant can ignore the truth that law enforcement members are only men and women; they are not superheroes. And they operate at a disadvantage, because what they call a job, I treat as a calling. Where they work, I worship.

"My friend the Wolf and I are members of a group known as the Horsemen. Revelation speaks of death angels on horseback, sowing the end of all wherever they rode. We may not believe in God or the devil, but we do believe in a narrower truth: that each individual death is an apocalypse of one. We are the Horsemen, and we have been riding for a long, long time without any of you knowing, bringing the end of the world, one death at a time.

"We have revealed ourselves by choice. It may not be the wisest choice, in the end, but I have never claimed or believed that I was a superhero, either. I do what I do because I must, and this is where the game has taken me. I have climbed all my personal summits, as has the Wolf. We planned for this inevitability long ago. We knew that if you allow yourself to indulge any appetite, a day must come where the food that once nourished you begins to taste bland.

"In my profession, boredom kills. I cannot lessen my need fulfillment; I can only move to the next level of it. What you call sickness I call true love, and I have acknowledged from the beginning that it might be a love that would end me. I accepted this without hesitation, not because I wanted to so much as because I needed to. I could no more turn away from the opportunity to embody what I am than the sun could stop shining or the wind could stop blowing.

"I foresaw this moment, this future time, and the Wolf agreed with me that it would arrive one day. It was in that moment that we planned the Contest—the day the Horsemen would reveal their existence and see who could most shock the world. Who could create the greatest dark wave of death and thunder? Who could cut the widest swath of destruction?

"This is why you are hearing my voice now. The Horsemen have arrived, and the world will be changed forever by the time we are dead or done.

"Don't misunderstand our intentions. We have made ourselves known. This doesn't mean we are now easily captured. Freedom is my goal, not suicide or prison.

"I have more screams to find and explore, new nourishment to seek. I can only do this outside a prison, and my love is as bottomless as it is pure."

He falls silent after this long exhortation. The young woman on the altar still doesn't speak, but she moans, low and long and loud. It sounds like butchery and murder put to voice, and it makes the hair on the back of my neck stand on end in the dream, much as it did when I heard it while awake. He's wrung this noise from her without even using his hands. What awful sounds will she make once he goes to work in earnest?

She knows, I realize, and this is a new understanding, belonging only to the dream. He's shown her. That's why she never speaks, even as scared as she is.

Watch enough horrors as they're being perpetrated against others, and you soon come to realize that all horrors are not equal; all pain is not the same. Agony alone is not the same as agony that comes as a result of your greatest fears being realized. Given a choice, the person who has a phobia about dental work will choose needles under the nails over having her teeth drilled into without novocaine. Both become unendurable, but they aren't equal. They don't lay the same waste to the mind.

He'd shown her videos of his "life's work" and had made her see. A life is a long time, in the end. The man who called himself the Torturer had time to try it all. Every depravity he could imagine had been visited, examined, and experimented with. He is incredibly detail oriented. This tells me he would document all his acts, every scream of terror, every beg. Each would be treated as its own intricate work of art.

He'd shown her the truth of torture, revealing its wordless horror. How it takes a person and turns them into an animal. The way in which it shatters all our civilized illusions and extinguishes any future permanence of hope.

Having established that he could provide her with her greatest fear or something less, he would have told her that the choice was hers as to which path he chose. She could choose to be silent and still die horribly—but without visiting that one, worst place. Or she could choose to speak and experience it all. Not only would she die horribly, she also would know her own worst fear as a part of that death.

My stomach jumps as though I'd just drunk a gallon of coffee. I know that I'm dreaming, but the sensation is so visceral, I have to wonder if it is happening in the real world while I sleep. The words she'll be screaming soon suddenly make perfect sense. The prior connections I'd made regarding them, the first times I'd watched the video, had been broad, vague.

"Now, let us turn to our sacrifice," he speak-sings in that voice made of ten thousand organs. "It is important to remember: Pain can kill. Move too quickly and cut too deeply, and your sacrifice will die of heart failure before the installation is complete." The camera pans to the left and zooms, revealing a cart at the foot of the altar. It's made of stainless steel and it gleams in the room's false sunlight. "The physical solutions must be considered, of course. I have sublingual nitroglycerin tablets, as well as syringes of Adrenalin that can be delivered right to the heart. I've taken classes in emergency medical techniques and am constantly studying up on all forms of medical and surgical techniques." He pauses, and I can almost hear an ironic smile. "I have ample chance for live practice, after all. I can put in stitches that would stand up to the scrutiny of any hospital and place an IV with the confidence of a nurse or a junkie.

"But then, there is the mind. It's important—very important—not to neglect the emotional aspect of torture. Some of the richest nourishment possible can be found not in the material pain of physical damage, but in the skillful destruction of identity. And how do you attack it? By ripping out all moorings of certainty and control, and then putting them to the torch as your sacrifice screams. You must show them they are like the frog in the science lab, its legs forced to hop with electrical current. Show them their own helplessness as an absolute truth, and all the things that fill them up will empty in a rush. They will shatter.

"Allow me to demonstrate."

It's coming, I think. The moment where she knows. And, oh, it's so so so much worse now that I understand what it means, completely.

The camera moves forward and jostles a bit as he works to ensure only her body and his hands are visible in the frame. The hands, like the Wolf's, are encased in gloves of supple black leather that end at the wrist. They reek of wrongness and confident violence.

His hands disappear from the frame, followed by a series of brief rustling sounds from off camera. They reappear holding packages of what appear to be sewing needles. When the young woman sees them, her eyes bulge so hard they look like they might pop out of their sockets.

"Wait!" she says, in a strained, horrified whisper.

"It's important to identify your sacrifice's greatest fears. They are the quickest route to helplessness." The hands leave the frame again; more rustling sounds. They reappear, bobbing in and out of the camera's view as they drag a leather strap across her forehead. Sounds follow, and I can tell from the way the strap tightens against her skin that he's attached it to something on the far side. "Head injuries from flailing can cause too quick a death. You must never allow a sacrifice to escape to death until you will it."

It's coming, I think again. I want to stop watching. The dream's become a nightmare, and I want to wake up, but I know that I won't.

"Wait!" she shrieks. "But you—you promised!"

"This one's greatest fear is to be blind and deaf. The idea of being blind and deaf while also being helpless in my hands was more than she could bear contemplating. To live in a dark, soundless room of the self, with no warning of what's coming or when, is a horror of impossible dimensions." He pauses.

"Isn't it, my little sacrifice?" he croons. "I'm going to blind you with these needles, my dear. I'll use ten for each eye, so it won't matter if they're open or closed. ... "

"No!" she shrieks, drooling in her terror like a rabid dog.

"Shh ... ," he says, patronizing and amused. "I haven't finished yet. There is some good news among the bad. Yes, I will use knitting needles to deafen you—"

"No! No! No! No!" she shrieks, over and over, until the words run into one another and have neither beginning nor end.

He'd shown her greatest fear to her, happening to another, and then he'd made her a promise: I'll do my worst, but if you keep silent while I speak, I won't do that one thing you fear the most.

Her mistake had been to believe what he said.

"But," he continues, speaking over her crazed shouts, "so long as you scream sweet music for me, I'll leave you your tongue. And if you beg me well enough, I might even release you early."

Her eyes are fixed upward, staring into his. She is seeing him for the first time—really seeing him for all that he is. Her screams strangle in her throat, coming out as nothing more than a series of awful clicking sounds.

"Now. Let's get started," he says.

The hand disappears from the frame. It appears again holding a needle. It looks wet.

"I'll dip each one in ammonia before applying," he speak-sings, confirming this. "It's incredibly effective in blindings."

I fall into the viewer as I blink my eyes, and when I open them, I am the young woman on the table. I stare up at the man, seeking his face, and choke on a scream when I realize he has no features. I'm staring at a formless mass of featureless skin with a grinning, hungry mouth. I scream, ripping the noise from every part of me that's human and alive.

The hand strikes down without warning, like a snake—and I wake up in my bed with a shudder.

I glance over at Tommy. He slumbers on, and I'm grateful.

I stare at the ceiling and wait for the dawn. It's hours away, but I won't sleep again.

I hope.

CHAPTER FOURTEEN

The Wolf's Latest Act—Leading by Example?
—*By Peter Muir, Staff Writer, Los Angeles Herald*

It began last Saturday, in the early afternoon. We can only assume that the Wolf chose that time and day because it provided some assurance that the mall in Glendale would be busy.

Which it was. Security video cameras caught the carnage, but they also caught the bustling crowds that came before it. It was post-Christmas, a time of clearance sales everywhere, and the open space near the food court was a friendly, moving mass of shoppers and young children.

No one had any reason to notice or even know that there were two extra trash cans. They'd been modeled to match the existing ones in detail, after all. The space was large enough to need extra receptacles, and the crowd prevented anyone from taking in the whole space at once.

The size of the cans let the garbage placed on top camouflage the fact that they were already half full. The Wolf had put together an unusual but deadly package. Custom-made one-hundred-liter canisters of liquid oxygen had been placed inside a slightly larger custom-made pressurized container. Inside each pressurized container: a mixture of lampblack and crushed porous silicon surrounded the cylinders.

The cylinders of liquid oxygen had not been built by the Wolf to allow for any pressure venting. Instead, he had designed two valves for each cylinder to rupture just before the pressure inside the tank rose to the point where it would compromise the cylinders themselves. He then assured that this rise in pressure would occur at the time desired by putting the cylinders on top of hot plates, which were on timers.

"On the one hand, it's incredibly simple," said Officer Tom Blythe, head of the Bomb Disposal Unit for greater Los Angeles. "At the same time, it's pretty damn sophisticated. LOX {liquid oxygen} is incredibly dangerous, highly volatile stuff. He not only designed and built the cylinders himself, but he also built them to the specific tolerances of expansion versus heat that he needed, and then presumably, he filled them himself. Again, that's no mean feat."

I asked him about the explosive mixture.

"LOX explosives have been around since 1895. They were used primarily in mining but abandoned because they're unstable and dangerous. The discovery of an explosive reaction between porous silicon and LOX is relatively recent. The Wolf's design was smart because it was simple. He used the LOX as the blasting cap by expanding the gases through heat. The valves popped before the cylinders ruptured, spilling LOX into a mix of activated carbon coated with kerosene and porous silicon. The expansion occurring also ruptured the cylinders, because it was too quick a reaction for just the valves themselves to handle. You have to understand, this is all happening in milliseconds, so these various reactions are all bumping into each other and increasing the overall rate of expansion of the explosion as a whole.

"This is all happening inside a pressurized container, and I'm not talking about some home-use pressure cooker you can buy at Kmart, or something. This Wolf character built that one by hand, too. It was designed to fail, but not until after an extremely powerful amount of pressure built up inside. Think of a hand grenade. He built it like that, designed to fail across multiple seams, so that the explosion would send force out in every direction."

This, as most know by now, is exactly what occurred. At 2:15 pm Pacific time, the two false trash cans detonated with tremendous force, sending the large steel ball bearings surrounding the pressurized container off in all directions, killing thirty-five people and wounding nineteen others, many critically.

Unfortunately, it did not end there.

One hour later, a hooded man shot his way into a mosque in Burbank, which was two-thirds full at the time, and tossed four cylindrical cans into different parts of the crowd. By the time he'd raced out the door, the cylinders detonated.

"Again, super-simple but not for the amateur," Officer Blythe noted. "He attached packets of home-made picric acid to cans of wasp killer, then set it off

with an electric charge on a timer. It wasn't big enough to vaporize the wasp killer, just enough to puncture the cans, which were pressurized. That stuff's basically a nerve agent."

It turned out that fatalities from the cans' contents were lower than the number who died in the stampede to get out. The person responsible (assumed to be the Wolf or an associate) had chained all exits from the outside and had electrified the metal doors using a chained series of car batteries.

"The can explosions were more of a psychological weapon than anything," Blythe says. He looks tired, with dark circles under his eyes. "They panicked, which drove them to the doors. They were packed in against each other when the first person contacted the door and..." He spreads his hands, apparently unwilling or unable to put what happened into words.

It's difficult not to sympathize. There were more than fifteen casualties of this action, and another nine seriously injured. One of those who died was a twenty-three-year-old pregnant woman, who was trampled by the crowd.

Less than a half hour after the incidents at the mosque, a machine designed to shoot tennis balls was trained on the front of a synagogue. Again, the Wolf's timing was impeccable in terms of its design for terror. A wedding had just occurred, and the new couple, as well as all attending, were beginning to file out.

Smiles soon transformed into screams of terror.

"He bolted it into the sidewalk," Blythe says. "The tennis ball machine. He powered it with a deep-cell battery and encased it all in bulletproof Lucite. The tennis balls were opened up, and then an aluminum sphere was inserted inside each one. Each sphere was full of a home-brewed nitromethane mixture, which he detonated using mercury fulminate.

These were more sophisticated in design than the other ordinance. He had a timer set up that synchronized the rate of fire with a signal from a bank of cell phones—about ten of them, I think. So in other words, ten balls would fire, and then about three seconds later, a call would go out, setting off an electrical circuit, and the explosives inside those ten balls would go off. Then another ten would fire, and the next cell phone would activate. Definitely not the work of your average electronics amateur. Or pyrotechnics amateur, for that matter."

Nineteen people died in this attack, with another eight seriously injured, including two still in a coma.

Three hours of war-zone violence in Los Angeles, and then it was over. I was at home when the explosion in the mall occurred. I spent the rest of the day chasing the story and heard the howl of sirens everywhere I went.

The Wolf claimed responsibility two hours after the last attack, releasing a video that was downloaded three million times worldwide before authorities managed to block it.

"This was not an attack on religion or political policy," he says. "It was an attack on ignorance and false complacency. I made sure to target both a synagogue and a mosque to ensure there was no confusion in this regard. Ignore any spin your government decides to spew: I did this, me and myself alone. I did it to show you how easy it is to do."

His introduction completed, the Wolf then says the following:

"I'm going to show you exactly how to do it, too, and provide you with some manuals on building weapons and explosives at home. It's easier than you could ever imagine."

I will not repeat those directions. It was just all too easy. Instructions on how to make the volatile explosive picric acid from aspirin were provided, for example, along with step-by-step directions for the home manufacture of RDX and its use in the making of C4—one of the most popular, stable, and powerful explosives in the world.

I think about those three million downloads and wonder what percentage of those who downloaded these instructions will be inclined to put them to use.

"This is an unparalleled era for the home manufacturer," the Wolf says, in an ominous voice. "Three-D printers, CNC routers that will fit in the parking space of a garage, and a nation packed full of hardware stores and markets. If you can envision it and have the will, you can probably build it.

I've given you what will be the missing piece, for most: various processes for the making of high explosives. If you're so inclined, the time has arrived to fulfill that deep-seated need.

"Make this the Year of the Bomb. Help me sow this society with acts of violence and destruction. Did someone steal your parking space? Turn their vehicle into a fireball. Did a bank foreclose on your home? Homemade hand

grenades and a pneumatic air gun will let you reduce every branch in your town to rubble.

"If you are inclined to bring death, if you have been teetering on the edge of yes or no ... the time for yes is here."

Three million downloads, with that message at the end? I'm sure you'll forgive me for being just a little bit afraid.

Violence, like suicides, can cluster. We're a social species, and sometimes, all one psychotic needs is the approval of just one other person with similar appetites.

Let's hope the opposite occurs, and that those who want peace outnumber those who don't, by far.

CHAPTER FIFTEEN

"So, how does it feel to be back in the saddle?" Alan asks me.

"Like it was way too easy," I mutter.

He grins. "Desperate times and all that."

"All hands on deck once the politicos start poo-pooing in their drawers, honey-love," Callie agrees.

I sigh and smile, nodding my head. "Yeah. Yes. You're right, of course."

I'm in my old office, standing in front of my old whiteboard, and though it's been only three months since I walked out of here to go to Colorado, it feels like three years. Or maybe thirty. I crossed the Rocky Mountains and my life changed, not for the better.

"I only need to know one thing, Smoky," Director Rathbun had said. "Are you sure you're ready?"

I'd been seated in one of the two chairs that faced his desk. Director Rathbun had been seated behind the desk, rocking slowly as he examined me. He looked like he'd aged overnight. He was in his early fifties, but there'd always been an undeniable vitality about him that erased his age, as though he were driven from within by some tireless engine. He's lost weight, visibly so, but it's not weight he needed to lose. He's gone gaunt.

It makes me trust him. Events don't take a toll on you like that unless you're emotionally invested. Rathbun's a politician—every director has to be—but I've always liked him anyway, because he's still always been a cop. It seems this hasn't changed.

"No, sir," I had finally answered. "I'm not sure. I do know that I'll never be sure about anything, ever again, unless I come back and fight."

His smile had been faint, almost wan. "You'd better be ready for more than a fight, Special Agent Barrett. This is not a single event. It's like having

249

a repeat of Sandy Hook every week. What you need to prepare for is a war. Homegrown, sustained domestic terrorism has always been one of the Bureau's greatest fears."

I studied him carefully. *What if this is all a trick? Maybe he's trying to see if I've gone over the edge, if I'm ready to go vigilante and become a hunter rather than a capturer.*

I couldn't find any evidence of this, though. All I could see was a tremendous weariness, a century of exhaustion packed into a quarter-year of time. Rathbun was a giant who'd dropped to one knee and was still struggling to rise.

"I guess that's true, sir."

He'd turned his gaze away from me, staring off in silence for a while. "Do you have a plan?" he asked. "A place to start?"

"I have some ideas."

Another long silence had passed. "Do you think he did it? Jones, I mean? Did he take that money, hand over evidence to psychopaths, and betray his own people?"

I sighed. "My gut says no. Jones was my mentor. He was there for me, after Sands—really there for me, sir. To me, he never read as being anything other than a dedicated agent and a truly great boss." I shrug. "But I've been through too many loop-de-loops on the roller coaster in the last three months. Up's been down; down's been up. So my mind tells me I need to hold it to an 'I don't know.' And then I need to go find out."

He'd nodded, still looking off. "He saved my life once. Did you know that?"

"No, sir."

"It was in the late eighties. I was posted at Quantico, and Jones was there doing some training. They were grooming him for the BAU at one point."

I blinked, surprised. "I never knew that."

The Behavioral Analysis Unit has always been where the rock stars live. The legends. It's not at all unbelievable to me that Jones could have ended up there—he had the touch. I just can't believe he never mentioned it.

"Yep. He's the reason it never happened. He wanted to stay in Los Angeles. I never understood why, but then, I never asked him, either."

I smiled a little. "AD Jones didn't exactly put out an 'I'm accessible' vibe, sir."

He chuckled mournfully, shaking his head. "Truer words, Smoky. It may be so that no man is an island, but Jones came close." He falls into a melancholy moment, then waves it off. "Anyway. There was a would-be agent who was getting drummed out of the Bureau while I was there. He was a young guy, ex-military, named Hobbs. Jason Hobbs. He couldn't pass the psych eval and had gotten into a violent altercation with another trainee which ended with him snapping the other trainee's arm."

I shook my head, frowning. "He's lucky he didn't get drummed *into* prison for that."

"I agree, but Hobbs saw it differently. I'd just finished a run and had entered the dorm building I was staying at. I got to the elevator and there was Jones. He'd just finished requalifying at the range and was headed home as well." He grimaced. "Lucky thing, that. Because about a second later, there was Hobbs, all wild-eyed and gripping his sidearm with both hands. Looking for blood." Rathbun had glanced over at me, his eyebrows raised. "My own weapon was in my room."

"Bad luck," I murmured, rapt. Yet another story AD Jones had never mentioned. The man had been a sphinx. *Or something a whole lot worse*, I thought.

"The baddest there is," Director Rathbun agreed. "He saw me first. Jones was standing at an angle and a little behind me. I don't think Hobbs even knew he was there. He knew I was, though, without a doubt." He paused, pondering that past moment. "His eyes met mine, and I watched them just ... shut down. Everything and anything that contained warmth or humanity disappeared, and his focus narrowed until I'm sure I was all he could see."

"Tunnel vision," I murmured.

Rathbun made no indication that he'd heard this. He was in the grips of the memory, staring into the black hole of a gun barrel pointed his way. "What I knew, right then and there, was that I was a dead man. Hobbs had his weapon in a two-handed grip and was already raising it to shoot. I had a pair of gym shorts." He shrugged. "I was going to die. I couldn't see any other way it would turn out."

"But AD Jones ... "

"Jones had just come from the range," Rathbun said, finishing the sentence for me. "But it was more than that, Smoky. It was *Jones* who made the difference. Think about it. Any number of agents could have been there or even armed, and I could still have ended up dead."

It's true. There is a world of difference between carrying a weapon and using it. Then another world of difference between using it and using it well. "Yes," I'd acknowledged. "I guess you're right."

"He was just so damn *fast*, Smoky. I'm talking, you know, action-movie-star fast. Or maybe a Western—that would be more Jones's style. He pivoted around me and double-tapped Hobbs in the head."

I raised my eyebrows. "Really? Two headshots?" I whistled. "He must have been pretty confident."

We are taught to aim center-mass, as opposed to going for the headshot first. Handguns are not the most accurate weapons in other than in the most gifted hands. This is never more true than when adrenaline is spiking through your body.

Rathbun shook his head. "I don't think it was about confidence so much as necessity. Hobbs's weapon was already up and pointed at my chest by the time Jones got off those shots. He told me afterwards that he thought headshots were my only chance." Rathbun grinned, and it had, for a moment, stripped the years off him again. "I was hopping around like a crackhead. I think I was shouting, too, just single words, as I recall, each one with an exclamation point behind it. You know: 'Oh! Shit! Fucker! Almost! Killed! *Shit!* Me!'"

I'd laughed out loud at this pitch-perfect imitation of his younger self. It had the vividness of truth. Anyone could see themselves acting in exactly the same way in that particular situation.

"What about AD Jones?" I asked.

Rathbun shook his head again. "Cool as a cucumber. He just stood there, waiting for me to calm down. 'You good?' he asked me, once I had." His smile faded. "Jesus. He looked like he'd just played a game of bridge instead of blowing a man's brains out. It made more sense to me later, when I found out he'd been a sniper in Vietnam."

I'd been struck dumb by this. "No kidding?"

"He never mentioned it to you?"

"No, sir. Not once. Not ever."

Rathbun had sighed. "I never got the idea he was all that proud of what he did in that war. I tried to draw him out about it, but all he would say was

'I got the chance to do some shooting. I was good at it. Some people died.' Something along those lines. Classic Jones."

"Wow. That's all news to me."

"When I became director, I took advantage of my position to dig a little deeper, just out of curiosity." He looked at me. "I was given a folder. A heavily redacted folder. When I asked for all those pesky black portions to be removed, I was told that I didn't have the necessary clearance."

I frowned. This made no sense to me at all. "The director of the FBI didn't have clearance? How is that possible?"

Director Rathbun had given me a wry smile. "Welcome to spook world, Smoky. My guess is that the missions Jones was on were run by our friends at the CIA. Everything's Chinese-walled over there, especially when it involves touchy subjects—like assassination, for example."

I sat back in my chair, dumbfounded. "I thought I knew AD Jones. Now, all I can think of is how little I knew about him, personally."

"You and me and maybe everyone, Special Agent Barrett. Which is why I'm going to ensure you're cleared to see anything in Jones's files that I'm allowed to see. I can't help you with the CIA, but I can give you access to everything the Bureau has on him." He'd stared me in the eyes, underlining the point. "Everything."

"Thank you, sir. That will be very helpful." This is what I had said aloud. Privately, I'd wondered if I would like what I found, knowing in my heart that I probably wouldn't.

The truth of other people was almost invariably a letdown. Supermodels shoot heroin, or they binge and purge. The wide-eyed, innocent high school valedictorian has given blow jobs to every boy in the school or is being molested by her father. The dead can't defend themselves against the secrets that crawl out once all the rocks have been turned over.

"Anything you or your team need, you get, Smoky," the director had told me, before sending me on my way. "Homeland and the ATF and everyone else are all jockeying on this, trying to get their piece of the pie. But I've promised the president that this is personal to the Bureau, and that we won't rest until the Wolf and that other psycho are behind bars or dead." He'd paused. "Just so you know, the president made it clear that dead was just fine, so far as he's concerned."

"What about you, sir?"

Director Rathbun had drawn himself up at this question, and for a moment, he looked like the man I'd known just three months ago. "The FBI doesn't perform assassinations, Special Agent Barrett. Not even for the president."

"Yes, sir," I'd agreed. "Understood."

It was an answer I was relieved to get. An answer I could be proud of.

Dr. Childs had provided my psych clearance. I'd spent a morning on the range, requalifying with my weapon. It had been difficult for the first two clips, but then something clicked, and my hands had stopped shaking. My breathing and my heartbeat leveled out, and I stood on a mountaintop, enshrouded by silence. Death felt close but unthreatening, and my hands were the hands of a gunfighter again, guided by the gunfighter's philosophy: Shoot till they are dead or down or you are, and never—ever—just shoot to wound. I passed well above all margins.

There were two highly experienced, highly intelligent predators roaming the land. They were intent on a plan of death and destruction, so I was allowed back in what had seemed like a heartbeat because Director Rathbun was right: This was more a war than a fight. Wars need soldiers, and necessity tends to blur administrative lines first.

If I failed or fell apart, someone would pay when the war was over. Probably the director, my team, and me. Until that time came, I was needed. More than that, I was in charge. I was terrified by this truth, terrified beyond belief.

I was also where I belonged. I knew this. I no longer believe in destiny as a metaphysical creation. I don't buy that we're born with a known end or path. I do understand now that at some point in life, this truth becomes a lie. We become a result of our own actions combined with life's actions against us, and it makes us into what we will be until we're dead.

I am a mother and a wife. I am a friend. I am also a hunter of the worst kinds of men, and as the Torturer had said about himself, I could no more stop being what I am than I could stop the sun from rising or the tide from coming in. There were times in the past where I could have turned in another direction, chosen another path. Those times are long gone. A mountain range bars the road back, and when it comes to ourselves, we can travel only by foot when it comes to change.

I have not been driven here. I am here by choice; it's the result of accepting a destiny I conspired to create.

I have briefed the team on my conversation with Michael McKay, and I am once again in front of a blank whiteboard. It's a familiar place for all of us to be, but at the same time, everything is different. We all know that this is not the same as other challenges we've faced. This is about more than hunting predators—we are looking for our enemies, in a battle for our lives.

It helps that my own team has welcomed me back without a fight or a hint of judgment. They only are happy to see me returned to them; they don't seem to need an accounting of the time I spent away.

Or maybe they don't want one, I think. *Who wants to hear about all that bullshit and pain, anyway?*

I pluck once at the band around my wrist and clear my throat, telling myself it's time to begin. I've picked up another disability along the way, it seems: a need for proof of the perfect starting moment. It never comes, of course. It's just another form of fear, an excuse to stay motionless. The only solution is to step off the cliff into the illusion of the void.

I uncap my black marker. "So," I say, "I've been thinking for a few weeks now about the different things McKay said. The problem is that this thing is such a big, fat mess."

"A collection of cataclysms, honey-love," Callie agrees.

I smile. "That's a good way to put it. Too many big disasters mixed together. It's an invitation to get spread all over the map. Every time I look at the whole, I get lost before I can register the parts."

"It does send you down conspiracy lane pretty quick," Alan muses. "Guy on the grassy knoll and his brother, too. But I sense there's a 'but' coming soon, right?"

"But—" I nod, grinning at him—"some of the points McKay made spoke to me. I think they're ways into the mess." I write *True Believers* on the top-left side of the board and underline it once. "He said that the true believers, as he called them, could be one of the weakest points of any conspiracy. This really rang true to me. One of the things that makes this big ball of mess a big ball of mess isn't just its scope, but the fact that it stinks to high heaven. It's impossible to know what's a lie and what's the truth." I tap the two words I'd written with the cap side of the marker. "But we have some of these mixed in with all the bullshit."

"The girl who pointed the shotgun at your stomach," James muses, nodding in agreement.

"Maya," I say, writing her name beneath the underline, followed by some of the details concerning her that we knew. "Looked to be in her late teens, confident, well-spoken, and handled herself like someone who'd been tactically trained. She was definitely a believer in what she was doing and saying. She was even willing to die because of it."

"She proved her word was good," Alan chimes in. "She said you'd find a bunker underneath the grass, and you did."

"She also predicted that someone would show up to kill her, and that happened, too," I point out. I write the words *family killer* next to Maya's name. "We now know that Maya was the one who killed and posed those families. According to her, they were bad guys. Clearly, that doesn't track with some of the victims being children, but I think we're safe in saying that she believed her own assertions."

"I agree," Alan murmurs. "I saw her face. She was ready and willing to die. You can't fake that kind of belief."

"The same can be said about the man who killed her," Callie says, consulting her notes. "Fred Carter, another resident of the houses on that street. He blew a hole through Maya before being killed by a sniper himself."

"Which turned out to be another teenage girl who took her own life after killing him," James observes. "That would place her in the same category. Also, both Maya and Carter's statements, while opaque, seemed religious somehow. Belief based." He consults his notes. "Maya: 'I fight without the knowledge of the Father, as a member of the Rose of Swords, against the hidden tyranny of the Black Gloves!' Carter: 'Death to all who fight under the Rose! Close the door! Close the door!'" He glances up at me. "And let's not forget that Maya predicted his appearance, that someone would show up momentarily and kill her."

I write *Fred Carter* and *Unidentified girl* under Maya's name. "The only problem with them," I say, "is that they're all dead."

"Maybe by design," James says.

I tilt my head at him, curious. "What do you mean?"

"I mean...all the things Maya and Carter said, they were pretty improbable. Meaningless without the underlying story. I agree that they *believed* they were true, but that doesn't mean they were actually true. What if it was all scripted? Maybe they were there to play their parts, muddy the waters, and die."

"Manipulation of opposing fanatics by a single individual or entity," I murmur.

"Yes," James says, nodding.

Alan frowns. "What was the point, then?"

"Us," James says, looking around to indicate the team. "Maybe the point was to get us to Colorado. So Maya enacts her part of the script by killing the families. This brings us there, and then Fred Carter plays his role, and the other girl plays hers, and—voilà." He snaps his fingers. "We're on site, all the loose ends that brought us there are tied up, and all the players involved in getting us there are dead. So now there's no one alive to lead us back to the guys who formulated the plan."

"I suppose that's possible," I say, "but I can tell you for certain that Ben wasn't just playing at wanting to kill me. If getting us there was a part of the plan, so was me ending up dead."

James shrugs. "Maybe that was the idea. To kill you off and to reveal the museum. It would be a pretty dramatic opening, and the Torturer did say the point of their competition was to solve boredom."

"It's telling that they went after both you and James so hard, honey-love," Callie points out. "They made it personal, toward either killing you or crippling you both emotionally. No one attacked my family or Alan's."

I hadn't considered this, and find myself more puzzled than afraid. "Why just us? What's the difference?"

"Because we'd be the most demoralizing," James offers. "You're the head of the team, obviously, but we're both symbols, too. We've both lost family to serial murderers, and we've both overcome that and gone on to capture more than what was taken from us." He smiles wanly. "It's brilliant, really. I'm guessing it was the Torturer who thought it up. I'm getting a feel for these two, and that kind of devastating subtlety is his deal. The Wolf would be more pragmatic about it. He'd just want us dead."

"One kills you slowly, while the other just kills you?" Callie asks.

"Something like that."

"I agree," I say, staring at James, who returns my gaze. "That feels right."

I suppress a shudder that threatens to overtake me. If it had been scripted, had been planned ... then Ben had to know he'd either end up dead or imprisoned. That being true—what would it have taken to convince him to stay? What had he been willing to risk imprisonment or death for?

Me, of course. The promise of his time with me.

I hadn't spent enough time with Ben to understand his depths, but there was no reason to believe he was suicidal. No, it was something simpler and much uglier. I was the end of the road of all his fantasies, the culmination of a life of dark dreaming. The time he'd planned to spend with me, the things he'd planned to do to me, were simply worth dying for.

"If it was that important to them to get rid of us," Alan says, "they must think we can catch them. Smoky didn't die; James didn't stay gone. Both plans failed. That's gotta irk them. Psychopaths make mistakes when they get annoyed."

"Good point," I murmur. "But let's not forget that it also makes them dangerous. I don't see these unsubs as the type to give up. If they really think getting us out of the way is vital to achieving their endgame, they'll probably keep on trying."

"There's a cheery thought," Callie says.

I nod. "No kidding. Anyway," I continue, "everything Maya said has panned out so far." *Bunker*, I write on the board. "She said there was a bunker under the grass, and there was one." *Two men*, I write, next to *Bunker*. "She said there were two men involved, and we've seen videos from both. It's been three months since Colorado. I think if there were more than just those two, they would have made themselves known by now."

"I agree," James says.

"She said that when she tortured one of the men—one of the fathers of the families she murdered, I guess—that he said something like: 'The Milgram experiment. Explanation wasn't a lie, it was the truth. *He* wasn't lying.'" I write *Milgram* on the board. "Does that ring any bells for anyone? Do we know who 'he' is?"

"No," James replies. Alan and Callie shake their heads.

"Let's assume there is something to know," I say. *"His explanation wasn't a lie.* Maybe a case, or something?"

"We'll search for it," Callie says. "If it is about a case, there can't be many that reference the Milgram experiment. Seems fairly esoteric for the criminal arena."

"She said these families, or at least the parents, were bad guys," James murmurs. "Maybe we should put that on the board, too. If it follows the rest, then we'll find evidence that she was telling the truth about them."

"Good point," I say, after considering it. *Dead Families—parents criminal?* I write, underneath the others, and then: *Find evidence.* "Now, let's move on to the next set of true believers."

Older couple, I write on the board.

"The ones you saw on video that committed suicide?" Callie asks.

"Yes." I write *Sheila/granddaughter* next to *Older couple.* Then I write: *unwilling; under duress. Said did "terrible things." Blackmail?* "They referred to their granddaughter as 'our Sheila' and inferred that something terrible would happen to her if they disobeyed." I pause, remembering. "But the husband's opinion was that the events on the street indicated the granddaughter was already dead or would be soon.

"Did they ever mention anything about the mother?" Alan asks. "Sheila's mom?"

"No."

"Strange," he muses, frowning slightly as he gazes at the whiteboard. "They're about to die, are focused on the granddaughter's future safety, but not a word about the mother? No concern for her at all?" He sighs. "I think Mom's dead. Not as a result of these recent events, but earlier."

"That was my conclusion, too," I say, nodding. "The important thing is: We know who these people were, or we can find out. Which means we can find out who Sheila is." I pause. "Or was," I amend, soberly. "It's not just conjecture, it's something concrete that we can know. That's what we need to do most: find the concrete facts, the anchors. We need to start filling out this picture with reality instead of their script." I turn to the board and raise the marker. "That brings us to our most important anomaly." *The survivor,* I write. "The only person on the block who didn't die."

"Her name is Rebecca Stoddard," Alan supplies.

I write this out, next to *The survivor*.

"Where is she?" I ask.

"The women's correctional facility in Denver," Alan says.

"Prison?" I frown. "Why?"

"She copped to killing her husband. But," he adds, "that's *all* she's said. I've been checking up on her. Apparently she's a sphinx. Never talks. She confessed to blowing her husband's brains out, agreed to go straight to prison without a trial, and then—clammed up completely."

"Maybe she's scared of what might happen if she said anything," James muses.

"Maybe," I allow. "What I want to know is why. Why is she the only person on that street that survived?" I write this out, next to her name: *Why survived?* I tap the marker against my front teeth. "I want to see her. Maybe I can get her to talk to me."

"You have to wonder if she disobeyed someone by staying alive," Callie muses.

"Hopefully, she'll tell us." I sigh. "Let's turn to our two offenders." I take the marker in a writer's grip and scrawl across the top of the board first: *The Wolf*, followed by *The Torturer*. I underline each. "What do we think?"

"Both are in at least their forties," James says, "but they could be older. Fifties or even their early sixties. If they are older, they'll both still be in good shape. Especially the Wolf. He's more ... " He searches for the word. "Physical. The acts that he enjoys require more effort and involve more strength. He likes that." He looks at me. "The Wolf thinks of himself as an engine of destruction. He doesn't kill—he obliterates."

"Okay," I say, nodding. I write these observations under the Wolf's name, in summary form. *40s–early 60s. Physically fit. Engine of destruction, not death—obliteration*. I add the same observation regarding age under the Torturer's name, and then add some notes of my own as I speak. "The Torturer is older and is the dominant personality of the team. He employs an exquisite attention to detail as a method of both heightening and delaying his own gratification." I think, then speak some more, writing as I do. "They've both been operating for a long time. They self-actualized early and probably met early, too. You don't build something the size of that museum overnight."

"They're wealthy," James adds. "The construction of that bunker would have been expensive, never mind the cost to acquire its contents. It'll be a quiet wealth, though." He glances at me. "I agree with you that they've been doing this for a long time. It's been their life's work. They'll have worked to hide their wealth, as opposed to flaunting it. And they won't have any criminal records to speak of. Maybe none at all."

"Both are very strong, honey-love, and they don't appear the slightest bit conflicted. These are highly organized, highly intelligent offenders," Callie says. She glances at James. *"Life's work* is a good way to put it."

I jot notes, moving back and forth between the columns developing under the name of each offender.

"They have an organization," I say, writing. "Maybe something related to import/export?" I snap my fingers as a thought occurs to me. "Who's in charge of inventorying the museum?"

"At the moment? That would be the CIA, honey-love," Callie says, flashing me a mirthless smile. "It was the locals first, then us, and then the spooks swooped in and took over. No one else in or out till they're done."

"What?" I can barely suppress my outrage. "What the fuck is that about?"

"I guess they'd be worried about a secret museum of atrocities, as a default action," James observes, wryly.

I blink, considering this. "Shit. I guess you're right." I sigh, deflated by this truth and my own impotence in the face of it. "Do we have any indication of when they'll be done with it?"

"Last time I asked, they said, quote: 'We'll let you know when we're done,'" Callie answers. She sniffs in contempt. "I told them that arrogance and evil were an unattractive combination and that they should choose one and then stick with it."

Alan lets his mouth drop open in mock surprise. "Really? Don Quixote was a redhead? Damn."

"He pretended it didn't matter, but he was crying inside." She sniffs, her voice haughty and cold. "I could tell." She drops the façade and sighs. "All I was able to get out of them was an assurance that they were only making sure none of the items involved 'matters of agency concern.' Those items would be removed, but only those items, if they were found."

"Do you believe them?" I ask.

She smiles faintly. "Of course I do. 'Matters of agency concern.' Could it be any broader? They've made it virtually impossible for anything they do to become a lie. So yes, I believe them." She mimes sticking her finger down her throat. "But I prefer my truth more 'truthy,' honey-love. You know?"

"I do. But let's not give up yet. I'll talk to the director and see if he'll help me rattle some cages in the Death Star." This is our nickname for Langley: the Death Star. Home of the dark side. "Vampires hate the light. Maybe he can arrange to hint how bad the agency would look if an effort to cover their tracks resulted in more civilian casualties, particularly while operating on U.S. soil in violation of their mandate."

"Oooo... hardball with assholes who deserve it!" Callie exclaims, clasping her hands in false prayer, as she bats her eyes heavenward. "Hallejah; hosanna to the highest!"

I glance at James, expecting some acerbic remark, perhaps about how we need to stop wasting time and get back to business. He's chosen to ignore us instead and is staring at the whiteboard, lost in thought.

Complete disinterest is a form of disapproval, I tell myself. It's a start.

"I guess the key question would be: Why now?" Alan murmurs. "Do we believe what the Torturer said? That they've decided to make themselves known because they're bored?"

This mirrors my own question, one I've been asking myself over and over again since the Torturer made that claim. It's always felt... flat to me. Unsatisfying, like French fries without ketchup, or a tongue kiss given with a bone-dry mouth. The pattern expected is violated, and you're left ultimately uninjured but slightly off-kilter. When incompetence creates a mystery, even the mystery solved fails to satisfy. Oh, those were just French fries; that was just a kiss.

"I think it's kind of like our CIA friends," I reply, my voice thoughtful. "Ultimately true, but deliberately broad. It's so far from being the whole story, in other words, that it sort of becomes a lie." I shake my head. "Of course it's boredom, because it's always boredom, in the end. Right? They live with an inability to endure the mundane. But this boredom is different. It contains another stressor that's forced them into their plan B."

James nods vigorously. "Maybe one of them is dying, for example. Someone got cancer, and this is the endgame they agreed on if that day, or a day like it, ever arrived."

"Could be," I allow. "For now, let's divide up our duties and start filling out that fact-based picture. We're getting on a plane, and we're going to Colorado. I'm going to interview Rebecca Stoddard. Alan, I want you to find out everything there is to know about everyone who lived on that street."

"Got it," he rumbles in agreement.

"James and Callie, I want you to pore over every forensic inch of every house on that street, millimeter by millimeter. I want any on-site visits to be on video; I'll want to see them later. Look for what's missing. Look for what's there that shouldn't be. Take special note of any anomalies. We're chasing ghosts here, and my guess is that we're going to find evidence of their existence more in what's missing than in what's there. You understand what I'm saying?"

"Probably more than you do," James retorts, and that impatience-driven bite in his voice does my heart good. "Look for what isn't there, and use that to figure out what was there, as a result. Reification, iteration, blah, blah, blah." He waves a hand in a gesture of dismissal. "We got it."

"The bad seed returns," Callie says, winking at me. "How wonderful. We've missed you, Mr. Satan."

"Please shut up," James retorts, rolling his eyes. "And once you've *managed* that, practice till it's perfect."

The earth turns again, I think.

It might not be permanent at first. We may lose James to his own battle with despair again. But at least the darkness has an edge of light to it, and that light is an alloy of hope mixed with possibility.

"I also want everything the locals or anyone else already has. Autopsy results, news footage from the cameras that were on site—everything. If someone recorded something on their cell phone and posted it to the Internet, I want a copy."

"I'll put in a call to the nerd squad at Quantico, too, honey-love," Callie says. "I'm sure they've gathered up records of all the residents' Internet activity by now. They're efficient little gremlins."

"That's good," I nod, approving. "If it turns out they've been less than efficient, though, feel free to scare them silly."

Callie gives her fingernails a preening stare and smiles. "I know the agent in charge. Lust before fear, honey-love."

"A little bit of both's even better, Red," Kirby contributes.

"Hear, hear," Callie answers, with a grin.

I glance at my watch and then list off in my head all the things I need to do: tell my family I'm going; pump my breasts so there's enough milk to feed Christopher; brief the director by phone on our current plan. Pack what I need for a two-day visit. Face my overprotective husband and daughter.

"Wheels up at dinnertime?" I ask. "Does that work for everyone?"

They all indicate that it does.

"One other thing," I say. I turn my attention to Callie. "I'll be bringing Kirby along. But I want you to talk to your hubby, and I want a pared-down tactical team traveling with us. If we were supposed to have been decimated, they're not going to like our sudden reappearance. I don't expect it, but I'm not in a gambling mood. You'll talk to Sam?"

Sam Brady is Callie's husband and the head of the FBI's CRT—the Critical Response Team. They're akin to city SWAT teams and are a reassuring mix of men with arms the circumference of my thighs, with eyes that never stop tracking their environment, along with hands that never leave their weapons. They are a tight, disciplined team of expert killers, and I'll feel safer knowing they're along for the ride.

"You got it, honey-love," Callie agrees. "It won't take much to convince him, anyway. He's been pouting about not being able to stay near me ever since these shenanigans began."

"Good. I'll feel better about it, too." I look over the whiteboard and study the face of each member of my team. I can think of nothing else to add or to ask.

"That's it, for now. We'll meet at the airport in five hours."

Back to Colorado, I think. *Back to where my center stopped holding.*

A pit in my stomach opens and squirms. I pluck at the band around my wrist and pretend that my strength is greater than my fear.

CHAPTER SIXTEEN

"Just like that, huh?" Tommy asks. He barely keeps it from becoming a snarl. "Back to work, back in the line of fire, and so what if it makes me crazy?"

I turn from the bag I've finished packing, forcing myself to face him fully. I tamp down the desire to snap back at him. Tommy is a true partner. This reaction on his part is not based in some caveman misogyny, but in the fears already proven to have a basis.

The last time I packed a bag and hopped on a plane to Colorado, I ended up thirty feet underground, at the mercy of a psychopath. Christopher had still been in my belly, and I had survived the encounter with a combination of luck and training, but it was mostly luck, in the end. At home, Tommy had battled for his and Bonnie's lives, and though he'd won, our home had been burned to its foundation.

He'd almost lost everything that mattered to him. He'd done his part, had put his own life on the line to protect Bonnie. Tommy had earned this anger and the right to question me.

I walk over, stand in front of him, and take his face in my hands. "I'm scared, too, Tommy. Truthfully? I'm terrified."

He grabs my wrists, and his eyes plead with me to reconsider. "Then don't go."

I push my fingers through his hair. It's like a dark, curly mass of silk. "We can't hide behind walls forever, Tommy. You know that. It's not just about me, or even you. It's about our children. We're supposed to keep them safe, but they're in danger because of me, because of what I do." I smile at him sadly, chiding him gently. "You know we can't trust these men. It's pure math, honey, think about it. They've already attacked us—our entire family—directly. So what's the only thing we can really be sure of about them?"

265

I watch his own experience and training battle with the desperation and stubbornness in his eyes. He knows the answer but doesn't want to give it. He drops his eyes, letting go of my wrists, and sighs. "That they want us dead and are willing to take action to make it so."

I reach up, gently pulling his chin down so that his eyes meet mine again. "Back when you were working for the Secret Service, if someone made an attempt on one of your principals but failed—what would you have done? Let them go because the principal survived?"

"No," he admits. "Of course not."

"Why?" I press.

"Assassination is a big step to take. It signifies deep commitment on the part of the would-be assassin. You have to assume that if they tried it once, they'll try it again."

"So?"

He stands now, hugging me loosely with arms draped around my waist. He looks down at me, and the naked fear and tenderness exposed in that gaze makes me shiver. Tommy is a deep feeler. He loves with his whole self, nothing held back, all-in.

"So ... I understand. That doesn't mean I like it. You want some more 'pure math,' Smoky? Put yourself in harm's way enough times, and one day you'll lose. That's what worries me."

I stand on my tiptoes to plant a kiss on his lips. "Me, too. But it's not like I'm trolling for enemies here, or something. They wanted me and my family dead, and we're all alive. I don't trust them not to try again. I'll never be sure we're all safe while they're still out there, faceless and running free."

Tommy's arms close around me, and he bends down to return my kiss. His lips linger on mine, and I feel the ferocity of my love for this man. Tommy fought a monster to protect Bonnie and came through. He'd rescued my listing heart from the boneyard it had wandered into after Matt's death. He made me feel, then believe, in the value of my own womanhood again. We have a son now, a new creation that belongs to no one else but us.

Husband, I think, kissing him deeply, as my toes tingle and my heart swells. *Father of my children.*

"I love you so much," he breathes, as we kiss.

"I love you, too," I breathe back.

This world is a stone, where survival is a bare affair, mostly a result of luck. The opportunities for loneliness, weariness, and suffering outweigh the chances of finding companionship that matters. Even a moment of love is the most significant thing most of us will ever experience.

We kiss, and as his soul fills my soul and I return the favor, I remind myself not to forget that it is this, right here, that matters.

"You ready to go, boss-woman?" Kirby inquires. She taps her watch. "We need to hustle if we're going to make it to the airport on time."

I look down at Christopher as he sleeps. He's as motionless as a stone, a totality of slumber. As we grow older, the pains of mere existence encroach, and we never sleep quite as deeply as we did when we were infants.

"This is the first time I've been away from him—really been away—since he was born," I murmur.

"Don't worry," Tommy says, putting an arm around my shoulders. "I'll take care of him. You left me plenty of milk." He kisses my cheek. "He'll be fine."

"I know." I force myself to turn away from Christopher. "What about you, honey?" I ask Bonnie.

She steps forward, hugging me once, then steps back. Her face is placid, a still, calm lake on a windless, breezeless afternoon. "Don't worry about us, Mama-Smoky. Just be careful. We'll be waiting for you when you get back."

"Yeah." It's all I can manage through the lump in my throat.

"Chop, chop, boss-woman," Kirby demands. "Gotta get this show on the road."

"All right, already!" I complain. I grab my purse, my bag, and my briefcase. "Bye, guys," I say, one more time, and then I head for the door before my heart can change my mind.

"Hey, Kirby," Tommy says, before we leave the house. "That's my life you're taking care of."

She cocks her head at him and smiles. "Don't worry. They'll have to kill me to get to her, and you know what? That's just not so easy to do!" She winks at him and then rushes us out the door.

I watch the house disappear in the rearview mirror of the car. "Do you think it'll ever stop feeling like I'm saying good-bye forever?" I murmur.

"Sure it will," Kirby replies, ever chipper. "Once these fuckers are d-e-a-d, dead, you'll be all fine and okey-dokey again. I promise."

I glance at her, smiling a little in spite of myself. "Prison's an option, too, you know."

She gives me a shark's smile, and her eyes glitter like knives in the gloaming. "Not if I get there first."

Her grip strangles the wheel, then relaxes. It's a wanting motion.

CHAPTER SEVENTEEN

I'm sitting in one of the prison's interview rooms, waiting for Rebecca Stoddard. Kirby stands guard in the hall outside, relaxed but ever watchful. It's not even 9:00 A.M. yet. My hair is still damp against my neck, and the faint scent of the hotel shampoo tickles my nose. It smells like apricots.

What I really want is more coffee, but I've learned not to overload on caffeine before an interview. An overwhelming need to pee is the last thing you want, particularly if it occurs at some crucial moment.

I recall my own lesson in this regard. The memory comes easily and remains cringe-worthy. Jackson Robert Caan. He'd killed twelve women and teenage girls but had revealed where to find only ten of the bodies. I'd been working on him for weeks, building a bond based on his love of my scars. He'd sit and watch them endlessly, gapingly at times, as though they were stars, not scars.

Finally, the time had come, and he agreed to tell me the details of where they could be found. He knew this would be the end of our time together, but he also knew that he'd spun it out for as long as he could. Still, he was dragging his heels, speaking slowly and with unnecessary detail. Caan had wanted all the last looks at my face that he could grab and file away.

"Life in prison is a hell of a lot longer than life on the outside," he'd once said to me, in a voice filled with self-pity. "All a man has on the inside is his mind." He'd glanced at me, winking. "His dreams, you know?"

We had been parrying like this for more than an hour when I felt it. It arrived without any warning that it was coming: a sudden, sharp, unbearable need to empty my bladder. I had to fight to keep my face calm, my eyes on his, as I recorded his directions and clamped my legs together like a vise.

When he was done, I thanked him and even shook his hand. I stood up calmly, left the room, closed the door behind me—and then bolted to the nearest ladies' room as fast as my feet would take me. I shuddered against the toilet seat with the strength of my relief, and it was as involving and pleasurable as any orgasm I've ever had.

I hear the shuffling sounds of constricted footsteps made by prison slippers against prison concrete, as well as the faint jangling of chains, heading toward the door, the sounds of a life turned inward. Prison is a man-made archipelago of concrete and steel, where the forgotten go to fade away under cold, fluorescent suns. I close my eyes once, then open them again. I force myself to sit up straight and empty my mind of all expectations.

The most successful interrogations begin with an acceptance of failure. It's not an attempt at Zen, or anything. It's just the way things are. Criminals or suspects enter the room with their own expectations of you and your actions. The best way through this first wall of armor is silence and stillness. If they speak first, that's best, but it's not a rule. What you're going for is rapport. That's something you approach, not something you pounce on, and the route to it can't really be mapped in other than the most general sense, because every journey's different.

The door opens, and Rebecca Stoddard shuffles in wearing an orange jumpsuit. Chains run from the cuffs around her wrists, hooking into the broad leather belt around her waist. Her ankles are cuffed together, the chain just long enough to allow her to walk but short enough to force her to pay attention, in order to keep from stumbling over her own feet.

She's tall, for a woman. Five feet eight or nine, I estimate, and she has red hair that hangs down to her shoulders. Her eyes meet mine, a flash of bright, emerald green. I sense the intelligence there. Rebecca is not a beautiful woman, but she's cute. She has a button nose; full, red lips; and creamy, freckled skin.

"Move to the far side of the table, Stoddard, and sit down," the female guard orders.

Rebecca does as she's told, shuffling her way over, then taking her seat on the cold steel bench. She doesn't speak, but she studies me with a gaze that's more curious than confrontational.

"Please uncuff her hands," I tell the guard.

The guard, a bulky blonde, shoots me a look of cool malice. "Be nice if you told me before I had her sit."

"Sorry," I offer, not meaning a word of it.

The guard sighs, shaking her head. "Stand up, convict," she orders.

Rebecca stands, and the guard steps forward with a key, keeping her eyes glued to Rebecca's as she unlocks the cuffs. She stands back, nodding at the bench. "Okay. Sit back down, but keep your hands on the table where I can see them."

Rebecca sits again and rests her arms palms down on the tabletop in front of her.

The guard turns to me. "You want me to cuff her wrists to the table?" she asks.

"Thanks, but that won't be necessary."

"You sure?" she presses. "She's got you by about nine inches and twenty pounds."

I smile, pointing at the scars on my face. "The guys who did this were a whole lot bigger, and they're all dead." I glance at Rebecca. "Besides, I don't think Miss Stoddard has any plans to escape, do you, Rebecca?"

She doesn't answer, but she smiles slightly and shakes her head.

"See?" I say, looking back at the guard. "We're good."

"Fine by me," she replies, turning on her heels and heading back to the door. "I'll be right outside. Scream real loud if she tries to kill you." She exits, closing the door behind her. I hear the grinding of the locks.

I raise an eyebrow at Rebecca. "There goes a real people person," I joke.

Rebecca chuckles. It's a light and flowing sound, like a stream passing over pebbles in the sun, and it surprises me. "You can't really blame her," she says. "She represents the system she's a part of. She changes it, but it changes her, too." She cocks her head. "Are you familiar with systems theory, at all?"

"Only in its most basic form," I answer, "but I'm a quick study." I wait, inviting her to continue, to teach me.

Rebecca Stoddard had been a teacher, after all, before coming to that fateful street in Colorado. During the plane trip here, I'd read the file that Alan had compiled on her. In fact, Rebecca had been a professor—a full-fledged PhD. She'd taught games theory and systems theory at Harvard and had been well respected for her work in both fields, until her life was upended by the abduction of her only child—a daughter, Emily.

Emily had been four years old. Rebecca had taken her daughter along with her on a trip to the market. They'd been idling at a light when a carjacker smashed in the driver's-side window, cut Rebecca's seat belt, and had dragged her out, kicking and screaming. He'd pistol-whipped her with the gun in his hand, dazing her into darkness for the space of two or three seconds. It had been long enough for her to wake up to find both her car and her daughter gone.

The police never found either. There was no ransom request; the assumption, based on the case notes from the detectives involved, was that the carjacker had probably killed Emily and dumped her body somewhere before offloading the automobile.

Rebecca had been inconsolable. She'd taken a leave of absence from the university that eventually became permanent. She'd handed in her resignation to Harvard, and then both she and her husband had disappeared.

Only to reappear, twelve years later, on what the news media is (so cleverly) calling "Murder Street, U.S.A."

What happened to you? How did you go from Harvard professor to convicted murderer?

I sense that the answers to these questions are a part of the larger, missing picture I'm trying to understand.

Rebecca is silent for a moment, studying me with a hard, stony gaze. I can see no trust, no self revealed, no evidence of hope for a future. They are executioner's eyes, twin chips of deeply rooted ice.

She sighs, looks off. "Systems theory," she says, "is the analysis of end-product production, with the goal of identifying the discrete components involved in the formation of the system as a whole. The system could be a literal, material system—such as an automobile—or it could be a model of isolated functions and recurring events—such as in a business or an economic system. So long as it produces some end result, whether desirable or otherwise, it can be analyzed and its components plotted."

I blink, letting this mouthful sink in. *"Okay,"* I say, nodding slowly. "I think I got that."

"There's no difference, really, between isolating the components of a material system and modeling the isolated functions and recurring events of a business. A car requires an engine, a fuel supply, wheels, and a driver. Yes?"

272

"Sure."

"Seems obvious, right?"

"Of course."

She nods. "Yes. So, then, since it's so obvious, why bother to map it out at all?" Rebecca pauses, letting this rhetorical question hang for a moment. "Because, when the car malfunctions, modeling the car as a system allows you to discover *why*. Were the tires flat? Was the gas tank empty? Did the driver fail to push the gas pedal down? Did the engine fail even when fuel was present?" She smiles, clearly in her element. "This correlates to nonliteral models, too. Once you isolate the discrete components of a business, you can identify points of failure. 'Supply and demand' is a broad, crude example. Those two components can be held as separate, discrete, necessary parts that together form a greater, holistic whole."

"That makes sense." I cock my head to indicate the guard who sits waiting outside the door of this room. "How does it apply to our surly overseer?"

"Many ways. Any number of ways, really. But the aspect I was referring to involves the phenomenon of feedback. This is the result a component gets as a returning force because of the component's operation. For example: As a boxer punches a bag over and over again, calluses develop on his knuckles. We concentrate on the effect of the punch on the bag but often miss that the bag returns a result to the knuckles, too. Follow?"

"Yes."

She nods, and it's the automatic, reflexive nod of teacher approval. "This prison is a system, and a complicated one. The COs are a component part of that system. They perform their function and receive feedback of various kinds as a result of that performance. Some of that feedback is good: a paycheck. Much of it is bad: being spit on; having urine or feces thrown in their faces." She flashes me a mirthless half smile. "She sees the worst of the worst, in terms of human behavior. Over time, her opinions of the incarcerated have been modified by this kind of feedback. It's probable her opinions of general human nature have been altered as well.

"It's likely she believed, when she took the job, that the environment wouldn't change her. She was wrong, of course, because that's ... " She spreads her hands, shrugs. "Well, that's impossible. Nothing's immune to feedback. All existence is the current result of varying forms of feedback."

"That's fascinating," I tell her, mostly meaning it.

"Thank you." She inclines her head toward the video camera mounted on the wall behind me. "I see we're recording this."

"We are. Is that a problem?"

She smiles mirthlessly. "Would it matter?"

"No. But if it bothers you, I'd like to know."

She raises an eyebrow. "Why, if the end result's the same?"

"Well ..." I consider my answer carefully. Answers—the right answers—are important to this woman. "I suppose because the systems I'm modeling are systems of individual behavior, and 'why' is the most important component to identify. Without it, you never reach the result you're going for."

"Which is?"

"Understanding."

She goes silent at this and seems to pull away. Whatever bond I'd believed we'd been building disappears, replaced by a broad, sardonic weariness. She barks out a laugh and shakes her head. "Understanding? Please." She looks off and away, not meeting my eyes. A thousand yards enters her stare.

"Rebecca," I say, softly, careful to keep my tone confident but nonconfrontational, "I've seen just about every kind of crazy you can imagine. I might be more ready to understand than you think."

She glances at me, looks away, scoffs. "Anyone can understand a statement in a literal sense. Belief's a different thing altogether."

"You think I won't believe what you have to say if you tell me the truth?"

She is silent for a time, staring at a spot in the middle of the table. When her gaze finds mine again, the hostility has vanished, as though it were never there. She smiles, and it is the impersonal smile of the professional, falling somewhere between aloof and friendly.

"Systems theory reveals universal, or relatively universal, truths over time. Examine enough systems, and no matter how different they are from each other individually, commonalities appear. Does that make sense to you?"

I consider it, nod. "Sure. The same is true when it comes to analyzing psychopaths. Every individual is an individual—and that's an important factor to remember, always—but they also share characteristics of behavior."

"That's right. Every snowflake may be different, but they're all made of frozen water. They all fall from the sky. Every unique fractal is cold and melts against the skin. In nature this is a material result of material actions. When the temperature is cold enough and the humidity high enough, snowfall occurs. If variables A, B, and C exist, D probably results." She looks at me directly. "*Probably* is always the potential wrench in the works. However slight the possibility, one must always account for the possibility of an unknown variable."

She's right, of course. Every serial offender is the same as the rest of his kind and yet also uniquely different.

"These system commonalities eventually become expected. The 'probably' drops as a considered variable. Result D becomes more than an expectation— it is assumed. These assumptions can become entrenched and permanent, at which point they transform into bias. Bias over time delivers error."

I quell my impatience and tamp down my desire to ask the questions I need answered. Rebecca is talking freely. It would be a mistake to pressure her at this point. I think about what's she just said, instead, and look for a way to contribute to the conversation.

"There was a study done once," I say. "Its results fit with what you're saying. The study took a group of seasoned law enforcement personnel with years of individual experience in solving homicides and paired them up against a group of mental health professionals with no real experience in profiling criminals.

"Each group was given the case files of a number of solved homicides, with all information about the offender redacted. None of the group members were familiar with any of the cases. Each was asked to profile the offender—to come up with the type of person they thought had done it—and this was then compared to the perps who were actually charged."

Rebecca's eyes are on me now, and they've sharpened. I have her interest. Good.

"Let me guess," she says. "The group composed of mental health professionals were more accurate, on average, than the group of experienced law enforcement personnel."

"You got it."

She nods. "They saw part of a pattern they'd seen before and assumed the same result. The mental health professionals expected nothing and worked with the unique aspect of the information given them."

"That 'probably/maybe' factor."

"Yes." She's staring right into my eyes now. "The flip side, of course, is that there *are* commonalities in patterns, and it's good to have a catalog of the patterns that do exist. Right-handed people tend to draw in a counter-clockwise motion, for example. A spy in World War II was once captured and tortured to reveal the authentication methods he was to use with his contact. He told them 'shave and a haircut.'"

"Knock-knockity-knock knock—knock, knock!" I supply.

Rebecca smiles. "That's the one. You might think it amateurish to use such a common code, but it was purposeful. The spy didn't know the name of his contact so could not provide it no matter how long he was tortured. The Germans went to the location the spy had provided, and they knocked—shave and a haircut." She gives me a lopsided smile. "Two seconds later, machine-gun bullets were whizzing through the door and walls and into those Germans. Because, you see—in the real code, the last knock was to be omitted."

"Smart."

She nods. "Very. Or, how about the behavioral impulse that directs us, on the average, to knock once for yes, twice for no? Why yes first? Because we are driven by bias and selfish interests first, and so the first questions we ask tend to be the ones we think we already know the answer to."

I barely cover my surprise when her foot taps mine once under the table, then taps it again twice. Rebecca gives no indication that anything has happened at all. A dozen courses of action run through my head, but Rebecca begins to speak again before I can choose one.

"You can conceal intentional anomalies inside larger, expected patterns. What is expected is seen first and is generally completed heuristically. That is to say, when the first parts of the pattern fit what's 'required,' the remainder is often assumed to complete as expected, without any action taken to verify."

"That missing last knock."

She nods her approval, and I feel—just for a moment—as though I am in a college classroom, not inside a prison. "Yes. That's an excellent corollary. There are thousands of examples. An older man with white hair, wearing a priest's collar, is generally assumed to be a priest, not an impostor. We are more likely to trust a policeman who is well-groomed, alert, and wearing a pressed uniform than we are to trust one with stubble on his face and alcohol on his breath."

"The individuals I hunt are definitely managers of expectations," I muse.

"Of course they are. They live in costume. Their true selves violate all patterns, and fundamentally so."

I decide to push a little, to poke and see what causes her foot to tap against mine again. "Rebecca, all that being true—why would the individuals behind all this suddenly decide to reveal what was so successfully hidden? Until I came to your neighborhood, no one in the outside world knew your street was anything other than a normal place to live. Yet everything so far points to my team and I being lured to Colorado as a deliberate act."

Her foot taps mine under the table twice. "I have no idea," she says, aloud.

Two taps for no. Why no? No what?

My earlier ideas of blackmail return, and I remember how she noted to me that the interview was being recorded. It had seemed casual at the time, but perhaps it was actually a clue. I'd told her I was seeking understanding—maybe this was it.

"I saw something when I was down in the bunker," I say, switching gears. "After I killed Ben. It was a kind of control center or monitoring station. There was a bank of monitors, and I could tell that I was seeing inside a number of the homes on your block."

"Really? I had no idea."

Her foot taps against mine once. *Yes.*

Yes, she is saying, *yes, I knew we were being watched there, and yes, I fear that I'm being watched now.* Along with that, unspoken but understood: *No, I will not speak freely or take even the slightest chance that what I say here will make its way to the wrong ears.*

"I watched an older couple hug each other and then I watched the husband kill his wife and himself. They talked about someone they clearly cared about whose name was Sheila."

Rebecca's foot taps mine once. A brief moment passes, and then, a single tap again. *Yes,* she is saying, and then *yes* again. There is something important here.

"I know who you're talking about," she says, nodding. "Tom and Carolyn Anderson. Lovely people. Sheila was their granddaughter, as I remember." Her foot taps mine once for yes. "I never met Sheila." Again, the single tap. "They never talked about her that much and always seemed sad when they did."

Tap. *Yes.*

"They spoke about her as though she were still alive. Did you get that sense?"

Rebecca shrugs, but again, the single, confirming tap. "I can't say. They were never definitive—never shared many details at all, really." She pauses. "I know from experience that no parent can ever really believe their child is dead without seeing the body." Her gaze on me seems more intent. "You can't give up hope without confirmation."

"Emily?" I ask, softly.

Rebecca lowers her head and sighs. No tap necessary this time. "She watched me through the back window as he raced off with her in my car. That man," she says, almost spitting the word out. "That filth." Her eyes rise to meet mine again, and all the distance, that thousand yards of staring, is gone. "Emily was screaming," she whispers. "My baby was so afraid, and I couldn't do anything for her. I saw her screaming, and then I saw nothing but blackness. When I got my wits back ... she was gone."

I hate this part of what I do. I hate it most. I'd rather see a dead baby than have to be the one to break the news to the mother. There is nothing quite as haunting as watching a strong man shriek, unaware that his wife has fainted next to him. I once told a woman that her daughter had been found axed to death. Her mouth had opened slightly, then her teeth had snapped together, shearing off the tip of her tongue. I rode with her in the ambulance, holding her hand, covered in her blood and tears, as she howled without stopping.

"I lost my daughter," I say, without meaning to.

The newly grieving don't want to hear about your old, settled loss. It becomes a kind of unwanted comparison, or even a form of twisted competition, in their eyes. People in agony have time only for themselves.

Rebecca studies me and nods. "Yes, I remember reading about that. I'm sorry."

"Thank you." I sigh. "But I shouldn't have brought it up. I'm not sure why I did. I apologize. This is about you, not me."

Her foot taps mine, twice this time. It catches me off guard, and I barely cover my surprise. No, she is telling me. I force myself not to frown. But why hide it?

"No apology's necessary," she says aloud, puzzling me further. "The only reason I agreed to see you was because I knew you'd understand about Emily. Emily is all that's ever mattered to me."

A single tap against my shoe. Yes? Yes to what?

"I read the case file," I say, my voice quiet. "The case is still open, but there's no mention of any leads about your daughter. Is that true?"

"Yes." Her voice is low, defeated.

The foot taps ... *twice*. It's a sucker punch to the solar plexus, and I freeze in place, using all the willpower I can muster to keep the shock I feel from showing.

A tear balloons in the corner of her eye, growing fat before it bursts. It slides down her cheek without purpose, like a dead man being rolled down a hill. "I never saw my baby again," she whispers.

But then—two taps again—and I feel the hairs on the back of my neck stand up.

No? As in, she's lying about never having seen Emily again?

"My husband's gone, too, now," she murmurs. "But then, he really died the day we lost Emily. He never blamed me, not even secretly. He just died inside. Emily was his wonder. That's what he called her. His 'proof that God exists.'"

She puts a hand over her eyes for just a moment and curls into herself. It's a spasm of agony, the bittersweet of all that once was and could never be again. Then, the hand drops, and her eyes are a dry, dead calm. "Now, all I do is read my books." Her foot taps mine once. She sighs, smiles, shakes her head in self-deprecation. "I read my books"—the foot taps again, insistent—"and pretend I'm still a professor, talking about systems theory and about anomalies hidden inside expected patterns"—another single tap—"when the truth is what?" She spreads her hands, indicating that to her, this is a rhetorical question. "I'm just a mother who couldn't keep her daughter safe and a wife who killed her husband."

"Rebecca ... ," I say.

She acts as though I haven't spoken. "I want to thank you for coming, Special Agent Barrett. I was there that day. I saw what happened to you. You're very brave, and I truly, truly appreciate you making the time to come and listen to me, and for being so kind in your responses." She gives me a dead soul of a smile. "After all—I'm a murderer. You might even find out soon that I'm much, much worse."

She taps my foot twice this time, signaling a no.

"But however it turns out and whatever you do learn about me, I hope you'll still believe one thing, at least: I loved my daughter more than I ever loved myself. There's nothing I wouldn't have done for her."

One tap for yes, and yes, I do believe this about her. I don't understand everything yet, but I do believe this.

"Is there anything you can tell me about the other people who lived on your block, Rebecca?"

The thousand-yard stare returns. I watch her shutting down, locking herself up tight again right in front of me, and I can't understand it. "I've said everything I want to say, or need to. I'd like to return to my cell now."

She taps my foot once for yes. Then again.

"Please, Rebecca—you're the only survivor. Don't go. There must be things only you could tell me, insights you could help us with."

"No," she says. "I'm sorry, but no." Two taps, definitive in their finality. "Guard!" she calls out. "I want to go back to my cell, now!"

The door opens, and I search for words to keep her from leaving, but I can find no confidence in it. Rebecca has delivered her message. It's up to me to understand it.

"Stand up, convict," the CO says, the flatness in her voice matching the boredom in her eyes.

Rebecca stands, and the CO frees her wrists from the table. Then, it happens. In that in-between moment, in that small space of freedom, it happens so fast that it's over before my mind understands what my eyes have seen.

Rebecca lunges, grabbing the key from the hands of the startled CO, and plunges the end of the key into her own throat. It's far from sharp, but she manages it on strength alone. I see the end of it plunge into her neck. I watch it rip a jagged crescent from one ear to the other. I blink, and by the time I understand what's happening, she is dying.

The CO is screaming for help, backing away from the spurting blood. I am rooted in place, transfixed by Rebecca's eyes and by the peace and relief I see inside them as she dies.

CHAPTER EIGHTEEN

I stand alone inside the six-by-eight cell that Rebecca Stoddard had called her final, solitary home. It was the last place she'd slept through a night she'd wake up from. The last place she'd been alone with her thoughts.

I hate prisons.

It's a modern, single-prisoner cell secured by a steel door instead of a sliding wall of metal bars. A square of safety glass is fixed at eye level, designed for the guards to be able to look in, used by the prisoners to peer out. Just below waist level is a rectangular steel hatch, through which items can be passed, including the prisoner's wrists for shackling. The hatch is locked from the outside, just like the door into which it's set. Prison has a single direction for its occupants. It accepts with open arms, hugs the guest tight, and then refuses to let go until told by another. The prisoner's voice is never relevant, never important, never heard.

I close my eyes, drawing in a breath. It's calm enough, I suppose, under the circumstances. My heart has stopped racing, and the initial bout of adrenaline shakes has passed. A vision of Rebecca's dying eyes swims into focus, and I see again what I saw there earlier, what I have at times thought of as either *the last detail*, or *the smallest worst thing*. It's the name I've given to the glimpse of a usually unpleasant, always unexpected but obvious truth. Sometimes they just surprise you, but at other times, they can shake you to the bone.

Rebecca's suicide had been both deliberate and planned. Her actions, once she put them into motion, were both decisive and doubtless. The pain hadn't seemed significant to her. Although the cut had been difficult, leaving a long and ragged wound, her face hadn't twisted as she cut, nor had it gone gaunt in a pose of endurance as she died. Initially, as the bright red blood (bright as red paint, so ridiculously red it looked fake) spurted from her neck, her eyes filled with focus, drilling into mine with an intentness that captured me. This action, too, was purposeful, a wordless demand to witness that would take away all your honor if you refused the duty.

Timeless silence followed, and for an unmeasurable series of moments, Rebecca's decline was almost civilized. The initial explosion of violence had been shocking and jagged, but her fall into the sleep of death had slowed into the smooth motion of a long, deep dive. The light in her eyes dimmed as the rate of blood flowing from her severed artery slowed, and in time with it. She focused on me; I was the witness her gaze demanded, and the future could be known.

Her eyelids drooped, then dropped, then closed, shimmering against the orbs of her eyes like butterfly wings, a beautiful shuddering of infinitesimal jolts from the waning yet still omnipresent and infinitely delicate tensions of life. The catastrophic blood loss she'd experienced had turned her white as paper just a moment before, but I thought I could see the gray beginning to seep into her skin. It was more a phase shift than a sharp change, kind of like trying to watch water evaporate or ice melt, but it was also far too global and much too relentless to hide.

I was watching the animus of life leave her. There was no other way to put it. It was an action I could see clearly, in that wobbling line that divided shivering, white, and alive—a person—from silent, gray, and still inside—a body. Watching with such intensity had forced me into sync with her, creating a kind of endless moment of horror-filled expectation. I couldn't look away, not even if I wanted to. I was entirely locked in and overfocused.

And then it came, the last detail.

Rebecca's eyelids had opened once, in a single, slow motion before bouncing smoothly closed again. Her breathing was shallow and languid and slow. She was being overtaken by her death pallor, the same as when the sun gets muffled for the day by a thick layer of clouds. Involuntary muscle motion had begun to flatten and fade.

Without warning, her eyes snapped open, wide and full of panic. Her hands flew to her ruined throat, scrabbling violently, and what was meant to be a scream exited her mouth as a horrible and sustained grunt instead. I couldn't help thinking that it sounded like the amplified groan of a person straining to move their bowels. It was an ugly, helpless, snorting, animal noise, and it thudded through me, drenching everything it touched in numbness, instantaneously, the way that adrenaline can anesthetize a traumatic injury even while it's happening.

She was looking into my eyes when I saw it: a nuclear, white-light flash of terrible, unearthly fear. It was as brief as a baby's heartbeat, there then gone, and once it was gone, Rebecca was dead. I had to fight down a shout and get a grip on the nearly overwhelming wave of terror that washed over me, drowning out the possibilities of thought. Understanding of what I'd seen—of what it meant—followed in the next half-glimpsed moment, bringing with it the resumption of time and self-awareness. I could taste my own spit, and was aware of doing so. I could hear my own heartbeat.

Kirby had been there, on the heels of it all, trying to protect me and control the moment. She used firm but gentle hands to make me stand, then turn and walk away. Her eyes roved and checked, roved and checked, scanning both me and the environment, searching for injuries and indications of danger.

"Smoky," she said, her hands on my shoulders, her eyes searching mine. "Are you okay? Are you hurt?"

I realized I was trembling hard, and that my mouth had dropped open and stayed there. I closed it, blinking fiercely as I fought to get my own muscles back under control. I could feel the shiver trying to reach my teeth and knew that if I allowed this to happen, it might become a clacking I couldn't stop, like magic shoes that make you dance until your feet bleed.

"Smoky?" Kirby asked again.

"Not hurt," I managed to whisper, shivering in a single, hard jolt as I did. My throat felt like a rusty engine. "Just surprised."

Kirby glanced at Rebecca's wide-eyed corpse and nodded. "That's definitely the clown jumping out of the cake with a butcher knife," she muttered, not meaning to be funny in the slightest.

I open my eyes again here, in what had been Rebecca's cell, and sigh. She'd been afraid beyond all reckoning because she was going to die, and that fear had been endless. No matter that she'd planned her suicide with a clear head; in that last, unmeasurably tiny increment of existence, the only thing she'd wanted was to live. This is what I'd seen and understood in that last instant before she was gone. Rebecca had recognized the approach of her own death. She saw the cliff's edge as it raced toward her, fast, but not fast enough that it killed her before she understood it for what it was.

A tear runs down my cheek. The result of this knowledge had been hideous for her, and it was this hideousness that had been that last detail I witnessed. Death is every deepest fear realized, and Rebecca had understood this fact just before dying herself. Unfortunately, I had been able to observe her in this state, and it was like taking a shotgun blast to the chest. My ears were full of senseless, roaring shouts, and sorrow was a hammer to the head, pounding me like a nail.

"I-I'm okay," I'd forced out, making myself look away from the permanently frozen image in my mind and into Kirby's eyes instead. I cleared my throat, clambering for the feeling of a firmer hold. "Really."

I kept the shivering from reaching my teeth, I thought but did not say. *So I have the reins. I'm the horse and the rider, and the rider's in control.*

Sitting here, alone in the cell, I can still sense the presence of that frozen hideousness. It sits at the edges of my vision, in the corner of either one eye or the other. I acknowledge its existence and the fact of its density, but only as an inverse of denial. It's important to accept their presence, the statues, once they've been emplaced. The action of pretending otherwise is just another form of interaction, really: that of pushing away, and the ultimate goal is to achieve noncontact without expending this strain of resistance, because you can't resist something that's always there forever.

The famous mathematician John Nash was afflicted with a full-blown case of paranoid schizophrenia, and it had come complete with a set of walking, talking, interacting hallucinations of other human beings. It was his interaction with these illusions that was both the cause and evidence of his insanity, and the results were ruining his life and career. They were real people to him. They spoke words and stopped the sunlight. He had contiguous memory of them and of his friendship with them, a record that, because it had felt "real," could evoke real emotion, resulting in an authentic sense of duty to respond, should they speak, as well as the desire to do so.

It was only when he realized there was proof they could not actually exist—that they never aged—that he was able to finally separate out from them. He apparently continued to perceive them at times, but he never again interacted with them. They became random ghosts, following close and yammering in his ears at first, then falling gradually quiet and moving slowly, farther and farther away.

"It's the dog you feed," I remember muttering at Kirby, as I gripped her shoulder with the thick, drunk fingers of one hand. "You understand?"

Kirby grinned, and that had been its own flash of light, steadying me further. Comforting. "Not a single, bonkers word of it, crazy-lady."

I grinned back, thinking that I loved Kirby. She was a true friend. "You're a true friend, Kirby!" I trumpeted, shaking her shoulder with the hand that was still on it. "You know?"

"Yeah, yeah, yeah," Kirby replied, rolling her eyes. "But you were talking about a dog."

I blinked, as a wordless thickness filled my brain for both a second and all time. I blinked again, and it had passed. "Right," I agreed, nodding. "The dog you feed." I frowned. "The two dogs we all have inside us? You've really never heard of this?"

"Not that I recall," is what she had told me. I believed her at the time but am less certain in retrospect. I think she already knew about the dogs but just wanted to keep me talking.

"We all have two dogs inside us. One is our urge to do good, the other is our urge to do bad, and they are always fighting. The one that wins isn't the one that's strongest, it's the one you feed the most."

"Deep," Kirby replied, rolling her eyes and meaning none of it, the perfectly executed misanthrope.

"No, no," I had insisted, realizing as I spoke that I sounded like a drunk with a mouth full of taffy. I pointed at Rebecca's corpse. "That," I said, pointing again. I tapped my temple. "What you see. What you *know* because of what you see." I stopped tapping, suddenly exhausted. "Looking at that stuff, thinking about that stuff—that's the dog you don't feed." I stared into Kirby's eyes and made myself smile, so she could see that I was, in fact, going to be fine. "Because if you do, he'll never stop growing, and then ... he'll eat you up."

Kirby had smiled, keeping the wattage just under that of her usual grin, so that I could see she was serious. "Refusing to feed the bad dog has always been my strategy, Smokes, don't you know? Think about it. You'll see, I'm right."

She *was* right, of course, and I smile a little, thinking of it. Kirby's refusal to go negative, internally or otherwise, was almost a constant. That did not mean it was all an accident, nor that it was all effortless or lighthearted. I think it is as much a choice for her as anything else, and an act of will requiring both discipline and strength.

I come to understand many wordless things, moments that freeze in place before turning into the ice statues that rove inside me, always ready to appear like the occasional ghost. Surviving these moments is about maintaining distance and managing what's required to make that happen. Closing them up in a locked room doesn't work, any more than speaking to them directly does. The balance to find lies in knowing they are there only exactly as much as I have to, and no further. I may always be capable of hearing them when they talk, but I'm equally capable of ensuring that I never answer.

A knock on the cell door cuts my musing short. The door swings open to admit Kirby, who is pushing a small, two-tiered bookshelf on wheels. She pushes it up against the wall and next to the stainless steel table that's bolted into the floor, taking stock of the cell as she does so.

"They painted the concrete gray?" she asks, pointing at the floor. She shakes her head. "That's like painting poop brown."

"It's prison, Kirby."

"It's the discouragement of individuality on a budget, darlin'," she chirps back. "Compassion at its barest and on the cheap."

I shrug. "Sounds like prison to me."

"My point," she says, flashing me a grin. "Prison is poop painted brown. It won't kill you, in other words—but it's definitely shit, and—oh my God—it sure does stink."

"As long as it won't kill you, I'm fine. Compassion on a budget is still pretty impressive."

"Oh, I agree," Kirby replies. "It should suck balls to be guilty." A wicked grin creeps across her face. "Now that I think about it, I betcha sometimes it really, literally does."

"Ew," I say, making a face. I point to the bookshelf. "Desperate, awful prison sex aside—are those all the books she checked out while she was here?"

Kirby nods. "Yep. Each and every one. They keep good records, and I side checked the books they pulled against the master records myself. It's complete."

"Great, thanks."

She pauses, examining me. "Everything good?" she asks.

"For the moment." I smile. "Thanks."

Kirby rolls her eyes. "I killed a prince heading up a drug cartel once," she grouses. "It took me sixteen months to get close to him. I imagine I can handle finding a bunch of the world's most boring books." She winks once at me, then leaves, closing the door behind her. I hear the sound of a few footsteps, followed by silence, and know that she's taken up position right outside.

A prince-killing bodyguard? I think to myself. I consider the environment I've found myself in, as well as my own potentials for anxiety, and smile a little. *Well, when it comes to feeling safe... Kirby being such a badass definitely doesn't hurt.*

I let this understatement lie, and I stand up, moving to the books. In the aftermath of Rebecca, once the smoke had cleared and her body had been carted away, I thought about the taps. One tap for yes, two taps for no. I had pulled a notepad from my purse, listing out the sequence of taps as I remembered them, followed by recalling what words she'd been speaking at the time. I had stared at the combinations till my eyes burned, searching for meaning.

Indicated she knew they were under surveillance, I had written. *Indicated she knew the older couple I watched commit suicide on camera, and was aware they had a granddaughter named Sheila. Made it clear through multiple taps with her foot that the story of this couple, and of their granddaughter, was one she knew well and regarded as relevant.*

I raise an eyebrow, nodding to myself as I read the next note:

It's an oddity that both this couple and Rebecca lost children and that they ended up as neighbors. Quite a coincidence; maybe too much of one (?).

And then:

Tapped no while stating that no further information ever appeared regarding her daughter after the kidnapping. Tapped no specifically while stating that she'd never seen her daughter again after that day (!!!).

I had circled this last sentence, and as I read it again, I feel goose bumps rise on my arms, from shoulder to wrist. It's a shuddering of the flesh, as though the skin was screaming as it tried to run away.

What does this mean? I'd written extemporaneously. *Is she saying she has seen her daughter since the day of the abduction? Is that possible?*

I'd circled these sentences, too.

Multiple single taps regarding reading her books, over the course of multiple statements. Why? She wants me to look at the books she read, I had written, answering my own question and then circling it.

Inferred I might find out soon that she was much worse than a murderer, but then tapped no as if to indicate what I found would be untrue. Blackmail?

Finally:

When I said to her "this is about you and not me," she tapped to indicate no. Why? Was she referring to Alexa and how we've both lost daughters? Or was she talking about me as an FBI agent? Both? I had circled *Both*, on instinct only, for reasons I could not yet define.

"I need you to get me all the books Rebecca checked out while she was here, and I need you to bring both me and the books to her cell."

"Consider it already done," she said. Her mouth had flashed a smile, but her eyes had been grim and worried. Violent death had occurred in my proximity, and it had put Kirby on high alert.

Ten minutes later, and here I was.

I scan the titles, seeing nothing that would interest me personally. They're all medium-to-thick volumes, mostly hardbound and obviously highly technical. *Advanced General Systems Theory*, I read on the spine of one, my head tilted sideways. *Comprehensive Game Theory* on another.

I choose the first at random and open it on the stainless steel tabletop that's meant to act as a surface-of-all-trades, as a dinner table sometimes, a reading desk at others. I have no idea what I'm looking for, so I decide to simply move through the book page by page, scanning as I go.

On page two hundred and twenty-five, I see a circle made by black pen around the word *My*. I blink, surprised by the reality despite my expectations. The gooseflesh reappears.

"How about that?" I whisper. "A genuine, real-life secret message."

I write it down in my notebook. I finish turning all the pages, but *My* is the only word she circled. The next two books yield nothing. On page one hundred and twelve of the fourth—*The Complex Math of Complexity Theory*—my breath catches when I see the word she'd circled: *daughter.* I write it down on the notepad next to the first word, and then I stare at it, hearing the two words together in my mind as a statement.

My daughter.

I lick my lips, feeling dread coil around itself in the pit of my belly. *What follows?* I wonder. Will I like what I find? I freeze inside this moment, but only for a moment because the questions are useless. I'm going to continue until all the pages in all the books have been turned, and every secret, circled word has been revealed.

I breathe deeply and continue turning pages. I complete the book without finding another circled word, then close it up and move on to the next. By the time I finish, I have a jumble of eleven words and a number. It's easy to solve the order they go in, and when I finally read what's revealed, adrenaline rockets through me, clearing away all the musings and fog and doubt.

"Holy crap," I breathe, reading the sentence again. I blink to make sure my eyes are clear, and read it again.

My lovely daughter died today by gunshot October 2015. I saw it.

"Holy crap," I say again, in something sharper than a whisper.

I get up and move to the door, but Kirby opens it before I can knock. She stands in the doorway, her face grim. "It's about the bunker—the death museum."

"What happened?"

"A bomb went off inside it, five minutes ago—Callie and James are fine, don't worry. The bang was big enough to move the house above the bunker off its foundation, and the shock wave shattered windows for blocks, but there were no serious injuries that we know of so far."

I gape at her, my mind reeling. "What—what does this mean, Kirby?"

She's silent for a moment, gazing at me. "An explosion that powerful inside an enclosed space?" She sighs. "Anything still down there was blown to smithereens, that's what."

CHAPTER NINETEEN

I am sitting in the conference room of the Denver FBI field office, watching video of the explosion's aftermath as I talk to Tommy on my cell. Outside the room's door, streams of agents are moving at a dead run. Anytime a bomb goes off inside the borders of the United States, it activates and involves—in a nearly unqualified sense—everyone.

"So you're fine? The team's okay?" he asks, for the third time.

"We're unhurt," I reassure him again. "The CIA team that was working inside the bunker was working in the same room as one of the explosive charges. They're treating it as a rescue operation, but ... " I let my voice trail off, indicating the obvious.

Tommy is silent for a moment. "Yeah," he says, then sighs. "They may not find anything. High explosives up close can vaporize a body. The more the blast energy is contained, the more catastrophic the damage to whatever's inside its radius."

"That's what the bomb expert they flew in from Quantico said, too."

"Do they know what it was? RDX? C4?"

"There's nothing official yet, but the guess is C4 explosive or some variant. The team inside the bunker was transmitting video when the explosion occurred, and I'm told that just before the big blast, there was a release of what they're guessing was a cloud of atomized copper dust."

Tommy whistles. "Bunker buster. When the primary explosion happens, it sets all the atomized copper in the air on fire and sends it flying outward at a jillion miles a second in every direction. No one in the same room as the blast could have survived."

I sigh. "Yes. I haven't seen the video yet—the CIA owned the agents who died, and they're still vetting it—but that's what the bomb guys told me, too."

The pause again. I can almost hear the oscillation of his worry, bouncing back and forth between desperation and pain. "I'll tell Bonnie, but she'll still want to hear it from you again later."

"I'll call her once school's out. Promise."

"Good. Kirby's still with you?"

I glance to my right, where Kirby is sitting in one chair, with her legs stretched out and crossed at the ankles. Her eyes are closed in a light doze, while one hand rests against the butt of her holstered weapon. "If I can't catch forty winks inside the FBI, then no place is safe," she'd quipped, smiling and then nodding off in what seemed like a blink. I knew she'd wake up alert and just as quickly.

"Right next to me," I answer, truthfully. "Lethal as ever. Sam Brady and two of his guys are here, too, parked right outside the door. Weapons bristle," I joke. "Hyperawareness reigns."

"Okay." Another pause hangs. His worrying hums through the phone lines.

"What about you?" I ask, trying to change the subject. "How are you feeling?"

"Rough," he answers, "but I'll be fine."

I smile, rolling my eyes. "A veritable wealth of information, thanks."

"Strong and silent, that's my plan," he jokes. "Keeps people thinking that I'm wise. Keeps me from saying something dumb."

"But ... you say dumb things to me all the time."

"Hardy-har-har," he replies, but I can hear the unspent laugh in the tone of his voice, and it lightens my heart just a little.

"I gotta go, Tommy. I love you. Give Bonnie and Christopher lots of kisses for me."

"Stay off that street, Smoky. You promised."

"Nobody's going near that place until bomb techs have cleared every home. Don't worry."

"Now there's a dumb request. But I love you anyway."

"I love you more. Bye."

"Bye."

I hang up and sigh, staring at the phone in silence.

"Is he wigging out?" Kirby asks.

I glance over at her. Her head's still down, and both eyes are closed. "Pretty much," I reply.

Her lips curl into a smile. "Must be love."

"I don't know. Director Rathbun wigged out a whole lot more, and it sure didn't feel like love."

Kirby holds the smile for another moment but remains quiet, her breath coming slow and steady. *You love Tommy, too, killer bunny*, I think. *Like a brother, not a husband, but still—you love him. I figured you out on that score months ago.*

It's a thought that both worries and uplifts me. On the one hand, I'm thankful that someone else would lay their lives on the line for my husband. Having that someone be a person like Kirby was especially reassuring. At the same time, I consider a more sober truth: The people Tommy loves and who love him back are all involved in professions that could kill them. Tommy has a warmth inside him, like a fire that can only comfort. He was built for competence and duty, like the rest of us, but he was mostly built for love. If anyone had ever deserved a family or needed one to protect and be responsible for, it was Tommy.

And if he were to lose us? I shake my head firmly. That was an injustice I couldn't allow to be perpetrated on the world.

The door to the conference room opens, and Alan, Callie, and James enter the room. Callie and James appear unfazed by having worked through the night, but Alan's eyes are red-rimmed and rheumy. He's clutching a jumbo cup of coffee in one hand, and a subtle but permanent scowl has set in. He reminds me of a mildly drunk but deeply pissed off boxer in search of a fight. It's not so much about age, for Alan, I know. He always looks this way when he doesn't get sleep; and I know, when he speaks, it will be as though he was possessed by the spirit of a seventy-year-old cynic with anger issues.

"Big juicy hamburgers!" Callie says, holding up the bags in her hands and shaking them as she does. "Piles of delicious greasy fries!"

"Shit on a bun," Alan mutters, darkly. "Heart attacks in a bag. Hurrah."

"Yum," I manage, but it's a halfhearted attempt.

I am distracted by the video playing out on my laptop's screen. It's all exterior, shot by the FBI agents who were there securing the street, but what it shows gives me a picture of how hellish it must have been inside that bunker when the bomb went off.

Every home on the street had been under constant video surveillance, with cameras focused on both the front and back of the houses. We're able to see and hear the explosion when it happens. The sound is tremendous, even coming from underground through tons of earth and concrete. Every video feed on every home jumps violently, like an infant being shaken by an enraged and psychotic parent.

"Holy exploding cow, honey-love," Callie mutters, pointing with a French fry at one of the split-screened images. "Look at the flame geysers shooting up behind the house over the bunker."

"Those are from the vent holes," James says. "When the bunker was constructed, Ben—or whoever—needed to recycle the air inside it. Running it through the home would probably have been too loud, so he had it piped up and out of his backyard through camouflaged exit vents. When the explosion occurred, the blast energy found its way up and out of the vent pipes, creating—" he nods at the laptop screen—"the world's largest Roman candles."

I turn my attention to the large flat-screen television that is mounted on one wall of the conference room. The sound has been muted, but the channel's been tuned to local news. The airspace above and around the street has become a predictable madhouse, as news choppers swarm, battling for the best point of view.

One of them catches a perfect shot of Ben's house from above. A ragged hole is visible in the roof, and the entire home has canted to the right. A tower of thick smoke rises into the sky, huge and immobile, like a swollen thundercloud or an unspent volcano.

"See the hole in the roof?" I say, nodding toward it. "I bet that's where the blast came up through the hatch in the pantry."

"Based on the fact the bunker was multilevel and compartmented by blast doors, the bomb techs are guessing there was more than one device," James says, "and that each one packed quite a wallop."

"Give me some of those fries," I say, holding out a grasping hand. Callie obliges, and I stuff three of them into my mouth, chewing as my eyes move between the story unfolding on television and the video feeds on my laptop.

It's a cacophony, a chaos, and a tragedy. The entire federal world is descending on Denver, along with the eyes of the world in general. Soon, I know, this

293

is a storm that will break. The deluge will bring the flood, and I'll find myself at the center of it all, dodging demands for answers like they were bullets.

In spite of this, a vague sense of excitement and expectation has been building inside me. It began at the intersection of revelations inside Rebecca's cell: the message from the words she'd circled in her books, followed by news of the explosions in the bunker. These things belonged together. They were related. I wasn't sure how just yet, but I was sure it was so.

It was as if all the disconnected pieces of a very large and very jumbled puzzle had fallen from their box into a pile on the floor, and in doing so, had given the sense of their order, like a conversation you have to strain to hear over the murmur of a crowd, or a blurred photograph. It was not yet possible to make out any edges or to give meaning to the shapes, but the most important step had been taken—the existence of a coherent pattern had been both revealed and confirmed.

In order to focus at all, you must have a point to focus on, and this is what we have been lacking. It's not enough to identify the fact of separation. In order to get anywhere, in terms of comprehension, you must identify the separation that's meaningful. In a thousand-piece puzzle, it's the parts that actually go together that lead you toward the prize, not just the knowledge that a thousand separate pieces exist.

This particular puzzle has existed, thus far, only as a fact. It was a multitude of parts known to be connected in some whole but lacking any thread of purpose to define it. I understood Ben's individual nature, in the most general sense, but I could not see how he fit with the bunker, or with the people on the street, or with his fellow monsters like the Wolf or the Torturer.

I didn't see it now, either. But I could smell it. I could tell that it was close. There was a reason behind this concurrence of events, and that reason reeked of timing. The death museum had been a trophy room to end all trophy rooms. No serial killer gave up something that precious unless it was an absolute necessity.

Blowing up the bunker? That was *running*, not attacking. It was a protective action, a destruction of connections. My growing feeling is that we're only an insight away from seeing the full picture with clarity.

Everything that has happened began in response to some concerned inevitability. I *know* it. Something or someone became revealed, or soon would be, and it couldn't be prevented; and because of this, endgames were put into motion.

For the first time since all of this began, I can feel a coherent image straining to emerge. It remains blurry, but then, these are birth shudders, as motion replaces the infinitely still and form replaces the broad, forever blankness of unconnected nothing. Soon, blurs will become clear boundaries, and all the stick figures will have faces.

And then, I think, *we shall see what we shall see, won't we?*

The door to the conference room opens, and a young female agent wheels in a whiteboard made of clear glass. "This is all we have, Special Agent Barrett. Will it do?"

"It's perfect. Thank you."

She nods, a quick, shy dip of the head. "It's Agent Monahan, ma'am. SAC Edward said to get you anything you need." Her eyes dart around the room, stopping to focus, briefly, on each of us in turn. "Is there anything else you require at the moment, Special Agent Barrett, ma'am?"

"No, thanks, Agent M. I'll let you know if I do."

She blinks for a moment before speaking, like a car warming up from a cold start. "Thank you. I mean, yes, ma'am." Another quick, shy dip of a nod follows, and she turns and leaves, trailing her youthful eagerness behind her.

"Awww ... ," Callie opines. "You gave her a nickname!" She clutches her hands together and looks up, presumably toward heaven. "Agent M will never forget this day."

"I think you mean, she'll never forget this day, *ma'am*," Kirby says, winking at me.

"Yes," Callie agrees with enthusiasm, nodding vigorously. "You're right, of course. Do you agree, Special Agent Barrett, ma'am?"

I shrug. "I don't know. I kind of like it. Very 'mature stateswoman,' don't you think?"

"The word you were actually looking for was *elderly*," James says. "As in, 'an *elderly* stateswoman.' Now, can we get back to work, please?"

"You can bite me, *and* we can get back to work," I reply. "How does that sound?"

"Like you're still talking and we're still not working," he retorts.

Before I can devise a snappy comeback, Callie's cell phone buzzes against the tabletop, followed by a ringtone of Queen's "I Want It All."

"Mr. Brady asked me what I wanted in the sex department on our next anniversary," she says with a smile, as she grabs the phone. "I chose that ringtone as my answer." She winks, answering the call as I roll my eyes and Alan groans. "This is Agent Callie Brady. Yes. They are? Excellent. Give me the quick-and-dirty details right now, but be certain to send copies of the actual reports to my email." She opens the thin, leather-bound folio in front of her and begins taking notes. "Right," she murmurs. "Got it. Got it." She stops writing and frowns, one eyebrow arching up in an expression of questioning disbelief. "Are you absolutely sure about this?" She pauses, giving me a gaze rooted equally in trouble and shock. "No, no—I'm not questioning your capabilities, Vanessa. Not in the least. I'm just surprised. I broke a mental fingernail, so to speak. Thank you for getting back to me so quickly. Don't forget to email me those reports. Goodbye." She goes quiet, contemplating some unknowable point in the distance.

"Callie?" I inquire.

She sighs. "That was Vanessa, a DNA analyst from Homeland Security. They flew her down here to do on-site analysis of any DNA they happened to find in the bunker museum and then kept her after the explosion to do the same as a part of the recovery effort. I used her as opposed to the local lab because she has treasure: a portable DNA sequencer."

"Fancy," James says.

"No," she replies, giving him her most withering gaze. "Clothes are fancy, James. This is a genuine technical marvel. It weighs one hundred and eighty pounds and can run up to eight samples every ninety minutes. It's DNA by drive-through."

"I apologize," he says, sounding anything but. "What I meant to say was *very* fancy."

"Vanessa also tends to be a little more flexible than the average lab-bound DNA tech," she continues, ignoring James, "because she actually gets outside under the sun and such—she's been packed off to Nepal and Pakistan in just the last year, as a part of the relief efforts following the awful earthquakes in those regions. She's all tennis shoes, blue jeans, and get the job done."

"Who cares?" James complains. "Less editorial and more information, please."

"Only because the information is far more interesting, my impatient misanthrope." She glances down at her notes. "Your hunch was correct, Smoky. DNA confirms that the girl who called herself Maya—the one who pointed that ugly shotgun at you when you were preggers—was in fact Rebecca Stoddard's daughter, Emily. She was kidnapped roughly twelve years ago and hasn't been heard of since. Until now."

"Holy *Jesus* cow!" Kirby exclaims.

"Curiouser and curiouser," Callie agrees. "But the surprises don't stop there: I also had Vanessa run a comparison between the DNA of the other young woman—the one who shot and killed Mr. Fred Carter after he shot and killed Emily Stoddard, and who then killed herself—against the DNA of the older couple Smoky saw on the video feed." She pauses for effect. "Also a familial match."

"Good Lord," Alan mutters, shaking his head, his eyes wide. "What the sweet shit have we stumbled into?"

"Nothing good," Callie answers, uncharacteristically sober. She looks down, reading from her notes. "The couple was Tom and Carolyn Anderson. The girl, Sheila, was their granddaughter. They took over raising Sheila after their son and his wife died in a car accident when Sheila was two. She was kidnapped two years later." Callie is looking at me now. "She was taken in the same year as Emily Stoddard but approximately six weeks prior."

"Wow," I whisper. I can feel my cheeks flushing with excitement. "So we have two kidnapped girls showing up twelve years later on the same street as their caregivers," I say, pacing as I talk. "Hardly an accident, and certainly no mistake."

"I agree," James says. "The odds defy coincidence."

"The question is … ," I muse, still pacing. "Why?" I pause, thinking. "Also, how? As in: How were the Potters and Rebecca Stoddard kept under control and quiet for twelve years on that street?"

"Had to be related," Alan offers. "The one preceding the other."

"Probably," I tell him, nodding as I do. "It's the logical point of control and a hell of an effective one, at that." I go silent for a moment, considering what I might do and how I might respond if I found myself in the same situation.

If someone bad had Bonnie and Christopher, what would I be willing to do? I press my lips together, thinning them into a grim line. *Just about anything, I suppose. Maybe not murder ... but even that might only depend on who I was supposed to kill.*

"That's the problem with family," Kirby observes. "You love 'em."

"Okay," I say. I stop pacing. I grab a black dry-erase marker from its box and face the glass board. My heart is racing in tandem with my mind. "Okay," I say again, to steady myself. I uncap the marker. "It's time to concentrate on the decision cycle. We need to get everything we know written on this board—*everything*—and see if an opportunity to seize the tactical advantage presents itself."

I stretch my arm and write out four capital letters in the upper-left-hand corner of the glass: *OODA*.

"It's OODA time," Kirby chirps.

"The OODA, she is a good-a," Callie chimes in.

OODA—observe, orient, decide, act—is the model of a combat decision cycle, and the one most used by the U.S. military. Each aggressor has his own OODA loop, or decision cycle, that begins again each time the last one ends. The idea is to keep your own loop short, and to either get or keep ahead of the enemies' decision cycle, thereby seizing the tactical advantage.

We almost always start out behind, when it comes to serial offenders. In the beginning of an investigation, the OODA loop is long, because the first step—observe—has little to narrow it down. So we focus on whatever we have—the victim, the methodology of the kill and its signature, the location. Then we orient: We search for whatever connections we can find between the information we have, and this leads to a decision regarding what our next action will be. At the start of things, this almost always becomes a decision to engage in more guided observation as the chosen action.

In the end, our strength lies in numbers. Some people are prone to calling law enforcement the largest and most well-armed gang in America. I don't find the comparison to a criminal gang apt, but it is true that we win less through violence than we do as a result of human parallel processing. Generally speaking, ten smart cops will outthink a single, genius offender; and a hundred set of eyes, backed up by access to a variety of exhaustive databases and billions of dollars in cumulative budgets, can close the gap on any decision cycle rapidly.

The usual weakness—cooperation and coordination of efforts between different echelons—had been substantially decreased, in our case, by the necessities of scale. It had been made even less of a factor by the presence and contents of the death museum, and was then rendered completely irrelevant by the explosion of bombs on U.S. soil, in a residential neighborhood, no less.

Other than a nuclear bomb, or the name of the guy on the grassy knoll, I can get you pretty much anything you request, Special Agent Barrett, Director Rathbun had told me. *Nothing makes politicians and bosses cooperate faster than the eyes of the world, and the eyes of the world are definitely on what's happening right where you are.*

It was giddily terrifying, pinballing me between feelings of elation and worries that I was going to wet my pants again, but this time without the excuse of being pregnant.

"I'm feeling more confident," I tell my team, "and there's a reason."

"The bombs," James says.

I go still for half a moment, looking at him, marveling, as I have before, at the synchronicity that we can sometimes achieve. Just because the truth is an inevitable conclusion doesn't mean it will be seen or become known. James and I both recognize by feel, the way a sailor can predict a coming storm by the movement of the ship beneath his feet. This is where most of our fellowship lies: in our reading of the waves.

I nod. "Yes. The bombs." I turn to the glass board and press the tip of the black marker to it.

What has changed? I write, followed by the answer: *The destruction of the death museum.* Next: *What possibilities does that reveal? That this is not about solving boredom, but about hiding things and destroying connection.*

"That would explain all the actions against us," I say. "Earlier we considered the possibility that we were attacked specifically *because* they think we might be able to catch them. It's a workable conclusion and a logical one. We were the first victims chosen, outside of the residents of that street, for example. We might assume this is because we fit their victomology, that it was a choice based on need and not necessity, but—" I tap the first heading I had written: *What has changed*—"considering recent events, necessity seems more consistent."

"I agree," James says. "The personal actions Ben took with you spell need. The killings done on video by the Torturer and the Wolf seem to fit victimology as well. Creating circumstances that cause us to come to Colorado, killing my mother, the attacks on Smoky's family; they make more sense when viewed as strategy, not desire."

"Exactly," I say, nodding my agreement. "If we build on that assumption, another question worth asking reveals itself."

The marker squeaks and squeals, slashing letters onto the glass. *Why now?* I write, followed by its answer: *Some recent, precipitating event we remain unaware of.*

"And there's a corollary," I continue, writing more.

If they are concerned enough about any connection(s) to take such drastic measures, then connections must:

—Exist.

—Be possible to discover.

I tap this last set of assumptions. "These should be our point of focus, which means we need to data dump everything and anything that could possibly be relevant to that discovery."

I reach out to the glass again, and the marker slashes. *Everything we know right now,* I write near the top edge of the glass and then, next to it, *Possible leads/No follow-up yet.*

"Nailing down the motivations behind their actions against us gives us a point of reference within the whole. It's a jumping-off point for perspective and framework, and might make it possible to correlate existing info into other parts of the whole, so we can start building a cohesive picture."

"There's a mouthful," Alan mutters, smiling a little.

"Big-word Sally and her big-word sandwich," Kirby jokes, grinning. "It's cohesively delicious."

I roll my eyes, accepting my deserved reminder that excitement about a line of thought can easily lead to pedantry. "Yes, fine, sorry. Can you forgive me and move on?"

"Enough of the roundtable Chatty Kathy," James snarls. "I have a lot of information to share regarding the investigation of the houses on that street, and I'd like to start being professional and effective before the decade's out."

"No need to get nasty, honey-love," Callie chides.

He turns on her, and I realize that James is not a part of this banter, not at all. His anger is sincere. "My mother might disagree with you on that, *honey-love,*" he snaps, each word dripping with bitterness and rage. "But hey, maybe I'm wrong. I mean, she only had her face burned off by a psycho with a blowtorch."

The squall vanishes as suddenly as it had appeared. James covers his eyes and does not so much slouch as he bends, in a quick, hurt motion, down, then back, like a green-wood sapling curved by the force of a single, freakish wind.

The hand comes away from his face. His eyes are downcast and subdued. "Sorry." He sighs, glancing around at all of us.

"James," Callie says, moving a hand to cover one of his own. "Look at me." He doesn't, at first, but then manages to drag his gaze up to a point level with hers. "I promise—me and just me, not as a part of the team or for the team—that I will never stop until we have the bastard that killed your mom." Her voice is gentle, but Callie's eyes are hard, clear, and cold. She leans forward a little and says it again. "I *promise*."

James stares back at her, silent as we all wait, holding our breath and trying to be small. "Me, too," he finally replies, nodding once. "Thanks."

Callie gives him a broad, bright, sunshine smile, full of affection and devoid of even a whisper of frivolity. "No thanks necessary," she says. "Don't you know that I'd do anything for you, sweetheart? And so would anyone here?"

He's unable to meet her eyes now. "I do," he says. "And I appreciate you saying it. But I need to move on from this conversation right now and get back to work." He hesitates. "I'm not built for this kind of intimacy, other than in short bursts, so ... please."

Callie chuckles, Alan coughs, and I hide a smile. Kirby breaks the silence with a snort. "I'm with you, Jesse James," she says. "I mean, validate my parking, baby, not my emotions—am I right?" She punches Alan in the arm. "Am I right, big man?"

"Don't hit me when I'm tired," he growls. "As a matter of fact, don't hit me, period. You always leave a bruise."

Because I am watching him when it happens, I catch James cracking a smile, small and fleeting, but the tension and pain have left him. It will return, of course, sometimes as quick and tiny thunderstorms, at other times as a single, freakish, giant ocean wave. We will be there, together or individually, to ensure that he always makes it back to shore.

"Why don't you go ahead and brief us on what you found, James?" I ask him.

"Yes." He clears his throat, shuffling through his papers until he finds the one he wants. He focuses on it for a few seconds and then looks up, closing the folder as he does. I know from past experience that he won't refer to it again, no matter the quantity of information involved or the number of details.

"Thanks to the swarms of agents from multiple agencies, including all their fancy toys, we got extremely detailed coverage of every home, and in record time."

"Unfettered interagency cooperation is like a sign of the apocalypse, it's so damn rare," Alan mutters.

"As a result," James continues, ignoring him, "some unusual data sets were discovered. I'll brief you on each one, and then Callie will brief you on the rest.

"First—every home had a surveillance system of some kind, except for four: the homes belonging to what I'll call 'the overseers.' This includes Ben's house and the houses of the three families murdered by Emily Stoddard."

I stop marking notes on the glass to interrupt him. "Sorry, James—quick question. Have we officially confirmed that she was the doer?"

"I can answer that," Callie replies, "and the answer is yes. That same swarm of agents came with half the FBI crime lab and two medical examiners, as well as all the portable processing they could carry. DNA from each family was found on Emily's clothes and on her body; and her DNA was discovered on the bodies of the victims, as well as in their homes." She sighs. "Unfortunately, little Emily was our killer. It seems she told the truth when she spoke to you at gunpoint."

I let this sink in, which it does, falling without stopping, like the world's densest stone. "Damn." I shake my head to clear the shadows, stifling my own sigh as I do. "Thanks. Go on, James."

"The majority of the remaining houses had the same surveillance system, and I mean exactly the same, down to consecutive serial numbers on the equipment used."

"Interesting," Alan murmurs, frowning in thought as he considers this detail.

I agree silently and mark it down on the glass.

"This included a total of twelve homes. The system design in each home involved two separate sets of equipment, both well hidden but with one hidden much more covertly than the other."

"Backup?" Kirby asks.

James nods. "Of a kind. Both were hidden well enough that we can assume neither was meant to be found, but I believe the less covert set was still meant to serve as a decoy in the case of discovery. This set could be discovered with some research and patience if you suspected it existed. The truly covert set was designed to defy professional detection equipment, including two features I've never seen before, anywhere."

"Do tell," Callie says.

"Average lens detection equipment utilizes an oscillating red laser beam. The refraction index of most materials is way below glass, so camera lenses— even those the size of a pinhole—show up through the viewfinder as bright red points of light that are easily visible in relation to their surrounds. Still, it's not foolproof, and you always get false positives, usually from metal, mirrors, or other types of glass. The cameras in these homes have light sensors specifically attuned to red spectrum lasers. When the sensor detects the presence of this type of light, a nonrefractive iris snaps shut, covering the lens. The first sweep with the laser will reveal those red dots, but then the irises close, and so a second sweep shows nothing, and neither will any visual inspection that follows."

"Holy crapola," Kirby says. "I'm not even aware of anything that advanced being used by the U.S. government."

James nods. "Yes. The techs involved believe they were custom-made and were of the opinion that the design is entirely unique. But that's not the only custom feature—the same sensors, activated, also power the unit down for one hour, which prevents detection by equipment designed to pick up the active presence of radio and EMF. Again, this design appears to be both custom and unique."

"I'll bet," Kirby says, bemused. "I've heard of shielding schemes but never a sensor-driven total power-down."

"Well, these systems have shielding schemes, as well. They cover any and all power sources, electric wires, and so on, and for the most part they exceed the TEMPEST standards used by the government, including the military and all the intelligence agencies. In addition, steps were taken both to shield and obscure the regular noise put out by wires and power sources, and the like. Thorough detection specialists won't only scan, they'll also listen, using extremely sensitive acoustic equipment—very similar to what plumbers use when they're trying to locate pinhole leaks from pipes running through concrete slabs. Not only were the components of each system soundproofed, any normal electrical wires running through the walls near each system were replaced with wire lengths deliberately designed to be louder than normal.

"The techs did tests on both systems using government-grade equipment, and they basically stated that detection of these systems would require either foreknowledge of their location or opening of the walls."

He pauses to let my marker catch up, and I consider what he's said so far, as I write. "Technical expertise aside," I ask him, as I finish, "I'd guess the expense for the design and placement of these systems would be pretty high, yes?"

"Yes," he confirms. "Try several million dollars."

I note this down and indicate he should continue.

"So far as the interior of the homes go, there was also a third, additional system, dedicated to audio only. This system becomes active only when the other systems are powered down as a result of sensor response. It's shielded just as thoroughly as the others and is also state-of-the-art."

Kirby whistles in begrudging appreciation. "So they're able to maintain full audio surveillance if the two other systems happen to be shut down in response to detection attempts. That's good strategy," she says, shaking her head. "NASA-level backup-schemes-type stuff."

A fuzzy awareness of some kind tickles my mind as she says this and as I consider these separate systems, the equipment involved, and their general design. I can't see it clearly, just yet—whatever it is—but it has made itself known, an emerging intuition not yet fully formed.

"All three systems provide total coverage, creating complete redundancy, and are either powered by active solar energy—Colorado averages three hundred days of sunshine a year—or by deep-cell batteries should solar become inadequate due to cloud coverage, snow storms, or physical damage.

"Finally, the output of each system is hardwired, from camera to digital video recorder, and the recorders were never placed inside the homes themselves but inside the bunker. Part of the installation of these systems involved the placement of an interconnected network of PVC pipes, including the running of pipes under the street and sidewalks." He shrugs. "It's a smart feature of the overall design. In the unlikely event that all the cameras are discovered, the most prosecutable content—the resulting video—can't be accessed without first following the wires to their terminus. This would require doing exactly what we did: digging up every lawn, breaking up the sidewalks, and jackhammering out selected sections of the street."

"That's a difficult warrant," Callie supplies, "when the only apparent crime is a perversion. Unless you have a reason to suspect that every house on the block is similarly wired, in the absence of murder, abduction, or the rape of a child—most departments won't invest in the time and trouble, especially considering the potential for liability and lawsuits."

"People do take their lawns seriously," Alan observes. "I knew a cop who trampled some woman's prize roses. She sued the department and won." He grins. "I doubt it helped that he apologized by sleeping with her, and then never called her after."

I rub the tip of my nose as I study what I'd written on the glass, letting my thoughts lead me. "Considering that aspect of things—running those pipes underground up and down both sides of the street—it makes the most sense that all the surveillance systems were installed at the same time."

"I agree," James says. "Now, in addition to the twelve homes I just talked about and the four with no surveillance at all, there was a final set of five houses with only a single video surveillance system installed, and it was the most covert version for each. Same equipment, same setup, same design. Each of the five in that group *also* had acoustic surveillance systems identical to the one I just briefed you on."

I frown, confused. "So…there were three distinct groups, then? Ben and the first three families who died—no cameras; twelve homes with three separate installations; and then a remaining five with just one set of video and audio; and in that last group, the most covert installation of the video surveillance was chosen?"

"That's correct," James confirms.

I shake my head. "I don't get it. What's the difference between each group of occupants?"

"Alan has some information to provide that illuminates the possibilities," Callie says, "but if you don't mind, I'd like to brief everyone on my data before we let that cat out of the bag. My findings are relevant to understanding some of the assumptions we later made, together, once we understood what Alan had discovered."

I uncap the marker again, poising it against the glass. "Hit me."

Callie produces her notes with a flourish. "First of all, for clarity, James and I initially split up the forensic targets, such as him on the surveillance systems, myself on the DNA, and so on. But with so many agents on site, that street was an anthill. We realized that the sheer volume of information being collected, combined with the scale of the crime scene as a whole, made collation of the evidence and the interpretation of its context a full-time job, even for two people. We ended up repositioning into oversight duties only and concentrated our efforts on accepting what they gave us and turning those findings into some possible conclusions.

"My point is," she says, indicating James with both hands, in the manner of a game-show model showing off a brand-new washing machine, "this was a joint team effort. So please ignore your natural inclination to give me all the credit. As he'd say himself, he couldn't have done it without me."

James rolls his eyes. "I never said anything even close to that. I'd rather die first."

"*Any*way ... ," Callie says, in an overloud voice, drowning him out, "I wanted everyone to know that James was possibly helpful, and not entirely destructive, in putting together the following."

"Noted," Alan replies, nodding. "Very generous of you."

Callie inclines her head, accepting the faux compliment as seriously as it had been given. "I know," she says, smiling sweetly and batting her eyes. "But then, enough about me—we have killers to catch."

She clasps her hands and clears her throat, her eyes going distant in thought for a moment. Like James, I know that Callie will not require her notes. She is, and has always been, a commodity much in demand as a witness for the prosecution; but these same qualities, combined with a propensity for public skewerings, have made her an object of fear and intense hatred in the eyes and hearts of the defense lawyers who were her victims.

"We continued to identify separate uniformities in those same three groups—the Ben group, the twelve-house group, and the five-house group. For example: All the members of the Ben group—the overseers, as James so dramatically anointed them—have the same brand and model of laptops, and each one uses the same encryption program, which I'm told is both off-market and proprietary.

"Each house in the twelve-house group used laptops of the same brand and model as Ben and friends, but the encryption software, while identical within the group itself, differs. It's an off-the-shelf, consumer program.

"The last group of five, interestingly, don't appear to share any common qualities at all, other than the broadest: They each had laptops, and everyone used some form of encryption. Unlike the other two groups, that's where it ends."

"Odd, again, so far as that group goes," I remark, as I pause my writing to shake a cramp from my hand. "Anomalous, even."

"Strange days, indeed, honey-love," Callie agrees. "And it doesn't stop there." She sniffs the air. "I think I might be getting a contact high from your magic marker. Are you caught up enough for me to go on?"

"Continue with impunity," I assure her. "These hands were born to take notes."

"Very well," Callie smiles. "We have not yet been able to gain access to the laptops used by Ben and friends," she continues. "The encryption program is very robust. Thanks to our crypto-fascist friends at the NSA, however, and the abominable actions they took to weaken a variety of cryptographic programs, access was gained to eight laptops in the twelve-house group and three of the laptops in the five-house group."

"Not a fan?" Alan asks, half smiling.

"I wouldn't trust any of them as far as I could throw the Constitution," she mutters darkly. "I don't want the 1984 version of life, everything mean-ing anything and the possibility of a helmet full of hungry rats on your head, thank you very much."

"Let's get moving, please," I say, keeping my tone gentle but firm, the voice of a friend who gives orders. "We're chasing something, here, so let's not fall further behind. OODA, people, remember?"

"My apologies," Callie says, nodding her head once, serious enough but unoffended—my friend who is also a fellow professional. "Of course you're right. Let's see … ," she murmurs, looking up as she gazes inward. "Right. We were pretty excited at first by what we were discovering on the eight laptops from the twelve-house group, but once the information on all eight laptops had been correlated against one another, our opinion changed."

"What did you find?" Alan asks.

"God-awful, soul-ending, hard-core child pornography. Admittedly, my exposure to that particular medium has been minimal, but this was the worst I've seen thus far. All of it was undeniably authentic."

"I'm sorry you had to see any of that, Callie," I tell her, meaning it.

"Not to worry," she says, wearing her smile like a shield. "It'll give me a few dark and stormy nights, I'm sure, but nothing that will last forever." She waves it off. *An unimportant detail*, she is saying, without saying. "The first scenario we considered was as obvious as it was satisfying: We'd stumbled into a nest of highly organized pedophiles." She shrugs. "It didn't fit every scenario, but it had a kind of... comparative badness that was very seductive."

I nod, seeing myself in the same situation coming to the same conclusion. "Understandable."

"Sure. But then—things changed. The correlation analysis had revealed identical anomalies on all eight laptops. Notably, the child pornography on each hard drive was almost never accessed. The most recent metadata we could find indicated that none of them had opened any of those files in at least six months."

"Well, that doesn't fit," Alan exclaims. "Kiddy diddlers are addicts. They eat at their trough because they just can't help themselves." He frowns. "And you didn't find any other caches anywhere? Not in any of the homes?"

"Nothing. That ant army was thorough, too. They used portable X-ray, metal detectors, fluoroscopes, and a few other pieces of equipment with twelve-to fifteen-letter names. They even searched under the tiles of every roof. They didn't find anything."

"Well, that makes no sense whatsoever." I sigh. "In terms of them as pedophiles, I mean."

"Agreed," Callie replies. "Once we had seen the contents on the hard drives belonging to the five-house group, we changed our hypothesis. Not to a certainty, exactly, but as a possibility worth consideration."

"Which was?" I query.

"Compromise for control." She purses her lips, conveying her disgust. "Blackmail. There's just no upside to having any connection with that trash, especially if you're a man. It's like plutonium for perverts. Radioactive to your reputation simply by virtue of proximity."

I consider this for a moment, turning the different scenarios over in my mind. I am sobered by the realization that I would probably be unable to prevent myself from hanging onto at least a shred of suspicion if I stumbled across the same material under similar circumstances. Child pornography is evil. Viewing it left a mark on the soul, creating a specific demand that was hard to put down: *Someone* had to pay. "You're right," I admit. "It's like finding out that your brother or sister is a cannibal that devours infants."

"Or hanging out with a bathtub of body soup in summer," Alan offers. "Hey, you didn't kill anyone. But, boy, you *sure* do stink of death."

"What was it you found on the hard drives of the five-house group?" I ask.

"Thousands of photographs of the people in the twelve-house group," she answers. "And hundreds of hours of video, too. Very little else, and nothing probative."

I jot this down and cap the marker for a moment, giving my hand a rest. "So the five were running active surveillance on the twelve?"

"Active and constant," Callie confirms. "EXIF information found in the photos and videos on the laptops alone go back almost two years, and they found encrypted portable hard drives that take that figure back a decade."

My mind is spinning, though not in a bad way. It's what accompanies a cascade of possibilities and ideas, as if the mind's eye was trying to focus on a thousand newly created connections a second and make sense of them. It was a stronger version of the same sense from earlier: We were catching up to something in the distance. We might not see it yet, but we could smell it.

"Smoky?" Callie inquires. Our eyes meet, and she grins. "We're not done with this ride, just yet. There's more, just as doozie-ish."

I uncap the marker again, eager, the ache in my writing hand forgotten. "Ready," I say, giving her a grin of my own.

"There were two other discoveries we made, both of them kicks to the brain. We weren't able to put them completely into context until Alan gave us the final piece, but be patient and, I promise, we'll get there quickly."

"Not quick enough," I assure her. "So stop delaying my gratification."

"It'll be my pleasure, honey-love. The next set of common items we found made no sense of any kind at all. In all twelve homes of the twelve-house group, taped to the underside of every bedroom dresser, the techs found a lottery ticket. They were all one-pick tickets; as in, they only picked one number to play, and they had all been purchased on the same day, though from different outlets, about six months ago. What we noticed when we took a closer look was an oddity in that single line of numbers on every ticket: The same four numbers were repeated from beginning to end. The sequence might not be identical on every ticket, but that repeating pattern of four was."

"I want to be able to look at it," I tell her. "How many numbers on a Colorado lottery ticket?"

"Well, it's six sets of numbers, with a maximum of two numbers in each set. That's a minimum total of six, and a maximum total of twelve. Each lottery ticket we discovered contained a string of twelve numbers—the maximum."

I pick at my lower lip, thinking this over. "What number was repeated on the ticket you found in Rebecca Stoddard's house?"

"Two-zero, and then zero-three, with a dash separating each set of two."

I write it out on the glass: *20–03–20–03–20–03*, and feel something tugging at my awareness as I do. It's like staring at the face of an acquaintance whose name you've been told but are unable to remember—the recognition of recognition.

"Why do I know this number?" I ask her.

"Why, because you do, of course." Her grin is back, and my heart is beating at the predator's pace, slower in excitement, as opposed to faster. "Listen to the last set of commonalities we found, and, I promise, it will come to you."

I turn back to the board and raise my marker. "Go ahead and shock me."

"By this time, we'd seen the pattern: Uniformities of different kinds, and in different forms, were being found within each home group. We asked the NSA goons to run correlation algorithms on every byte of recorded data related to each and every home. They came back in under an hour with another anomaly, and when we added it into the others, it made something clear.

"The run of the algorithm had turned up a commonality in movies rented through the television cable company used in each house. First of all, every rental had occurred on the same day in each home, and that day just happened to match the date of purchase on every lottery ticket.

"The second thing we noticed was that every member of the twelve-house group had rented the same movie.

"When we looked up the title of the movie online to see what it was about, we noticed the last and most important thing: The plot of the movie revolves around the abduction of a child."

"Oh my God!" I exclaim, involuntarily, not quite a shout, but close. My eyes snap wide and I can feel a prickling on my scalp, like a slow trickle of electric current is passing through it. "The number—it's a year!" I circle the first two sets of numbers, isolating them from the others. "Two thousand and three," I whisper, as butterflies trampoline inside my stomach. "That's the year Emily Stoddard was kidnapped."

"Yes," Callie says, enjoying the evidence of my epiphany as it shakes my whole body to its metaphorical bones. "Now get this: All the numbers fluctuate between 2001 and 2003."

It takes me a second to grasp the meaning of this, as my mind is still reeling. When I do, all the confusion inside me—the random motion and cacophonous noise—stops, and stops dead. I go from screaming to silence, from seizure to stillness, inside that infinitely small space of time in which action precedes understanding. This is finding out you've slammed your foot down and locked the brakes on your car only after it has already happened, or ducking from a bullet before you consciously recognize the sound of a gun being fired.

"The twelve-house group," I whisper. "Each one had someone they love taken from them."

It is Alan who speaks up this time. "Smoky, each one had a *child* taken from them. Just like Rebecca Stoddard."

CHAPTER TWENTY

I stare at the glass board, letting the reverberations of this latest revelation work their way through me. "I've never seen anything like this," I say, in a voice just above a whisper. "I'm not sure *anyone* has."

Kirby raises her hand, pumping it in the air with exaggerated excitement. "Oh! Hey! I can chime in on that if you'll let me!" She waves the hand back and forth. "Pick me! Pick me!"

"I guess everything's a joke to you," James says, sounding as cold as I've ever heard him.

"No," Kirby replies, without missing a beat. "The truth is, everything is very, very serious to me—that's why I joke. It's okay if you don't get that, since I'll never give a ding-dong-dang what you think of me, Mr. Snarlyface."

"Ha!" Callie snickers, pointing a finger at James. "Mr. Snarlyface! It's perfect!"

"Go ahead, Kirby," I tell her. "Any insight you can provide is welcome."

"My *pleasure*," she says, sticking her tongue out at James. He rolls his eyes in disgust but manages to keep any other retort to himself.

Perhaps "Mr. Snarlyface" hit a little too close to home, I muse, smiling a little.

"Well," Kirby begins, "it's just that we have a saying in the field: 'Luck kills.' Every act of violence between at least two human beings is an exercise in probability. Roll the dice often enough, and you are guaranteed to lose, eventually. Experience without training can be worse, since maybe all you'll learn are bad habits, with the only kind of confidence instilled being confidence that you *suck*.

"I mean, saying that you've been in two hundred fights without ever taking a single boxing lesson might only mean that you've gotten really, *really* good at losing. So a lucky win with training is a win, but a lucky win without training is always a lose, unless you never, *ever* end up in a similar situation again." She leans to the left, smacking Alan in the arm again. "Do you follow, fella?"

"I follow that I sometimes wish I had it in me to punch a girl," he mutters, scowling as he rubs the spot she'd hit.

"No you don't, big guy," Kirby replies blithely, "and that's the basis of your mojo. All the girls dig on that big ol' grumpy, teddy-bear style. *Anyway*," she says, turning her attention back to me and away from Alan's nonplussed gaze, "thing is, violence is stressful. Violence is scary. Even when you've done it a lot, because that's the nature of the human animal.

"Fear won't submit to the intellect, and all violent acts will make you feel at least a little bit afraid, even when you have the upper hand. Fear activates adrenaline, which might as well be called the dumb-dumb clumsy drug, since it puts your thinking underwater and can turn all your fingers into thumbs." She shrugs. "It's why cops can empty their guns at a suspect only fifteen feet away and still miss with every shot."

"Sure," I agree. "I had an instructor at the academy who liked to say that you could aim and fire at a target, but when it came time to put the bullets into people, all you could do is shoot." I grin. "*We call thinking in training, proficiency*, he would yell at us. *We call thinking in combat, being dead.*"

"A man after my own heart," Kirby says, smiling. "I like 'a good killer can't count to four.' My point, which is more likely: Kidnapping twelve children and twelve families without getting caught—because you're lucky? Or because you're trained?"

As I consider this rhetorical, James raises both eyebrows in what appears to be genuine surprise. "That's actually insightful," he says.

"Of course it is, Mr. Snarlyface. I don't make promises I can't keep, in bed or in life."

"Time will tell," James replies, but he manages the smallest version of a smile. Kirby grins back, winking at him.

"That's not it, though," she continues. "I used the small example first so you'd really grasp the larger one. Even with training and experience, the flawless capture of twelve kids in mostly public urban settings is crazy good. Add in the parents—on the surface, sure, it seems cut and dry: You can count on the average parent to do almost anything if the life of their child is on the line." She shakes her head, and I realize that Kirby is all business right now.

She's as serious as Kirby ever is, and while that might not be quite as rare as diamonds, it's at least as rare as gold. "But no. It's just not that simple.

"First and always, you have the X factor of fear. New kidnappers operating without the benefit of someone more experienced have a much higher rate of failure on the initial grab than a group run by someone who knows their stuff, and their captives also die more often." She nods for emphasis. "A *whole* lot more often. Newbie abductors are big ol' walking, talking piles of confirmation bias. They fail to account for fear because, hey, they know they won't knock off their captive—they're in it for the money, after all, and no one pays for dead. They make a point of telling this to the girl or guy they've got tied up, and figure that they're covered.

"Fight or flight, though, is one of the strongest set of motivators a human has. It stifles thought, focuses attention to the diameter of a pinprick, and when it makes demands, it's always going to be the loudest voice in the room."

"I've been in a shit-your-shorts situation or two," Alan says, nodding. "What struck me about the worst of them was discovering that my memory of the event wasn't always that reliable afterwards, either. Pretty powerful."

Kirby makes a gun with her fingers and shoots an imaginary bullet at Alan. "Spot-on, big guy. Adrenaline overwhelms the body and skews every response or decision that follows. What that newbie doesn't realize is that the tiny little brunette with cuffed hands and a gag in her mouth never even heard him. What she heard was the ocean roaring in her ears and the sound of her heart trying to beat its way out of her chest. Mr. Newbie kidnapper? His reassuring little diatribe was just the 'wah-wah-wah' of an adult from some Charlie Brown television special.

"So the moment he unties her feet so she can go potty—the tiny little brunette makes a break for it; and since she's in a panic, she trips over her own feet, falls down a flight of stairs, and breaks her neck. Or maybe he shoots her before she reaches the door, and the outcome is the same.

"Then again, maybe he makes a different kind of error. He not only fails to cut through her fog of fear, he doesn't make the boundaries clear, or the penalties for crossing them. He doesn't convince her she'll survive. So once again, heading for the toilet—she jumps him. Since all that adrenaline has basically turned her into the Hulk on a rampage, he kills her by accident, while he's trying to keep her from removing his balls with her fingernails or from tearing his eyelids off.

"Could be he does fine at the start but allows himself to get complacent; assuming that if she wasn't terrified yesterday, the same is true today. Only today, she woke up from a nightmare where he's decided to rape and torture her. So—" She shrugs. "Brand-new adrenaline rush, followed by an escape attempt and death.

"These guys?" Kirby raises an eyebrow. "Twelve sets of parents for twelve years, and they never say a word, never die early as a result of their own actions. Factor in twelve houses, plus the rest—the surveillance systems, piping wires under sidewalks and streets, et cetera, and we're talking about a level of tactical planning and execution that is world-class.

"Think of it this way: You're looking for a group of bad guys who can do what I do, at my skill level or better. They have at least as much experience as yours truly, probably more."

I consider this assertion and sigh. "Super un-reassuring, Kirby," I tell her.

She grins. "No shit, girlfriend. On the other hand, consider this: No one grows that skill set in a vacuum, and they definitely don't get that good without acquiring some kind of reputation for it."

"Very true," Callie says, "and a good point. I guess it's not just all guns and comedy with you, honey-love."

"Oh, they're always around," Kirby says, grinning, "they're just not the totality of my repertoire, so to speak."

"How would you do it?" I ask. "Correctly control a fearful captive, I mean. Give us an idea of the mind-set involved."

"Attention, intimidation, and open negotiation. That's my personal trifecta. They have to hear what you say, believe you mean what you say, and be able to believe you will let them live and go free, based on a logical argument which they can understand."

"Examples?" I ask.

"Attention is making them hear your voice above that screaming in their heads. This could be grinding the open end of your handgun barrel into one cheek while you look into their eyes and shout in their face, or it might mean slapping someone who's gone into hysterics hard enough to leave a bruise in the shape of your hand.

315

"Intimidation is about credibility. They must believe that there is no doubt whatsoever you will kill them dead should they force that hand. At the same time, they also need to believe in your professionalism, and that you're not psychotic. If you hurt them, it won't be because you like to watch them suffer. It'll be because they broke a rule and forced you to do the professional thing.

"One generally complements the other: If you give them what's clearly a preplanned explanation of the penalties they can expect for breaking your rules, make the penalties horrific, and deliver it in a calm voice and with a deadpan face, you'll get their attention, too, brothers and sisters. Nothing says 'Do what I say or else' like explaining you'll cut off their nose if they run, as though you're reading from a grocery list and are explaining that you want tomatoes, please and thank you, *not* carrots.

"Open negotiation is being honest about everything other than your personal details, and making a logical case, based on relatable self-interest, for belief in your assertion that they are worth more to you alive and unharmed than tortured or dead. One of the best ways that I've *heard* of doing this— since of course, I've never done it myself—"

"Of course," Callie purrs, smiling.

"—again, that I've *heard* of doing this, is to give the abductee the same lecture I just gave to your bright and shining faces." She counts off on her fingers, running it down for us again. "Tell them about fear and its effects; the difference in outcomes between an amateur and professional kidnapping; the attention-intimidation-open- negotiation cycle." She pauses, seeing something. "If you can make them believe that their survival is tied to following your rules, and even your actions of intimidation are based on a professional plan and not a psychotic impulse—then half the battle's won.

"Even so, nothing is permanent, and it's just as important to remember this fact as any other. The longer an abductee is held, the greater the chance that doubts will start growing in the worst place, the place you can't see—inside their heads. Even in a smoothly running abduction, your ongoing observation and judgments play their part." She shrugs. "People have their own internal systems of rules and beliefs, plenty of which lie below their immediate awareness. We don't always know *why* we dislike the greasy-looking dude with the bull-style nose ring, and if someone asked, we probably couldn't put it into words—but it's true.

"Trust is the big-daddy example of this, and in spades. Some abductees will never trust you when you tell them they'll walk out alive. This is usually because they try and put themselves in your shoes, and when they do, all they can see is the potential end result of prison. They can't see any of your professional confidence, so it seems pretty clear to them that you must be lying. Either you haven't thought it through—which means you aren't the professional you claim to be, or you have, and you're keeping them appeased until it's time to put them in the ground.

"It's the calmer abductees, usually, that tend to be this way," she muses. "The ones who listen closely and ask questions based on logical ideas, not fear.

"The point to remember is that you can never believe in the trust of someone you're victimizing, and you can never underestimate what someone is capable of when they're fighting for their life, even if the only place that's true is in their heads.

"So you have to watch closely and give them the same rap daily. And whatever you do, never—*never*—forget the ironclad laws: Don't harm an abductee who's playing by your rules; and, if punishment can't be avoided, be clinical, not angry, while you're causing them pain. It's never personal, because personal is always bad. Personal can't be professional, you see—so any failures in this regard make you a liar in the abductee's eyes.

"The only other thing that seems important is pesky probability itself. No matter how good you are, no matter how cooperative your abductee, grab enough folks enough times, and you'll eventually end up with a dead abductee—from a heart attack or stroke, maybe, if nothing else." She purses her lips, thinking, and nods in self-confirmation. "I guess that covers it." She flashes a grin. "In terms of what I've heard, of course."

"I'm not sure I enjoy having such things broken down into some kind of successful actions checklist," Callie murmurs, her voice subdued. "The top ten ways to use your abductees' fear against them." She shakes her head. "Do not like, honey-love. Do not want."

"Nobody sane likes it, Red," Kirby replies. "It's just the best way to do a bad thing, if your genuine goal is a successful exchange involving a live abductee."

I consider something, based on all that she's just told us. "Let me ask you a question, Kirby." I gesture toward the glass board. "In your opinion, would holding the children over their heads be enough? To keep twelve sets of adults compliant for twelve years?"

She frowns, looking at me as she ponders my question. "No," she replies, after a full minute of silent thought. "At least, it's not what my brain-food betters would term 'statistically viable.' If the children are the only leverage, you're counting on the one component in the abduction equation hardest to guarantee and maintain—trust. Worse, you're asking them to trust a person with their kids—you—who is the scum-of-the-earth sort of individual who's willing to murder, and maybe torture, children." She shrugs. "That's some pretty heavy cognitive dissonance, and it'd only get worse the more time that went by."

I chew on my lower lip, turning this over in my head. "Okay, but the thing is—it *did* happen. It *was* successful." I turn my gaze on Kirby again. "So, put yourself in the position of planner. How would you work it out?"

She gives me a lopsided smile. "Kind of 'I didn't do it, but here's how I would have, if I did'?"

"Give me your best O.J.," I reply, with a grin.

Kirby contemplates it for a few moments, her eyes gazing upward at some nothing in the distance. "Okey-dokey, Smoky. Two answers to that one. First—the biggest challenge is keeping their trust about a single, simple question: If they continue to do what you say, are the lives of their children in better shape, as a result?" She gives me a querying gaze. "It's a balance, do you follow?"

"Sure," I reply. "It makes sense."

"So there would have to be regular proofs of life, and they'd have to be undeniably real. Considering that, as time passes, satisfaction with the balance itself can degrade—sooner or later, seeing your kid in prison or shackled to a bed will become a source of pain, not relief—I'd do the proofs of life on video. I'd make sure that the parents saw both that the munchkins were under my control, but also that they were thriving in some way. I'd definitely make sure that the kids were happy, if not immediately, then eventually."

"Why?" I ask. "Why this method?"

"It lets them be parents, vicariously. It proves to them that in spite of the time that's flying by, their children are not being irreparably damaged. Nothing proves this more than seeing that their child is still capable of smiling."

"Good Lord, Kirby!" Callie exclaims. "That's absolutely the most vile, Machiavellian thing I've ever heard in my life."

"You're not wrong to judge it, Red," Kirby agrees. "It's diabolical. I can do all kinds of bad, but I couldn't do this, not in a billion years. It's how I would see it and plan it, though, if I did."

"What else?" I encourage her.

"I mentioned two answers, and this is the second one. The problem you're addressing would be that, no matter how well you executed the solutions in part one, if they believe that going for help could end well, they just might take the chance. In other words, if any other solution than keeping their kids in your care has viability, the more time that passes, the greater the likelihood they will go for it.

"It's the basic issue: No parent worth a crap is ever going to see their children in your hands as other than dangerous. Period."

I consider what she's saying against how I might feel if it were Bonnie or Christopher in that same situation. It chills me to realize that Kirby's one hundred percent right: As a parent, I really am that predictable. Even with all that I know about perpetrators and poor survival rates in kidnapping cases, I am ready to have my own hope used as a weapon against me, should my children fall into similar hands.

"How might you accomplish solving that problem, then?" I ask, not really wanting to hear the answer.

"Well..." Kirby's voice trails off, and she sighs. "Threatening the worst wouldn't be enough. You'd have to show them the worst. Video of a child the same sex and age as their own getting raped, for example, then tortured to death." She gazes down at the tabletop. "High definition, with the audio turned up loud."

"For shit's sake," Alan growls.

"Hang in there, big guy," Kirby says, but there is no true lightness to her tone. She sounds tired instead. " 'Cause it gets worse. You'd also have to do something that completely destroyed their credibility as parents, and that they believed did just that. It would have to be impossible to explain, something so bad that it isolates them.

"It would have to convince them that, even if they were to go to the cops or whoever, once this surfaced, they'd be done. D-O-N-E, all caps and nothing else. Maybe have them rape and/or kill a child on video, for example. It would have to be something on that level of horror to make a parent give up all hope of ever being believed. Such that, if they did go to the cops, the only results would be the parent in jail and the child in the ground."

"This just keeps getting better," Alan says, sad eyes perched over a scowl.

These answers have sickened me, too. I feel the instinct rising to put the meeting on hold, so I can call home and check on my own children. I battle it back, forcing myself to focus on Kirby and the business at hand. "Do you think that might work?" I ask her. "In terms of real-world application?"

"It's the best plan for some successful inhumanity," she replies, clearly not excited about this answer. "If I was a fully committed psychopath without a shred of a soul, that's how I would plan it. It would be a good plan, under those terms."

"It wouldn't be a plan everyone involved could know," Callie murmurs. "It's far too demonic. Even criminals, by and large, have their limits when it comes to children."

"That's because pedophiles aren't just criminals," Alan says. "They're enemies of the species."

I face the glass board, my eyes moving from one island of information to another. "Are we profiling them as pedophiles?" I frown. "I don't know. It's possible. On the other hand, it's not necessarily required."

James's eyes narrow, focusing on me with sudden interest. "How do you mean?"

"Well, if we're building a profile using Kirby's assessment of best-guess scenarios, the children's primary purpose is for use in controlling the parents. Based on her model, sexual abuse of the children is the least desired outcome for the unsubs. They need the kids happy and thriving, not visibly traumatized; and young children aren't good at pretending to be healthy and happy when they're frightened of their general environment." I glance at James and shrug. "It's not really in their skill set. Certainly not enough to fool the parents, who know them best."

He nods. "That's true. In the scenarios Kirby hypothesized, torture and rape of a child was a specific act, a means to an end. The goal being to destroy the parent's credibility in the most utter sense possible, in a manner they'd find insurmountable, on the one hand, and as an intimidation tactic, on the other. Those are functional examples, not pathological ones, at least in the sense of profiling them as pedophiles."

"Exactly," I agree. "Still, the willingness to use the torture, rape, and murder of children as a tool is fairly outside the general envelope of behavior, even for the criminal community. It's quite a commitment to make for the sole purpose of control." I frown. "I have to say, I'm not familiar with any examples of it, personally, though I don't doubt they exist."

"The Russian mob has a history of dealing in kiddie porn," Alan observes. "But the guys who make the material and star in it aren't generally mobsters. In fact, one reason the Russkies got known for selling that shit is because up until fairly recent times, Russia was one of two or three countries in the world where the possession of kiddie porn wasn't criminalized."

"Really?" I ask, astounded.

"Yep. It was illegal to make it or sell it, but not to own it. That makes for all kinds of loopholes, like, you know, 'prove I am the man who make this film, comrade.' The same was true in Japan, up into recent times, though the laws have changed in both countries by now. The point being, the Russian mafia probably got into that market because it was profitable, they're soulless, and they had a unique legal environment in relation to that trash. It's still an atrocity, without a doubt, but like you said, the motivation is more about making money than filling a personal need there."

"Even so," I muse. "Pedophiles or not, these kinds of horrific crimes involving children won't be a feature of most criminal organizations. They're too dangerous; they run the risk of bringing down too much heat. More than that, the average violent criminal offender doesn't profile as a child killer. Not even the average serial killer. It's one of the few nearly universal anathemas. So, if what Kirby's posited is true, we're talking about some relatively unique individuals."

"Actually," James says, speaking slowly, "it's a lot more unequivocal than that, if we're running with a profile based on Kirby's assertions. If you consider all the factors involved and required, the sheer existence of this group—or gang, or whatever you care to call it—goes way beyond being unique or even rare. It's a *singularity*. It's a concurrence of events and individuals so improbable, the possibility of its emergence is only known to us as a result of its occurrence."

"Okay, James," I say, encouraging him. "I follow that. How does it help us?"

He points at the glass board and all its markings. "There are only so many ways the convergence of personnel, training, access, and pathology required to create all this could have come about. Not only the training required to execute flawless abductions, for example, but a training environment that attracts the *kind* of individuals capable of becoming world-class at it.

"And," he continues, on a roll now, "as another factor, an environment where men operating at this level of expertise would collect and find each other. Or, drawing it out further, where they might have the opportunity to recognize their similar pathologies." He shakes his head. "Every individual convergence needed will be a rarity of its own. And while these individual instances might have more than one candidate environment capable of their creation, the *chain* of necessity—the 'convergence of convergences,' let's say— will be a singularity, too." He lifts a single finger of one hand for emphasis. "There will be only one possible configuration of connected environments that allows for the creation of this group."

He looks directly at me, his eyes boring into mine. "You were right, Smoky. The puzzle's revealing itself. It's just that it's so big, the only way to understand it is to view everything together instead of reacting to each part as it appears. It's the *structure* that's the signature, with these guys, not the manner of the individual killings themselves."

The room goes silent, as everyone considers what James has said. It is the kind of truth that becomes obvious once it's been uncovered by someone's brilliance. It makes me remember one of my favorite quotes, ever, by Thomas Kuhn: "You don't see something until you have the right metaphor to let you perceive it."

The investigative process employs this continuously as a way of revealing and understanding the otherwise unknown. In my job, I begin at the end. I start at the result, examine the evidence, and then do my best to contextualize it. "What is this like?" "What does it remind me of?" "What is it similar to?" From generalizations of similarities, I'm able to proceed toward a recognition of any differences, and if a generalization won't lead me to anything specific, I can abandon it.

Under normal circumstances, I'm applying this method to the acts of an individual. If a woman's been stabbed fifty times, I can ask myself a series of questions: "What does this look like?" "Rage." Then: "Rage at who, or what?" "Rage at women." "What kind of women?" "So far, women who are redheads, or women who are prostitutes." We pursue these hypotheses of similarity until they either dead-end or lead us to the most distinct difference of all: the individual killer. The previously "unknown subject."

Everything unknown is the same, in terms of its existence in a state of non-definition. Metaphors transform this equality of nonidentity into the differences of what something resembles, as opposed to the absolutes of what it is. James's "chain of necessities" is an application of this on a larger scale. He's put my intuition, that we're closing in on a revelation, into words.

"Do you already have a theory, James?" I ask, gazing at him intently. "You do, don't you?"

He nods. "Yep. But I want to finish laying out the evidence we have, first. It'll help clarify, and continue narrowing our field of focus."

"Makes sense," I acknowledge. I uncap my black marker. "So, what's next?"

"The actions of the various members of each group just before everybody died," James answers, inclining his head toward Alan. "And an overview of the individuals comprising the five-house group."

Alan raises his eyebrows. "Oh, me? Sure. Just a second." He flips through Ned, his notepad, until he reaches the page he wants. "I couldn't find any connections between the members of the five-house group to each other, or to any of the other residents on the street. The NSA's supercomputers chewed through every piece of information about their lives available to be found. *Nada.* They were different ages, different ethnicities, and the balance between men and women was fairly even: three men, two women.

"There were variations in credit rating, and they all had different jobs, with different incomes. None of them shared hobbies or addictions." He flips a page. "No member of the five-house group had any history of mental illness, and outside a parking ticket here or there, none of them had a criminal record, expunged or otherwise.

"Now," he says, looking up from the notepad, "there were some interesting similarities, given other things we know. For example: All the members of the five-house group moved into their homes within the same two-year period and—get this—prior to the arrival of the twelve-house group but *after* Ben and friends had already set up shop. Ben and his fellow assholes were there first, before all the others, by about a year."

"Really?" Callie muses. "That's interesting. And it gives us a timeline that helps confirm causation."

"Yeah," Alan says, nodding. "The monsters came early." He flips to another page. "What's really interesting, in the creepiest, most fucked-up kind of way, is what the members of the five-house group did the day all hell broke loose. One of them we know already: Fred Carter."

"The man who killed Emily Stoddard," I supply.

"Right. Now, we found burner phones either on the bodies or in the homes of every member of the five- and twelve-house groups. All of them had been sent the same text message just before things went to shit: the numeral one. Thing is, the last four members of the five-house group—the ones left after Carter died—got the text a full ten minutes before the twelve-house group did.

"So, what happens?" He sighs. "Those remaining four get a second text— the numeral two—one minute before the twelve-house group got their first texts of the numeral one. The four head out of their own homes and into homes belonging to the twelve-house group, with full-auto MP5s hidden under their coats, and open fire on the residents, once they find them."

"Preplanned synchronization," James notes.

"Smooth, efficient, and effective," Alan replies. "Looks like they were each assigned three houses in the twelve-house group as their responsibility, because they went through the front door of the first home they entered, shot to kill, then exited the back door, moving directly across the backyards and through back gates installed in the fences of every yard. Then they moved at a dead run to said back gate in a neighboring home and repeated the same process in reverse, cutting across the backyard, entering the home through the back door—*blam-blam-blam*—and then out through the front.

"Once they were in motion, the MP5s stayed out, and the cops with the best reaction times noticed and drew their weapons. Pretty soon, everybody was shooting someone. A few police went down, but the rest of the cops there made short work of the assassins. Cut 'em to pieces."

"It was a turkey shoot," Kirby confirms. "I even got to shoot my *own* fish in a barrel."

"No kidding," Alan says. "A real *High Noon* meets *The Magnificent Seven* scenario, for sure. But hey, the crazy doesn't stop there. It turns out, these four psychos didn't fire the kill shots in every case, because about half the members of the twelve-house group blew their own brains out right after getting the text messages on their burners."

"Like the older couple that I saw," I say. "So then ... " I frown, thinking. "What? The assassins were insurance? In case anyone in the twelve-house group lost their nerve and couldn't pull the trigger on themselves?"

"It fits," Alan says.

"It fits with the structure of the scenario as a whole, too," James observes. "Efficent preplanning that translates into smooth, almost flawless execution. Redundancy. Backups of backups."

"And lots of plan Bs," Callie chimes in.

"You know," I muse, "these four assassins were executing what was essentially a suicide mission." I look at Alan. "Any of them have children who were abducted?"

He shakes his head. "Nope. No kids. No marriages, either."

"So, fanatics, then." I contemplate this. "True believers, willing to die for their cause—whatever *it* was." An image of Emily Stoddard comes to me, joyous with certainty as she points a shotgun at my stomach. "Emily knew she was going to die, too," I say. "She was happy about it. Ecstatic and doubtless. Then there was all that stuff she said, which seemed religious to me."

"That lunatic Fred Carter got his God gab on, too," Callie notes. *"The Black Glove,* I believe he said?"

"Uh-huh," I confirm, nodding as I do. "And like we've said before, Emily was a true believer. Every piece of information she gave us has panned out, so far. I think the only lead we haven't discussed yet is this thing she said about the Milgram experiment."

James taps a folder lying on the table in front of him. "Right here. It forms a part of my overall theory."

"Good," I reply, "but what *about* the belief connection? Alan, did you find anything that points to a religious group of any kind? At all? Anywhere?"

"As a matter of fact—" he answers—"I did."

James interrupts before I can encourage Alan to continue. "Do you mind being patient about that answer?" he asks me. "Just for a little while? It will factor into my overall theory, which I'm ready to share, now; but it will all make more sense if you get the relevant information in a certain sequence."

"Of course," I reply, seeing no reason to disagree. "It's a huge volume of data to put in context. If you've got a road map, then you have the floor."

"Thank you. I—"

Callie's cell phone alerts to a call, and Freddie Mercury shouts James down. "This is Special Agent Callie Brady," she answers. She frowns. "Excuse me? I see." She looks at me with troubled eyes. "Which channel was that, again? Got it. Thank you very much." She flips the phone closed and grabs the remote for the television hanging on the conference room wall, changing the channel to Channel 4, then unmuting it. "Something's happened," she tells us, eyes glued to the screen. "Something big." She glances at me again. "Something bad."

CHAPTER TWENTY-ONE

"A bombshell from the now infamous residential street known to many Americans as 'The End of the Road'—allegations that an enclave of pedophiles had made it their home; allegations backed up by video, which appears to show members of the group abusing each other's children."

"Oh my God ...," I say, gaping at the television in disbelief.

"Hello," the perfectly put-together, middle-aged blond female anchor begins, speaking with a studied gravity and an appropriately serious expression: "I'm Kathleen Dickerson. This afternoon, Channel four received an anonymous package containing a USB stick. On the USB were twelve different video clips, which we at Channel four have verified as authentic footage depicting the horrific sexual abuse of children.

"Further investigation by Channel 4 into the occupants of twelve homes on the street has revealed shocking information: These twelve sets of residents were the parents or relatives of twelve separate children thought to have been abducted more than a decade ago. In each case, the supposed kidnappings were reported by the parents or relatives raising them; and in every case, none of the children were ever recovered or heard from again.

"More than a decade later, these same individuals—coming from different parts of the country and without any obvious connection between them— have turned up as neighbors, along with evidence that their children might never have been missing at all. Instead, it appears that they engaged in a ritual of sharing their children among one another, for the purposes of sexual use.

"Although it is not legal for any employee of Channel 4 to possess these video clips or to examine them in detail, a member of the Denver Police Department has confirmed for us that no indicators have been found in the footage thus far, supporting the possibility that the parents involved were acting under duress.

"As this source reported to us: 'They were laughing, smiling, and chatting it up. If the children resisted or became upset, the adults involved would administer some form of corporal punishment. I saw children slapped in the face, spanked with a heavy wooden paddle, and worse. In no case did I see evidence of guilt or shame in the adults involved. The sex included intercourse, and while the children appeared traumatized, in every case, the adults seemed to enjoy it.'"

"Turn it off," I say, in a voice thinned by rage. "Turn it off now."

Callie hits the off button on the remote, and the appropriately somber face of the anchorwoman, with her correctly saddened eyes, disappears.

"Thank you," I murmur.

The room is silent but seething. Anger and outrage thicken the air, and I imagine that everyone else can feel their heartbeats thudding away in their ears, too.

"Well, that's just god-awful," Alan mutters, clenching and unclenching his fists, unaware he is doing it. "It wasn't enough to use their own kids as leverage against them. They had to destroy their reputations as parents and human beings, too." He shakes his head, clenching then unclenching his fists, over and over, again and again. "Son of a *bitch*," he growls, looking and sounding like a man ready to commit a murder.

A thought occurs to me, bringing with it a thrill of displaced fear. "You know ... if I hadn't seen that couple on video, grieving without an audience, or if Rebecca Stoddard hadn't lived, we might be reversing our hypothesis right now instead of getting angry. We'd have no reason to question the evidence, if it's as convincing as they're representing it is." I stare into nothing, while a warm, tight knot twists in the pit of my stomach. "Jesus," I breathe, considering this potential.

"Well," James says, sounding tired, "thankfully, you did, and she did; and so we've confirmed our hypothesis instead." His eyes are just as angry as Alan's, but in a colder, deader way. This rage has given James a terrible focus, and his commitment to the chase bakes off him like a violent sun, endless and inexorable. He clears his throat. "Does anyone feel like they need to see any of this video right now?"

"I don't," I answer. "And I don't want anyone else to, either. Let's make sure it gets into the right hands in the FBI, and let them verify. There's no reason to subject yourselves to that, so don't." I look around the room, catching the eyes of each one of them, in turn. "Consider it an order."

No one dissents. They're all grim-faced, and the absence of banter is deafening.

"The way we'll right this wrong is by keeping our focus where it belongs. We're on the right track, clearly, so now is not the time to stop. OODA, people. Learn it, live it, love it."

"Well, live it at least," Callie replies, with a half-cocked smile. It doesn't quite reach her eyes, but I love my friend, in this moment, for the effort alone.

"Good. Now—James," I say, "you were about to make your case. Why don't you go ahead?"

The size of what we're confronting means that its distractions are to scale, as well. It is one thing to theorize a horror, another entirely to see the results in reality, and on this case, the horrors have been huge and personal. James's mother; the attack on my family, and our home being burned to the ground; the devastation of the bunker as well as the mere fact of its existence—the reasons to stop and gape have been continuous.

It's only when we've adhered to our own procedures that progress has been made, and the unknown has begun clarifying. This latest act might be more disturbing than the others, but in the end, it's just more evidence.

Motion reveals a network through delineation of its paths, and in terms of those we hunt, much has traveled recently. We are closing the gap on the decision cycle, and continued forward motion is the only reasonable answer, even if the road we travel on rises up from time to time and becomes our temporary enemy.

"Let me start," James says, "by summarizing what we know so far. I'll be revealing some additional data that's relevant, as I do."

"We're all ears, honey-love." Callie smiles at him. "Dazzle us with that big old brain of yours."

"I don't practice accuracy to make myself look good," James murmurs, barely registering her existence as his eyes scan across the glass board.

"Yes, my lord Satan." She chuckles.

This, too, is one of our procedures. We know who we are, as a team, in relation to one another. Rocked too hard by the truly awful, we look for the behavior in one another that we expect; and when we find it, we find ourselves, and are comforted.

"Starting roughly twenty years ago and continuing until approximately twelve years ago, the ownership of twenty-one homes shifts from an unknown entity into the names of the residents we're familiar with."

"Unknown entity?" I query.

"Yes. The construction of homes within the tract of land that residential block was built on was the work of a different company than the other ones in the same neighborhood. We know this because records exist for the other homes, from purchase of the land to construction of the houses themselves, to their various individual sales. No similar record of any kind can be found for the houses on our street. Nothing detailing who owned the tract, who it was sold to, or of any company involved in the construction."

Alan whistles. "That's an impressive cover-up."

"We initiated a massive computer search for financial transactions throughout the state during the time periods that fit, and also found nothing. No block transfers, in whole or in part, that add up to the approximate purchase value of the land itself or of estimated purchase and material costs for construction of the houses."

"You know," Callie muses, "land purchases are one of the last frontiers of privacy, even today. In many places, the records of purchase, transfer, and ownership are still stored on paper. Cash sales, purchasing with gold—even barter—are not at all uncommon. In fact, that's the attraction for some of our less savory groups, such as militiamen, white supremacists, and other groups whose membership is comprised of individuals with bones for brains. It allows them to either use the land themselves for their own needs, while remaining somewhat anonymous, or to sell it for guns, gold, or other shiny objects."

"What's your point?" James asks.

"The point, oh great Satan, is that perhaps the land was owned by our unsubs for years prior to the construction of that neighborhood. The bunker itself would seem to support this, as I'd imagine it would have to have been built first, before the house above it."

James blinks rapidly, considering this, then nods. "That's reasonable. It would fit the timeline, and might help to explain the decision, on the part of the unsubs, to invest in building all those houses in the first place. Maybe they became aware of plans to build on the tracts nearby and worried that someone might stumble across the bunker during the construction process."

"I also noticed that the homes our unsubs oversaw fit the design of the other houses in the neighborhood," Callie supplies. "It speaks to a desire for blending in." She shrugs. "Camouflage."

"That supports the more embracive picture I'm attempting to explain," James allows. "Seems sound."

"Thank you, great Satan," Callie opines. "I live for your praise."

"There are also no records of the home purchases themselves," he continues, ignoring her. "Rebecca Stoddard, for example, just ... owned her house on that street one day, and moved there not long after. But there's no paper trail leading up to her ownership of the home; it seems to have materialized out of thin air."

He glances around the table. "I worked financial crimes, and I can tell you, it's not simple to bury paper trails so completely, even when you're dealing with hard-copy records and the pre-computerization era. Purchases, ownership, and the movement of money is all about the documentation of every step in the process.

"In many ways, it can be easier to hack into a computerized database than a warehouse, and it's certainly easier to zero in on the records you're looking for. The real challenge digital records provide lies in their backup, and the ease of copying databases. You can burn a warehouse full of paper records to the ground and leave no copies. It's virtually impossible these days to achieve the same goal in terms of digital records, because someone, somewhere is going to have a copy.

"It all adds up to different versions of the same refrain, regarding our unsubs: tremendous sophistication, supported by confidence and competence in terms of execution."

"Freaking super-villains," Alan mutters.

"No," James admonishes. "They're anomalous individuals. Maybe 'extraordinarily outside the norm,' if you want, but this is the exact point I'm moving toward: *They're not something new.* At least, their abilities aren't."

"Okay, okay," Alan placates. "My bad. Lead on, McDuff."

"We then have a series of twelve flawlessly executed abductions over a period of two years, and the use of the children to corral and control their caregivers. An aspect of this being—as we just had confirmed—the use of extreme blackmail. Even here, the sophistication in planning and the confidence and competence in execution is evident. Forcing the parents of one child to abuse the children of another is not just diabolical, it's behaviorally brilliant.

"Think about it," he says. "It creates a shared trauma—a kind of built-in support group. Any instinct one set of parents might have to hate another for participating in the abuse becomes nullified by their own identical actions. It isolates them completely, but it isolates them *together*."

"Right ... ," I murmur, seeing the logic of it take shape in my mind.

"This goes beyond competence in violence," James continues, "it's advanced strategic thought, involving multidimensional considerations."

"You can say that again," Alan jokes.

"The unsubs continue to demonstrate their abilities in the design and administration of their 'prison without bars,' as we've already covered. Multiple, highly customized surveillance systems," he reminds us, holding up one finger. "Layered redundancy in personnel," he continues, holding up a second finger. "Compartmentalized hierarchies of personnel, with the overseers—Ben and friends—at the top, followed by the fanatical group of assassins, and then the prisoners that comprised the twelve-house group." Another finger goes up, continuing the count. "A preestablished, highly choreographed response plan, set off by innocuous texts to untraceable phones."

He takes a moment to look at each of us, in turn. "What does it all add up to? Well ... I think I know. It's an idea that started forming when I discovered something very interesting in the backgrounds Alan had done on Ben and friends. It wasn't stated as a commonality, but it would be hard to see without some prior knowledge."

"Really?" Alan says, raising his eyebrows in surprise.

James nods. "Yes. You noted they all had military backgrounds, remember?"

"Sure. They were all combat veterans, too. Vietnam. Though I wasn't able to find any overlap."

"Exactly!" James says, in a tone of controlled excitement, stabbing a finger in Alan's direction. "There was *just* enough information for a verifiable history. Given the military's tendency for documenting everything, however, there seems to be a surprising dearth of documents releated to Ben and the other three men."

Alan grows silent, considering. "Now that you mention it ... " He nods, slowly. "I take your point. Sure, the basic facts were there. They painted a continuous enough picture to give a timeline without any gaps I could see. But yeah ... really, not more than that. If I think about it, it ends up breaking down, mostly, into a series of arrivals and departures organized by date. Maybe that'd be the norm for some PI running a cursory background check, but it's pretty damn sparse when you consider the tools we dug into their pasts with, after that bomb went off."

"It's beyond sparse," James confirms. "It's a ridiculously improbable event." He pauses. "Unless they also share another commonality that helps to explain it."

"Which is?" I ask.

"I followed a hunch, which I was able to confirm with a little digging. It seems that Ben and the other three men who made up the group of overseers had other files detailing their military service, but in each case, all their files were consumed in the National Personnel Records Center fire of 1973."

"Oh ... crap," Kirby says, drawing everyone's attention. "Are you one hundred percent certain of that?" she asks James, staring at him with an odd intensity.

For his part, James appears to be unsurprised by Kirby's sudden outbreak of concern. "Completely," he answers.

She falls into a troubled silence in response to this. It's a state absent of all levity, and I strain to remember the last time I'd ever seen her this way.

"Do you want to fill the rest of us in, James?" I ask.

He sighs. "It was a fire that burned through the NPRC on July 12, 1973. It destroyed between sixteen and eighteen million official military personnel records, and in many, *many* cases the data was not duplicated elsewhere. The cause of the fire was never officially determined."

"Really?" I ask, dumbfounded. "Never determined? That's ... ridiculous." I pause, frowning. "Isn't it?"

"Do you mean," Kirby says, "is it ridiculous to think that a fire which wiped out a gajillion records belonging to the United States military, a group that demands that blame be assigned for every mistake as a matter of policy,

333

has never had the matter of its causation resolved?" She gives me a sardonic, death's-head grin. *"Nawwww..."* She waves me off. "Of course not!"

I look at James, still mystified. "So? What am I missing, here?"

"Seconded," Alan says, raising a hand.

It's Kirby, not James, who answers. "Well, Smokers, there's a persistent rumor in some circles that the fire was no accident but instead that it was part of a massive cover-up by a certain intelligence agency—*not* the CIA, of course, just exactly like it, bearing the same name and employing all the same personnel."

"So, the CIA, then," I reply. "But a cover-up of what? And why?"

"Think Watergate," James answers. "The original break-in happened in June of '72. The operators known as Nixon's White House 'plumbers' included intelligence operatives with long-term ties to the CIA, or to U.S. intelligence in general. Frank Sturgis, for example, was a part of a military intelligence unit tasked against the USSR in the late 1940s, and then he turned up to help Castro in the Cuban Revolution of 1958. He was rumored to have been connected to Oswald.

"Another, E. Howard Hunt, was in the CIA from 1949 until 1970. He was a personal assistant to Alan Dulles for a while—the first director of the CIA, and was involved in the Bay of Pigs fiasco. He was also the architect of a plan in the early 1950s to overthrow the elected president of Guatemala—which was successful."

"Connected," Kirby murmurs. "He would have known a lot."

"That's right," James agrees. "And the CIA wasn't as compartmentalized in those early periods, so the opportunities for exposure were greater."

"So I've heard," she says.

"At least two other members of the 'plumbers' were employed by the CIA prior to working for the White House," James continues, "including another involved in Bay of Pigs, and James McCord Jr., who at one time was in charge of physical security at Langley headquarters."

"Okay...," I say, nodding slowly. "I'm starting to get the picture. A bright light was about to shine on Watergate, and the CIA had ex-operatives involved in a conspiracy to subvert the democratic system of the United States."

James shrugs. "You say 'ex,' I just say 'operatives'; potato-potahto. But yes, that's the essence of it. One standout, as evidence of how worried the Agency was about the fallout from Watergate, is the order from Richard Helms, the director of the Agency at the time, to destroy any document concerning MKULTRA."

"What—the mind control stuff?" Alan asks.

James nods. "Yes. Human experimentation without informed consent, both here and abroad. It was black, black stuff. The *New York Times* caught wind of it in late 1974 and reported on it, resulting in the creation, separately, of the Church Committee and the Rockefeller Commission."

"Both of those were giant anal probes into the Agency," Kirby supplies. "Heads rolled. People *burned*. The CIA was gutted for decades."

I nod my understanding. "I see. So, the records fire in '73 is assumed by some to have been a part of preparation for the coming of that great, white light they knew would be shined on the Agency as a result of Watergate."

Kirby grins, without humor. "Gold star, Smokers."

"By that time, the Agency had been running wild in the world for a while," James points out. "They'd built up quite a collection of atrocities, and it might have made sense to take a wholesale view of personnel record destruction, in the interests of making various correlations impossible."

"Okay," I say, "let's get back to Ben and friends. You said the fire at the NPRC ended up destroying between sixteen and eighteen million personnel records. But there's no way that many people were involved in covert ops, or even connected to them. Not even close. Why assume it's probative?"

"I'd agree with you on that basis alone," he replies, "but then I thought about the single greatest contradiction in all the events connected to our investigation."

"Which is?"

"The girl," he says, spreading his hands out, palms up. "Emily Stoddard. She doesn't fit. Think about it: Emily's actions in killing the three overseers and their families are what brought us to Colorado in the first place. She's also the one who directed us to the bunker. It seems obvious she was a cutout, but then—why would the unsubs use a cutout to expose *themselves?*" He shakes his head. "It's not logical, and it stuck in my mind from the beginning."

"Good point," I agree.

"I actually hadn't made all the connections until Kirby briefed us on the complexities of kidnapping. It was a pretty impressive demonstration."

"Of course," Kirby chimes. "I only do impressive."

James actually smiles. "Well, it was, this time. After you briefed us, I took all the variables and put them in single-question form. It's a long list—what environments encompass the following: world-class training and experience in arenas of violence; advanced and multidimensional strategic thinking; multiple redundant systems as a matter of course; confidence and competence in the command of personnel; use of layered and compartmentalized systems of obfuscation and denial; confidence and competence in the design and execution of large-scale operations; contact with and access to individuals in the FBI; global access, over time, to the kind of unique items we discovered in the bunker museum; and finally, that not only puts a bunch of killers together, but also enables them to know each other *as* killers?"

"The mouthful of all mouthfuls, James," Alan says, smiling a little.

"It certainly narrows the field," I murmur. "I see why Ben and friends' records being part of those lost in the NPRC fire fits." I cock my head, looking at him. "Did you really formulate all of that after Kirby's talk?"

He frowns. "How else? Why?"

I give him a faint smile and shake my head. "Nothing. It's impressive, James. That's all."

It's easy for me to forget, sometimes, just how smart James is. How truly brilliant. I can see what he sees, now—the entire, connected system of it—but only because he'd shown it to me, first. I might have muddled through in my own time, perhaps even assuredly. A thousand years could pass, however, and I'd still be unable to transform the same massive volume of information into a coherent body in the space of time we've all been sitting here. It's not merely impressive: It's a permanent impossibility for the rest of us.

"I'm not seeing Emily as your catalyst yet," Callie says. "If Ben and friends were involved in her initial abduction, why would they use her as a weapon against themselves? How is she the key to your door of revelation?" She smiles. "So to speak."

"I'm getting to that." He pauses, considering. "Imagine you're the CIA before Watergate. You've spent the last quarter-century operating with impunity and without oversight. Your budget is what you make it, and your power has no boundaries in terms of its application. You've been rampaging through the world, toppling governments, engaging in secret wars, assassinating heads of state, and funding human experimentation.

"This is all occurring pre-Internet, long before the advent of email, cell phones, and even most satellite-assisted communication. A station officer or case office is given a lot of latitude to operate independently because communications are so much slower than today. Daily decision authorization can't be made policy, as it's simply not workable. There are no portable computers with encryption software, and so all reports are hard copies, moved through diplomatic pouches, trusted couriers, or through various mail-forwarding networks to their destinations.

"Imagine, for example, finding out that the Bay of Pigs had failed not in real time, but as a result of relayed communication—local human resource on radio to local human resource with a phone, who then places a call—or the monitoring of local media.

"Compartmentalization isn't, primarily, a decision-driven activity, as is mostly so today, but occurs organically. If you are not on the ground, you just don't know, unless you are the designated person back at Langley, receiving the reports from the field. If you are that person, you read the original reports before anyone else and perform your redactions prior to any copying—if anything is copied at all."

"Mr. Snarlyface isn't wrong," Kirby interjects. "A guy I knew worked in those simpler times, and he told me that he once spent a year in the wild providing only a report a month. If you waited a month to report in today, they'd assume you were either captured, dead, or had gone over to the enemy."

"I guess that would make security harder in some ways," I muse, "in terms of interception, for example. On the other hand, you could probably hide a lot in those gaps of time—and distance."

James nods. "That's right. That's my point exactly. So again, you're in the CIA, and Watergate hits. You predict the coming storm, and the call goes out worldwide: 'Oversight is coming, and it's got teeth, this time. The glory days are over.' And the cover-ups begin. Bonfires of top-secret and incriminating documents become the order of the day. Money is moved into secret accounts, assets who know too much and who can't be counted on start dying, and so on.

"Consider the possibilities—all the things that might have been concealed in those 'gaps of time and distance.' Entire networks set up on the ground over a period of years, designed to move money, people, weapons, intelligence, and more. But what if, during those glory years when everything could be justified, a group of monsters found each other and hitched a ride on the CIA express?" He looks around at us, his eyebrows raised in emphasis. "Maybe they mostly did the job they were supposed to do, but it was a job for monsters, after all. And since that's exactly what they were, they also did more than what was asked." He shrugs. "Perhaps they were in it for themselves more than any patriotic ideal, and so they used all that boundless permission and endless resource to fuel their own hobbies on the side.

"And perhaps, when the call went out, they obeyed ... for the most part. Everything that belonged to the job only was jettisoned and destroyed, but their private resources—already firewalled—were excised, isolated, and kept for themselves."

"Like the bunker museum," I say, nodding to myself.

"Yes," James agrees, "like the bunker museum. Or the money needed to construct twenty-plus residential homes. Maybe you are especially far-thinking and strategically minded, and you use the confusion inherent to the post-1973 purge as a cover for the assassination of any Company agent with specific personal knowledge of your existence and/or activities. Then, hidden, organized, and funded, you move into the next phase of your life: being all the monster you can be."

"That's a lot of supposing," I say. "What makes it more probable they'd be on their own than still attached to the CIA?"

"The risks. The behavior we already know. The general response from within the CIA was global, and more importantly, it was absolute. MKULTRA, for example? The order was that every document related to that program be destroyed, no exceptions. In essence, any evidence of proactive atrocity, where direct defense against an actual attack was not involved, was to be burned to the ground."

"Right," Alan murmurs. "So a death museum full of the worst shit in history would be a no-go."

"Inside the United States, especially?" James shakes his head emphatically, expressing his belief that this question is as ridiculous as it is rhetorical. "No way."

I can feel James's logic bearing down on me, hemming me in. On the one hand, in almost every conceivable instance, what he's proposing would be the most improbable answer possible. But I keep returning to the factors of scale, access, and ability. I consider the litany of variables forming that run-on sentence of a question he'd expressed to us and feel the pull toward the improbable, too, even when it's the *most* improbable. It is true: The incubators in this world capable of containing all those factors are as rare, and as few, as the most unlikely probabilities themselves.

"We're still talking about serial offenders, at the base, are we not?" Callie asks.

"Sure." James nods. "Why not? The monsters may be more accomplished in this scenario and more organized, but individually, they're still just monsters. The motivations behind their actions can be expressed in terms of personal, pathological needs, versus national security."

I sigh. I want to reject the concept as a whole but am finding it more and more difficult to see differently. "So," I say, "Emily Stoddard. Explain."

"It's twofold," he replies, continuing without hesitation. "So far as her as the cutout: Why wouldn't it make sense, in this scenario? I just said they were fundamentally the same as other monsters, in terms of their individual existence. But why wouldn't some hierarchy exist, in a group like that? Whoever has the gold—and resources—generally makes the rules. If we assume the scenario I'm presenting, of a personal network gone rogue, it would also be reasonable to assume that some broke away with more resources than others." He gazes at me intently. "Trust would be just as much an issue in this private scenario as it was when the network was still attached. Wouldn't it make the most sense to preserve the same responses to those issues?"

I blink. "You're talking about monsters with bosses."

"Isn't it plausible? Think about it: That's exactly how a network like the one I'm proposing would have been designed. It would have been top-down, structurally. Systems of layered deniability would have been built in. I mean, if you really consider everything, it's not out of the question that even the monsters wouldn't know who their 'big boss' is."

"Right," I murmur, taking this in. My mind has begun spinning in its own firmament, and I feel something huge and fully realized trying to shiver into place. My intellect has been straining to encompass it all, to see what James sees, and I have finally reached the cliff's edge of my own revelation. It calls me forward. "Go on."

"If you were a serial killer building a network like that for your own uses, with a background in the CIA way of doing things, wouldn't you have built in your own controls, too? As in leverage? Something to club the monsters under you into place and keep them there, and to use as a nuclear option should they become an unacceptable liability?"

I see it then; the last piece shivers into place. The hurricane of variables, which had been battering my mind's eye to and fro, coalesces, becoming an edifice in place. I can view it now, from the top, from the ground, and from every side. I can enter it and walk the stairs that lead from basement to attic and all the floors in between.

"So ... ," I say, thoughtfully. "Ben and friends are in charge of the bunker and all its contents. The potential for exposure becomes imminent, and an operation is designed to deal with it. Emily and the other children are used to force the parents to play their part, and then disappear from the locality of the operation, moving into some other compartment or level of the group."

"That's right," James replies. "Removing them increases security in terms of the operation itself. It also allows them to be utilized as leverage by who-ever's running things from above, should that become necessary."

I startle, my eyes opening wide. "The precipitating event," I breathe. "Emily's the clue to it?"

"She's its messenger," he replies, nodding. "The nuclear option of leverage."

"And you figured out what it is, didn't you?" I ask, feeling my own excite-ment begin to build. *The OODA loop*, I think to myself. *The decision cycle's about to close in our favor.*

He grins like a boy, in a way I've never seen him do. At the same time, though, the boy is starving, alone, and he carries a loaded gun. "I think so, yeah." He pauses for effect, but only for a moment. "It's what she said about the Milgram experiment. Something turned up."

James opens the folder he'd tapped earlier and hands out copies of a sta-pled, three-page summary. "I'll give a full picture momentarily," he says, once we all have the pages in our hands. "But how about this for an overview: In the early 1990s, long before anything happened on our Colorado street, a man was charged with serial murder, including rape and torture. It was a slam dunk. When he was arrested, he first claimed that it was a CIA operation and that he was being framed.

"Within a week he'd reversed himself completely. He said he'd been lying but that once he'd understood the overwhelming nature of the evidence against him, he no longer saw the point. He held to this story from that point forward and spent the next twenty-five years quietly serving out a life sentence.

"Then, about a month ago, his son died of pancreatic cancer. Two days after hearing this news, he hung himself in his own prison cell. He left a suicide note that was only two words long: NOT GUILTY."

CHAPTER TWENTY-TWO

"In 1961, Stanley Milgram was a psychologist working at Yale University," James begins. "He was interested in what gap existed, if any, between person conscience and obedience to authority. In other words, are we willing to subordinate our own beliefs when the person asking us to do so is an authority figure?

"Just a few months after he started his investigations, the trial of Adolf Eichmann began. Eichmann was one of the primary organizers of the Holocaust, and a consistent question in everyone's mind at the time was: How could so many German soldiers fall in line with the implementation of institutionalized genocide? Even the most emotionally vested person had trouble concluding that the German people in general were just prone to being evil as a majority behavior. At the same time, the atrocities were undeniable, and the soldiers involved did their jobs, while the German civilians living near the camps ignored them."

"'The banality of evil,'" I murmur. "Always one of my favorite observations."

"Mine, too," James agrees. "Of course, Milgram was a scientist, so he wasn't dealing in conceptual absolutes like good or evil. The problem in his perspective was the seeming ability for highly developed systems of authority to easily move the behavior of large groups of people away from what are, otherwise, fairly universal norms. The extermination of millions of unarmed, law-abiding fellow human beings, who were not involved in waging war against their country, went against essential cultural and religious mores.

"Milgram decided to design a behavioral experiment that would answer specific questions that had been formulated in response to the Eichmann trial: Could it be that Eichmann and his million accomplices in the Holocaust were just following orders? Could we call them all accomplices?"

"That must have been popular," Callie observes.

James nods. "There was criticism on this point, of course. But less than you might expect. Milgram was looking for a replicable, behavioral answer, not a morally culpable one. Lots of people were able to grasp the larger concern—that if it is possible to make otherwise 'normal' people do reprehensible things, humanity needed to know this, as a part of ensuring that an atrocity like the Holocaust could never happen again. Far from being an out, it was, potentially, preventative knowledge."

"Six million dead creates an onus for truth in all directions, not just revenge," I supply.

"Perhaps," James allows. "Milgram's design for the experiment was genius. It comprised three people: the Experimenter, who oversaw the test; the Teacher, a genuine volunteer expected to obey the orders of the Experimenter; and the Learner, a confederate posing as a fellow volunteer, who would be the recipient of effects resulting from the actions of the Learner.

"The Teacher and the Experimenter would be in one room, and the Learner would be in another. They could communicate but not see each other. Under the direction of the Experimenter, the Teacher—the only actual volunteer—would read off a list of word pairs to the Learner. He would then read just the first word of each pair, along with a list of four potential choices for the second word of the pair. The Learner would choose which of the four were correct by pressing a button. If the choice was correct, the Learner would move to the next word pair and repeat the process. But if the choice made by the Learner was wrong, the Teacher was ordered to give the Learner an electric shock and was told the voltage would increase by fifteen volts every time a wrong answer was given."

"I remember this one," Kirby says. "The volunteer believed the shocks were real, but it was all a con, wasn't it, Mr. Snarlyface?"

"Wrong term, right idea. There was no actual shock being administered to the Learner—but the volunteers acting in the role of the Teacher didn't know this. Instead, a tape recorder was connected with the electroshock generator, and it played prerecorded shrieks, screams, and so on that were prematched to the voltage level.

"Once a certain threshold had been crossed in regards to the number of shocks received by the Learner, the confederate playing that part would also start to bang on the wall and would complain about a preexisting heart condition. This would continue until the Learner eventually stopped responding at all. No shrieks or complaints, and no more banging against the wall."

"But that wasn't the end of it, right, Mr. Snarlyface?" Kirby says, grinning a little. "They kept right on roasting the nuts of the Learner anyway, didn't they?"

"More or less," James confirms. "The researcher acting in the role of Experimenter had four successive responses he was allowed to give to the volunteer, when and if the volunteer started objecting to continuing with the process. They were verbal escalations of authority, like: 'Please continue,' first; followed by, 'The experiment needs you to continue'; then, 'It's absolutely essential you continue'; and finally, the most emphatically worded response, and the one most approaching a direct order, 'You have no other choice, you must go on.'

"If they wanted to quit after the fourth response, that was it. Otherwise, the experiment carried on until the volunteer in the role of the Teacher believed three successive 450-volt shocks had been given to the Learner." He shrugs. "There were other tricks, various prods the Experimenter was allowed to give in response to questions, but that's an essential overview of the experiment's structure."

"As I recall," Callie says, "something on the order of sixty-five percent of the volunteers carried on until the maximum shock limit was reached."

James nods. "Twenty-six out of forty. The results have been replicated, too, including across cultures. There are some percentage variations, culture to culture, but the essential result has always remained the same." He picks out a paper from the ones spread in front of him. "Here's how Milgram put it: 'Ordinary people, simply doing their jobs, and without any particular hostility on their part, can become agents in a terrible destructive process. Moreover, even when the destructive effects of their work become patently clear, and they are asked to carry out actions incompatible with fundamental standards of morality, relatively few people have the resources needed to resist authority.'"

"Comforting," Alan mutters.

"Illuminating," James counters.

"That was then," I prod. "So what happened in the nineties?"

"Police raided an abandoned industrial park in Los Angeles, based on an anonymous tip. A caller claimed to have been casing the buildings in the park for the purposes of robbery, when he stumbled across, quote 'a bunch of god-damn stinky-ass corpses.'"

"Ah, a poet," Callie murmurs.

"The cops took him seriously," James continued. "They got a warrant and entered heavy."

"Always advised when dealing with bunches of bodies," Kirby supplies. "Especially the stinky-ass kind."

"They found a lot more than just the corpses, according to these briefing sheets James gave us," I say, reading from them. "'Discovered supine on the floor of one room: the corpses of eight different couples, laid out together in pairs. The couples had all been reported as missing within the last year, and foul play was suspected.'" I frown, and then continue reading. "'The women had been sexually assaulted and tortured. The men had not been raped, but had been subjected to extreme forms of torture, including being burned with acid, removal of their eyelids, and disarticulation of their testicles. Severe electrical burns were found in the palms and on the bottoms of the feet of all the victims, as well.'"

"Gross," Kirby observes, sticking her tongue out. "Super-yuck."

"'In another room,'" I continue, "'two chairs were found bolted to the floor, arranged so that anyone seated in them would be facing each other. Police-issue handcuffs were attached to each chair, at the arms and at the foremost bottom legs. The presence of blood was visibly ascertained on various portions of each chair. The scent of what the officer assumed to be the presence of human urine was detected.

"'Forensic tests later showed both assumptions as true; additionally, human blood and flesh were found on the metal of each set of handcuffs, in various places, including within the ratcheting mechanism. This indicated to the coroner that the victims had strained against the handcuffs violently and repeatedly, likely as the involuntary reaction to electric current being passed through their bodies.'"

I continue scanning through the information but revert to summarizing rather than reading the various reports aloud verbatim. "They continued to clear the interconnected office spaces. They found the perpetrator—Andrew Beckman—passed out drunk in front of a television that was playing a VHS tape. The tape was a recording of a couple being tortured." I scan further, nodding to myself. "The couple on the tape was matched to one of the pairs of corpses discovered earlier. Similar tapes were found and matched to the remaining bodies. Beckman's fingerprints were everywhere; they lifted them from the chairs, the cuffs, the tapes, and the bodies." I pause. "They also found his semen in and on the bodies of the women, as well as skin and hair evidence, variously."

"When they examined the recordings in detail," James interjects, taking back the reins of the narrative from me, "they found that Beckman had re-created a twisted version of the Milgram experiment, using the couples in the roles of Teacher and Learner, variously. Unlike Milgram's setup, Beckman ensured that the current used was live and that the shocks delivered were actual."

"Jesus," Alan breathes, shaking his head.

"Digging into Beckman's life turned up evidence of a man in long-term crisis. He was a failed surgeon. He lost his medical license after an investigation of a botched routine surgery turned up that he was drunk and under the influence of painkillers while he was operating. He had a son in his teens and an ex-wife, both estranged." James sighs. "He had no friends, and no one who could account for or confirm his whereabouts for at least a year."

"A nearly perfect fit," I muse. "He was a walking checklist of everything you'd expect to find in a serial killer. Organized when he needed to be, disorganized and drunk, otherwise. Hell, he probably couldn't account for all of his own movements even to *himself.*"

"It's true," James says. "He was nearly in a state of overdose when they found him, though the doctor's report stated it didn't appear intentional, at the levels involved. He was still incoherent when he woke up, and was, in the words of the cop guarding his room: 'Raving about a conspiracy against him by some guys from the CIA. Suspect stated that he'd been kidnapped from his own home one year earlier, in the middle of the night, and had been forced, at various times, to observe the torture of kidnapped couples, which he described in detail. Suspect stated he'd been forced to observe sexual assaults against the women, and to participate in them on threat of death. He described these incidents in detail. ... ' It goes on from there."

"He was confessing, without knowing it," I say, shaking my head in amazement. "Beckman was revealing that he knew all the details of the crimes, by putting himself at the scene of them. The story he gave must have sounded ridiculous to the prosecution."

"It is ridiculous," Callie points out, "in the absence of any prior knowledge to the contrary. Even patently so, I might add. With the overwhelming presence of forensic evidence pointing to only Beckham, combined with the complete absence of similar evidence pointing to anyone else ... "

"Finding him at the scene, drunk and stoned," Alan adds. "I mean, sure—cops can get lazy. 'Occam's razor' is code for 'Who gives a shit?' every now and then. But if I look at everything they knew at the time, I can't honestly see how I would have concluded any different."

"Me, too," I agree.

"Well, everyone else agreed with you as well," James says. "The prevailing theory being that Beckman was either trying to lay grounds for a psych defense, or that it was the world's worst SOGDI ever."

"SOGDI?" Kirby queries.

Alan grins. "Some other guy did it. Also known, at different times and places, as SODDI, with two *D*'s."

"Some other *dude* did it," Kirby decodes, on her own.

"Bingo," Alan says. "Some of the best cop stories ever are the crazy stories drunks or crackheads or just plain old dumb-dumbs come up with about the Invisible Man. One thing they almost all have in common: He never leaves a trace."

"I'd imagine our current unsubs—assuming they were there, or involved—knew that already, and counted on it," I muse.

"I think it's clear that they were," James says. "Consider this: The moment he sobered up completely, he recanted everything and confessed. He claimed his plan had been to commit suicide, and that when he woke up in the hospital alive, the combination of drugs, alcohol, and fear had gotten the better of him. There was no recurrence of these claims from that point forward—ever. Beckman waved the right to a trial and cut a deal to plead guilty in exchange for life in prison with no parole, in lieu of the death penalty."

I mime dusting off my hands. "And that was that."

James nods. "Until his son died a month ago, after a protracted battle against pancreatic cancer. The suicide note—where he wrote 'not guilty'—was his first and only reversal since being sent to prison."

"What about the ex-wife?" I ask.

"She died in a car accident ten years ago."

I hold up the stapled pages James had provided us, shaking them with one hand. "This is it—the precipitating event!"

"It does make sense," James allows. "They'd have had the son under surveillance and would have known about the cancer diagnosis, including that it was terminal."

I frown. "Doesn't it seem like kind of an extreme reaction? On the part of our unsubs, I mean. Sure, if Beckman's son was their leverage against him, he'd be free to tell the truth again. But there's no reason I can see for them to worry about that." I shrug. "Why would anyone be more inclined to believe him today than twenty-five years ago?"

"Yes," James replies. "That occurred to me, too. The fact is, the only reason we've come to believe Beckman's story at all is because of what we've been able to piece together as a result of what happened on that street, and what it's revealed. What they started. If Beckman's son dying was the precipitating event, then all their actions since to hide their existence have ended up revealing more than if they'd chosen to do nothing."

I look at him. "Then ... that's the clue. Some detail made it matter to them."

James looks off, thinking. "Why not kill him in the first place?" he asks. His gaze returns to meet mine. "When the original setup was conceived, why would letting him live be a part of the plan at all? Look at where we are now. Wouldn't they have predicted the current series of events or at least considered the possibility of them?"

"What if that wasn't part of the original plan?" Alan posits. We both look at him, and he raises an eyebrow askance. "*Maybe* the plan was always for him to OD on the booze and pills in the first place."

I frown, considering this. "Why not just have him killed in prison, then?" I ask.

"I don't know," he answers, shrugging. "Moving parts and probability, maybe? Our unsubs like preplanning, attention to detail, redundancy—all that dotting the i's and crossing the t's, along with a carbon copy, right?"

"Sure," James replies.

"So, after Beckman woke up alive and was already in custody, they had to make a new plan. They had to contact him and make the threat, using his son.

This means someone had to crawl out into the sunlight and meet with him, and that they had to cross various lines of law enforcement presence to get to wherever he was. No layers. No redundancy. We're talking direct contact." Alan leans forward, for emphasis. "Face-to-face."

As with James earlier, I can feel the idea unfolding in my mind, spreading wings, taking root. "What if it wasn't the first time?" I ask, excitement edging my voice. "That he came face-to-face with—well, whoever—I mean?"

"Maybe ... ," James allows, nodding slowly.

"Go back to basics," I say. "Every choice an unsub makes tells us something about him. In terms of serial offenders, we call their signature the consistent series of choices unique to them. Some aspects of signature are methodological, while others are pathological; but whichever one applies, signature is not just unique, it is *revelatory*."

"Go on," James replies, not urging me to skip the obvious.

"If you apply the concept of signature to our unsubs, what's revealed?" I ask. "What qualities are shown as important to them, that involve the act as a whole?"

James considers my question. "Power," he answers. "Control."

"Right," I acknowledge, smiling. "How might that manifest to someone in Beckman's position? What function does he serve, in terms of victimology?"

"He's the patsy," Kirby offers.

"Yes," I say, nodding once. "Absolutely. But I'm referring to something else, something before that. He was more than a means to an end—how was he supposed to suffer?"

James blinks, staring at me, seeing it. "The unsubs would have told him. They'd have explained that he'd be blamed, after he died, for all their actions."

"Bingo," I say, grinning. "And don't you think, that being the case, that they'd show him their uncovered faces? Since he was going to die, after all, wouldn't it make sense to increase the intimacy by removing every barrier between Beckman and themselves that they could?"

"Of course," he agrees. "So when they realized Beckman had survived, that meant that someone was out there who could identify them, or at least one of them." He frowns, momentarily lost in thought. "If they had Beckman on lockdown for a year, they would have followed some version of the same model they utilized with the twelve-house group, to keep him controlled and compliant."

"The son," Alan murmurs.

"The son," James agrees. "So, when Beckman sobered up, he would have understood that the same threat held true. Maybe the unsubs hedged their bets with an additional visit, to remind him, but..." He shrugs. "Not necessarily. Not even probably. Why bother? Beckman was screwed. No one was going to believe him, anyway."

"Not to mention," I point out, "a face-to-face wouldn't even have been necessary, strictly speaking. A 'letter from a friend,' with a photograph of his son could have sufficed. There's no reason to think the risk of exposing themselves directly was required in order to shore things up."

James mulls this over. "The question still remains, though—why take the risk at all, then? After twenty-five years, any reversal on Beckman's part would make even less sense. He'd have no credibility. And even if his captors had shown him their faces—so what? People change over the course of a quarter-century, and there are three hundred million people in the United States." He looks at me. "Why worry?"

"Maybe..." I pick at my lower lip, thinking deeply. "Maybe there's a reason for them to worry, then. Something that would give them a reason to believe Beckman might be able to steer law enforcement in their direction." I straighten, struck by a possibility. "Maybe one of the unsubs has a public face. Or was recognized by Beckman in the real world, at some point."

"What?" Alan asks. "In prison?"

I spread my hands. "Why not? The unsub could have worked for law enforcement at some juncture, or been a lawyer, even a counselor or administrator. Granted, it makes more sense, in this model, for the public persona to be a generality of some kind to the society at large, but still..."

James nods after a long space of silence. "It would fit," he murmurs. "Not just in terms of signature, but it would also explain the death of Beckman's son as a precipitating event important enough to justify what went down on our street. With the son dead, they would have lost their leverage on an individual who could identify them. Or at least one of their number."

We have reached a jumping-off point that I recognize, in the depths of me. It is the sense of having closed the gap between myself and our prey to an arm's length. I feel that, if I were to just run a little faster and strain a little further, I would find my outstretched hand tangled in their hair. This is the second wind of any investigation race, when the finish line becomes visible as the shape of a person's shadow.

"We need to dig through everything about Beckman's life, both before and after he was arrested," I say, scanning through the summary James had given us. "Every piece of evidence, every dollar into and out of his bank accounts, every phone bill, every drug arrest, and anyone he's ever had the remotest contact with, in or out of prison. I—"

I see it on the last page, toward the end, housed in James's summary remarks. It hits me like a bomb exploding: instant and global, involving every atom. My bones are water. My legs are lengths of string. I want to shriek, but my mouth is full of bile, and my stomach follows its lead. I have fallen to my knees and am vomiting on the floor.

Kirby reaches me first, pulling back my hair as she grips my shoulder. "Smoky," she says, her voice low but urgent next to my ear. "What is it? What's happened?"

I shudder, wiping puke from my mouth with the back of one hand. My eyes go to the pages of James's summary, still clenched in one fist. The white paper is stark against the carpet.

"Help me up, Kirby," I whisper, "please."

"Of course I will," she answers, still at my ear. "Just take it slow."

She pulls as I push, and together we manage to lever me back into my chair. I am drenched with sweat.

"Smoky?" James inquires, looking into my eyes. "What did you see?"

I place the flat of one hand against my belly to steady the roiling within and blink to clear the shock fog that's begging me to lie down, to give up, to sleep. I drop the three crumpled pages of James's summary re Beckman down onto the table with the other, and point to it, feeling myself begin to shiver.

"At—" I gulp and close my eyes, trying to steady my voice. "In the summary paragraphs, on the last page," I finally manage to get out. "You mention his father. The summary says ... " I close my eyes, fighting a wave of dizziness, and succeeding. I open them again and can feel my strength returning, as the shock begins transmuting into rage. "It says that his father was a researcher in the field of child development, specializing in orphans and children with parents who were criminals."

"That's right," James responds. "Richard Beckman. Arrested when Andrew was in his early teens for sexually assaulting the minors under his care. He was sent to prison and was murdered a year later by his cellmate, after stupidly admitting to his crimes in a conversation between them. It seems his cellie had been raped as a child and wasn't interested in sharing time with a pedophile."

I nod. My stomach has stopped heaving, and my eyes are clear. "In my last session with Dr. Childs, he shared something personal with me. It was out of character for him, but I appreciated the intimacy." I shake my head, feeling my blood seethe through me hard enough to make the tips of my toes and fingers pulse painfully. The space between my ears has become a pounding, savage drum. I slam a fist against the crumpled pages, startling everyone but myself. "He told me about his father. The researcher in child development." I grimace. "Who worked with orphans and the children of criminals, and who was arrested for child molestation."

There is a shock of silence, like the calm of stillness after a flash of lightning, as the moment quivers in anticipation of the coming thunder. James's eyes fly open wide, and I feel Kirby's hand, still on my shoulder, stiffen into stone.

"It ... " James gapes. He closes his eyes, clenching them shut tight for a moment, and then opens them again. "It fits," he breathes, not believing what he is unable to deny, simultaneously. "He fits. Oh my God. He fits." He shakes his head, expressing the certainty of disbelief. "Are you sure?"

"No," I say, somehow managing to smile a little, however grimly. "I always puke at *maybe's*, James."

He closes his eyes and shakes his head again. "Yeah. Of course. Sorry." His eyes meet mine. "It's just ...*Jesus*."

"I doubt he's involved in the slightest," I mutter.

"We need something else," James says, regaining his focus and equilibrium. "Something probative in addition to your conversation with him." I can see his belief, backed by his intellect, and the cold anger that's rising in him in response to it.

"We'll find it," I say. "I even have one idea. It's only a hunch of a possibility, but ... " I shrug. "It's worth checking into, based on his pathology, if we're right."

Callie speaks up. "It's not worth considering that Childs might be a victim, as well?" she asks, her tone cautious. "Is there any chance he dropped that clue as a warning to you?"

"No," I answer, without a second's hesitation. "There's not." I grind my teeth together and feel a longing in my hand to hold my handgun.

"How do you know?" she queries, forcing herself into the position of devil's advocate one last time.

I stare at her. I imagine that my eyes have gone dark and black, like bottomless holes or a twinned eclipse. "I just know."

She returns my gaze without flinching, searching me for doubts. My friend-as-peer. "Fine," she says, after a moment. "That's good enough for me."

I stand up, collecting my things as I speak. The time has come to be in motion, to move forward without stopping. To not only feel my fingers in his hair, but to cover his body with mine and bring him down, to ground. "We're heading to the jet now," I say. "James, we'll check my lead from the air. Callie, talk to your husband. I want Childs seized and held—now."

"On what basis?"

"My say-so," I retort, more forcefully than she deserves but unable to control myself. "If I'm wrong, the Dr. Childs we know will understand, once presented with all the information to hand, won't he?"

She inclines her head in acknowledgment of this truth. "You got it, honey-love."

"Kirby—contact Tommy. Brief him on things, ensure he understands to keep it to himself, and then get my family surrounded by every able-bodied killer you and Tommy can find. Our unsubs are advanced strategists, remember? Long-range planners." I run a hand through my hair. "We can't be sure what fail-safes Childs might have put in place in case of discovery."

She gives me a terse nod. "Done and done, Smokers," she replies. She places a cautionary hand on my shoulder and looks directly into my eyes. "You just make sure to turn that flame cold, you hear me? You need clarity here, not a killing rage."

I realize that I want to slap her for saying this to me, so in the next instant, I understand that she's right, of course. "I promise," I tell her, keeping my voice steady. "You're right. I see it. I promise. That's going to have to do it, for now."

She spins away from me without another word, pulling out her cell phone as she goes.

"Not a word of this to anyone, other than as I've already directed," I say, speaking to everyone in the room. They show their assent, using nods or murmurs. "Good. Wheels up in thirty minutes. I want sirens on, heading to the airport. Let's run some red lights."

I breathe in, breathe out, and let my mind settle around my rage. "Let's go catch a monster."

CHAPTER TWENTY-THREE

I walk into the conference room of the FBI's Los Angeles office and take a seat in a chair facing Dr. Kenneth Childs. His hands are cuffed behind his back, and his ankles have been cuffed to each other, hobbling him. Sam Brady, Callie's husband, stands behind Childs, handgun at the ready. He's taking no chances, which I can only appreciate.

"I stationed my best men outside," Sam tells me. "And the good doctor understands my ample willingness to make him dead."

"He was very convincing," Childs confirms, smiling.

His frivolity's a horror, but I don't rise to take the bait. Instead, I study him, forcing time to move at my pace. Confrontation of any kind is still conflict, after all, and conflict brings fear. I focus my attention as an act of will, steadying my mind with the crutches of abstraction.

Does he look different to you now? I ask myself. *And if you answer yes—is that actually the truth? Or is just impossible to see him as anything but different, now that the mask's been pulled away?*

I've kept my word to Kirby. The plane ride had given me the time needed to traverse the gap between impotence and acceptance, and I am grateful. My rage has died down and become embers of anger. I let it warm me from within.

Childs appears at ease. His eyes look into mine with a familiar curiosity, and it's a gaze I can return without artifice.

He looks the same, I decide. *The same as ever, as always.*

"How are you, Smoky?" Childs asks, speaking softly. He squints his eyes at me, peering. "You look well. I see hunter's eyes again."

I stare at him, caught for a moment in our pasts together. I am thinking of his private offices, the wall-length picture window, and my own revelations as I spoke and sobbed while he sat and listened. "It's strange," I say. "Your eyes look the same."

I've chosen honesty, on instinct. Playing chess with Childs is a waste of time. He's just too good.

He half smiles, inclining his head in acknowledgment. "That's because they are. I don't have two faces, Smoky. I am myself, no more nor less, and have always been so."

I consider him, pondering this. "And how does that work, doctor? Explain it to me." I give him my own lopsided smile. "I know you want to—right?"

I'd thought a lot about Childs, on the way here. On the one hand, that brilliant mind, the one I'd be a fool to match wits with on a head-to-head basis. On the other, that tiny, biographical hint—the mistake that had caught him. Finally, the question tying both together: Why?

If there is a single quality that all those who engage in cruelty for pleasure share, it has to be their narcissism. The decision to step outside the firelight of their own shared humanity is an act of self-permission only the largest of egos can afford. After all, what could be more egotistical than the absolute certainty you can survive without empathy?

I felt, more than saw, that it was Childs's ability to blend in among the very people who should have known what he was, that he'd be most proud of. The mistake he'd made was not necessarily a reflection of some subconscious desire to be captured. But it was the result of his choice to hide in plain sight, among the hunters, and it was this choice, I felt, that had defined him.

"You just had to get close and stay there," I muse, out loud. "Being one of us was your most constant, fundamental cruelty, wasn't it? And not as a pretense—you actually made it *true*." I look into his eyes, searching for but finding no horizon. "You were one of us, in all the ways that matter." I pause, considering. "Then again, who knows? Maybe it all amounts to nothing more than a leveraging of the banality of evil."

Childs raises one eyebrow. "You're quoting Hannah Arendt? I always appreciated her insight. A little talky at times, but she had a way of seeing things, without a doubt." Childs shifts in his chair, staring off at some event horizon, with a gaze unfocused by reflection. "I can't say you're entirely wrong, in terms of the point you're making," he murmurs. "If you ever want to truly understand me, however, you'll have to reach a point where you can grasp the following statements as true: When I was your friend, I was your friend in truth; and I valued you for your own ways, and without reference to my own purposes. This was not made less so by the fact that I also had my own purposes, which I was willing to suborn our friendship to, should the choice become inevitable."

I smile, leaking malice. "So you loved me as a friend, you just loved yourself more?"

Childs laughs, and once again, I recognize this sound. It's his laugh, and it's him, as always, the man I've known for twenty years, who mentored me to what I can only think was the best of his ability.

Does he lie when he laughs? I wonder.

I brush it away, because it's an unimportant question, of course. I can wonder if I like, but in the end, I already know the right answer: Of course he does—*most* of the time, and certainly in all the ways that count.

Not all the time, though, I think, considering his smile. *You can fake a laugh, but it's much harder to fake true mirth.*

Sometimes he laughs to lie, because lying is what he does, but sometimes—he's just happy, or something's just funny.

Dogs play for no reason. They seem to be having fun when they do, and it appears to make them happy. That doesn't mean they're not dogs.

"That's why I took an interest in you from the first, Smoky," Childs tells me. "It was that *insight.* You have a way of cutting to the bone of things that I've always admired." His face grows serious as he focuses in on mine, the perfect presentation of a man striving earnestly for honesty. "But here, so you know: In almost every way, I've *never* helped you to hurt you. Your successes in therapy, under my care, were my accomplishments, too, and for the most part, they stood alone."

"How noble," I say, softly.

"All I am attempting to convey," he replies, ignoring the barb, "is the actual presence and position of banality in terms of individuals like myself. It's the secret, really." He leans forward, intent. "Banality forms the guts of life. It's work, then sleep, and two-thirds of the day is gone. Then there is walking, here to there; driving, here to there; urinating; defecating; and let us not forget to remember eating."

He shakes his head, amused. "It's not that hard to learn 'normal.' All you really need to do is imagine that you're eating, or sleeping, or walking, or shitting, and then—imagine that you *care.* That these most boring things matter, and that 'mattering' is *you*." He smiles at me. "Take a firm grip on that, inside yourself, and when you speak of the things about which all other human beings care, let that blandness be your guide. Find the one connection we all share, killer or not: *the ways in which our bodies make us care*. From that one connection—the seeds of kinship, without the necessity of lying."

I contemplate what he's told me. "So," I say, frowning, "what? Physical need is your path to some kind of...artificial empathy?"

He shrugs. "Why not? All empathy is modeling. Think of it as a muscle. Anyone can take the weak arms they were born with and make them muscular, over time. All exercise is artificial, ultimately. Are the end results something less than actual reality? Of course not." He smiles. "This is what I meant when I told you there were times I only helped you, and where no agenda was involved. They were no less real than the times I was acting to harm you." He leans forward a little to underline his own emphasis. "Passion is passion is passion, Smoky. If one's passion includes living side by side with those who should see you for what you are, then one's pursuit of understanding empathy will be driven by that passion and inform its results, as well." He leans back, his eyes gleaming. "But then, we have always shared this pursuit, haven't we? You and I simply come at it from opposite sides and for different reasons. You seek additions to your own library of empathy just as deliberately as I, because you know the more you understand, the greater your chance to know the predators once you see them, while I did the same to ensure that I could hide."

The shapes of truth, I think, marveling a little. Childs is a ghastly, repugnant horror. His existence is a crime. But his assessments of himself are the closest to the truth of any monster I've ever known.

He is a calculated creation of the inner "self," guided by his genuine passion for cruelty toward an understanding of the genuine human need to care about others and feel their pain. He'll never experience love as love, or feel any true burden of responsibility for another, but Childs had found a way to grasp the shape of their truths through approximation.

His own true loves—love of himself, and his own pursuit of pleasure—had been leveraged to allow for an understanding of the rest of us, from a distance. Childs would never be capable of feeling my love for my child, but he understood: I loved my son like he loved himself; and the pleasure that love gave me matched the pleasure he experienced as he reaped the fruits of his own cruelty.

Not everything is a manipulation, I had once heard drawled by a man I was interviewing. He had been a quiet, small monster who liked to eat women's breasts. "Everyone just needs to converse, now and again. You know?" He had blinked his rheumy eyes at me, and I caught a flash of his graying teeth, in what I assumed was his demented version of a smile.

How nice to eat you—oops, I mean meet you! I imagined him saying, in a cannibal's version of the Freudian slip.

"Not talking to any particular end, you understand, just jabbering so's you can be sure you still exist." He'd knocked on his head lightly, and I recall that it had sounded hollow. "Make sure who you think you are is actually there, that you've not got caught in some fucked-up nightmare of your own devising."

The cannibal had nodded once, primly, calling up some moment from the past. "I talked to all those girls, lots, before I ate their titties, and it wasn't something special. We was always just jabbering before I got them started screaming. Just shooting the shit and killin' the breeze. Not a thing that involved them being natural-born whores, or joking them about, you know: 'which one would I prefer—a chicken or a wing?'" He'd cackled at that one, enjoying a little cannibal humor. "Just normal shit, the shit everyone fills up their time with. TV shows, sports, and jackin' off. Boxers or briefs, and how all mullet-wearing motherfuckers must die. All that contemporary-type, cultural shit.

"I remember one girl told me all about some Broadway show, even, and I got her to sing me a song from it. I was still thinking about that song when I started in on her.

"My point I was making, though, is that if all you'd saw was the talking before the killing, you'd just think we were a mismatched pair. You know? You might've thought she could do better than me, but nothing we were saying would have tipped you off about the eating, and the titties, or any of those later things. Because it wasn't something I was doing just to calm 'em or to make some time. I needed some conversation, that's what. My brain needed to hear a different voice than my own to get itself *right*—one that wasn't me."

The rheumy eyes cleared for a moment, glittering with hunger, as he'd stared at my chest. "Just like now," he muttered, listing away from his own shore and into deeper waters. "Just you and me—*jabbering.*" He nodded to himself, talking to me but no longer talking *with* me. He'd gotten lost. He licked his lips and goggled at my boobs like they were burgers. "*Shooting* that shit. Yes, *ma'am. Killing* that fuckin' breeze."

Childs thinks he's superior to the booby-burger man. But he's not. He's just smarter, and he's not as crazy, so he can put on a better face.

And why? Because most of life is the filler and not the fight. Childs wasn't *ultimately* special, true, but he also wasn't wrong. We have more in common with the monsters, in terms of day-to-day experiences, than our differences. The divergences are everything, in the end, but they are singular.

That sword cuts both ways, of course. Because fundamentally, whatever approximations they might make, Dr. Childs and the booby-burger man are each just a different version of the other. While the rest of us share a thousand qualities in humanity, they can share only the one.

They're both that same sheen-eyed, gray-toothed, blood-hungry cannibal, and the only thing they'll ever know about love will be found inside the moment of the kill.

"I just realized that you can't grasp what help really is, in terms of what makes it valuable, Childs," I murmur. "Caring isn't a differential equation or a deliberate act. There's no 'sum' to rightness. It's not just about moments versus moments, because it's never only about what's rational. Sometimes, it's just about what is." I shrug. "The way things are. A wife or a husband can wake up one day, realize they're unhappy for no reason they can explain—and leave. No weighing of any score other than the one that matters most: the number they *need.* The one that will give them permission to do what they *must.* You may be able to approach it, but you'll never, ever, arrive."

I want him to understand that he is missing something within himself, something he can know about and calculate endlessly, but which he will never understand. I want him to long for an aspect of himself that will never exist, because it cannot be replicated by the process of weighing "everything."

"The truth," I continue, "is that bragging about this fictitious ability of yours, to live in two worlds, reveals it as your own concern. You're not proud because of what you accomplished to this point—you're relieved, now that it's over." I sit back, considering him. "What you're really grading yourself on is how long you survived free, being yourself, and how much damage you got to do. Some part of you knew from the beginning that the only sane plan would be no plan at all, because the moment you gave yourself permission once, you'd have given yourself permission forever." I lean forward, my hands clasped together. "But you *couldn't*. You couldn't decide not to. Because the thing you are isn't a 'newer and better,' it's a 'broken and missing.' A sickness. Which is why the sane part of yourself, the part that does nothing but find the right functional answer, made you afraid for your life the moment you decided to give it up and enjoy your first kill."

I lean back, crossing my arms. I shake my head. "You *knew*. You knew, the moment you understood this was something that you could not decide *not* to do, that every other thing you had always believed you were the exception to, was in fact *exactly* what you were about. Mr. Calculator ran the numbers and came up with every answer that you never wanted."

I count off on my fingers. "Such as: That you're a murder junkie, which means your mind will deceive itself, if that's what's required to make the next fix 'logical.' That you're prone to tunnel vision, to making the facts conform to the thing you've already decided you simply *gotta* have. That you are incapable of empathy, incapable of guilt, and incapable of love—and that none of these are strengths, at all. They're stumbling blocks of missing information that you can never know, and each understanding that exists in others, which is absent in you, could always contain the one idea or perspective that gets you caught." I raise an eyebrow. "Like the inability to resist dropping that itsy-bitsy biographical detail, when doing so was the one thing that would allow me to cut through any doubts I might have had and become certain."

Childs stays silent. He doesn't seem angry or sad—or anything. He's just there, a creature of focus, listening.

I chuckle. "What? Are you trying to calculate it out? Are you listening so closely because you want to ensure you don't miss a variable, because you still believe, so long as you have the most complete description of all the parts, that you'll be able to make a model of the whole that's real?"

He frowns and then breaks out laughing so suddenly, I recoil. It's genuine laughter, happening because something's got a grip on his funny bone, not some planned reaction designed to mock and unsettle me.

"Smoky, you disappoint me so," he manages to say, once the laugh's slowed from its run to a crawl. "And at the same time, you astound me." He grins, another dogtoothed display of what funny means to a man like Childs. "I'm never going to regret whatever I'm missing, because I believe that what I'm missing is what would be required to regret it. I'm not sad. Neither am I overjoyed. I know what I am, as what I am, and I'm never going to get a more 'right answer,' as you put it, than that. Trying would only involve me in solving something I'm incapable of doing, and besides—I have no interest at all in becoming capable of guilt, or regret, at this juncture." He laughs again, clearly tickled by the thought. "I can't see a good result coming from that, considering all that I've seen and all that I've done, can you?"

I stare at him in silence.

"In fact," he says, his voice pitched low and conspiratorially, "watch this."

The laughter drops away like a man falling down a well, to be replaced in an instant by the coldest eyes and the most humorless face he's ever deigned to show me. He seems soulless to me, a representation of guilt as both a total and permanent result.

There you are, I think, frozen into stillness by this moment of discovery. *Your real face. The true you.*

I remain silent and still, trying not to move a muscle. For me, Childs is like a rare bird, some species with feathers that change colors every hour, never repeating except in one case—when every feather turns completely black. Once the bird is black-feathered, it becomes the predator it was actually born as, but which, otherwise, it is not. It hunts only its own kind, in the dark, and it never kills slowly, because the dying shrieks of its own species are an irresistible source of pleasure. The problem with this bird: Its feathers will turn black only in the dark. Sightings are the rarest of all animals alive, and even this rarest state is indescribably fragile.

If Childs was such a bird, his feathers had just turned black, bringing every part of his truest nature into the starkest possible focus. One shift of a shadow—even blinking my eyes—and, *poof*—the truest version of the blackest bird might have blinked away, taking all its secrets with it.

"I once skinned an infant, just to see what that would sound like," Childs says, in a voice that sounds like the cold water of an underground river sliding over smooth stones as it races through the dark. The smallest smile appears, and its aspect terrifies me. It fits his eyes: two marbles of ice made from flesh and filled with awareness but emptied of life. Every aspect of him is fearless and confident and devoted to its own ends, to filling its own belly. This Childs will never fail to decide for himself, regardless of what this means for others. He will never deny himself, not even to entertain the possibility. He'd eat others to live, for example, if this became the only solution to his own survival, and it would be a choice he could make without any need for debate.

I clear my throat, still afraid to do anything that will send pure Childs away. "And? What did that sound like?"

He cocks his head barely, first to one side, then the other. The little ghost smile stays in place, exactly the same from one moment to the next. It makes me think of a corpse that chose to smile, and then left it at that. "It was like listening to the birth of all the world's pain," he whispers, dead-eyed and frozen-lipped, smiling that moue that promised everything cruel would come, if you could only sit in one place long enough. "In the sounds of those screams, you could hear it wishing for words to beg." He chuckles, tiny dark pieces of some horrible, low noise. "It hadn't matured enough to develop any concept of death. It only knew that it suffered in the now, and that the now would go on forever." The chuckling stops, and the smile returns to its endless and unconcerned stillness. "Infants can take much longer to die than you'd ever have expected," he muses. I understand he's not saying this to enjoy its impact on me but because remembering brings him joy, as the experience of ecstasy.

He turns his head ever so slightly and gives me all his attention. The smile persists in a maddening state of sameness, and I can feel it even when I'm not looking at it, like an itch in the center of my brain. "I *loved* skinning that infant slowly," he croons. "I *loved* it like you love your husband and your children. I loved it like a man facing death longs for his own life." He grins, finally, like a zombie jack-o'-lantern, and I quail on the inside. Looking into that grin feels like waiting to be murdered while you still have the opportunity to run. It makes me want to whine without words, to moan like an animal. "Missing?" he cackles. "I don't care what I'm *missing*—because there is no 'care,' there." He taps the tip of a finger against his chest, above the heart. "I never worry about things I can't fix, or can't know, or can't control. I let them go. And then, they are gone."

The grin persists, neither lessening nor fading. Gazing on it now makes me feel like I'm food. As if Childs is a cat, and I'm the mouse he's tricked into believing it's in control. The moment I finally accept that those cat wrists will slide free, whenever he wishes, will be the moment *after* he's already begun murdering me.

Get a grip! I scream to myself. *He's just a guy! A really, really super-scary guy, but still—just a guy!*

It doesn't work much, but it does work a little, which is enough. Terror is like a wild horse: If you can find a way to put its back between your legs, you can tame it. You'll just have to grip with your knees, grab the mane with both hands, and hold on for dear life.

I force myself to stare directly into that horror of a face and its murder of a smile. "I understand," I tell him, softly. "Not the way I would if I were you, of course. But I understand the way you want me to. I'll be able to explain you to others in a way that will meet with your approval." I pause, letting my words sink in. "In fact, if you'd be willing to discuss some other matters and help in providing some clarity—I promise to do so. I'll make sure you're understood for what you are."

The true Childs ... this *thing* ... stares at me with its unblinking, black-button eyes. The lips move, sliding against each other, turning first up, then down. That awful moue, like the most secret smile of a murderous child, forms in one moment and is gone the next. It transforms without stopping to become the jack-o'-lantern grin of clearheaded madness once more.

This merry-go-round of monster faces cycles through itself for another few moments before coming to a complete stop as a single motion. To call it sudden would be a misnomer, as it would imply an ability to recognize the slowing moment just before the end. But there were no ragged, trailing edges of trembling motion to follow with my eyes, only a face that had been in constant, labile motion, suddenly struck to stone by a state of change too fast to follow.

Childs peers at me with the flat, dead gaze of a self-aware corpse or a shark. I feel seen, but there is no contact between us, no projection of *him* that then reaches *me*. His eyes drink the light in, drink it down, drink it gone.

"Do you think this face is an accident, Smoky Barrett?" he asks, speaking from the hollow of his throat.

I frown, puzzled. "I'm sorry. I'm not sure I understand."

"Do you think it's the face of madness, something outside my control?" he asks, watching me. "As in, a kind of me that takes over, functioning as a sin eater to corral all the horror into one place for the health of the system?"

"No," I answer. "I don't. I think all the other faces you show to the world are contrived creations, but I believe that this face means I'm seeing *you*. And what I see is far too controlled to call crazy. Also—" I nod at his torso—"your breathing is deep, slow, and steady. You're not sweating under the arms." I glance at his face. "Not sweating anywhere, that I can see." I nod downward. "Your feet almost never move. On the rare occasion that they do, the movements are smooth and relaxed, without any visible evidence of conscious pre-planning." My gaze bounces back up to meet his corpse eyes again. "There are generally lots of precursors involved with physical motion. Especially after long periods of stillness." I shake my head. "Not for you."

Childs watches, still not projecting, never blinking. "It's not that you're hypervigilant—"

"It's that I'm permanently alert," he interrupts. "My mental awareness never idles. I never doubt, and I'm never afraid."

I frown, surprised. "You never doubt? At all?" I stop, dipping my head once as I smile ruefully. "Sorry. That sounded like a challenge, which it's not. I don't actually doubt you, it's just ... surprising." I lean forward, letting my interest show openly. "How does that work? You make one plan of action, once, and never worry about it again?"

"No," he intones, slowly, his attitude implying that I had missed something obvious, and must thus be an idiot of the first order. "I didn't say I never review, recheck, or replan. That would be *stupid*," he says, spitting out the last word. "It would also be insane ... *dummy*."

The change that's swept over Childs is shocking. It is still true Childs, clearly—feet that never tap, and that drawn, still face—but he's been seized by a disproportionate rage, and it's pulled him taut, like a bowstring. His formerly cold eyes have gone hot with hate light, brimming over with wordless, molten shouts of bare-fisted violence. "I said I never *doubt*. Doubt is a feeling. A sensation of anxiety. And I am *never* anxious." He tilts his face to one side. "Does that clear things up for you, Mrs. Ima Stupidcunt? Or do you need me to explain it using only three-letter words?" His lip curls, twisting his face into something between a sneer and a snarl. "There's nothing quite so vacuous as a fool who takes all things literally," he tells me, glowering.

Since the appearance of true Childs, I have adopted a strategy of deference as good manners, guided by the permanent understanding that he never actually exists outside my borders of control. It's the concept of 'not kicking a man once he's down' put into practice, and it's a reasonable general choice when dealing with offenders who define their lives in terms of measuring where they are on some value-driven scale of dominance.

Because everyone's value is judged, by them, against this same scale, it's also true that no serial offender is capable of respecting you if you never assert your control over them, and prove it. I consider the aspect of this outburst and decide it's time to remove the implication of the carrot by reminding him of the stick.

I stand up and move to a position behind my chair, putting myself above him. I cross my arms and choose what I've always called the 'lawyer face' as my expression. It's completely attentive and professionally friendly, but he is not personalized by me one iota. He is an obligation. A job I'm required to do both professionally and, well, nothing else.

"You said to me earlier," I say, tuning the tone of my voice to my affect, "that you were harming me only when harm was the object of the exercise. I understand the concept you were communicating: that as a matter of principle, you weren't cruel to me just because you could be. Would you agree with my interpretation?"

"Aside from the fact that I was *literally* cruel to you, when I was, because I could be," he says, smiling with the bow-tie lips of a fallen cherub, "yes, close enough. Though I suppose the most truthful answer would be that I was never cruel to you if I did not need to be."

I nod. "Fine. In the same way, I will always strive not to remind you of your position within my boundaries of control, unless your actions make it necessary." I pause, gazing down on him. "I'm concerned you've lost sight of your obligations in this regard. That you no longer agree with the maintenance of an essential level of self-control as necessary, on your part." I cock my head. "If this is true, maybe we need to take a break and give you the opportunity to regain your composure." I raise my eyebrows in query. "Is that the best course of action? For us to take a break?"

Childs's face grows purple for a moment, and his eyes bulge with rage. He struggles visibly, however, and manages to get a handle on his emotions, dialing them down from their upper range, that of stampeding elephants, to a more acceptable level of polite, icy terseness.

"Done," he says, with a stony gaze.

"Excellent," I reply, nodding my agreement with his choice. I uncross my arms and move around to the front of my chair again, retaking my seat. I search his eyes silently, giving him a decent interval of my regard.

Childs has calmed himself fully now, returning to his former state of unblinking, lizard-eyed stillness. I use this observation as a bridge, a way of returning our conversation to its prior level of collaborative pretense.

"So ... what was that about?" I ask him. "You present with an impressive level of self-control, and then lose it in an outburst of rage based on a single misunderstanding?" I frown. "Is this how you are when you're most yourself? No patience, when it comes to women?"

He glares at me and then closes his eyes for a few moments before opening them again. "I'm like a sword that has to be blooded, once it's been drawn," he intones, calm again. "I'm a weapon. That's my purpose. Very simple. And no, it's not exclusive to women. It involves everyone." He gives me a steady gaze, returning my own. "Think of it as putting distance between yourself and your hungers, so that you're required to travel—just a little—in order to eat that most favorite and forbidden fruit. It's a discipline concerning coherence of identity. I live my life in the day-to-day, engaging in all the things that make us similar. I only wear *this* face in the singular moments. Outside those moments, this face, and the person who goes with it, *do not exist.*"

"I don't really understand your whole—" I indicate him with a flourish of my hand—"thing. Are you claiming that you have multiple personalities?"

One side of Childs's mouth twitches, and he narrows his eyes at me. "Not at all. Not remotely. Think of them as non-competing paradigms of personality, each one encompassing a distinct set of behavioral impulses, all of them enclosed within a hierarchal heuristic structure designed to ensure none of them can conflict, and that they all run smoothly. Behind all of them is me— let's call my position the 'master personality.' It's the creator of any others, as well as being their controller, though that's really not an accurate metaphor."

"Why?"

He mulls this over—or at least I think he does. His preternatural stillness makes gauging his emotions difficult. "It's the metaphor of relationship that's bad, I suppose. There is, of course, only one 'me,' which is my identity as a whole." He glances down at himself. "That's me. The here and now."

"I understand."

"This is because human beings are a collection of competing and cooperative urges. In most cases, the division between the two isn't necessarily of note, as the competition is not between survival-level instincts, but between a survival-level instinct and our intellectual rationalization and integration of it. In reality, no competition ever truly exists between our abstractions—which are the product of what human beings tend to term as *mind*—and any physical instinct, because no competition is possible. Sense data, including the sensations of perception, precede our abstractions of them. You see?"

"Sounds logical," I allow. "Go on."

"In this same wise, then, the way to create paradigms of personality is to create an explanation for ourselves that allows for their existence in a noncompetitive state, to ourselves."

"And? What's the benefit to you?"

"Separation," he replies, without hesitation. "That would be primary. There's me, and there's the paradigm of personality you know as Dr. Childs. This personality can know all about me, because it *is* me, but it can also function in service of its own rule sets only, without expending any consideration or concern on my behavior—as the primary personality—at all. He can maintain a complex, consistent cover much more easily, and hold it all in his head with more accuracy and less effort, as well."

"I see," I reply, contemplating these claims.

"It's about operating different sets of behaviors separately, in terms of their relation to one other, not operating them in literally separate locations. And when one paradigm is in use, the other is never concurrently *behaviorally* active; but if needed, the memories of either can become 'known' by the other. Since this is not an attempt to overwrite a personality or to force a change in a behavior through the use of abstraction—which requires that a conflict be created between competing paradigms—there are no difficulties involving issues of integration.

"I can 'know' what Dr. Childs knows, when I want to, because Dr. Childs *is* me, and I *am* Dr. Childs. It's only the *behaviors* of each personality which never coexist."

I stare at him blankly, waiting for my mind to get its mouth around all those concepts and their entireties, but it's a futility from the start. "I'm not even going to try and pick all that apart right now," I tell him. I point to the video camera that's been recording everything from the start. "I will review it later, though. It seems to be an important aspect of your identity."

"It was a factor in my freedom, from the beginning," Childs confirms.

"I believe you."

Childs looks up toward the ceiling and then around, finally returning his gaze to me. "I'm not communicating from this perspective anymore, for now," he says. "I've spent too much time being this version of myself without killing anyone. It's not difficult in short bursts, but pretending that I care about anything else, from this viewpoint, is exhausting if it goes on too long."

"I see," I reply, fascinated by this admission and by all the things it might reveal about him. "Would you be willing to let me interview you with this personality as the dominant one, in the future, as long as it's kept short?"

"We'll see," true Childs intones. His eyes lose their focus for a moment, stepping him away from sight and its connection to his surrounds. As the next moment arrives and becomes, both focus and connection resume. Childs smiles once again, with a Dr. Childs smile. He chuckles briefly, delighted. "What did you think of that, my dear Smoky?" he asks, grinning. "Did you like the Dark Man? Or did he only disturb you?"

"I'd have to say a little bit of both, I suppose," I reply, giving myself a moment to marvel at the construct he'd created for himself, of himself. "I can honestly say that I've never met anyone like you."

He laughs, pleased. "I'm glad to hear that. It's good to be something that's new and not boring. It will keep me relevant."

"I imagine it will."

I pause to gather my thoughts. The direction of the interview had been knocked off course by the sudden appearance of true Childs. I consult my memory, thinking through the mental list I'd made earlier of the subjects and details I wanted to be sure that I covered.

"I'd like to continue with the general interview now, if that's acceptable to you," I tell him.

"Of course," he replies, beaming. "Onward."

Do the difficult one first, I tell myself, looking at Childs across the space that separates us. I sigh inwardly. *God, I'm tired of talking about Matt and Alexa with serial killers. ...*

I force these thoughts away and demand my own focus. Childs is so much less now than what he was when we started. Something about meeting the truest version of himself, how he'd hidden it away inside himself, bringing it out only when it was time for violence—it had been a long time since I'd been so content to be inside my own skin, no matter what the costs of my life, so far.

It was good to be me. Good not to be him, too, of course; but I didn't need the comparison anymore. It was good to be me without reference to anyone, least of all Childs.

Get to it, then, I tell myself. Finish it up so you can walk away and leave him to his lifetime of small, locked spaces.

"It was you who *actually* put Sands onto me, wasn't it?" I ask, starting without thinking or needing to. "Who told him how to get into my home, so that he could kill Matthew and Alexa—and me?"

"Guilty as charged," he agrees, appearing neither jubilant nor guilty. "It was an experiment, after a fashion. I thought it likely Sands would succeed, but..." He shrugs. "I couldn't discount the possibility of you turning the tables on him. And so you did, so you did." His eyes sharpen, focusing on me even more intently. "And how *strong* surviving that challenge to your life made you! How formidable! You went from child to woman in the space of a day, and afterwards, never saw the monsters more clearly."

I cock my head at him. "Do you expect that to hurt me?" I ask him.

Childs frowns, confused. "Not at all. Nor is that my desire. I enjoyed playing God with you, in my own way, Smoky, it's true. But it's never been your suffering that's sustained me."

"So?" I ask. "Then—what?"

He settles back in his chair. "I loved you as the result of my efforts."

"The way that you loved Beckman?" I ask. "Was he also a result of your efforts?"

Childs grimaces in disgust. "Beckman was a spineless worm. He could have risen above the shadow of his father but instead chose to fail everyone who ever loved him, from his mother, to his wife, and finally, to his son."

"To be fair," I point out, "in the end, he came through for his son, didn't he?"

Childs nods, acknowledging this without any evidence that it mattered to him in any way. "I suppose that is fair. He did manage to keep his mouth shut, didn't he? If he hadn't, his son wouldn't have lived long enough to die alone. So—kudos to Mr. Beckman, on that front, at least."

"Isn't it also fair to say," I continue, probing for a weakness in Childs's impervious affability, not from anger, but just because, "that Beckman was your biggest personal failure? I mean, you can call him spineless and weak—but in the end, Beckman's why you're sitting here."

It draws no negative response. The affability remains, untouched. "As I said before—alas!" Childs sighs in acceptance. "Perhaps I shouldn't judge Mr. Beckman so harshly, after all. He did earn me twenty-five good years, did he not?"

"He did," I allow, feeling myself begin to hate Childs again, just a little. Some aspect of myself wants to slap him with my open hand. I want to yank something sorrowful from him, some evidence of regret at his defeat, but so far, in all his guises, I can find no chink in his armor.

"I'm curious," he asks, "when were you completely certain of my guilt?"

"I was ninety-nine percent sure after I saw the biographical information on Beckman's dad," I reply. "One hundred percent came on the plane flight here. I followed a hunch and checked to see if Beckman had ever been approached to participate in the interview initiative."

I refer to the FBI's program for the interviewing of serial offenders. They're asked to participate in a series of interviews that include diagnostic tests and questionnaires, as well as one-on-ones with behavioral analysts. No bargaining is involved, and the offenders must agree freely. Not all are willing, but ego does win out in many cases.

"I knew that he would have refused, under normal circumstances, because of his worry for his son. If the right person approached him, though—someone he recognized and who could provide a guarantee that the conversation wouldn't be penalized, should it occur—he might." I shrug. "It was a shot in the dark. I couldn't be certain you'd have tried." I smile, feeling Cheshire. "You fell inside my predictions. We got you in the visitor logs prior to the series of interviews you did with him—I assume that's when you pitched it to him in the first place."

Childs inclines his head in assent. "You assume correctly."

"Why?" I ask. "Why expose yourself like that?"

He tilts his head, regarding me, and I see a single flash of depthless darkness fill his eyes and then vanish. True Childs, perhaps, peering out into the world through one of the windows of his mind, feeling clever to hide so well, when in reality he was a prisoner of his own creation.

"Why do you think, Special Agent Barrett?" he asks, watching me.

I knew the answer to this question, because it was the intuition that had driven me to have and check this hunch in the first place. It had been only further confirmed by everything I'd seen and heard so far. "I think ... you had to. That you just couldn't help yourself. The idea of walking right into prison and letting him see your face ... of making him submit to a series of falsified interviews about crimes he never committed, interviews that would become part of a permanent record branding him as a serial killer for the purposes of study ... " I nod, half to myself, in confirmation.

"I think you were like every other one of your kind, in relation to what drives you. It was just too perfect for you to pass up, even with the risk. Maybe you even resisted it for a while, but in the end, you are what you are—aren't you?"

"You continue to be an A-plus student, Smoky," Childs says, speaking softly. "You know the rules and don't doubt them. It's the hardest thing, you know. It's as you said: the banality of evil. Given enough opportunities to doubt the black and white of me, even the most hardened can feel the pull to believe that lie." He smiles. "But not you, Smoky Barrett. Never you. I could talk for a thousand years, and you'd never go blind to my hungers."

I shift in my chair. "Well, I've been given lots of reasons to be sure."

"I suppose that's true. I suppose it also makes my claim of contribution to that state of alertness irrefutable, does it not?"

"I suppose," I allow. I lean forward. "I have to tell you, though ... I *do* see you differently. I can always see him now, when I look at you—like a black circle around the edges." I look at him, watching what I'm describing appear, then fade, only to reappear again and again. Childs sees me watching and says nothing.

"Let's move off of you and me for now, doctor," I tell him. "I want to talk to you about your cohorts. The Wolf. The Torturer. Your past."

Childs pauses, regarding me. "I will never lie to you, while I'm still alive, Smoky. In a choice between being untruthful with you, or silence, I will always choose silence."

"Very noble," I say.

He ignores this riposte, as he'd managed to ignore all the others. "The relevance of this to the questions you just asked: The only thing I will tell you about my brothers or their plans is that they will continue. My imprisonment changes little, except as such change applies to me. If anything, they will pursue their agendas more aggressively. They are my brothers, but ... well ... let's say that I was the oldest. Each of them is brilliant, in their own way, but one thing both share with me is a healthy respect for your abilities." He sighs, an acceptance of some inevitable truth. "They know they can't outrun you forever, and both are aware that you'll never give up. But, with my capture, more than ever, they'll hear the ticking of the clock marking their time, and will thus redouble their efforts."

"What can you tell me about those efforts, doctor?" I probe. "Do you know what they're planning? Do you know who they are?"

He shakes his head sideways. "I do not know their plans, other than broadly, as you know them, too. Each of the Horsemen designed their own paths of destruction and kept the details to themselves, as an action of security."

"Horsemen?" I ask, frowning.

Childs rolls his eyes. "Melodrama, I know. But symbols are important, even if only to ourselves." He shrugs. "It's the name we were given. We are the four Horsemen, if not of the world's apocalypse, then of someone's, that's certain."

"The name you were 'given'?" I query. "By whom?"

Childs smiles. "I can honestly tell you: I do not know. He is the smartest of us, without a doubt. Smarter than you," he says, inclining his head toward me. "Smarter than me, too. If you win this war—because it is a war, Smoky, not just one battle—you will only catch him last. Even when you do, if you do, the price of discovery will be ... *very* high, I'd imagine. Very high, indeed."

"You sound like a Bond villain, Dr. Childs. You do realize that?"

He laughs out loud, startling me. "I can hear my own voice, Smoky. I take your point. But consider this question: When is megalomania not megalomania?" He pauses, raising his eyebrows as though waiting for my answer. "When its reach does not exceed its grasp," he answers, completing his own riddle. "And the senior-most Horseman—I call him the Machiavellian—can reach quite far before that effort becomes ego."

"He's just a man, doctor. No more, no less."

"So is a billionaire," he scoffs. "Or the president of China. That doesn't make you their equal in influence. Or resource."

I shrug it off. "Maybe, but it'll never be my job to arrest the president of China, or of any other country, for that matter. So far as billionaires go, the prey's just bigger, not different."

Childs is grinning at me now, in purest appreciation. "Hear, hear!" he exclaims. "Spoken like the terrifying hunter you undeniably are!" He leans forward a little, moving closer by sliding to the edge of the seat of his chair. Sam Brady reaches out, placing a hand of caution on Childs's shoulder. "But Smoky—I acknowledge all your strengths, openly. And yet, even so, I wouldn't put my money on you."

Childs means for it to frighten me, but I feel impervious to fear, at least for now. It's difficult to define the exact point my fear left me, but I know it had begun to drain away the moment I was sure about Childs. It had grown only more true as I continued to close the distance.

Ex-CIA, the death museum, and a full residential block of hostages and madmen and gunfire and death. My house burned down—the last place that held my oldest memories—gone. Tommy was almost killed, along with Bonnie—except that she had played her part in saving them both, of course. ... I had a shotgun put to my pregnant belly, and later, I had a son.

All that chaos and misinformation, and most of all—towering above it all—the sheer size of their monstrosity ... and yet, in the end, I *had* pierced the veil. Childs was like an ancient nightmare, the monster other monsters feared. But I had chased him down and put him in a cage, and there he'll sit forever.

It had restored my confidence and erased my fear. I feared some possibilities always; it was a feature of this job. But I no longer feared *them*. Instead, I knew that they feared me. I had taken one of them and started the death-clock ticking, the countdown of their final days of freedom.

I had also regained my equilibrium as it related to their actions. Large scale or small scale, whether in the form of domestic terrorism that murdered by the tens or hundreds, or as the Torturer's terrible one-on-one—I would capture them by chasing the individuals, not their acts. *Passion is passion is passion*, Childs had said to me earlier. Well, horror is horror is horror, too, if you can only make yourself accept it. Hitler seems like Satan only when you contemplate his works. Remember that he died by his own hands, and that his corpse was left burning in the mud, and it becomes simple to remember he was, ultimately, nothing but a man.

"I probably should be afraid, Dr. Childs," I tell him. "But when I look at you, all I can hear is my own voice in my head, saying: 'One down. Four to go. Back to work tomorrow.'"

I might expect him to react to this badly or to try and diminish it with humor. Childs surprises me instead. "Indeed," he agrees. "And well done. No one could ever make a rational claim to the contrary, Smoky Barrett, and any man who makes you his enemy? Well...that man's probably already lost the war." He inclines his head to me, one slow, deep dip. "I'm glad you were the one who caught me."

I look at him, momentarily nonplussed. His compliment means nothing to me, and won't, ever—but, how strange; how *odd* that he gave it because he meant it. Childs was a living Pandora's box, and I wonder, briefly, if all the Horsemen will be this way. The feeling in my gut is that they will. If there's any reason to be afraid of them all, it's to be found right here, in Childs. Whatever else he is, Childs is a truly, uniquely formidable monster. If the other Horsemen are nothing more than the same, the future's not guaranteed.

"You don't have to thank me, Dr. Childs. It's my job to put you in prison."

He laughs out loud once more, in response to this. "Hear that, Mr. Brady?" he crows, talking to Sam, who's still standing guard behind him. "Strength from every part of her."

"Everyone already knows that, you puke-filled piece of rotten dogshit," Sam growls. "Smoky's a genuine badass. Has been for years. You haven't had a goddamn thing to do with it, and you never will."

Childs stiffens at this, and I imagine that I can see the dark corona that surrounds him widen. He lets it go, though, and I remember his dense diatribe of description about how to build a better monster. It sounds like insanity, and it seems that it should be, particularly when I consider his inward schisms of the self. But then I watch him bite down a rage that's probably as natural to him as blinking, and realize that he did so because the following of his own rules of conduct demanded it. The Dr. Childs part of him doesn't engage in blind, dark rages.

Maybe, with a man like Childs, it's less about his method than his will. Perhaps the fact that he can conceive of it always guarantees some portion of success.

"Were you in the CIA, Dr. Childs?" I ask him. It's a sudden question, and he's caught by the moment, though only briefly.

"I would neither confirm nor deny that I was or was not," he answers, using what could be an old joke, except that he's not smiling. "I will only say that I've done many things."

"Can you explain the purpose behind stockpiling hostages for twelve-plus years, and of having them live side by side on the same street?"

Childs leans forward again. "I really wish I could, Smoky. Truthfully. But I cannot. Just as I cannot tell you anything, however small, that might lead you toward my brothers. I can tell you one thing," he says, nodding as he does so. "There was a reason, and it wasn't any of the most obvious ones that will come to you. You'll have to think smarter, to outthink the Machiavellian."

"I'll do my best," I murmur, considering him and this strange steadfastness, which shouldn't matter to him at all. Unless...I straighten in my chair as an idea flashes behind my eyes. "Are you afraid of the other Horsemen?" I ask, watching him closely as I do.

It had been minute, just a trace of a reaction, but I had seen it. Childs had frozen for less than a heartbeat, if that—but still, he had frozen. "Well, of course I'm afraid of my brothers, Smoky. They're each virtuosos, in their way, of hunting, murder, and pain." He chuckles, shaking his head with amusement. "Have you seen the Torturer at work?" Childs grimaces. "Wonderful to be the spectator, but you'd never want to be the star."

"You don't worry they'll come after you anyway, as a part of tying up loose ends?"

He shakes his head, grinning now. "Not in the slightest, and it's not wishful thinking. However, if I were to talk about anything, out of school, so to speak? I'd be in the hot seat, screaming like that infant I once skinned, and going just as mad."

"Sounds about right for you, in my opinion," Sam Brady mutters.

I catch Sam's gaze and shake my head from side to side, slowly. *Don't do that, I'm saying. Don't insert yourself into my interview.* He dips his head, letting me know that he'd heard me and understood.

"You may be right, Mr. Brady," Childs says. "When the judge presiding over Edmund Kemper's trial asked Kemper what he thought a just punishment would be for Kemper, in light of his string of rape and torture-murders, Kemper said that the families of the girls he'd murdered should probably be allowed to torture him to death." Childs smiles. "It's a hard argument to overcome. Particularly if you truly know what that means, in real terms—what it's like to be slowly tortured to death. I would hazard a guess that it's a common worst fear for many, if not most, serial murderers." He shrugs. "Live by the sword, I suppose."

"Is there anything else you can tell me that you think I might want to know," I ask, "or that might be helpful to me in any way?"

He ponders me, and I watch his imaginary black corona writhe around his head like a crown of snakes. "Just one," he replies. "You'll take it as a form of cruelty, but I can assure you, that's not so." He sighs. "Alexa. I do regret her death and my part in it. I'm not sure why, exactly—to be honest—but ... I do. Even in the planning of the event itself, Sands was meant for you. He'd been told not to touch Alexa and certainly not to kill her."

I wait, watch. I raise one eyebrow. "Is that it?" I ask him.

"Yes," he says, smiling. "Thank you for listening. I've wanted to tell you that for years."

I search for the rage that I recognize, of the burn-down-the-world, no-survivors variety, but all I can find is the usual anger, the kind we are all capable of, for a multitude of reasons. It's not that I don't care. Nothing will ever become more worthy of my anger than his participation in her death, when weighed against Alexa's life and the sum of my love for her. I still mourn, from time to time, and I know that I always will. It's a problem the world can't solve. It's just not ever again going to be worthy of my *rage*.

I stand up and look down at Childs. I explain the truth of things to him, using three sentences and a bland tone of voice only just above boredom. "You'll never matter enough to be included in any of my good memories about Alexa," I say to him. "And over time, it's only the good memories that will remain. Which means, so far as she's concerned, you'll just be forgotten."

I turn and leave, not watching for his reaction, or needing to.

CHAPTER TWENTY-FOUR

We are home.

Christopher slumbers away as I hold him close, no bones in his body, it seems. If I weren't certain he was breathing, I'd worry that he wasn't.

"Wow, he really commits, doesn't he?" Tommy jokes, in a whisper.

I smile. "It's like he just drank a six-pack of baby beer," I whisper back. "Now he's sleeping it off."

"Good thing he doesn't smoke. If he fell asleep with a cigarette, the whole place would go up before his eyes ever did."

"Babies don't drink beer," Bonnie points out to us. "Or smoke cigarettes."

"Thank you, sweetheart," Tommy whispers. "I really wasn't sure about that."

It happens, that rare thing: One corner of Bonnie's mouth tilts up, almost very much like something you'd call a smile.

"Look!" Tommy whisper-screams at me, pointing at Bonnie's face with a series of exaggerated gestures. "Did you see that?

"I did," I whisper back. "It was really, *really* close to being something that any blind guy would call a smile, you know, if you described it to him using *all* the same words you'd use to describe any smile."

Tommy hugs Bonnie close, weeping mock tears of happiness and sobbing in a whisper. "I'm just so happy, Smoky! I mean, I hoped and I prayed—but I never thought this day would actually come! Hallelujah! Oh, happy day! Our Bonnie did something with her mouth that someone, somewhere might call a smile ... if we paid them enough money ... and threatened them a little!"

"So cornball," Bonnie whispers to Tommy. "So *sad*," she finishes, patting him on the shoulder with a comforting hand.

Christopher executes a mighty stretch, burbling as he does, and then resumes the strategy of using *all* of his body for sleeping. No resource left unconsumed.

"You sure he won't hurt himself, sleeping that hard?" Tommy jokes.

I nod. "No, we're good. He's got those bendy baby bones, so he's like that man in the Fantastic Four, the one who stretches."

"Cool, cool," Tommy whispers, showing his approval with two thumbs up.

It is midevening now. The darkness has dropped its curtain and is busy shedding the last layers of its connection to the light. I had walked through the front door still tired, trailing the ghost smoke of my interview with Childs, and they were all there, my family.

Tommy was on the couch with Christopher in his lap. Christopher was flailing with all four limbs—just not all of them at the same time or in the same direction—but he seemed determined, and he was working on it. Bonnie was curled into the EZ recliner set by the couch, reading a book. I couldn't tell, from her expression, if it was an awesome read, an average read, or the worst book ever; but, like Christopher, she seemed determined.

"Mama-Smoky!" Bonnie said, jumping up from the recliner to hug me tight.

Tommy turned his head, his eyes lighting up as he gave me a big, beautiful, clearly spontaneous smile that reminded me of joy. "Hey, baby," he said, maneuvering Christopher off his lap and into his arms so he could stand up and come to me, too.

A moment later, I was completely engulfed, encircled by arms that squeezed me sometimes, crushed in others. I stroked Bonnie's soft, silky hair with one hand, gripping one of Christopher's tiny, kicking feet with the other, feeling the warmth of it through the foot of his pajamas against my palm. Tommy kissed me, and then I kissed him, too; and I felt the light scratch of his stubble on my cheek and smelled his scent in my nose: mostly clean man, with a hint of baby barf and hand soap. I took Christopher in my arms, closing my eyes as I nuzzled him close and was renewed by the scent of life itself, before all the unnecessary additives.

They took me in, held me close, and loved me without words, and I let their scents and kisses and sounds wash me clean of all the evil I had seen.

We are home. Not just a literal statement, it was also a metaphor you could feel.

I wake up in the wee hours, around three o'clock, from an otherwise untroubled slumber. I crawl out of bed as carefully as I can, so as not to wake Tommy.

Once I'm up, I stand there for a moment and watch him sleep. Tommy could never be called boyish, but the way his face relaxes so completely when he sleeps makes him look much younger.

I pad off on my bare feet to the bathroom and sit on the toilet with my knees pressed together and my eyes closed, taking all the time I want in the process of emptying my bladder. My mind dwells on many things lightly, but nothing at depth, because it's three o'clock in the morning, and the deep dark's found its way to all the places it's allowed by now. There are no sounds of people or vehicles or the working war of life. This is the calm, still quiet of a world not being rushed to all its destinations by the hustle and bustle of daily life.

I exit through the doorway that leads into the hall, straining to turn the knob quietly and to walk without making a sound. These are the hours that wake babies before their time, and I do my best to move without touching anything and to reduce the weight of myself against the creaking floor to nothing.

In the living room, I peer through the drapes and check to make sure that the moon's still there; and then I move to the kitchen, making myself a cup of coffee, clutching it close as I find my way through the half dark to the rental sofa we still haven't replaced with one we like. I sit down and take my first sip of coffee, closing my eyes to listen to my home.

I hear the rattles from a gust of wind across the roof, the hum of the refrigerator in the kitchen, and the ever-ongoing creaks and small shudders that are the sounds, my father once told me, of the house protecting us.

All those creaks and groans and rattles, he told me, *are how you can tell that it's a home and not just a house. Because those sounds are made when the house resists different pressures against it from the outside. Wind pushes and pulls, rain patters and makes everything weigh more than it did before; even the earth moves, deep down in the dirt. For any house to be a home, it first has to find a family to protect, and then it has to prove it can keep that family safe.* He smiled at me, and I had smiled back up at him without speaking, made far too helpless by my love for my father to do anything else of substance. *That's what those noises are all about: It's our home, using its entire body to protect us from the things outside that we don't want in.*

I sip my coffee and feel my father, not in any physical sense, but with me, loving me. Always using his entire body to protect me from the dangers of a world equally ready to bless a young girl or devour her whole, depending on the nature of the world in every given moment.

Something has changed in me again, this time for the better. Tomorrow I have to wake up and resume my search for the Wolf, and the Torturer, and the other Horsemen. Dangerous monsters who view the night's qualities in much different ways, and who both know and hate my name.

Anything could happen after I leave my home. Innocent people might die, or I could be forced to take a life to save others' lives, or even to save my own. Success is not a given in any such endeavor. On any given day, I could walk out my door and not return. I could fail to make it back home through the darkness for any number of reasons. Instead of waking up in my own bed, I could wake up in a hospital after having been shot, or wake up in some killer's basement, tied down against a table while I watch him make his preparations from the corners of my eyes.

There were other dangers, too. Loss is dangerous, and its possibility omnipresent. Any of my team could be killed on any day for reasons fair or foul, with the need for concepts like *justice* or *fairness* to ever play a part in the final outcome. We could lose James one day, not because it was a bad day, but because on that day he woke up and couldn't find anything to think about besides his mother's and sister's eyes.

The monsters take their share, too. Even if they never get the chance to do us violence, each and every one of them work hard to ruin us with their presence. To make us believe in things that aren't true, to doubt things that don't require it, and to steal the beauty from our world ingeniously—not through theft of the objects outside us, but by crippling our ability to see it.

I sip my coffee with closed eyes and listen to our home. I find my family in their beds by thinking of them, and each one I take the time to think of brings every memory of their presence to my imaginings. Every opportunity that I have to dwell on their existence in my life becomes a prayer for love that's just been answered.

This is our secret power, and it is the comparative truth that's healed me. That I am so much luckier than a man like Childs, lucky to a degree that seems impossibly miraculous. I have people who I love and who love me back; and they will always be glad to see me when I come home, and they will cover me with their kisses, scents, and touches, while allowing me to do the same.

This is the difference that I have found between happiness and the void: to choose people who choose you back, over and over, in an endless circle of being loved for who you are, loved for how you make them feel by the simple fact of being in their lives.

Yes, I could die tomorrow, but even in that unlikely outcome, I would die without any doubt that I loved my people, and they just couldn't seem to get enough of me, too. This is not something any monster could ever steal from me by killing me or any other person who I care for. It is not our weakness; it is our reason. Our permanent advantage.

War is coming, but I'm okay. I have a house that is a home. I have hot coffee in the wee hours and can hear my family slumbering above me, safe, alive, and all of us still loving one another.

I sip my coffee and hear my father's voice as he smiles down at me and lets me know he loves me. *It's a metaphor, sweetheart,* I can hear him say. *Don't just hear it,* feel *it.*

And I do.

We are home.

Printed in Great Britain
by Amazon